SECOND SIGHT

HK SAVAGE

Book 1, The Admiral's Elite

Chapter 1

It was dark. She could hear the heavy rhythmic pounding of the drum moving steadily nearer to her position. She cast her eyes about, frantically searching for a source of light or a weapon. If she could not escape, at least she could fight.

Out of the darkness, a luminescent, spherical shape drew near. As it came closer and she could finally see, she gasped. A man's face floated, seemingly disembodied in front of her. Craning her neck, she felt a surge of fear crash into her, nearly knocking her backward with the force of it. The face was not that of a human, none living anyway. It was skeletal, bone white with dark circles beneath his hard black eyes. When he smiled, her heart froze. She tried to run but could not. Her feet were rooted, her eyes locked on his, unable to look away. For the first time in years, she screamed. It ripped from her throat uncontrollably, her shriek echoing in the quiet of the night.

Becca woke gasping, sitting bolt upright in her bed. This one had been so real she had to blink repeatedly while she gulped air, trying to reassure herself she was in her bed and it had only been a vision. Again.

Visions were different from dreams, and somehow Becca always knew upon waking which was which. Heart still racing, she reached over to turn off her alarm not due to go off for another half an hour. She feared what she would see if she were to close her eyes again. Rising, Becca peeled off the tank top, stained a deeper blue from her sweat. Her dogtags slapped her on the chest, a reminder of her servitude, a life chosen more out of self-preservation than actual patriotism yet both were equally strong components of her character makeup.

"God I hate sleep," Becca mumbled, stripping the rest of the way to climb in for a quick shower before breakfast.

In accordance with what her mother referred to as her "need to live in a constant state of denial," Becca limited her shower to necessities only and kept the water warm instead of the luxurious, steamy heat she would have actually preferred. Dressing was simple considering the fact that she worked in a few hours. The blue fatigues or "digies" the Military Police wore while on duty, hair pulled back into a simple bun and hat pulled down to its regulation level required no decision making on her part.

The predictability and constant external direction was a draw for her given her determination to live outside her head as much as possible. If her superior officers knew why she was so good at her job, they would have her court marshaled immediately for falsifying information upon enlistment and most likely have her out on a Section 8 before she could say looney bird.

When Rebecca Sauter had enlisted in the US Navy at the age of nineteen, she had failed to give full disclosure in the section on mental health. She had never told anyone what she could do, knowing it would earn her a one way ticket to the same place her grandmother had eventually ended up in *her* later years. Becca made the connection after her first few "dreams" and chose to keep her mouth shut and stay free of that awful place.

Becca had been too young to know the particulars of how her Grandmother ended up there but whenever anyone spoke of her, there had always been the pregnant pause and eye roll that said, "never mind what *that one* says". She remembered Gran calling and her mother arguing that she wouldn't tell her husband *not* to go on a business trip because of some *feeling* Gran had. Her mother had been upset, reminding Gran that he was no longer on active duty, that he would be fine. When he'd called from the hospital to tell her about the car accident, things had been different. Gran became a thing to be feared and was avoided but for the rare guilty visit in her twilight years, but not for Becca. Gran had been the only one who could have guided her and she was out of reach, dying before her granddaughter was brave enough to tell her they were the same.

Becca was left to worry in private if she had inherited some sort of familial mental imbalance, if the ability to dream the future would eventually bring her to the same end as her Gran. Her older brother Kyle was straight as an arrow but her little brother Jared was a flake and Becca often wondered if he was like her, but she couldn't imagine asking even if she could catch him straight for long enough to have a serious conversation. The times between his "bake sessions" were few and far between; the man loved his chemicals.

***

Breakfast was served early on the base. Becca had no worry that she would have to wait for her dry toast and even drier eggs washed down by surprisingly good black coffee. Her trip to the mess hall was limited to eating only. There was no visiting beyond a curt smile at the very few enlisted men and women who noticed her forgettable figure in the halls.

She'd never liked the fact that she was small, but after discovering she was different, she craved anonymity and for that she was grateful for her appearance. Becca was gifted with unremarkable sandy brown hair that hung straight to her shoulders on the rare occasion she wore it down, and large hazel eyes that sat atop a small, slightly upturned nose splashed with a few light freckles. The effect, combined with her slight build and modest height of five foot, three inches, often got her confused with a teenager despite being twenty-two years old.

Becca finished her breakfast, grabbed her cap from the seat beside her, and made her way to the front doors where her partner would be picking her up in the Charger they'd gotten last year when the base had finally upgraded from jeeps to sedans. Under normal circumstances the San Diego weather they enjoyed at the Naval Air Station at Miramar was conducive to an open topped vehicle, however, with the addition of laptops to their gear, the occasional rain had become a real problem.

As was typical, Becca heard the powerful engine before she actually saw the black vehicle pull up alongside the curb. She climbed in and flashed a quick smile at her partner.

Danny Yamamoto was a perfect partner for a wallflower like Becca. He was a California native and well liked by most everyone despite being an MP, an oft hated presence on the base. Especially on Friday and Saturday nights when the enlisted men liked to blow off a little steam.

His coal black hair was clipped in a standard high-and-tight and he was only a few inches taller than his partner, but his lean, muscular build marked him as someone to be left alone. Despite Danny's strong presence, there was sincere warmth in his deep brown eyes and his lips formed a perpetual smile, lending him a welcoming air that put most people at ease.

Danny's insistent way of burrowing his way into her life was the only reason Becca had a somewhat steady boyfriend. He had been more upset than he should have been eighteen months ago when they had been assigned to each other and, after much prodding and poking, he had learned of Becca's strict regime of no excess and no social life. Almost immediately, Danny started trying to lure her to parties and the apartment he shared with his girlfriend Michelle, forever trying good naturedly to draw her from her bubble of isolation to meet some of his friends.

On occasion she relented, mostly out of annoyance, but still her aloofness kept her from really being accepted. Then, three months ago, Danny introduced her to Terry. Terry was the youngest of five children, all girls. He knew how to be patient and was more than willing to take the reins when she appeared at a loss for how to proceed with an adult relationship. He had been nothing but kind since their initial meeting; her cool exterior had not turned him off. Quite the opposite, he had become infatuated with her.

It was this odd infatuation Becca credited with the relationship she now shared with him. They saw each other a few times per week with intermittent phone calls sprinkled in.

It was more than Becca had done before and she saw it as progress. Not Terry. Though the relationship had become physical well over a month ago, Becca had yet to stay the night or invite him to stay at her apartment. It was a stalemate each silently refused to budge on.

"Hey Danny," Becca greeted her partner warmly. His peaceful nature automatically relaxed her. She didn't know if that was why he was assigned to her after her first partner said she was a cold bitch, but she appreciated him regardless.

He eased the car slowly away from the curb. Danny gave her his usual dimpled smile, flashing his artificially straight white teeth at her. "Are you coming to our barbeque this weekend? I talked to Terry last night and he said you still hadn't committed one way or the other." He was cheerful though she could hear the anticipated disappointment in his tone. "Michelle said to tell you she hopes to see you there, otherwise Terry will be in her kitchen the whole time and that is *not* where a man belongs." He annunciated the last exactly as she would, including a head weave. "Her words, not mine."

"I don't know. I haven't thought that far ahead," she deflected.

The car slowed causing her to look over at him. Danny was staring at her in disbelief. "Bec, it's the day after tomorrow."

"Oh." She felt her cheeks warm. "Um, when is it again?"

Danny blew out a gush of air in frustration. "Saturday at two. My place. We're going to grill and maybe head over to the courts for some volleyball."

Battling the way her lip wanted to curl at the thought of being around so many people she didn't know, Becca gave him the answer he wanted to hear. "Okay. I'll be there."

Danny had started to ease back out away from the curb while twisting his head to cast her a sidelong glance. "Think you're coming solo?"

"I can call Terry but he might have made other plans," she offered lamely, knowing that as much as she wished he hadn't, she knew he would have set the date aside for Danny even if she had refused, as was frequently the case. She was a crap girlfriend. If it wasn't for the sense of normalcy it gave her, she wouldn't let the charade continue. It wasn't fair to Terry.

Looking quite pleased with himself, Danny hummed happily, bobbing his head in time to a few short bars of "I Kissed a Girl." They were not supposed to have the radio on anything except a few approved stations while on duty, none of them good, so the two had gotten used to leaving it off.

"So how's it going with you love birds?" Danny asked her innocently. Though by rights, he probably knew better than she. Terry had been Danny's best friend since the sixth grade and she knew they often spoke of her. Both professed a deep need to see her happy, serving only to irritate her all the more.

Annoyed at the image of the two of them discussing her in her absence, Becca growled, "You tell me. The two of you are worse than a couple of old ladies."

"Bec, I can't tell you anything you don't already know. The man's smitten and you are the object of his affections whether you like it or not." What he couldn't tell her was that Terry was completely gaga over her. If Becca suspected the intensity of Terry's feelings, he knew she would head for the hills. Danny had told Terry to play it cool if he didn't want to scare her off, although he doubted Terry could keep himself in check much longer; the man had it bad.

Becca didn't answer. She stared out the window at the sparse landscape surrounding them. San Diego was one of the most temperate climates in the world. It was usually in the mid to low seventies, sunshine most days and a slight breeze off the ocean year round but for the twice annual gusting Santa Ana winds. The base was mostly flat. The military need for a grid justified the razing of most of the trees at its inception, yet Becca had learned where to look to see remnants of the stark desert beauty.

The dry winter landscape had caused most of the plants to go dormant; the base didn't water like the surrounding suburbs. Becca let her eyes slide over most of the brown vegetation. The naked twisting branches of a small copse of trees just beyond the base's fence line behind the airfield was one of her favorite places within sight of the base and her eyes focused intently to catch as much as she could before they passed. The trees overlooked a semi-wild patch of ground that would be dotted with native wildflowers in the spring and summer. Becca found rare and invaluable peace sitting in the trees after a run and enjoying the smells of dry ground, the bark of the Cypress trees, and the occasional whiff of jet fuel.

"He's a good guy, Bec. It wouldn't kill you to give him a little more." Danny spoke softly, bringing her mind back inside the car. "You know he'd treat you like a queen if you'd let him."

"What? I know, Danny." She struggled to keep the rising aggravation out of her voice. Her partner knew her tendency to be a loner but he was a bit of a romantic. Becca was going to be lonely in life and that was that. She'd accepted it, why couldn't he? It didn't help her mood that every time she turned around either Danny or Terry, or even Michelle, was at her about her feelings. Soon she'd have to end things with Terry or she'd lose her partner's respect and that was something she couldn't do. Danny was too important to her.

Becca felt a pain in her stomach and had a sudden flash of Terry's face, twisted and white with pain. The flash was strong and she inhaled sharply at the image. As was usually the case, there was too little to use to figure out any particulars as to when or where this would happen and Becca was left to pick apart the minutiae of what she had seen in

11

that brief premonition. Initially, she thought she was seeing their breakup only she couldn't imagine he would take it *that* hard. Thankfully, if Danny sensed something he kept it to himself.

She spent a lot of time in her head and Danny was used to her odd behavior. In a way, he was the closest friend she'd ever had. He let her strange gasps and exclamations at her thoughts go without question and went with her when her gut instinct gave her direction. It hadn't steered them wrong yet and her partner trusted it as much as she did, even if she did give him the willies.

It was a Thursday and not much would happen that day. Some speeding, the occasional traffic stop for distracted driving but no big occurrences. Those were the problem of the night MPs. Danny and Becca were day shift for another week yet, meaning they would have a relatively easy time of it. She knew it was a reward for their smooth handling of several potentially severe issues the month before.

One incident had been at a bar just off base involving several Marines and a lot of Tequila. The call came in that they had gone from having a good time to being belligerent. Danny had started to enter until Becca unexpectedly stopped him from going in the front doors. Instead, when they went around back, they saw one in the process of smacking his girlfriend around outside her car. Danny had taken him into custody and Becca went in to escort the other two outside, where they could be handcuffed and delivered safely and without further incident, to sleep it off. The bartender had commented to Danny how fortuitous it had been that they had come in the back; one of the men had been planning to jump them when they came in the front door. Only Becca knew it had nothing to do with fortune or luck.

Their shift was up by five and Danny dropped her off at the mess hall to get dinner. Becca thanked him, grabbing a light dinner before heading home to change for her nightly run off base. Knowing the guards on duty had its privileges.

The meal sat like lead in her belly, but she prepared for her run regardless. The conversation with Danny about Terry had been bothering her, as had her vision of him in pain. Being out in the crisp night air would clear her head.

Becca adored the long, cool nights. They gave her the ability to run hidden in the evening shadows, to let herself melt away and be free for a short while. Soon they would be gone with the impending spring but for now she enjoyed what was left of them. She took different routes to change up the scenery, except for the end. In the end she always ended up in the same place, her Cypress trees behind the airfield.

This night was no different. Becca wore dark running pants and a black long-sleeved shirt with a black fleece pullover tied around her waist to keep her warm when she would be sitting in the wood after she'd finished her light five mile circuit. The similarly colored stocking cap on her head would help her to remain warm in the cooling desert air.

At the outset of the run Becca felt her dinner, albeit light, pressing at the back of her throat. Swallowing her discomfort and maybe something extra, she set out and focused on her breathing and patterns of her footfalls. Within minutes, her stride was steady and Becca felt her head clearing, concentrating on the smooth way that her muscles propelled her forward.

Once out, Becca was glad she had chosen such dark clothing. The moon was full and she felt exposed in the few sets of headlights that touched her before she got off the main road. Running alone at night did not make her wary like it did other women because Becca's instincts had always kept her safe, as she trusted them to do now. If a path felt wrong, she turned down another. She wasn't sure why but somehow she just knew no harm would come to her as long as she listened.

Halfway in, Becca felt her dinner at the back of her throat again. A twisting knot in her side threw off her stride. She pushed on, determined to be in command of her body. Another mile clicked past. Becca clutched her side to hold the searing pain that had planted itself there, unwilling to be moved. By the time she smelled the Cypress trees, Becca had stopped and vomited in the underbrush twice. She'd given up all pretenses of running and was now walking briskly toward the peace she craved in the small oasis.

Reaching her destination at last, Becca sat down heavily in the leaf litter, pausing only long enough to remove her pullover from her waist. She donned the clothing from habit, not need. She was overheated to the point she worried she had a fever. The fear that she had food poisoning crossed her mind fleetingly and Becca quickly cast it aside. Dinner had not sat well from the get go, food poisoning took longer to set in. Her best course of action was to catch her breath and then see where she was at physically, before deciding what to do. The idea that she needed to be home was foreign. The four walls that made up her housing were in no way as relaxing as this spot. All things being equal, she would rather be here.

Becca pulled her knees up to her chest and wrapped her arms around them, leaning back against the rough, partially peeled bark of the tree. Her head spun and her stomach clenched again; Becca breathed deeply to avoid retching though she doubted anything remained in her stomach. The last mile of stomach-emptying run had taken care of that. Her slow breathing, combined with the earthy smell she drew in through her nose and mouth, was comforting and she rested her spinning head on her knees.

Chapter 2

A distant coyote howled and another answered, closer. Becca remained still. She knew the base was surrounded by a coyote fence. It was chain link with razor wire on top that kept out more than coyotes. That would have been more soothing if she was actually *on* the base and not paralleling it. But by the sound of the howl, the coyote was far off and not a threat to her.

She kept her eyes closed, listening to the mournful cries of the pack. The light outside her closed lids faded and Becca felt the moon slide behind the clouds, the complete darkness welcome to her splitting head. Another howl sounded, closer this time. She fought down the primal urge to cringe at their predatory night chorus. She was relatively safe here. No healthy coyote would attack a grown human and her body still screamed at her for her exertions. She felt no compulsion to move.

Something canine barked, big, harsh barks nearer still than the coyotes' howls. They didn't sound like the dogs she had grown up hearing. She wasn't an expert in wildlife and couldn't be sure what she was hearing but Danny had told her they did not have wolves in this part of California anymore. Only coyotes and wild dogs, some of which she seriously suspected she would be meeting soon. Becca scanned the darkness nervously.

As would be expected, her eyes found nothing. Her gorge rose again and she stood hurriedly, stumbling out a few yards, not wanting to soil her place of solitude. Stomach now certainly empty, Becca staggered back to resume her prone position on her nest of leaves and soft moss, resting her head against the tree trunk at her back.

Heavy, rhythmic pounding reached her ears. Becca sat bolt upright, her mind digging down to its subconscious level to identify why hearing the mixture of sounds was so alarming. Neither alone was alarming but put together they caused her chest to tighten painfully, and then it came to her. Her vision from this morning. It was here, confronting her head on. The visions were coming faster and more frequently of late, seemingly undeterred by the fact that they were entirely unwanted. Now wasn't the time to analyze why this was happening.

As soon as she made the connection to her vision, Becca's felt stupid for not seeing her symptoms for what they were. They often preceded an "event." It was clumsy of her to have assumed the nausea had been from dinner, even if it had been reminiscent of eating a shoe covered in butter sauce.

In that instant, she was afraid. Memory could guide Becca home but she knew the fastest route was still nearly a mile back, along roads that would be deserted this time of night. Anyone going out was already there and wouldn't be coming back until well after midnight. That seemed to be the routine. As an MP, no one was more aware of the daily patterns of the men and women living here than her.

Having decided against the inevitable failure of running, she began to shuffle around on the ground, feeling for a fallen branch or rock, anything she could use as a weapon to defend herself. She prayed silently for the clouds to pass and the moon to return, and with it her sight. Meanwhile, she listened to the thumping. It was familiarly cadenced; something in the way it moved told her it couldn't be human. The footfalls were in a four beat rhythm. A loud rhythm. It was a big, heavy animal. She would have thought a horse by the thunder, except the odd muffling of the sound and lack of clattering on the many rocks said paws, not hooves. Becca tried to remember if anyone had a large dog near the base. She had patrolled the perimeter for over a year and could not recall anything larger than a Labrador. This was big. This was no Labrador.

When the footfalls were nearly upon her she deciphered a second set closing in as well. Simultaneously, Becca's hand touched a branch as long and thick as her arm. She hoped it wasn't so old it would break when she tried to use it; it would have to do. The sounds became slower as the paws reached

16

her trees. Loud snuffling came from nearby off to her left.
Becca pressed her back against the broadest part of the trunk
and opened her eyes as wide as she could. In her head, she
reached down trying to find the extra sense that had kept her
safe all her life. Unfortunately, it had been screeching at her
for so long its initial trigger had gotten mixed up with her fear
and she couldn't separate the two. It was not going to give
her a better idea of what she faced. Feeling abandoned,
Becca waited with her makeshift club poised.

She did not wait long. A small yip sounded right beside her
and she swung her club where she thought a large dog's head
would be. She was rewarded with a surprised yelp and the
feel of the repercussion as it connected solidly with a dense
mass. Having some direction, she followed the first blow
with another shorter jab. This one again resulted in a
satisfying connection and she heard the debris under their feet
shift as the dog retreated.

The other one reached them. She heard more scuffling in
front of her and a low whine. The other dog yipped back.
Becca raised her club, opening her eyes still wider to no avail.
With no external light there was nothing for her eyes to work
with. But just as she felt a cloak of dismay beginning to
weigh her down, a glimmer of light broke through and shone
from above. The cloud covering the moon moved on, leaving
it to shine once more. Although as soon as the light came,
Becca wished it would disappear again.

The icy fingers of fear, true and awful, mind-numbing fear
clawed its way into her spine. A stone's throw from her
position stood two enormous shaggy beasts that had to be
wolves, though where they came from she could only
speculate. Part of her brain believed them escapees from the
zoo while discounting it in the same passing stroke. Another
part of her brain told her these were more than just animal.
She watched them look at each other, one tipping its head as
if listening and the other appearing to nod in agreement.

Shaking it off as a hallucination in her agitated state, Becca
raised her club again like she was up at bat, positioning

herself against a tree to keep her back guarded. Speaking her thoughts aloud often acted as a therapeutic device for Becca and was a byproduct of too much time spent alone. Now she did it hoping it would give her strength and also hoping her human voice would sooth the large creatures.

"That will teach me to ignore my gut," she began in a low voice. "I *saw* you coming last night and I didn't listen. Now that we know both of us can hurt each other let's agree to part ways, huh? You go your way, I'll go mine." She gave free rein to her thoughts out of a need to hear something other than their heavy panting, which just made her focus all the more on the two sets of large white teeth well within leaping distance of her all too fragile flesh.

The wolves closed their mouths, tipping their heads in her direction, and blinked. Becca foolishly thought it looked like they could understand. Nervous yet hopeful she was soothing them at least, Becca continued talking. Better to have them calm than seeing her as a threat.

"Well, I guess I didn't see you. I heard you, but I saw something else with you in my vision." A chuckle, high pitched with strain, leaked through, "I had no idea you'd be quite like this though. Where in hell did you come from and why are you so damned big?" Seeing them temporarily captivated, Becca made the decision to try to reach the road. She pushed herself smoothly away from the tree and began to take small, careful steps backward.

"Don't follow me. Stay where you are," she said in a singsong chant she found comforting. It sounded like a soothing tune her mother used to hum when she was doing chores around the house. Becca ignored the picture of her mother, not needing the distraction. "I'm nothing interesting, nothing to follow."

Her feet were making minimal noise as she carefully stepped back, over and again in high exaggerated steps in an effort not to get caught up on anything and trip. By her recollection she should be out of the trees in another few feet.

18

Then she would have a quarter mile of relatively flat desert scrub to navigate before she'd be behind the safety of the fence. She worried she would get hung up in any of the low lying tangles of brush that were impossible to walk through, or fall into a nest of snakes or scorpions in the process.

Not giving up and pushing aside the fear clouding her senses, Becca tried to feel for any guidance her instincts might be giving her. Giving herself over to her faith in her instincts, Becca closed her eyes and breathed steadily in and out, quieting herself so that she could listen.

Calmer now, she was more receptive. As soon as her eyes closed, she heard not the sound inside her head warning her, but a sound outside which crept in, distracting her. It was the sound of paws crunching the dried matter beneath them as they slowly stalked after her. Becca heard the paws beginning to fall in more rapid succession. The wolves were curious again.

She opened her eyes and focused on those now closing in on her. The wolf in the lead was a rich chestnut color, regarding her evenly with green eyes far more intelligent than a normal animal should be. As she stared into them, she felt her instinct telling her this was okay; this was not what she needed to be afraid of. As crazy as it sounded, she didn't question it.

Becca stopped moving backward and the wolves halted with her. The only sound in the ensuing silence was the soft sound of their breathing. Her gaze was drawn to the green eyes of the lead wolf. Letting her body do what her mind should have screamed at her not to, Becca extended a hand out to the large cinnamon muzzle inches from her fingertips.

At her gesture, the creature cocked his head and blinked. Becca got the impression he was deciding how to take her advance.

"That's right, don't be afraid, wolf. I think you're a good wolf. You won't hurt me." She kept up the singsong cadence, humming after the words were gone.

19

The large black nose closed the distance between it and her hand, touching her and snuffling loudly on her palm. It tickled and Becca smiled. The green eyes rose to hers again and she swore she saw him wink. Yes, it felt like a *him*. Her shoulders eased in increments while she kept her hand extended, not sure what to do from there, afraid to break the truce they'd reached.

A low growl erupted from the creature moving up beside the green eyed wolf. This one was slightly smaller and more honey brown with amber eyes. A female perhaps? As it approached, Becca's guiding instinct told her this one did not share the same forgiving nature as its counterpart.

Becca didn't dare glance away to see how far she was now from the road that would lead her back onto the base. She was certain as soon as she broke her stare the smaller wolf would leap and Becca did not entertain any illusions what her future would be from there.

While Becca stared at the amber-eyed threat, she felt the low vibrations from the larger one's rumblings through her fingers, still a hands breadth from its teeth. Fearing it was now in agreement with the smaller one that Becca should be eaten, she shot a quick glance at it to see how close the big one had gotten, certain it would be the last thing she would ever see.

Except when she looked, she saw that its giant head was turned *away* from her. His growls were aimed at the other one, not Becca. She let her instinct guide her again and took a quick step that put her at the shoulder of the big one, creating a barricade with his body.

Becca standing that close to its comrade pushed the smaller one over the edge. Her growl rose to a snarl and she stood up on her hind feet, the male rose to meet her and their bodies collided with a bone jarring crash felt through the earth beneath her feet. Becca stepped back too quickly and her heel caught on a low bramble, bringing her down hard on her back. The momentum carried her head to the ground where it struck a rock with a dull thud.

The snarling kept her attention on the immediate threat of the female wolf and Becca ignored the pain knifing through her head accompanied by the warm flow of liquid now traveling down the back of her neck to soak into her shirts.

The female stopped snarling, lifted her muzzle in Becca's direction to sniff, and her lips pulled back into an eerily human smile. In a feat of acrobatic beauty, the honey colored female pulled up her front legs, twisted her front half and leapt over the male's larger form. She barely landed before lunging at Becca who rolled out of the way just in time.

Teeth grabbed her shoe and, reacting automatically, Becca mustered all the strength she had and kicked the tender nose with her other foot. Roaring in pain and fury, the female reared back and threw herself at Becca. The male bit her side but it did not hinder her attack in the least. Instead, she dropped lower until her teeth were inches from Becca's chin and her teeth locked onto the neck of her shirt. The shock of the female's hot breath on her skin made Becca jump, tearing her pullover open to her undershirt. Her dog tags flashed in the moonlight.

"Stop," a dark, firm voice called out of the darkness.

The wolves fell back a full body length and sat on their haunches. Becca couldn't see where the voice had come from and was only half certain it hadn't been imagined, due in part to the blood leaking in thick, steady drops down her back.

One of the wolves whined. Becca hadn't seen but guessed it to be the male because of the other's snarling response.

"That is enough," the voice cracked out deep and commanding.

The wolves lay down on their bellies, muzzles stretched out before them with their ears flat to their heads, their supplication total.

Becca was dizzy; the moon was again slipping behind the fast moving clouds and her vision was rapidly disappearing. Fearfully she tried to scurry backward, putting more distance between herself and the multiple threats facing her before she lost all ability to see them. There was no cover here at the edge of her trees. Her hand groped beside her in vain trying to locate the makeshift club she had lost when she'd fallen.

The darkness that engulfed her was immense. Her eyes widened, trying to catch a glimpse of the source of the mysterious voice and saw nothing. Becca put her hand behind her head and pulled it away, sticky and wreaking of salty iron. The amount on her hand did not bode well for her endurance even if she could see to run. Protectively, she pulled her legs up, making herself as small as possible, and stared out into the night. Waiting seemed to be her only option.

It felt an eternity, though in reality it was probably less than a minute, when Becca finally saw something. At first she thought it was the moonlight shining on an object. When it moved steadily nearer, the terror she already felt doubled to a paralyzing level even her military training could not overcome.

The white orb from her vision, the one she had neglected to remember in the wake of the wolves, shone of its own accord, gliding forward ever closer. As it drew near she could make out the two dark holes were actually a pair of eyes sunken into a bone white face, absent any sign of hair or color. The eyes focused on her and Becca could not stop the frightened whimper that escaped her lips. Their obsidian color stole their spark, the only sign of life, from the light above. None came from within. She was as obedient as the wolves who so clearly called this nightmarish creature their master.

"Forgive them. They lose much of their reason when the moon waxes full. We did not know you were one of ours." The voice, so bold before, was now silky smooth, gliding over her mind and covering it with a haze to make all else foggy and unclear.

Becca could not speak to him; only gape in wonder. She thought she saw him scenting the air as the female wolf had done, but in the darkness it was hard for her to be sure what she was seeing. A passing thought of her likely concussion had her wondering if any of this was even real.

His face drew nearer and Becca felt an urge to pull away while the powerful macabre allure of his dead eyes held her firm. When he was hovering over her, Becca's neck craned back to see a white hand come forward from the darkness and felt it stroke her blood slick neck. His fingers were ice cold, sending shivers down her spine not just from temperature, but from the revulsion that twisted her insides at his touch.

With his hand still on her flesh, the white figure felt her cringe and, instead of retracting his fingers, he let them trail down her neck to follow the curve of her collarbone, leaving them there in a silent assurance that she breathed at his whim. Seeing Becca's comprehension, he smiled.

His long pointed canines were the last thing Becca saw before the looming darkness inside her mind enveloped her.

Chapter 3

The sound of shuffling feet and crackling paper amidst the general hush surrounding her told Becca she was not dead, unless she had died and gone to the DMV. Her ears picked up the beeping and whirring of monitors, her nose filled with the light scent of disinfectant, and she knew she was very much alive.

Before she opened her eyes, she did a mental diagnostic of her own. The pounding in her head from the impact was still there, though it had lessened to a dull headache. Assuming they had something stronger than a few aspirin lying around, she could handle it. There were no injuries beyond a few aches and pains she could feel. Her last memory coming back to her in a flash, her hand flew to her throat and her fingers felt carefully for the punctures she feared would be there, then laughed at herself for believing the impossibility.

Becca let her hand find the injury that *was* real. Easy to find, it was marked by a shaved patch on the back of her head and tape covering the rough ends of what felt like stitches. The tape ran the length of her thumb. No wonder she had seen all of those things, she mused. That rock had really rung her bell.

Her muddy brain started to chug back to life and tried to put order to the chaos within. She had obviously been in such an altered state that she had seen two large dogs out walking with their owner, the one who had found her and brought her here after she slipped and cracked her head. Only her imaginings could have given the dogs the wolflike traits she imagined or the man such a nightmarish image. A little nudge was all her overactive imagination needed to turn the ordinary into the paranormal.

Her explanation made sense, except for the nagging detail of her prescient dream. Becca justified it away as a premonition of what she thought could have happened, not the reality. Not entirely satisfied with her thin attempt to mollify her unquiet mind, she had at least put things in some sense of order, enough to be tucked away for the present, when the doctor entered.

He was an older man, gray receding brush cut, a carbon copy of her father and marking him as a Marine. She knew without a word that he would be buried in that cut.

"Rebecca." He addressed her without her rank. Only the doctors did that on base. "Glad to have you back with us. That's quite a nasty gash you have on your head. Care to tell me what happened?" His attempt at a warm smile fell short. The doctor was a little too clinical to have a good bedside manner. Becca might be the only patient who didn't mind such a lapse, she didn't care to discuss her situation in too much detail.

She nodded without thinking and stopped when her vision glazed from the motion. "I was out for a run and slipped. I hit my head on a rock and I must have passed out." Becca gave him the version of events she had settled on. "Did the man who brought me in give you his name? I wanted to thank him."

Dr. Kinch, according to the tag on his white coat, knit his brows and cocked his head at her. "The MP's found you next to the road about a half mile from your quarters. Did you see a uniform? Maybe remember his rank or what branch?" Miramar was home to Navy and Marine as well as some occasional visiting personnel from other branches waiting on ships.

Her explanation struck down, she found herself at a loss and shook her head dumbly, waiting for everything to make sense. Nausea made her stop moving and lay her head back against her pillow.

"That's too bad. It was a good thing you got here. That gash on your head took ten stitches and you have a good concussion." He referenced the chart in his hands. "We'll be keeping you overnight, just in case."

A knock on the door stopped any further uncomfortable questioning. Becca was glad for it, until she saw to whom the knuckles belonged.

"Hey Bec," Terry's gentle voice called out softly.

She sighed, tired, and had to force a smile. Luckily, the doctor saved her.

"You can only stay a few minutes, son." The bars on Terry's sleeves gave anyone familiar with the uniform instant recognition of his rank while the medals on his chest spoke to how he earned it.

Doctor Kinch outranked him, he could call him what he wanted.

Terry nodded his head at the doctor, barely taking his eyes off Becca to do so. As soon as they were alone he rested one cheek and thigh on the edge of the bed, taking her small hand in his larger one. The concern in his crystalline blue eyes was genuine, and what else Becca saw there caused her great discomfort.

As much as she wished she could, Becca could not return the depth of the affections of the gentle soul who obviously loved her. She winced at the thought that she would inevitably hurt him and Terry mistook her discomfort for something else.

He shot up from his precarious perch on her bed. "I'm sorry Becca, did I hurt you? Are you okay?"

She was so small he often worried he had caused her injury, never mind she had gone through the same rigorous training he had. Eye rolling would hurt so she refrained. A delicate flower she was not, but try explaining that to her big strong boyfriend.

Becca stared at Sergeant Terry Schnackenberg, Schnack to his friends. He was an impressive man at two inches over six feet, regulation brown hair and lean fit body from years of soccer before a life in the Corps. At twenty-seven he was five years her senior and, with the same self-assuredness that was going to make him an officer, he guided their relationship. Hanging back and balking were her only necessary communication skills. It worked for her in a broken way though it was not enough for someone like him. He deserved more and it pained her to admit it to herself. Their time together had been pleasant, even if limited by necessity.

Becca shook her head in at his query. The movement pulled at her fresh stitches and brought back her dizziness in spades. "I'm okay. Just fuzzy that's all."

Concern gave way to one of Terry's other impressive traits; his investigatory skills. He should have been the MP, not Becca, though he was destined for a higher command. Something Becca was avoiding like the plague, much to her father's enduring disappointment. They were already grooming Terry for his commission. "Tell me what happened?" His tone was gentle enough, but Becca knew from experience he would not relent without some form of explanation.

With as little detail as she could muster, Becca told him the same as she'd told the doctor. "I was out for a run and slid on a rock in the dark. I hit my head and must have passed out. When I came to, I was here." She gestured at the bed beneath her weakly with one hand.

Terry frowned, then his features relaxed. He had his doubts yet, to his credit, he was not going to grill her just yet.

Grateful, Becca smiled at him. The investigator was gone, replaced by the loving boyfriend Becca knew she was going to have to wound all too soon.

He tried to joke with her. "You know, if you had been with *me* none of this would have happened."

Becca bit back her groan. They'd talked earlier this week. Terry wanted her to come over tonight for dinner and a movie. He'd tried nearly every combination of events to orchestrate a sleepover, all to no avail. She didn't see why it was so important to him, except that now it must be a battle line in his head. Honestly, it was in hers too. Sex was one thing, but sleepovers were quite another. With the high probability of giving herself away, unguarded sleep was something she could not share with him, ever. As dear as Terry was, comfortable with strangeness he was not. He was a lot like her father. She was sure a therapist would have a field day with that one.

Her father, Corps to the end, was a hard but a good man. He wanted one of his sons to follow in his footsteps and had been disappointed when they had both declined. Seeking his approval, Becca had been the one of the three kids who had enlisted. Except it was in the Navy and not in his beloved Corps; strike one. Plus the fact that she blatantly refused to seek a commission as an officer; strike two. Becca didn't want to risk strike three; they rarely spoke anymore.

Forcing a smile, she kept her reply innocuous. "You know I have to work tomorrow. I can't be over when I have to work in the morning. It exhausts me to be up so late."

His proud grin rewarded her well-aimed comment. Predictably, he took it as a compliment to his sexual prowess. His vanity was a useful tool if manipulated properly. Becca found it helpful since he'd begun to pressure her for a more serious level of commitment. Terry leaned over and kissed her lightly on the mouth, sending out his tongue in a slow sweep to remind her what she'd missed this night, when a throat cleared in the doorway.

The pinchy-faced nurse did not warrant any arguments, her message was clear. Terry stood, gave Becca a warm smile, and promised to return in the morning. She twisted her mouth up at the corners holding a false smile until he spun on his heel and her positive exterior crumpled. Becca promptly slunk down into her pillow wishing morning would not come.

28

Alas, it did. Morning sunlight broke through the white metal blinds prevalent in every building on the base. Apparently the military's adversity to sleeping in extended to the unwell. The window dressings did nothing to blacken the room and Becca's faced east. Fortunately she was not a late sleeper, but the sunlight did bring her headache roaring back.

The morning nurse stopped in to read her machines and agreed to bring her something for the pain. Becca closed her eyes again, willing the man with the hammer in her head to stop smacking the backs of her eyeballs. In record time, he did.

In one magical instant, Becca's pain in her head stopped and euphoria swept through her. Giddy was not a typical feeling for her so what to do with it eluded her. Becca felt her expression lighten as her entire body relaxed. Keeping her eyes closed, reveling in the release from the pain that had been a regular part of her consciousness for the last twelve hours, she breathed a deep sigh of relief. She had never had a painkiller kick in so fast, nor appreciated one so greatly.

Chapter 4

The stranger that walked into the woman's room had never set eyes on her before. He'd been given a name and strict orders by his Commanding Officer to bring her to him at once. That was not an order to be disobeyed. The officer had come to retrieve her at his CO's behest, "even if she requires prodding," were his exact words. The officer did not like his mission but it was not his place to argue. The CO dealt harshly with dissenters.

He had excellent eyesight, better than most, and as he approached from the hall he saw the face of the woman he was to escort. Her forehead was crinkled up, the marks of chronic strain easily readable in the lines on her face to a man as observant as the officer sent to retrieve her. Drawing the breath necessary to make his words heard, he entered the room.

When his foot crossed the threshold the tight expression he beheld in his first sighting transformed from tense and bitter to light, relaxed and, arguably very attractive if one were into the type. Drawing nearer, he reassessed the words he had been readying for his charge. The small, serene face he looked down upon having lost its edge now had the countenance of a mere child. Certainly this could not be the woman he was sent to claim. Opening his mouth, he asked more gently than was his usual curt manner.

"Petty Officer Sauter."

The long medium brown lashes fluttered and the refreshing smile faded to a memory, visible only at the edges of her pale pink lips in an instant. Her hazel eyes were large and pronounced as they opened in her heart shaped face. The eyes themselves were unremarkable, but the few seconds that had transpired when she opened her eyes and had not yet closed herself off showed him a tiny glimpse into a soul he had not anticipated in one so young. The deep sadness housed within such delicate features inspired a protective feeling in the officer's breast he'd not felt in a lifetime. She was so small and weak, more so than others of her kind. The sentiment was wholly unexpected and gave him an uncomfortable twinge. The admiral wanted her for something, it wouldn't do to get attached.

"Yes, Sir." Becca's exterior shifted in a heartbeat to lose all remnants of pleasure. Upon realizing she was being addressed by a superior officer, her body exhibited all of the human signs of stress. Her heartbeat accelerated, sweat appeared on her upper lip and her pupils constricted. She began to rise out of respect, face paling at once with the effort.

Before she could move more than a few inches to swing her leg over the edge of the bed, a cool hand; a very *strong* cool hand gripped her calf and stopped her in her tracks.

The cerulean blue-eyed, black-haired captain, her quick notice identified him from force of habit, who had addressed her had an unreadable expression on his smooth face. Becca was embarrassed. The captain was holding her leg firmly and Becca felt her face flushing at his familiar touch. Yet even with her elevated stress level, his touch soothed her. Once his hand was on her, she felt her head clearing of pain and her heart decelerating. The ensuing peace she felt was foreign and she felt nothing other than relief washing over her at its unexpected arrival. It did not disappear entirely when his hand slowly eased itself off her limb. Becca blinked at the strange effect the drugs were having on her.

Head clearing, she examined the captain at her bedside. He was a good-looking man, if a little pale, and she was imagining what she looked like at the present. It was no comparison. Self-consciously she ran her hands through her hair to make sure it wasn't sticking up. It wasn't but that could have been due to the amount of sand she felt beneath her fingertips. Great. Finger combing her dusty locks, she managed to sneak a glance or two at his long, lean form and had a momentary flash of seeing his pale chest, naked and hovering over her. Heat rushed into her cheeks and her fingers dropped to her side.

By the bemused expression on the face of her attractive visitor, she assumed her awkwardness hadn't gone unnoticed. Not being able to stand, Becca did not completely forget herself. With as much dignity and respect as she could muster, she raised her hand in a smart salute, lowering it only upon his command to be "at ease."

"I have been ordered to escort you to Admiral Black. If you will accompany me we will be on our way." The captain adjusted his cap, tucked securely under his arm. His raven black hair, long enough to hint at a soft wave, caught her eye because of its unusual length. The tag on his breast announced his name was Rossi, terribly Italian for such deeply blue eyes.

Becca masked her confusion well behind her blank sailor's face. An outranking officer did not request, he ordered. This one spoke to her as a gentleman, not a superior. She watched him closely for signs of sarcasm, thinking she was missing something with her head being so rattled. Had she seen Admiral Black's name in a recent report, or had any dealings with Captain Rossi she wondered, searching her memory. No, she'd never seen him before. She would remember someone like him, and she had no recollection of an Admiral Black. Her pulse quickened in apprehension. He had asked her to go with him but she was supposed to stay in the hospital for another day. Not that she wanted to mind you, however the doctors had ordered her to do so and orders were orders.

"Sir, I'm not supposed to leave today. Doctor's orders, Sir." Becca hadn't meant to be rude, still it sounded rather abrupt to her ears.

The strong jaw tightened and Becca heard his teeth grind, evidencing a quick temper. He was not used to being denied. "I have my orders and the admiral outranks your doctor, Sauter."

Three years in the service had done much for Becca's ability to take an order and not get ruffled, but the way this

Captain Rossi asserted himself rankled her. It was difficult to keep her upper lip from curling into a sneer.

"I am sorry but the doctor has advised me his orders are to be followed until I am returned to the command of my commanding cfficer, *Sir*." Her disrespectful tone was nothing short of insubordination and Captain Rossi knew it.

His teeth ground, jaw whitening from pressure as he replaced his cap firmly on his head and spun on his heel to retreat from the room without another sound.

As her migraine came galloping back, Becca was left to wonder what that was all about, although not for long. On his heels arrived Terry, eager to pick up where he left off the night before as doting boyfriend.

"Hey Bec. I wanted to stop by before breakfast and see how you were doing." He glanced around sheepishly. "I'm not supposed to be here, you know. But I had to see you." He leaned over and kissed her lightly, fearing he would break her if he applied any pressure at all.

"Thanks Terry." When she was out of here she was definitely going to have to put an end to this. "I just woke up and I think I'll be okay as soon as the nurse brings me my aspirin. She's taking a really long time." Becca forced a pained smile, hating her manipulation, yet needing to keep a distance from him.

The mention of a task gave him purpose. Terry held up a finger, telling her to wait, and strode out of the room on a mission to retrieve aspirin for his wounded lady. Chivalrous to a fault, that was Terry. Also chauvinistic, she reminded herself. He'd made several comments about females as officers that were all too telling of his opinion on the subject. Becca let them go. Her desire to remain *out* of the rank of officer meant it would not be a subject for them and she'd always known theirs would not be a long-term relationship. She wasn't capable. Poor Terry, being old-fashioned wasn't a crime.

Just as Terry left the doctor returned, rushing to keep up with the captain striding, no gliding, a few steps in front of him. His face was again completely calm and smooth, no visible signs of the frustration he'd exhibited before his exit.

"Rebecca, Captain Rossi has orders to remove you from my care," Dr. Kinch stated in a bland voice, his hands twitched indicating some level of unrest while his face remained lax. "Are you feeling well enough to travel?"

Nodding her head gently, not trusting the feared mallet in her skull that had just disappeared, again at bay, Becca replied. "Sir, if the captain insists and you approve, I can sign your release." Risking a glance at Captain Rossi's figure standing what must have been just shy of six feet and more imposing than many men larger than he, Becca met his steady blue gaze already studying her pointedly. A chill, not entirely unpleasant, tickled down her spine. Embarrassed all over again, Becca turned her eyes back to the doctor.

He grunted and began to fill out paperwork in the chart. Dr. Kinch noisily flipped back and forth between sheets on his clipboard and clicked his pen repeatedly whenever he had to think. Several times he glanced at the Captain, appearing to seek approval.

The captain gave him none. He stood completely still, hands at his sides. Becca was beginning to feel stupid with so much attention on her. She was almost relieved when the captain spoke again to give her purpose. His voice held a minor gravelly rumble to its depths, which in her state, made her think she could almost feel it grating across her skin and raising goosebumps on her arms. Again, worried he could sense the direction of her thoughts, Becca felt her face flushing.

The captain was enjoying watching the expressive young woman run through so many emotions at once. There was something amusing about her constant embarrassments and frustrations. It had been a long time since he had allowed himself to be in such close proximity to a woman like this one. Her internal struggle captivated him and he felt the unusual need to hear her voice again. Deep within him his nature stirred.

He shot the doctor the sideways look he had apparently been waiting for, and his pen raced furiously down the pages. "If you will dress, we will be better able to leave here."

Becca blanched as a detail came back to her. "Sir, I apologize but I was informed my clothing was discarded. It was ruined in my accident and I forgot to request a change be brought up from my quarters. I didn't think I'd be leaving so soon." Her hand ran up the back of her neck to touch the rough thread holding her scalp together. She could only imagine the amount of blood she had lost; the recollection of it dripping down her back made her shudder.

The jaw did not clench this time when the captain spun and left the room without a word. She wondered at his strange behavior. He was impersonal while generally exhibiting proper decorum; an odd combination.

While he was gone, Terry returned victorious with Becca's aspirin. "Here you are." He held a tiny plastic cup of water as well and presented them to her with a staged half-bow.

The euphoria she felt when the doctor and captain made their appearance had now completely dissipated and the tiny man was back in her skull pounding away. Without argument, Becca accepted his findings and downed them both, handing back the empty cup.

Terry took in the doctor's frantic note scribbling and Becca sitting up on her bed. "What did I miss?"

Captain Rossi chose that moment to return, an immediately recognizable bundle of shades of blue in his hands. His lips tightened, eyes hardening when he saw the man sitting familiarly on the edge of the woman's bed. His voice was sharp this time. "Sauter, you will need to put these on."

35

Terry spun to face the new voice, taking the man in with a nervous tweak to his stomach as something base within him told him to fear this captain. Clearly not one to back down, Terry straightened his back and raised his chin. Outranked but needing to stake his claim, Terry kept his voice just within the respectful range. "Sir, might I ask where you are taking Bec, er Petty Officer Sauter?"

"No you may not. My business with Sauter does not concern you." His instant dislike of this man had him struggling to keep his voice even. It would not do for him to lose his temper here; people would get hurt. Starting with this one. He was reading the young man and did not like what he saw. The man was used to getting his way and preferred to be in control. He had more than likely chosen the young woman as his companion because of her diminutive size and, he was guessing, non-argumentative personality though he was not so sure about that last bit. Captain Rossi felt his urge to protect the young woman rising again in the presence of this bully who was making obvious his claim on her. Rossi understood being under someone's thumb.

Turning his attentions back to the woman, he held out the fatigues he had obtained from the nursing staff without difficulty. His charming influences over their kind were handy at times. "Please."

Becca was pleased to be shut of whatever was going on between Terry and the captain. She started to swing her legs down again, this time unimpeded, only Terry jumped first, twisting his body to block her.

"Becca you have a concussion, you can't be up yet." He shot Rossi a look that blasted well over the line well into dangerous territory. "I'm sure the doctor has explained that already."

The doctor did not so much as slow his pen. Becca started to feel like she was in Wonderland, and equally as confused as young Alice just come down the rabbit hole. Did she exist? If she spoke, would it have any bearing on this exchange?

Captain Rossi had not considered the reality that she could still be effected by her injuries or that she could be harmed by leaving. He assumed the doctor's wish for her to stay was solely due to some sort of protocol. Years had passed since he'd been in close proximity to someone like her; consideration for her fragile condition failed to cross his mind. That bothered him more than it should.

"I will find a nurse to help you dress, then we must go." Rossi was adamant. The admiral was even less understanding of human frailties.

Terry saw his opportunity and took it. "No need, Sir. I can handle this." He cracked a smile at the shadow that crossed the captain's face at his mention of helping Becca dress.

Becca had been watching all of this, wondering what the hell was going on. Gone from blissful to all jumbled up in a matter of minutes, she was feeling more than a little out of sorts. Being with both of them and the entranced doctor was starting to creep her out. Eager to be free of all of them, she struggled to her feet. The wave of nausea she expected, though not the dizziness. "Whoa," she cried out as her knees buckled.

Terry's hand swept out to catch her and he tried to brace her against his body. Becca was already embarrassed at being in a hospital gown in front of an officer she didn't recognize. Now she was swooning, bad enough without the additional insult of being *handled* like a weak little girl. Concussion be damned, Becca angrily smacked Terry's hands aside. She couldn't be certain but she thought she saw a flash of teeth from the captain and an unpleasant light in Terry's eyes. That tore it. Becca was a sailor and a good one. A far cry from the child Terry was treating her as. She lurched forward and took the clothing the captain offered as she made her way unsteadily out of the tiny overcrowded room, down the hall, and into the large bathroom to be all by herself.

The visit took a little longer than expected but she emerged feeling more prepared to meet the mysterious Admiral Black who commanded a significant amount of respect if the doctor's lack of argument was any indicator. The bathroom had a shower with wall mounted dispensers and a hand held sprayer. She took the opportunity to wash up, being careful of the stitches, and finger comb her hair. Dressing in the borrowed fatigues, she blushed when she uncovered the fresh underthings tucked under the t-shirt. The visit took a little longer than expected but she reappeared feeling more prepared to meet the mysterious Admiral Black, who commanded a significant amount of respect if the doctor's lack of argument was any indicator.

When she emerged, head spinning wildly, Becca felt like she was going to float off into the atmosphere. She held tight to the handrail running the length of the wall, letting it guide her back to her room.

Upon her arrival Terry leaped up to help her and she tried weakly to object for a second time, but in a very unsailorlike fashion she found herself unable to see straight or stand. Most of her reserves had been spent cleaning up, and, stubborn only got her so far. His arm wrapped around her waist and she extricated herself from his possessive grip to hold his arm instead. She was not by nature a cuddly person and certainly not one for public displays of affection, especially in front of an officer. Fortunately, Terry did not force the issue.

Dr. Kinch broke his silence and grumbled something low, Becca could not make out the words.

The captain did. "Be assured, Doctor, we have medical staff available at our facility. She will be properly cared for should it prove necessary." Rossi's irritation was barely concealed at this point.

"With all due respect, Sir, she clearly needs medical attention. I would like to request that her doctor be given a chance to speak to your CO to explain." Terry tried one more time to keep the two of them apart.

The captain's answer was a disparaging glance at Terry. With that, he wrote off everyone in the room but the woman he was sent to collect.

"Miss." His voice was not as smooth as it had been originally, though he had ironed out quite a bit of the anger the others had helped put there. "May I escort you?" He held out his arm.

The fall must have done more damage to her senses than she thought. Becca had an image in her head of curtseying to the captain but refrained. It was a welcome change that he asked, that he didn't force himself like Terry did. She gave Terry's arm a pat and smiled unsteadily at him, or at least at the one of him in the middle of her increasingly blurry vision. She concentrated on putting one foot in front of the other and crossed over, taking the captain's arm; purely out of practicality, she told herself. Nothing more. Quite honestly, her head was so turned around that was actually believable.

They walked only a few feet before the captain stopped them and looked down. He heard her bare feet padding along the linoleum floor. Changing their course, he aimed for the nurse's station and asked about shoes. They dug out her trainers they'd kept for her. Becca slid them on with a borrowed pair of socks from their bin behind the counter and allowed the captain to escort her out of the hospital. A black Charger waited out front for them. Captain Rossi opened her door, allowing her to climb unsteadily into the vehicle by herself. Having seen her independence upstairs he allowed it, knowing his reflexes were quick enough to catch her should she fall.

Her head was spinning and she worried she would throw up in the car. Rolling down her window and laying her head back on the seat helped ground her only slightly. Before they'd gone a half a mile Becca felt she was losing the battle with herself and, for the first time in years, without the assistance of nauseating drugs such as she'd used in boot camp to quell her dreams, she felt herself drowsing in the presence of another person.

Chapter 5

Unaware of how long she slept, Becca startled awake, the echoes of her scream still raw in her throat. Visions of the white-faced man had come to her again. Dread roiled in the pit of her stomach, its presence as strong as it had been before. She could feel the perspiration beading on her lip and running in tiny lines down her back. Becoming reacquainted with her surroundings and car companion, Becca was mortified realizing she'd had a prolonged vision and said who knew what right in front of this stranger. Quiet and unmoving, she sat with her eyes closed, waiting for him to say something. He did not, though she knew he had heard some sort of ranting in the radio-free silence.

The car slowed a short time later, the smell of jasmine wafting in the windows over a faint smell of fresh water. Becca heard his door open and reached for hers, stopping when she felt it opening seemingly of its own accord before the sound of his door closing was even gone from her ears. Her eyes flicked up and she saw the captain standing, again offering his arm to her without any readable expression on his face.

Accepting it, she made no effort to hide the fact that she was taking stock of her surroundings. They were inland on a plateau part way up in the foothills overlooking a small lake below. A large gothic mansion stood in the foreground, its architecture entirely out of place here in heavily Spanish influenced California. Although with no visible neighbors, it was doubtful anyone had noticed the discrepancy. The sound of the central fountain bounced off the hard surfaces as they made their approach to the large grey stone steps across the crushed white rock.

Her feet were frustratingly unsteady and remaining upright required complete concentration on Becca's part. She was not able to give her destination the more prolonged examination she desired. Nor did she catch the curious glances the captain was sneaking as he escorted her. She had no way of knowing that her vision in the car had given the captain some insight as to why his superior would be interested in her. It did not, however, explain why *he* was drawn to her.

Together, with Becca leaning heavily on her chaperone's arm, they mounted the stone steps and strode through the heavy wooden doors opening before them. Becca's body froze. Her knees locked and would not move.

Feeling her stop, the captain twisted his head to see if she was going to faint. The damage to her head was worse than he had initially thought and he was upset with the admiral for taking her away from doctors before she was ready. He did not understand the urgency, unless her longevity wasn't of interest. He did not like the idea of her being disposable. But the woman's face was pale white, her eyes wide, and the small mouth set in a tiny "O."

"Sauter, we are expected." Placing his hand over where hers lay on his, he pulled gently. Or so he thought. At his tug, she leaped forward and crashed into him.

Becca felt her arm nearly separate from her shoulder and her stomach twirled at her indelicate handling. Staggering, she barely kept her feet. Superior officer or not she planted her feet, put her hand on his side, and leaned back while tugging on the one he was holding. Inconveniently, it was at the same time Captain Rossi decided to loosen his hold on her. Becca fell backward, landing hard on the stone and wishing she had more padding on her posterior.

Captain Rossi was frustrated at her antics but held his temper in check. Her human inability to balance herself thus far had become a problem and would keep her from being much use to them. Admiral Black's interest in her must only be for her prescient abilities. Her vision in the car and subconscious understanding of the CO's true nature was impressive.

She rose unsteadily to her feet, pointedly ignoring his proffered hand. Her features hardened into a well-practiced mask and she stepped forward slowly and with obvious effort, but admirable fortitude.

Becca entered the palatial home and felt small in the large, dark interior. It was illuminated only incrementally by the light coming through the iron grated windows and a light source above. Everything about the residence felt cold. The paintings on the walls showed severe-faced men and women in clothing from periods long gone; the lack of rugs on the gray stone floor lent the building an institutional air. The chandelier above was large and black, the light only radiating out a short distance, leaving the area beyond too dim to see the room in any great detail.

Becca wanted to ask what this place was, why she was here, but she thought better of questioning Captain Rossi and kept her mouth closed, mask firmly in place to hide her trepidation. The knotting in her stomach had extended into her legs, rooting her to into place, and it was taking great physical effort to ignore. She feared she would be sick and humiliate herself even more in front of the captain, or worse yet in front of the admiral.

A low growl emanated from the darkness just beyond her sight and Becca held her breath. She stopped to wait for the captain a few paces behind her. Her limited experience with dogs did not extend to guard dogs. The memory of the dogs from the night before made her shiver.

He saw her fear and had, of course, heard the growl before she had. "Gabrielle, that will do." The steel behind his cautioning words was palpable.

The growling stopped and a golden haired woman stepped out of the darkness dressed in black cargo pants and matching t-shirt. Becca studied the woman's features with the momentary wistfulness a lesser woman feels when face to face with superior beauty. Her heart skipped when the woman turned her face from the captain to her. Her eyes were bright amber, the shade somewhere between orange and yellow. Somewhere in Becca's brain a cry of danger rang out. With little outward show of her misgivings, not knowing if she was a superior officer, Becca took her arm from her escort with a sliding step away from him, snapped to attention and saluted. Better safe than sorry and she did not want to offend this woman. There was a dangerous air about her.

"Petty Officer Sauter, Ma'am." Shamefully, Becca's leg had to step out behind her to catch her as she swayed drunkenly. By some miracle, she recovered herself before falling. The hard eyes of the woman she faced told her she would let Becca fall without a move to help.

Giving Becca a cursory nod, her amber gaze slid back to the captain. "He's been waiting, Michael." Her voice was lower than expected. It cast her in an even more seductive aura than her long locks and shapely body.

Becca was completely outclassed. Her juvenile features, lack of curves and childlike stature could never be considered sexy, maybe inspiring a "cute" at best. Her twisting stomach, induced by her instincts, told her in no uncertain terms that she should be running away, not toward this place or these people. The only exception was the man beside her. His presence did something to calm her in some weird, inexplicable way.

"Where?" Captain Michael Rossi asked calmly, unaffected by Gabrielle's purring voice or familiar air.

She motioned with her head to her right, blinking slowly. "Downstairs." Her glance pointed off into the darkness and Becca shuddered, thinking the downstairs would be even colder than where she now stood, chilled and marveling at the blonde's comfort in merely a t-shirt.

Her escort nodded and closed the distance between them to stand directly by her side, only their clothing keeping their flesh from touching. Becca neither missed the fact that he continued to stare straight ahead, nor the daggers Gabrielle shot her direction. How could Becca possibly threaten *her*? Maybe she had a claim on the captain and mistook his

44

assistance as something it was not. Her body leaned away from him for propriety sake.

Leading her silently into the darkness, the captain lent only the occasional assistance when Becca, who had again rejected his subtle offer of support, stumbled. For her part, she was painfully aware of his every move though she could barely see more than the pale profile of his face. The only illumination in the hall was cast by the candles and sconces lining their path.

Captain Rossi used the darkness to study the stubborn woman more closely. Humans varied widely in their strength and stamina. This one seemed to be stronger in character than most females he had encountered, braver as well. He respected that for what it was worth. She was still human and, although one of a populace he was sworn to protect under the admiral's command, not a part of his world.

The curving stairs leading into the lower chambers were harder for her to navigate with her balance still impeded and Becca allowed the captain to take her elbow. His touch was feather light yet she felt every shift of her body against his. By the third step Becca felt the cold reaching up to her from below. It was like the thermal layer her feet would hit when she jumped into the pool on one of the first warm days of spring. The combination of cold and her protective sixth sense screaming at her to leave, put her on edge. By the time they reached the bottom step, Becca was struggling to keep her teeth from chattering.

Chapter 6

While the upper floor had been straight out of a history book, the downstairs was a cutting edge command center. The walls of the large open room were lined with digital technology. Several large computer screens as well as a forty-two inch flat panel TV glowed from the wall opposite the bottom of the stairs. A number of tall bo staffs brought her eyes to the wall on her right. A change in the lighting revealed a doorway on the other side of the weapons rack. In the center of the room, several black leather chairs surrounded a long black table. Direct lights shone down in six glowing circles on the darkly shining surface.

Her lower level rank kept her from most of the command posts on base but once, when delivering a prisoner to a Federal holding facility outside Los Angeles, she'd seen the inside of what could only be described as a "war room." This had that look to it as well although the black walls absorbed the light, giving it far more dark shadows than the brighter agency building had. Her eyes were having a hard time picking out all of the details.

With some reticence she straightened her arm, removing it from the captain's and took a step sideways standing "at ease," her hands clasped behind her back.

A silky smooth voice oozed out from one of the shadows in front of her. "Petty Officer Rebecca Sauter, I presume?"

Becca's mind and stomach screeched in debilitating unison. She had to grit her teeth and swallow hard to keep herself upright. Her pulse raced and she worried she was going to pass out. Her vision began to dance with white spots of light. Carefully, she pursed her lips and blew out, trying to calm herself without being too obvious. She failed. She saw the captain out of the corner of her eye tilt his head slightly in her direction, watching her sway.

All of this happened in only a few short seconds. Her body finally did as it was told. Her feet snapped together, her hand flew to her brow. "Yes, Sir."

He did not release her from attention, instead coming completely out of the darkness and approaching her at a painfully slow speed. Becca felt her body bobbling and stretched her toes inside her trainers, trying to give herself a firmer base. It worked temporarily. Keeping her eyes up to the ceiling, over the bone-white face she knew she would see if she looked, Becca was able to keep herself from going into a full blown panic attack.

"I am pleased with your recovery after last night's adventures." He moved around her and she heard him sniff at the stitches in her head. "You have lost a good amount of blood. We will need to take that into consideration." Coming around and stopping in front of her, she could no longer keep her eyes from him. The ghostly face stared at her from more than a foot over her head, his obsidian eyes reflecting the red glow from a nearby light giving him a demonic appearance. "You might be wondering why you are here. In our chance encounter, something I heard you say intrigued me."

Becca searched her head for ideas and found nothing. She had been talking just to talk last night. None of what she'd said had stayed with her since it was nothing more than babble. She waited still and silent for him to continue. The spots were starting to grow in front of her eyes. She could not breathe herself calm with him standing right in front of her. It wasn't acceptable to faint in front of an admiral and that was surely who this was; Admiral Black at last.

"Do you not remember telling my wolves that you knew they were coming? Did you foresee *my* coming as well?" A hint of a smile played at his mouth while his eyes remained cold. "I think that you did."

Her body wobbled but whether it was because of the concussion or the shudder that ran through her, she couldn't tell. She'd kept her secret all her life and in less than a day exposed herself to two strangers who could end her career.

"At ease." He chuckled without warmth. "Rebecca, I would like you to tell me exactly what you saw *before* we met and how these visions come to you." He asked her to tell him about her visions as mildly curious as one would ask another about the weather.

Those cold eyes stared intently at her, unblinking. When she let her gaze run over him she saw that he was not entirely hairless, only bald with white eyebrows not from age but naturally; the palest of blondes. Her first impression that he had been an old man was untrue. He was in actuality more likely only a few years older than Captain Rossi. And he was an admiral? With his lack of pigment she thought he might be an albino except his eyes were not right for that. They weren't right period. Still, try as she might to tear her eyes from his she was not able. In fact, she did quite the opposite. Becca followed her urge to step toward him.

The cries of caution within her body fell to the edge of her perception under the power of his stare. Swallowing once in an effort to find her voice, Becca spoke in quiet wonder as she fell further under his control.

"I dreamt of them and of you." Her entranced voice was distant to her ears, its softness that of a stranger's.

The chilling smile did not repulse her as it did last night, nor did the icy fingers that reached out to her. His large hand wrapped around the back of her neck, thumb pushed against her jaw, tilting her head and exposing her throat to him.

Captain Rossi had been watching closely despite his appearance of disinterest. He already figured out that she was prescient and sensed the extent of her power from her body's reactions to Gabrielle as well as the CO. She stepped from his side, falling under Black's control and he felt an unexpected irritation. When he saw his commander's intentions, he interrupted, surprising himself as well as the other two who had forgotten about him, being so focused on each other. The thought of her being bound to the admiral by blood was unacceptable to him. Black was his commander and no one knew better than the captain how utterly merciless and cruel he was in his methods. Part of him winced in memory of one in particular. The human woman could not be subjected to that. It would destroy her and Captain Rossi could not abide that though *why* remained a puzzle.

"Sir, she is weak and has already lost a lot of blood. This is not the time, Sir." He kept his tone respectful to avoid offense.

The warning in his tone was deceptively bland. "Michael, you forget yourself. This is my command and I will run it to my satisfaction."

Michael nodded agreement, his face deceptively calm. Not for the first time he was grateful he did not have a pulse to betray him. "Yes Sir, however if you are planning to use her for her ability, I would suggest waiting until you know she will survive the exchange. If she is too weak her mind will not endure it. We have seen it before, if you'll recall."

Cold eyes stared flatly back at him before Black finally responded. "And if that is the case, would it prove more problematic than the last?" His thin lips pulled back to reveal his prominent canines. "Are you certain your request is not of a more selfish nature?"

"No, Sir." Michael did not want the admiral to think he was lying. Still, he could not deny a certain amount of validity of Black's question. At present, he wanted to believe he was only attempting to preserve her physical and mental stability for her own good.

Black flicked his hand and Becca felt herself released from his draw. She couldn't remember if she'd answered his questions or not, it was all confused. Her head was fuzzy again just as it was last night after she hit it on the rock. The concussion had to be a bad one and she worried about going to sleep again. Who would wake her during the night to make sure she didn't slipped into a coma? Why did she leave the hospital? Terry had been right, damn him.

"Take her upstairs and assign her quarters." Black ghosted away and moved to a cabinet at the edge of the room, arms moving as he opened and closed drawers. "Michael, take something up to give her. It will move things along more rapidly," he called out over his shoulder.

Captain Rossi did not salute, responding instead with a respectful, "Yes Sir."

At the end of her endurance, Becca watched the captain step forward to take something from the admiral's outstretched hand. He returned to her and she let him take her elbow to guide her back to the stairs. The fear she'd felt since ascending the front steps faded, leaving in its place only exhaustion. Her leaden legs failed her when she attempted to mount the stairs.

After the third stumble when the captain only barely saved her from splitting her face open on the steps, he released her elbow in favor of a more secure hold. A ghost of the giddiness she felt in the hospital came back as his arm slid around her waist, drawing her close to keep her from falling.

The captain felt her heart flutter at his touch and wondered at the cause. Humans confounded him. His own memory of being one had faded with time, taking his understanding of them with it. This one was not pure human though, which might have been why he felt drawn to her. Both details were becoming more disturbingly apparent to him the longer he was in her presence.

His first instinct was to avoid her and yet the need he felt to protect her in her weakened state kept him close, as did his curiosity for what Black had in mind for her. He did enjoy a less formal position with the admiral than the others in their unit because he had been under his command for a very long time. He also knew that to question him was to challenge him, and few survived such a transgression. Rossi would have to tread lightly where the woman was concerned. Another risk to her rode within him. He alone could keep that threat in check.

Becca watched the shadows come and go in a confused haze as the captain guided her. First, up the stairs then back toward the front entrance, then right to go up a grand staircase lined with intricately carved wooden banister posts and into a hallway at the top. The hall was lined with ancient wooden doors the same style as the wood lining the stairs. The dark door Captain Rossi opened led to a large square bedroom. He deposited her on the full size bed with wrought iron headboard and footboard and she felt her consciousness slipping away as her eyes fluttered shut.

Cool fingers unbuttoned her cuff and Becca felt his fingers sliding up her arm as he pushed up her sleeve. Her skin tingled at his touch.

The captain heard her pulse accelerate and assumed she was frightened. Once again operating out of a strange place in his long silent heart, he let his fingers fall more solidly against her flesh, stroking it to ease her distress. "Don't be afraid, Rebecca. I have something that will help you to heal quickly."

A pinch in the crook of her arm and Becca felt the medicine enter her vein. Immediately, her eyes popped open and she began screaming, her fingers clawing wildly at her arm.

The captain's hands captured her wrists to stop her from injuring herself. Already blood was welling to the surface of her skin where she'd torn at herself. The scent assailed him, his body fought him as did hers though for different reasons.

"It burns!" she screamed, her eyes shone with tears of pain as the fire spread through her arm.

Captain Rossi lowered his head to sniff the injection site and growled. It was a serum he recognized instantly. Black had tried to begin binding her to him anyway, despite his officer's objections. Rossi had been right her body was too weak. His cold blood boiled.

Knowing he was putting himself in great peril by his actions, he opened his mouth and sank his own fangs into her warm flesh to remove the serum intended to make her a servant to the admiral. Without his treasonous bite, she would surely perish.

Becca cried out at the captain's bite then felt the fire receding and assumed he was sucking out the poison as they were trained to do in the case of a snake bite. She hadn't seen his fangs, their entrance hidden by raging fire coursing through her veins before he removed it. In any case, her burning veins sought only reprieve from the torturous medicine flowing rapidly up her arm. It didn't matter to her how it stopped, only that it did.

The serum's recession left Becca beyond fatigued. She felt floaty and disconnected from her body. The pain in her head was growing more distant and even with her eyes open she could barely see for the blackness encroaching on her vision.

Captain Rossi watched, relieved at Rebecca's liberation from pain. His reprieve was short lived, quickly replaced by anxiety as he heard her heart slowing. It slowed too much. Her eyes were becoming distant, beginning to glaze over.

"Rebecca." He tried to get her to focus on him. "Look at me," he ordered.

"I can't. I can't see anything."

The woman's small voice was not afraid and sounded too weak to his practiced ears. The captain had seen death in many forms through his existence and recognized its appearance now.

A solution was available downstairs. He'd assumed that was what the admiral put in the syringe he'd given the captain, not the serum he had just injected. They always had some on hand for their own purposes and it was useful for humans as well. Her eyes rolled back in her head and her body tightened, back arching as a convulsion contorted her painfully rigid body.

Cursing under his breath, the captain began to run through the explanation he would have to give his commander. His trespass would not be taken lightly, at least he could argue he knew the admiral wanted to keep her and acted upon that assumption. That might be enough to save him too severe a reprimand. Captain Michael Rossi ignored the whisper in his head that told him he wanted to keep her as well.

Sinking his fangs into his own wrist, he watched the blood flow at once to the surface. He'd fed well before going into the human hospital knowing it would be taxing, even with his years of practice at control. The dark red streams stained her rapidly bluing lips as he held it to her mouth.

When the first drops made their way through her tight lips her convulsions began to ease, though they could not stop without her ingesting more; an improbable task with Becca's throat locked tight and her uncooperative mouth clenched shut. He wriggled his thumb between her jaws and pried her mouth open enough to allow his wrist greater exposure.

He was cautious not to use too much force and tear the mandible off entirely. Humans are fragile, he continued to speak in his own head. It was a mantra he repeated to himself as he fed her his healing blood, stroking her throat softly to encourage her to swallow. Unconscious as she now was, she could easily choke. He slid an arm under her shoulders to cradle her against him and elevate her head.

Finally her heart beat stronger and the specter of death was beaten back from her body. The captain removed his wrist and licked it to seal it, ignoring the sensations he was experiencing from tasting her blood and now her saliva. For a creature like him, blood exchange was very personal though not quite as much so as sex. That was good. It would not do to become aroused by a woman the admiral intended to mark. He used his free hand to shift his trousers and willed himself to stop picturing her mouth on other things.

The question of what would happen to him now brought his body back under his control. The mark on his wrist would be gone within minutes but the scent of his blood inside her would linger at least a day. He sat back on the edge of the bed to watch the woman responsible for inspiring his insubordination and impending punishment. It would be brutal, of that he was certain. Whether it would be fatal was yet to be determined.

A small spill of blood lay at the corner of her mouth. The admiral would already punish him the second he smelled her blood in him. Wanting to taste her again, he leaned forward and licked at the spot on her lip. Her heat combining with the taste of her blood was heady and he drew his tongue slowly across her lip, torturing himself by taking what was forbidden. When his tongue reached the corner of her mouth, her head turned toward the stimulus and his lips were on hers. He could have moved in time. He didn't.

In that dreamlike place between asleep and awake, Becca let her lips linger on his before she twisted her face away to rest her face on the coolness of the pillow. He remained unmoving, watching the young woman for a few minutes as she slept and marveling at his own insanity. Humans are fragile, he told himself again, but found it only served to draw him to her more.

Chapter 7

Becca woke in the night; something felt wrong. Sitting up slowly, she looked around her quarters and remembered where she was. Focusing inward, she felt no hint of dizziness or nausea from her concussion. As she sat up she glanced about at her room with its dark blue bedding and sparse furnishings. Again it struck her that something was terribly wrong. Her clothing was still on with the exception of her shoes and someone had put a thick blanket over her in the night.

Becca recalled the captain bringing her to bed and injecting some sort of medicine in her arm. Her allergic reaction had been severe. Her hand trailed over her sleeve with the memory. She felt a bandage under her clothing. Shamefaced, she remembered screaming and writhing in agony. He had only seen her at her worst so far and for some reason she could only guess at, Becca wanted desperately to show him her better face.

At the thought of him, the feeling of disquiet her instinct was sending grew to an urge and she hopped out of bed feeling better rested and stronger than she had in a very long time. Knowing her instinct was guiding her Becca gave in to its direction and let her feet follow.

It guided her down the stairs and into the entryway. Instead of going down the hall toward the command center, she went the opposite way. Interestingly enough, she had little trouble navigating the dark, unfamiliar hallways without a light.

Up ahead, a cracking sound reached her ears accompanied by a terse male voice. She followed through a large sitting room with a fireplace and several racks of antlers mounted on the wall, through to a large kitchen with a warm fire crackling in the hearth, and down a step where the walls narrowed into a chilly stone-walled hallway that turned abruptly to the right.

When she turned she saw what, or rather whom, had drawn her, and froze. The room was small, about the size of a walk-in closet with high ceilings and well lit by overhead halogens. The sudden light made her blink as her eyes attempted to adjust. It must have been a storage pantry in the days when supplies were purchased in bulk and vegetables put up for the winter. Several exposed ceiling beams held hooks for drying herbs and possibly even for salted meats. At present, one held something more.

Before her stood the admiral; illuminated properly for the first time she saw that he was a tall, lean man approaching six and a half feet, possibly the tallest man she'd ever seen in person. His face was eerily complacent with long canines making indentations in his lower lip, and in his hand he held a short wooden club.

The captain was hanging like a side of meat from a metal hook, his hands bound by chains shining brightly in the light. Facing her were dark purple bruises covering the captain's broad back and, what she was guessing were broken ribs, distorted the flesh on his side, looking like they were going to go through the skin at any minute. This punishment was a common occurrence by what she could see of the stages of the discolorations on the pale body. The club came up for another blow.

"Stop it!" she cried out, stepping forward.

The white hand paused as he turned his head toward her and smiled, sending a chill through Becca's heart. That sealed it for her; the admiral was a truly heartless man. He was beating a man half to death and still showed no emotion. She swallowed hard, tasting bile.

"Rebecca, what perfect timing." He turned back to his target and brought the club down swiftly, striking the captain on an already purple splotch over his kidney. His body pitched violently but he made no sound.

Becca could not see his face, but she could guess at his consciousness by his clenched fists. "Please," she pleaded in a strained whisper. Admiral Black's cruelty was unconscionable to her, a woman who had grown up in a home with clear rules and gone into a field with those same boundaries and moral codes. Whatever the captain had done, she was sure this went far beyond a justified punishment.

The club fell from his hand onto the hard ground with a heavy thud and he stepped toward the captain, reaching up to turn the hook and the hanging man to face her. Becca gasped at the bloodied skin and broken nose she saw in place of the handsome face that had been her brave savior a scant few hours ago. More dark bruises in the shape of the ugly club covered his chest and one cheek was broken open, the flesh flayed like a lobster tail. She took a step toward him until a disapproving cluck from Black halted her mid-stride.

"I was just about to ask Michael a few more questions. You might be able to fill in the blanks should he prove unable." He stared at Becca while he questioned his victim. "Michael, tell me again why you felt it necessary to act against my orders?"

Michael's words were quiet, making it hard to hear. Becca saw flashes of white as he spoke. His head was down and she couldn't be certain of what she saw. Maybe his lips were swollen, changing their shape. It wouldn't have surprised her and again she felt her temper flare. With great difficultly she kept her mouth shut. She couldn't help Michael if she was escorted from the premises for questioning a superior, or hung up next to him.

The instinct she trusted for guidance had calmed to a strange lull and didn't warn her of any danger to herself so she listened and feared only for the captain's safety, not her own.

"Speak louder so that we can all hear you," Black commanded darkly.

She strained to hear him.

"I told you." His voice was terribly rough, more gravelly than she'd come to expect. She could see him trying to hold his sides steady when he spoke, only those same muscles pushed against his broken bones causing him more agony. His words came in short gasps as he took shallow breaths. "I gave her the injection you gave me. It was killing her. Her body rejected it. I told you she was too weak."

The cold stare bored into her soul. Becca felt violated. She fought the urge to turn and run and not to stop running until she reached Mexico.

"Is that why you presumed to take my place as her Master?" Black asked casually.

"No Sir. I knew you wanted her alive and there was not enough time to make it to the supply for the counter agent. I made the decision to save her, for the unit, Sir. No disrespect was intended, Sir."

Becca didn't understand what they were talking about with masters and who was serving who, but she heard that she nearly died and remembered the captain giving her something even if the details of the what and the why were fuzzy. He saved her life. Though she had known it, hearing him say the words made it more real. She warmed to him, intent to do the same for him now.

Admiral Black's smile made Becca's skin crawl. "Then show me you have not made her your servant."

"What?" The captain's head shot up, his eyes widened in alarm.

Becca had no clue what they meant about making her his servant though his reaction frightened her. Her warm feeling cooled. She didn't look over when Black chuckled.

"I see she fears you. That is a start but the question remains, does she obey?"

Captain Rossi hung there, unable to do anything to stop this punishment. His shoulders ached and his wrists burned where they touched the silver-infused chains the commander had made centuries ago. The mixture was just right; it incapacitated the monster within without killing and burned without scarring long term. As far as he knew, the admiral was the only one who had perfected the blending. The bruises would heal as soon as he fed; the broken bones would take longer. Some of the bigger bones could take up to a full day to mend at his age. He was valuable to his master though not enough so that he doubted his willingness to kill him. The question of whether or not he had claimed the admiral's prize as his own remained. The captain was fearful; for the first time in decades, he would die.

The look on Rebecca's face at the commander's words sent a pang through his thawing heart. Her presence there had begun to awaken feelings in him he had long thought dead. Not all of them pleasant. He knew he had given her more blood than he would have thought necessary except her injuries, plus the amount he had to take out with the serum, left her desperately anemic. Panic stirred at the thought that he gave her too much and bound her to him. He did not want that for more than the immediate reason of the admiral's wrath.

The captain hadn't bound a soul before and didn't want one now. They required a level of involvement he avoided. Captain Rossi avoided closeness with anyone since his turning, not wanting to harm anyone else he might care about. He preferred instead to follow orders, protecting humans from less scrupulous creatures like himself and the other members of their unit.

"Call her to you, Michael," Admiral Black prodded contemplatively. "I would like to see if your blood is strong. You have never bound anyone to yourself, let us consider this an experiment."

Inhaling painfully to make his words, Captain Rossi searched for Becca's eyes. She had been watching him and her frightened stare easily met his. Halfheartedly, he tried to pull her to himself with only his eyes.

Shrewdly, his master curled his long fingers into a fist and a flash of white streaked down to snap his collarbone. The blow jolted Rossi's body and he grimaced with the new pains.

Becca sucked in her breath, torn between helping a man who had been kind to her and fearing the man between them.

"Give it an *honest* effort, Michael."

Her wide hazel eyes watched the captain's battered face and saw his bright blue eyes darken. They were the night sky without stars. Not black like the cruel admiral yet scary in his own right. She saw the darkness in him and knew he was capable of terrible things. Still, her instinct did not warn her against him.

Captain Rossi knew that to compel her he had to reach into what she was to him and "feel" her. His memories tied two images together. Both strong. The first was the smiling face he had seen at the hospital at their first meeting when she appeared so happy and free. He wanted to know what brought her that joy. And the second was of last night. It was the more powerful of the two because he had a tactile component to the memory. He had touched her lips, tasted her blood, stroked her soft skin. Feeling the draw of her being, where it had begun to reach down into his soul, he locked onto her eyes and, using the powers inborn in his kind and strengthened by age, whispered her name. "Rebecca."

The darkness in the captain's eyes changed. They remained without light, only now in the place of anger, she saw hunger. It was a powerful hunger, one she'd never seen directed at her before except for the occasional drunk with a penchant for violent sex. They sometimes gave her a look nearly half as strong when she handcuffed them and led them out of a bar, swearing they would do things to her, certain that was what she "needed."

Becca hadn't seen anyone want her this way before. There was no overt threat of violence, although it felt like it could be close. A surprising twinge made its way through her lower areas. This display was raw power; she could feel it. And his wanting made her work to keep her knees from buckling, there was no stopping the warm wetness she felt but thankfully no one could see. Stubbornly, she held firm in her resolve. Whatever was going on between the two men, she understood that it was critical to the captain's wellbeing that she not make a move toward him.

The intimate way he spoke her formal name brought back the giddy feeling she experienced at the hospital. Chalking it up as an odd combination of her internal warning system and an unhealthy attraction, Becca tried to calm herself. It was to no avail. She felt her heart pick up speed, her breathing followed and she kept her feet in place with the greatest effort.

In the next instant, before Becca's will could fail her, the captain brought his lids down, his whole body sagging in exhaustion. With the breaking off of his stare, Becca felt herself cooling and her pulse slowing accordingly. The absence of his hunger in her head left a hole it had created for itself. The backlash of the vacuum rocked her forward, following him as if he had pulled himself back out of her like a wet piece of clothing from her body.

"Hmm." The white hand went to his pointed chin and Black regarded Becca curiously. "That is an interesting turn of events. It might be worthwhile to use that as well." His long fingers snaked up, and in a flurry of clanking chains, the captain slid down to the ground with a soft whump.

"Rebecca you have the day to yourself." The chains hung ominous, noisily clanking above where Rossi lay on the cold floor, freed from their grasp. "I will summon you after the evening meal."

Admiral Black left her with the beaten, unmoving body of her only ally in this cold place. Becca moved to his side as soon as they were alone, unsure what to do from there. Her medical training on broken bones was limited. The ribs caused her the most concern because of the damage they could do if they punctured a lung or kidney. Several of them were threatening to break through the skin with the least amount of additional pressure, and she knew a compound fracture carried a high risk of infection. Keep the bones and blood inside the body was the medic's mantra when he taught them. After breathing and circulatory system functions were established, the next thing to worry about was blood and bones. And both were best left on the inside. She already knew that the captain was breathing; he was still conscious.

"Roll me over," the captain mumbled into the stone floor.

"I can't. Your ribs are broken and if I move you they could put a hole in something."

Holding his body pinched tight, his words came out a strained whisper and Becca had to lower her face to his to hear him. "You can. Do it." The scent of blood on him was strong but there was a lack of something else on him. Sweat. All of that stress should have had his adrenaline pumping. He should have been soaked. Instead, she noticed only a faint scent of soap and maybe light cologne, his scent was musky and earthy. Strange but not unpleasant.

Her panic at his injuries pushed the observation aside as nonessential. For now she was considering trying to find Gabrielle to see if she had access to a backboard or could help her to lift him. Where was this medical care Captain Rossi said they had available? She hoped to hell it wasn't the captain or he was screwed.

Becca realized she was shaking her head and he couldn't see. "No. Stay here, I'm going to find help." Her voice trembled and she reached out to touch his shoulder in an effort to reassure him. The instant her fingers touched him, she felt the giddy feeling return. "What the hell," she mumbled, pissed that she would be getting turned on right now.

Not getting the desired response from Becca, Captain Rossi pulled up the elbow on his unbroken arm so that he had his hand palm flat on the floor like he was going to do a sideways pushup. Disregarding Becca's frantic suggestions that he stop moving, he gave one shove and rolled himself over. The movement did indeed send a rib through his lung, and another skidded across something else if he wasn't mistaken, but they didn't give him concern. He hadn't needed either one since nineteen forty-two when he died the first time.

The hazel eyes he'd captured before were wide and wet with tears. "Captain, Sir. What have you done?" Her anxiety for him gave him a thrill of pleasure.

He smiled crookedly, his crushed cheek stopping the one side of his face from moving properly. "I would prefer you call me Michael. Now please help me up. It will hurt a lot less than if I do it myself."

She blinked back the helpless tears moistening the corners of her narrowing eyes. "You have a death wish." His actions made no sense to her unless that blow to his cheek had caused brain damage, and for that she had no training. Would helping or restraining him hurt him more?

Exasperated, Michael raised his good arm. Becca stared at it, unmoving. "Help me up, that is an order," Michael commanded.

"Sir," she said, not bothering to salute. Frustrated with his self-destructive goal, Becca stood and held out both hands to take his extended one. Being five foot three and one hundred twenty hardened pounds did not give Becca much power to deadlift a prone man from the ground so it was a shock when he clasped her hand and she saw that her suppositions had been false.

Michael was not a helpless man. Despite his injuries, he provided more than a little assistance. Becca also found she was back at her full strength. In two smooth movements

Michael was on his feet and standing on his own, even if he was clutching his side painfully. "Thank you," he squeezed out.

"Sir, can you breathe?" She eyed him warily, his ashen pallor more white than previously. He looked like death. Becca listened closely for any wheezing in his breathing or signs that he had indeed just committed suicide by his reckless actions.

Again one side of his face grinned at her. "Michael," he reminded her. "I'll be fine, I only need to eat something."

Her mouth dropped open. "You're hungry?"

Michael was enjoying her frustration with him. The voice in his head told him to be careful. She would fear him when she saw what he was and he wanted to put that off for now.

He tried to allay her concerns for him. "Yes, I'm stopping in the kitchen. Why don't you go upstairs? Get some sleep." Speaking so much hurt. "There are still a few hours before dawn and we don't know what he has planned for tonight. You'll want to be at your best."

He heard her pulse pick up but he saw no change in her expression. His estimation of her was under constant correction. Maybe humans had changed since he'd been around them. She was stronger than he remembered them being. Or had they always been so, and it was his opinions that had changed? Had convincing himself he couldn't be around them for their weaknesses made it easier to accept what he was? Accept his weakness?

She was shaking her head. "No, I am going to stay with you, Michael." She tried his name out and found it suited her. Becca dropped her eyes, giving herself a moment to erase the smile that put itself there. It wouldn't do to flirt with him even if he had given her permission to address him informally. "It would be irresponsible to leave you alone with injuries like those." She pointed at his chest and furrowed her brow. In what must have been a trick of the sparse lighting, his bruising appeared to be fading already.

Michael caught her curious stares at his chest and knew she had seen what he could feel happening. His body was repairing itself as much as possible although it would require fresh nourishment soon to completely heal, especially if the admiral needed him this evening. He was growing more desperate to be rid of her before feeding, an unbidden memory of her taste flashed through his mind and he felt his body responding. Michael made a conscious effort to hide his discomfort as well as his body's desire with a painful shift of his trousers. Standing taller, he hoped that she would see he was capable and leave him to take care of himself.

The strain the damage was placing on him taxed his control. It had been a long time since he had lost control of his urges with a human, though it remained with him; the image of the poor girl's face burned in his memory forever. She was naïve to the existence of his kind and thought herself wicked stealing a kiss from the strange soldier, not knowing he had saved her from the Germans but could not save her from a greater danger. Himself.

He shook his head trying to be free of the memory. He was young then, freshly turned with limited control. He'd avoided close contact with humans since.

To Becca, he nodded curtly and turned the corner to enter the kitchen passageway. Michael entered first and smelled the occupant before he saw him. He was sitting at the roughly hewn wooden table on the long bench near the door. Michael signaled him with a series of subtle hand gestures to distract his companion for him.

Seconds later, Becca turned the corner and saw the man as well. Seeing him similarly clothed in black fatigues like Gabrielle, she saluted.

Faster than her eyes could follow, he leaped backward off the bench and saluted her back, perfectly poised and serious before breaking into laughter. There was no sign of rank that she could see on his garb as she did a visual appraisal. Why was Captain Rossi, er, Michael the only one wearing a recognizable uniform? Maybe because he was on base. She pondered what that meant.

Auburn hair, thick and shaggy, hung past his ears. His look was better suited to a skateboard than military service. His tall body, built more for power than speed, made his display of grace all the more impressive. When Becca's gaze came back to his face she saw green eyes that were too familiar, then dismissed the feeling just as quickly as impossible. She didn't feel threatened by him, however she did find it off-putting to be confusing him with a large wolf.

If Becca tried to make sense of what was happening, she figured she'd decide she was crazy. There had to be some reason for her continuing déjà vu moments as well as some sane reason she was here with this odd unit. A vision had never come back as anything but an exact replication in real life and always clear. This one was confusing her as its elements crossed between reality and fantasy. Maybe it was because of the concussion that it was all jumbled in her head. Maybe these people were some special forces unit, except they didn't let women in, and Gabrielle was definitely a woman.

She calmed herself. It would all be explained in time she was sure. She had to trust her instinct to keep her safe and she would do whatever the nightmarish Admiral Black needed her to do until she was returned to her post. After that, life would go back to relatively normal and she would leave this behind. A quick glance at Michael's damaged back gave her a twinge and she stopped herself from going too far. This was a post and he was her superior. She needed to keep that in mind if she was going to keep herself or him from getting into any further trouble. There were politics here she didn't understand and getting a little action wasn't worth her career. An image of Black's smile as he stood by Michael's beaten body helped to shut down her lusty thoughts.

"At ease, Rebecca." Michael released her, seeing that his compatriot was enjoying her nerves far too much to consider her discomfort. He shot a warning glance at the joker. "Petty Officer Second Class Rebecca Sauter, this is one of the men on my team, Captain Ryan Hallbeck."

Becca was confused by his rank being equal to Rossi's but did not question him. Ryan spoke up, his suntouched face breaking into an easy grin that looked like it belonged there.

"We're pretty casual around here with each other, even Mike here." He nodded at the man in question, his admitted leader even if not in rank. "The only exception is Admiral Black. I'm *not* going to use your rank, so what do you want me to call you?"

Trying to fit in, she offered the only name anyone used for her when not on duty. "Becca, Sir."

Deep rumbling laughter erupted from his large barrel chest, "No 'Sirs' for me. Just Ryan, okay Becca?" He stuck out a large hand.

Accepting, Becca saw how tiny her own appendage looked in his overly hot grasp as she shook his firmly and without hesitation. He tipped his head approvingly and let go slowly. "It'll be good to have another woman around here. Hopefully this one is less moody." Ryan grinned again.

Michael snorted and clenched his teeth at the pain that knifed through him, drawing Ryan's attention. Another series of gestures with his hands by his hip reminded Ryan of his job. Ryan shifted his focus to Becca and began to ask her about how she was liking it here so far. Ever so subtle, he began to shift his weight and step sideways, interposing himself between the two and hopefully herding her to the table to allow Michael some privacy.

She decided not to comment on her opinions of Admiral Black. Better to keep her observations limited to those less likely to inflame. "Yes, S...Ryan. I'll be curious to find out what I'm to do here and for how long before I return to my post." She caught Michael's gestures, assuming he signaled Ryan to take her off his hands and bit back the disappointment that went with the snub. Twisting to face Michael, she kept her face blank. "If you will excuse me, I think I will take your advice, Sir, and rack a few more hours." Uncomfortable not saluting as she left them, Becca turned sharply on her heel and strode efficiently out of the room to nurse her bruised ego and extrapolate what she could from the details she knew to be true of this bizarre place in private. She'd done her duty and gotten Captain Michael Rossi to another person either to help or witness his demise. There was nothing more she could do.

Chapter 8

Sleep was a joke. Becca was wired and spent the next few hours alternating between pacing the room and flopping around on the bed out of frustration.

The theory she had for the similarities she kept encountering from last night to today was partially explained by head trauma and partially her instinct. It must have superimposed hints of what was to come and the people she was going to meet on her running accident.

The only complication was the Commanding Officer, the one she knew as Admiral Black, though she doubted that was his real name. She doubted any of these people she was temporarily reassigned to was on the grid. The whole setup reeked of Black Ops or some other form of ghost operation. The concept itself did not bother her. The question was why had they chosen *her*? She was just an MP. She worked hard, but never gave it everything unless she thought she wouldn't be singled out or win. She didn't want to stand out.

After she proved herself a worthy sailor, her relationship with her father had enjoyed a brief renewal. Her father, Ed Sauter, even seemed to forgive her strangeness. That is, until he had started to push her to try harder for an officer's commission. Terrified of having people under her command and facing more intense scrutiny, Becca avoided it. Her father again considered her a disappointing underachiever and had been distant these past two years.

At dawn, when Becca was starting to wonder if she could get a cup of coffee, she heard a sharp knock on her rough wooden door. She answered it before the sound left her ears.

Standing there was Gabrielle, a stack of black fabric in her hands, boots and toiletry bag on top. "Michael sent these. While you're here you can wear them. Bathroom's down there. She twitched her head toward the far end of the hall.

It hit her that she would be there for a while and Becca felt the smile fading from her features. "Thanks Gabrielle." Becca offered with a forced smile, hoping to make nice with the woman Ryan termed "moody." However, her propensity to display more than one mood, anger, was yet to be seen. She took the pile and tried to make conversation. "When's breakfast?"

Uninterested, Gabrielle turned away and mumbled something unintelligible.

"I'm sorry, what?"

Raising her voice so that Becca could hear without having to turn back or break stride, Gabrielle repeated, "I said this is not the Holiday Inn. Breakfast is whenever you make it."

Her friendly overture rebuffed, Becca shut her door harder than was necessary and lay her pile on the bed to take inventory.

Five pair of fatigue style black pants, five black t-shirts, two black fatigue jackets, two black belts, five sets of standard issue underthings, socks and boots. Her toiletry bag was basic, nothing less than she lived on in training. Gathering what she needed, putting away the rest in the small dresser in her room, Becca took the time to shower before breakfast.

Feeling refreshed, if not informed, Becca made her way downstairs to find coffee and toast, if that was possible. It was. The kitchen was relatively well stocked. Nothing fancy, just lots of basics such as: bread, peanut butter, cheese, fruits and vegetables. Doing a mental tabulation, Becca figured the men were big eaters or there were more people here. There was too much food here to be eaten by the five of them before it all went bad.

A few more minutes of scrounging revealed a coffee pot and the necessaries to make the stimulant her body told her it needed. Lots of late night patrols had gotten Becca addicted to the stuff. It could be worse, she figured, letting herself have that one vice.

Once the pot was percolating, Becca dug up a loaf of bread but could not find the toaster. Instead settling for a cold peanut butter sandwich and a pear. She had just taken a bite of sliced pear still lying on the cutting board and was pouring her first cup into a plain black mug when she heard a shoe on the stone behind her. Startled, she jumped and her hand holding the mug twitched open releasing the mug to fall to the floor. The hand that went with the boot flashed around her and snagged the mug before it hit the stones with only a small amount of coffee spilling on the ground.

"Settle down there, new guy." Ryan's jovial voice was just about in her ear. The heat from his body radiated in waves onto the back of her neck above her jacket as she leaned away from him and into the counter. The mug went back on the counter beside her but the heat did not move away.

Growing uncomfortable with his proximity, Becca made a point of looking over at the spill beside her before announcing, "I should clean that up." When he didn't move his arm she put her hand out and gently wrapped it around his wrist, applying a slight bit of pressure.

"Where are you going? It can keep," he rumbled from behind her, his voice closer than it should have been if he was standing at his full height.

Becca did not want to make waves on her first day but wouldn't be intimidated by Ryan. He might have a superior rank but if he wasn't going to use it, then neither was she. Besides, this was pretty common in her field; surrounded as she was by men ninety-nine percent of the time they used their size to make her feel inferior. "Back up, Ryan. I'm moving."

She heard him sniffing in her hair, "Just wait." He sounded distracted.

Her hand on his wrist slid around, placing her thumb on the tender underside, which was very sensitive to pressure. Becca applied sudden strong pressure and felt the limb buckle, surprising its owner. When his body came forward, she ducked under the other side and took several rapid steps back to the wall, giving her room to maneuver if it came to that.

But Ryan didn't look upset; instead his expression was one of amusement. "That was pretty good." His eyes twinkled mischievously. "Let's see you get out of this one."

He darted fast to her outside and she was ready. Ryan's arm snaked around her shoulders in an attempt to wrap around her and pull her into his chest for a bear hug. It was a standard move and one where she found her size gave her an advantage.

All of her sparring partners were tall men like Ryan with only a few exceptions. Becca's height difference made them have to adjust their attacks just enough to throw them off. Ryan was no different; albeit faster and stronger, he was still a tall male used to fighting other tall males.

Becca spun around, twisting her hands to clasp his wrist as he altered it mid-reach to her lower shoulders. Using his forward and downward momentum, she spun his wrist around his back and up, shoving him forward into the wall. Ryan growled at her, the sound throwing her off, but she held firm.

"You're stronger than you look," he chuckled, a hint of annoyance creeping into his voice.

Before Becca could answer, Ryan swung his long free arm around and struck her in the side with a fist. It was not a full force strike but she had not been prepared and her muscles were loose, unguarded.

Her grip loosened and he spun around to hold her tight against his chest in a bear hold again. Arms pinned and her face stuck into his chest, Becca took a few breaths and felt out of place for a moment. The smell of him filled her nostrils. It was a blend of outside, more specifically cedar, reminding her of her cypress grove by the base. She stomped on one of his feet and he chuckled, pleased with himself now that he was back on top.

Ryan's smugness riled her and she considered her options. In hand-to-hand combat anything goes, she remembered her instructors telling her. Becca leaned her head into Ryan's chest and he looked down to watch her curiously, no hint of suspicion until she struck.

"Ow!" He howled and reacted instinctively, shoving Becca and her teeth away from him.

Unfortunately for Becca, Ryan was incredibly strong and his knee jerk reaction propelled her into the counter where the whole mess had started. Her back struck the edge, hands trying to catch her on the surface behind her and she felt the wind rush from her lungs. What had to be the kitchen knife she had used on her pear pierced the underside of her forearm at some point in her slide to the floor.

"Damn," Ryan exhaled loudly, rushing to her side. He lifted her arm and she saw the small slice and the thin stream of blood now leaking out.

It was small and he reached into a drawer to take out a white kitchen rag to wrap around it. Becca leaned against the cabinets, waiting for her breath to come back. No matter how well trained a person is, there is no fast or dignified way to recover from having their wind knocked out. Becca heard the gasping sounds her body made in an effort to bring the air back.

To make matters worse, Gabrielle chose that moment to come rushing in. Becca was still making sounds similar to a sick seal when she saw the amber eyes narrow and her full lips purse.

"What did you do to her, you overgrown pup?" Her eyes ran over Becca, making her own damage assessment. "She's here for a reason; don't break her. She isn't a toy." Her acidic tone cowed Ryan, his demeanor even more remorseful with her correction.

Ryan's green eyes turned back toward Becca, his hand pulling at his shirt where she bit him. "We were just screwing around. She surprised me, that's all."

Gabrielle's nose went up, she looked like she was scenting the air. "Ryan you need to get that looked at." She spun on her heel and stomped out. "You don't know where she's been."

Becca's lungs were working again and she sucked in a few grateful breaths. Feeling like you're suffocating is horrible even if you know it's just temporary. She was not going to apologize. Sparring on base often led to a few bloody bouts but she felt bad about his being chewed out for it. "I thought you said she was moody? All I've seen so far is pissed."

Ryan's broad smile rewarded her efforts at levity. "Yeah, the shifts are subtle. Pissed is one, annoyed is another, sometimes we see angry." His hand pulled his shirt away again.

She laughed at that, Ryan did as well. Standing, he held out a hand to her and she took it, letting him pull her up. Removing the rag, Becca saw her slice was still bleeding but she had been lucky.

"Just missed the important stuff." Ryan pointed to the blue line in her wrist not half an inch from the damage. "Have a seat, there's a first aid kit in here. I think we both could use it." He rubbed his chest.

Easing down on a bench with her back to the table, Becca watched Ryan move. He was graceful like Michael but had a more rolling gait whereas, the captain glided. She felt clumsy next to these big men but as she'd seen, she could hold her own with them, a fact that astounded her. She felt strong and her instincts had told her who she could trust and who to watch, though she didn't necessarily need it here. It was pretty clear she could count Admiral Black and Gabrielle among those to watch and Ryan as an ally. Michael was less clear. She would have called him ally except for the cryptic exchange this morning with the admiral. Maybe the admiral was one of those paranoid types who tried to keep total control of his troops and had the idea Becca was somehow more loyal to the captain because she met him first. Still there had been something to that little seduction attempt of his. Maybe that was it. Maybe he'd seduced women before and it caused problems in the chain of command. Becca felt a quick pang of anger that this might be coming down to a pissing match between the two, it was something she had grown sick of in her testosterone-filled reality.

Ryan set the kit he dug out on the table and sat down next to her, holding out his hand. Obediently, Becca gave him her injured wrist with her jacket sleeve pulled up. She couldn't bind her own wrist one-handed and was grateful he would help. He quickly had her wound cleaned and wrapped with gauze and a protective tape outer wrapping.

"Thanks." She examined his handiwork. "You do good work."

"I've been around a cut or two in my time." Ryan stood up and took off his shirt.

In a male dominated world one gets used to seeing men shirtless, although this one was a particularly fine specimen and gave her pause. How could it not? Ryan had a body any professional athlete would have given his soul for. He was big, well muscled, and tan. Many a woman would go weak over it. Becca had to admit she was impressed.

"Nice," she commented. He started to puff up for her until her finger extended to the small oval, just below the center of his pectorals, showing him to what she was referring. The skin was torn and there was a faint line of blood around it.

"Yeah, not bad. I don't really need to clean it up it's just that my shirt keeps getting stuck to it."

Becca looked back at the wound and swore she saw the indentations popping back out. Sure she was seeing things, she stared.

"Like it?" Ryan flexed for her.

She put out a hand, touching his chest beside her bite mark. Sure enough, it was receding. The purpling of the skin was fading back to tan and, right in front of her, all that remained was a trace of blood with no indication from whence it came. Bewildered, Becca's wide eyes took in Ryan's amused expression.

"Cool, huh?" He smiled and, up this close, she saw that his canines were slightly longer than they should be. An image of a large cinnamon colored, green eyed wolf interposed itself in her mind.

Shaking her head, Becca ran through the logical explanations of what she'd just seen. "What was that? You can't heal that fast."

"Maybe you just don't have as strong a bite as you think," he teased her, reaching down to grab his shirt on the bench beside her, bringing his face intimately close to her own. His lips were inches from hers and he stared into her eyes, tipping his head and breathing in, closing his eyes in the process.

Becca mistook his move and her fist shot out, striking him directly in the jaw. It was a natural reaction borne of repeated efforts from years of being around nothing but men, some of whom had similarly inflated senses of self-appeal.

His eyes hardened and he roared, loud and inhuman. It was more enraged beast than man. Becca scurried back but the table stopped her from going more than a few inches. Ryan's face came down to hers, his hands on the table behind her.

Two points of white protruded from behind his upper lip, his mouth and nose started to lengthen.

Feeling like she was in a horror film, Becca lashed out again, this time aiming for his nose. Her fist looked like a child's against his large head so close to her, but the blow served its purpose. He closed his eyes and shook his head, snorting. Becca ducked and ran for the door but by some twisted miracle he was there before she reached it. Her momentum carried her straight into him. Icy fingers of fear wrapped themselves around her heart. The face staring her down was not Ryan's; it was the face of a wolf. The one she had seen that night. Only this time it was not friendly. Things had changed too fast for her instinct to warn her before the attack. Late to arrive, its warnings hit her full force, splitting her vision with its dancing spots of white light.

Becca struck his chest and bounced back, landing on her butt in front of him. Ryan fell down to his hands and knees and in a sudden rippling of light, his human form was no more. The beast now at her feet and approaching fast was a full wolf, lips pulled back and snarling his fury.

The wolf was at her feet, her body frozen with fear. Then, in an instant, her mind quieted. Becca thought that meant she was going to die; she'd heard of soldiers experiencing peace in the face of death and was fleetingly glad she wasn't going to die screaming like a frightened rabbit.

A sound like a rifle crack reached her ears and the wolf nearly on top of her shot sideways. Shocked, Becca's eyes tried to track him as she heard snarling and the sickening sound of flesh tearing. Cinnamon flashed against black and white, swirling so fast she couldn't make sense of what she was seeing.

Another crunch and the swirling stopped. The wolf lay panting on his side, a paw twisted awkwardly under him and Michael sat straddling him, utterly still. The upper half of

Michael's arm was bloodied under what was left of his shirtsleeve.

Becca could only stare at the wolf, trying to see Ryan in there. His eyes were closed and without them she saw only an animal. Not typically one for tears, Becca found herself overwhelmed, alone, and in a situation she couldn't understand. A sobbing moan tore out of her. She put her hands up over her face and felt the hot tears wet her palms.

Low murmuring and the scraping of something being dragged across the floor reached her ears yet she couldn't bring herself to look at it. Her psyche was in a tenuous place, threatening to break. Mentally hardened by years of training and a lifetime of self-control, Becca had no experience with men who turned into animals. There was a word for it but she felt like a fool even thinking it. This wasn't real.

Other sounds reached her periphery, unable to process any more she didn't look up. The sounds went away and Becca felt a body settle beside hers. Her muscles tensed until the light feeling in her head told her who it was. He had protected her, but how? Just hours ago he'd had any number of broken ribs and collarbone to name just a few of his injuries. Now he was wrestling with a wolf? She tucked her head in tight to her raised knees and wished that when she opened her eyes she would be in her apartment, never having met any of these people.

"Rebecca." Michael hesitated, "Becca." His husky voice was gentle. "I want you to know that Ryan wouldn't normally hurt you. It's just that with it so close to the full moon he has limited control, especially with a human." His cool fingers touched her wrist, pushing back the sleeve covering her newest bandage. Cursing under his breath, he added. "*And* when blood is spilled. He should have known better than to horse around."

His words made sense if one were to allow for the impossible to be possible. But Becca was raised in a world with strict rules about black and white, logical and illogical and this was very illogical. She pulled her hand back from his light grip and curled more tightly inward, wanting this to all go away.

Michael watched Becca go into shock. Humans weren't allowed to see them and this was exactly why. They couldn't handle the fact that they shared their world with such creatures as these. Never mind their unit's sole purpose was to protect humans from others of their kind, those who didn't respect the rules. It didn't mean they understood the risks his unit took on their behalf. Michael bit back the urge to march down to the admiral and demand he be allowed to return Becca to her other life. Her preternatural ability could not be worth destroying her mind over. She was stronger than many, however she was still human, and she was fragile. The scent of his blood in her called to him and he ignored it. His desire to keep her with him for his pleasure was selfish. This was not the world for her, plus, his blood and its pull would fade in time. Where would that leave her? The beast within him didn't care. It only knew want.

"Come on, Becca. Let me take you to your room."

She felt him move away and did nothing. She couldn't have moved herself if she tried. Very gently, he wrapped one arm around her shoulders and one under her legs as he carried her easily from the kitchen and up to her room. He pulled back her covers and set her down.

After laying her down and covering her up Michael backed away, turning to go and was halted by the sight of her small body curled defensively into a ball. He'd seen the effects of severe shock on the battlefield back when he was human and worried that was the case with her now. If he left her she would be alone, and without monitoring, could suffer for it. Justifying his actions as caution for her wellbeing, he took a step back toward the bed.

Michael went around the other side of the bed and lay down beside her, outside the covers so as not to chill her. He imagined he felt her relax the slightest bit at his touch. It was some time before her breathing became more even and he heard her heart keeping a strong and steady rhythm.

Michael knew she was out of danger yet he remained with her, enjoying the sensation when she stretched her body to fit his outline. He placed one hand on her arm, wanting to touch her skin as he inhaled her scent thick in her hair. Worrying he was taking liberties he should not, Michael stopped himself from going any further and removed his hand, backing away. One leg was off the bed when he heard her cry out his name in her sleep. If he had a heart, it would have been pained. There was fear in her voice when she spoke his name. Chastising himself for allowing the illusions he'd had, he slipped out of her room and went down to fill himself again with blood, hoping it would help him heal the ribs he re-cracked in the scuffle and hopefully give him the strength to win the more difficult battle he now fought within himself to leave this woman alone. Creatures like him could not be with humans. Only a fool would try.

Chapter 9

Becca stirred, sensing the day was nearly gone. She shied away from thoughts of what happened in the kitchen, clinging instead to the feeling of Michael's body when she lay against it. She liked it. She slept. The realization rocked her reality.

If Michael could be around Ryan, whatever form he was in, would he possibly be open to her brand of strangeness? It wasn't like she turned into anything, she snorted. She only had visions and gut instincts about things. That was mild by comparison. When she considered all that happened, his being her superior didn't seem such an insurmountable obstacle. Assuming he was interested, of course.

After a few hours of reassurance and rest she was better able to process Ryan's transformation. He was a creature she never knew existed beyond movies and books. So what? She had unusual abilities too. When taken that way, she found it far more palatable.

She rose and brushed her hair in the small mirror hanging over her dresser. Comfortable she was as good as it got, she walked out to join Admiral Black and find out what she was doing here.

The halls were silent except for her steady footfalls down the dimly lit corridor. Winding her way down the stairs, Becca heard nothing until the stairs spilled into the room in front of her. She saw Gabrielle, Ryan, and Michael seated at the table, the admiral stood at its head. She tried hard not to let her disappointment show when she saw Michael glance at her and quickly turn his head away again without changing his stern expression. Eyes flashing to the admiral, Becca thought his distance might be for his benefit.

Silently she joined the table, pulling out a chair at the admiral's gesture and trying to ignore the warning flashes starting in her head as soon as she was in his presence. "Be seated, Rebecca." He had a way of making her name sound creepy.

She kept her eyes on him, avoiding Ryan's guilty hangdog expressions noting his arm hung in a sling, Gabrielle's apparently characteristic nasty glares, and Michael's unresponsive face pointed directly at Admiral Black.

The admiral spoke. "Since you have all met already, I will skip the introductions. Some of you might question why I have brought Rebecca to our facility." He leveled a stare at Michael who didn't flinch. "I feel she has a valuable skill set that would make her a useful addition to our team." He smiled at her; his canines nearly normal sized gave her a chill.

Becca felt her stomach flip at the thought of being on a team with a woman who hated her, a man who turned into a dog, and a superior officer who had her completely turned around.

"Sir," Michael came to life. "With all due respect, Petty Officer Sauter has no place on this team. She is ill equipped for our missions and I cannot have my team walking into danger with a liability slowing us down."

Each word pelted her in a hail of duplicity. Her temper burned hot on two counts: insulted woman and insulted sailor. She rose from her chair bristling. "Sir, all due respect to Captain Rossi, he has no idea what I am capable of as a sailor. I believe I have a lot to offer the unit and would be honored to continue in my post here, Sir."

Admiral Black nodded approval at her tenacity. "I am pleased you agree, Rebecca. It would behoove us to have a woman of your abilities alongside us as we head into hostile territory." He surveyed the faces of the discontented team surrounding the table. "You bring up a good point as well. In order to properly utilize your abilities, I would like to know more about what you can do."

Her sixth sense kicked into overdrive and blinding pain lanced through her eyes. Training or no, she couldn't hide her wince. Holes punched themselves in her vision leaving large blind spots.

"For example, what was that?" Black studied her, fascinated. "Were you using it just then?"

"Using what, Sir?" Becca asked slowly, not liking the way the admiral was staring straight through her. She was a curiosity to him and it rubbed her the wrong way. Still she intended to follow the guidance her instinct was offering.

"Your second sight," he offered. "That is what it is called, is it not?"

Becca wanted to get up and run, not walk, from this table. "I'm not sure what you're talking about, Sir." That was definitely true. She had never heard a name associated with her visions. Had he recognized it that night in the woods? Now, faced with laying all of the details of her ability bare, she was finding it difficult to start.

"Don't try to bullshit me." His face was serene despite the waves of power rolling off of him. "You have the sight and you reek of preternatural. Now, tell me what you can do." He rested his fingertips on the table, inclining at the waist to bring his face closer to hers.

Afraid to ask what preternatural meant and felt abandoned in the face of Michael's blank expression. Michael, who had done nothing other than protect her up until now was discounting her. Ryan couldn't be trusted during the full moon and Gabrielle would probably lead any sort of charge against her. Becca felt more alone than she had in a very long time. So why did she insist upon proving herself to these people? *Maybe this is where you belong*, a little voice said. Seeing no other options, she surrendered to the absurdity of the situation and confessed the extent of her ability so long hidden.

"Sir, I'm not familiar with the terminology, but if you are asking what I meant about the wolves in the wood I can explain."

He nodded that she should.

"I get visions of what is going to happen, sometimes a few days out, sometimes more immediately. They come usually when I sleep but sometimes during the day too. Beyond that, I have what I would call an instinct for who or what situations are dangerous, and who I can trust." She hadn't meant to yet found her eyes touched Michael at the last. He stared steadily at his hands, the only hint he was listening was the tension in his shoulders.

Admiral Black was mulling over what she had told him. "Do you always remember your visions or do you speak them in your sleep and have someone record them? How does it work?"

"I sleep alone, Sir," she said flatly. She was not going to go into any more detail than that. "I remember my visions, I just don't always believe them." Becca's head turned toward Ryan sitting across from her and Gabrielle beside him. Her amber eyes took on new meaning after Ryan's change and now Becca was twice as leery of her, recalling those teeth snapping inches from her face. Michael, on the opposite end of the table hadn't moved. "Not everyone out there is as accepting of the unexplainable," she added.

Black laughed. It would have been more pleasant if she could get the image of him smiling with the club in his hand out of her head. "Too true Rebecca. Many a witch has burned for having the sight. Have no fear of that, your ability is welcome here." He straightened, his attentions back to the team as a whole. "As you all know we have been monitoring a series of thefts in the desert not far from the base where we discovered our newest recruit. We had a shipment of special weaponry arrive today and I would anticipate these thieves to strike again tonight. I think that would be a good place to take Rebecca for a test run." He looked to his second in command. "Michael, I trust you can manage her? I would like to keep these two in house for another day lest there be another accident."

"Sir." Michael did not argue nor did he look pleased.

"Gather what gear you need, you leave in one hour at sunset." The admiral turned and all eyes followed him out what had to be a side door hidden in the dark. It was the same area he came from when Becca met him initially; she assumed he had an office hidden back there somewhere.

Ryan and Gabrielle pushed back their chairs. He caught Becca's eye and gave a tight smile. She responded with a tense smile and nod in return. Accepting that she was different too helped her to cope with what he was. It didn't make it easy, although it was a start.

Soon it was only Becca and Michael at the table. A sideways glance showed his face turned dark and stormy. With the admiral gone he no longer had to hide his emotions. His request that she not be a part of the team irked her. She was eager to prove herself to all of them on this mission tonight.

Rising, she pushed her chair back. "Where do I get my gear, Captain?"

He did not miss her formal address and understood that how she would mistake his reluctance to have her on his team. It was better that way; she had no idea the dangers they faced on these missions. He did not take risking her safety lightly. He heard how frightened she'd been when she spoke his name in her sleep and seen the shock when faced with Ryan's beast. She would hesitate when the time came and hesitation killed. She had no place in their world.

Seeing he wasn't going to answer, Becca took matters into her own hands. The room was a large one, and open. The light seemed brighter tonight than it the night before and she could easily see another room off to the side, the one by the bow staffs. She took a guess and headed toward it. Sure enough, it led her straight to what she needed.

She had a vest, helmet, sidearm, knife, and secondary sidearm as well as some extra clips by the time Michael joined her. "Should I grab a bigger gun?"

Surveying her outfit, Michael approved. She chose enough to protect herself while still allowing for movement. She was ready for close range as well as distance fighting. He respected her thinking. All the more to lose should she face a real monster; none of this would help if she was too frightened to use it.

He nodded to the 9mm in her hand. "Are you a good shot?"

Her jaw lifted. "Yes."

"Then no."

Michael stalked out and Becca followed, irritated that she had to jog to keep up while she stowed her second gun.

The base was nearly an hour away, giving them plenty of time to talk if either one was so inclined. The first half hour was silent.

"We're tracking thieves targeting our special weapons. They're shifters. They change often and have been difficult to track in the past since we don't always know what form they take. I believe Black's plan is for you to use your sight to see what form they're in tonight and then get out of the way." Michael explained briefly without looking over. He saw the way she watched him at the briefing when he voiced his opinion. Her anger was useful. It would be better if she hated him.

Werewolves who couldn't settle their minds often had trouble changing, others couldn't tap in to their abilities. He wanted to throw Becca off. If he could show Black she

86

couldn't help them, this would be her first and last mission with them.

"What's a shifter?" Becca was annoyed with his elitist attitude. She didn't know what happened but it looked like his initial kindness was both false and short lived. If this was the real Captain Rossi, she wasn't interested. This mission would tell her what kind of officer he was and whether or not she could accept his command.

"Picture what Ryan did but into any animal he wanted."

Becca was nearing the end of her tether, the compilation of bizarre events stretching her to her breaking point. Her head pained her severely and she couldn't feel anything from the realm of her sixth sense or "second sight" as the admiral called it. She couldn't tell Michael that or he would say he was right and she couldn't do the job. Becca had no idea what was blocking her or if she was just not going to be able to perform on command. Honestly, she'd never *tried* to have a vision on demand before, only accepting them as they came.

The Charger stopped past the south gate of the base. It was infrequently used save for the occasional daytime deliveries. Michael stepped out and Becca did the same. Tensely standing outside her closed door, she awaited direction either from inside or out.

Michael was still.

She stood, hands on top of the roof, staring at the blackness of the car window. There was only the slightest of reflections in it from a distant light on the outer perimeter of the fence line. Not sure how to call her visions, she went with the best approximation of a sleep state she could muster out here. She rested her head on the cool metal window frame and closed her eyes.

In an effort to steer her ability, Becca thought about the shifters and imagined them with no specific form, merely as free form shapes for lack of a better form to conjure. Her mind reached for something dishonest, linking it with weapons. Slowly, she felt her heart slow, the sound of its heavy thudding reverberated against the inside of her eardrum as the external sounds of nighttime fell away. Michael's presence became extraneous. Conscious of each breath of air flowing through her mouth and nose, she let her body relax and her mind have its freedom.

Coyotes howled, three sets of feet padded across the road. They ran under the fence, one remained lookout until the others were under and waited at the fence for them to return. The other two ran across the grounds directly to the weapons supply.

The larger dark-furred coyote carried something in his mouth. As the coyote shifted, she saw the black rat drop from its jaws and race through the warehouse, darting into a specific aisle. Once in the aisle, the rat stopped part way down and wiggled up the leg of the metal scaffolding to the third level. He emerged with a small bag in his mouth, now heavy with something inside of it, and retraced his steps to the coyote waiting for him and they shot back across the base. Two coyotes arrived back at the fence where their shoulder mate awaited their return.

Becca blinked back to herself and straightened. Not sure what she might have said aloud, she gave Michael clear direction. "They've gone to the weapons supply across base." Becca was in awe of what she'd seen and couldn't hide her excitement over her premonition knowing it was real. And useful.

Michael spoke flatly from across the roof of the car, sounding disappointed. "Wait in the car. I'll go check it out."

Rankled, Becca didn't argue. Instead she let herself back into the vehicle and, watching for Michael's departure, still missed it entirely. He was directly across from her when he told her to get in the car and by the time she got in and closed the door, he was gone. A small voice in her head reminded her that he worked with werewolves and an incredibly scary man whom she was fairly certain was not entirely human, either. That left her with the question she wasn't sure she wanted to answer: What was Michael?

Chapter 10

His name in her head refueled her anger. He was treating her as if she didn't know how to find the business end of a gun and couldn't apprehend a criminal. Becca was Military Police and had been for the last three years. That was her job, to apprehend criminals, and she was very good at it. Even her former partner who hadn't liked her had to admit that much.

Rolling her eyes, she got back out and shut the door behind her to head down the fence directly to the section she had seen in her mind's eye. The open hangar doors provided the light by which she saw the creatures. Just in case her timing was off, it would be better to have a second person waiting at the fence when they returned, or if they were yet to come.

Becca's jog was a practiced pace she could maintain for several miles without fatigue. A human's answer to the dogtrot wolves use to travel great distances. Her pace brought her to the desired section of fence within minutes. Practiced eyes scanned the line of chain link, searching for movement or a flash of fur. She had no way of knowing if she was looking for one or three coyotes.

There, up ahead, was movement. Becca ducked and froze, reaching under her jacket to remove her backup weapon, fearing the click from her sidearm holster might spook the creatures.

Something struck the dirt with a soft thump and Becca held her breath. The other two coyotes had returned and the last one approaching the fence dropped the purse-sized bag she saw in her vision. What was in it was unclear but being from the weapons supply, she would assume explosive was possible. She aimed high.

When all three were through and on the same side as her Becca rose, holding her gun at the ready. "Halt. Police."

The coyotes froze and it was hard for her not to laugh at the picture of three coyotes obeying human commands. Would they put their hands up?

"Drop the bag and step aside," she commanded, approaching them slowly. The one who dropped the bag still had the strap in his mouth, preparing to swing it back up toward himself. He was refusing to obey her orders. Becca repeated the command, the unmistakable sliding action of her gun cocking giving them further warning.

One of them, the one who had remained behind, gave a yip and the largest with the bag snarled back. The middle creature licked the big one's muzzle. Becca watched the interplay of pack and human behaviors, fascinated.

The bigger one gave a low growl as his only warning before tossing the bag to the smaller, Becca's mind said female, beside him and continued his spin until he was facing her again. He was staring directly into Becca's eyes, snarling his intent.

She stared back, amazed to be looking into such human brown eyes. It could have been her experience with the wolves that changed her perspective or it was her sight, she swore the others weren't aggressive. Only the largest was a threat. His snarl rattled out menacingly into an angry series of yip-like battle cries as he rushed her.

There was a small distance, less than ten yards, between them in which he wove and darted unpredictably, adding a dizzying spin twice before he changed direction again and ran around her back. Becca turned with him but he was faster. She lost him in the dark of the surrounding shadows. Heavy clouds covered the moon tonight. If she had been able to find a flashlight among the supplies she would have been able to see. However, frustratingly, they hadn't had one and here she was facing a shape shifting coyote virtually blind.

Becca kept an eye darting back to the other two behind her and had to call for them to halt again, ordering them to lay down this time. Cautiously, she crab stepped toward them, splitting her attentions between the two she saw and the one she thought she had seen flickering through the shadows on her other side.

Reaching them, she stretched her arm down and put her hand on the bag beside the female. She whined and Becca looked at her face. Her expression was pleading. She feared for the male.

"I don't want to hurt him either, ma'am." She didn't question why it felt right to address her in that fashion. Somehow she sensed a maturity and wisdom about the female.

Throwing the strap over her chest like a messenger bag with its bulk twisted behind her, Becca removed her other weapon from its holster, bringing it to bear on the darkness to her right, the other remaining on the prone figures in front of her.

Her straining eyes caught a flash of movement running alongside her. She spun to track it, leaving her other side temporarily unguarded. The smallest of the three hopped up from the ground at her feet and rushed her, hitting her in her shoulder and knocking the gun from her grasp, bringing her hard to the ground.

As soon as she was down the coyotes were on her in a snarling, yipping, writhing mass. The large male came at her chest, mouth agape and she brought the butt of the gun still in the other hand down hard on the top of his head. Backing away, he shook his head and roared back to her. No longer cowed, the female worked with him and snatched at Becca's gun hand, holding the sleeve at the wrist. Becca's fingers tightened, the gun went off, and she heard a pained yip as her hand was liberated.

Freed, she trained the gun upon the large male now standing over her, tugging at the bag strap. The impact of the smaller animal when it threw itself at her neck in an attempt for her jugular was completely unexpected. Becca had underestimated the threat of the smaller creature. The injury to the female seemed to bring it to life.

Only the thick collar running the sides and back of her flack vest stopped the animal's teeth from penetrating her skin more than superficially. Training overtook conscious thought and the gun went up by her shoulder, the muzzle tucked under its throat where the bullet found its mark. Without hesitation her arm, wet with the spray of the animal's blood, whipped back to the larger creature. Shifting it away from his face, Becca pulled the trigger, landing a bullet in its side.

The sudden silence let her breathe, although it was not from relief. Around her lay three bodies, a quick check revealed they all still lived. Gauging by the lack of wheezing or bloody bubbles, the smallest one's survival was nothing short of miraculous, the bullet having barely missed the windpipe.

Michael's arrival while she was checking the others caught her unawares. She'd forgotten he was here with her and realized he probably thought she sent him off on a fool's errand on purpose.

Michael had been hunkered down, waiting outside the warehouse where the theft was to occur when he heard the first shot. As soon as the familiar noise reached him, Michael took off at a dead run, his beast riding him to go faster. He arrived just after the third and saw Becca hunched over the form of a body with several others scattered nearby; she was seemingly unhurt. Michael could barely control his temper as he jumped the fence and stepped out into the partial light. He was furious with her for facing the shifters alone. Too angry to be impressed by her results.

"What do you mean by shooting on base? Don't you know you're going to bring security down on us?" he barked at her. Michael wasn't really concerned about the patrols Black would take care of any complications. His clout allowed them to do whatever they needed to succeed.

Her head flew up affording Michael a view of her distressed state before she carefully tucked it away. With great difficulty, he held himself in place. She was pale and obviously shaken by the fact that she harmed three creatures. It couldn't be helping her that they had now taken their human shapes and lay naked and bleeding all around her.

"I'm sorry," she snarled, her voice barely cracking, "but the only alternative was to let them *eat* me."

On cue, the sound of a siren accompanied by a set of headlights approached them fast. Becca continued to apply pressure to a neck wound on the teenaged shifter, bleeding profusely. Michael didn't move. He could hear all of their hearts beating strong and knew they would heal. Becca, however, was fearful she had just killed her first man. Her heart beat the fastest of them all. If they had time he would reassure her. They didn't.

The first one out of the car yelled for them to freeze and Becca shouted back they needed medics. Three wounded, one severely.

"Becca?" The second man hopped out from the driver's seat.

Her head jerked up again, the details of her features washed out in the glare of the lights. "Danny?" Was it two days ago she sat in the car with him? It felt like a lifetime since she'd seen her partner.

"What happened? Where did the shooter go?" He obviously trusted her; he had no question of Becca's innocence.

"Um," she looked down at the blood now slowing, staining her hands. "I don't know, I didn't see anyone else."

Michael felt his lips twitch in amusement. She told the honest truth. She was not a liar. Good to know.

"Can you call for an ambulance?" she asked again, shooting a quick inquiring glance at Michael.

He gave a barely perceptible nod of his head. The medics wouldn't have the bodies long enough to ascertain their differences. They couldn't shift with their injuries, given the fact that the rounds Becca shot them with contained a solution that would keep them in stasis until they were given the antidote. It was a silver solution, the supernatural equivalent of a stun setting. When on a more dangerous mission, Becca would carry the deadly version they otherwise kept locked up- pure silver. It was the only guaranteed killer for all supernatural creatures.

Danny nodded to his new partner who ran back to the vehicle to call in the request. Meanwhile, he strode toward the fence and locked his fingers on it.

"Becca, where'd you go? Terry said you had some sort of accident and then some guy," he gave Michael a curious once over, "took you out of the hospital. He's been checking. Nobody's willing to give up any particulars on whoever authorized it. No one's seen or heard from you since." Danny dropped his voice, trying to be private. "Terry's worried sick, Bec. So was I. You're not in any sort of trouble are you?"

She sat back on her haunches, fingers still pressed against the wound that had all but stopped, and felt very tired. With an exhausted sigh she pushed her hair back off her forehead with the back of her wrist, unwittingly leaving a thin blood smear on her pale skin. Terry. She hadn't thought about him since leaving the hospital.

"What are you doing working tonight? Weren't we on days through the month?" Becca diverted. By her count he shouldn't be on nights for another week.

He shook his head. "Remember? I switched with Glen tonight to have tomorrow off for the barbeque." He gestured with his head back at the car. "They gave me Martin since you were missing. No one said anything about it being weird you were gone."

"Oh, is that tomorrow?" Becca had completely forgotten.

"Actually, it's today now." Danny made a show of checking his watch.

The flashing lights of an approaching ambulance drew their attention and Becca watched them turn at the gate where they'd parked before redirecting back her way. Another followed close behind. Becca stepped back to let the medics take their charges. The teen went in one ambulance, the other two went together. All three were unconscious and naked. A detail not missed by the medics when they attended them.

Becca, seeing their curious expressions, commented simply, "Nudists." There was a beach that catered to their crowd not far from the base making Becca's statement not as farfetched as one might think. Some of the service men were all too willing to believe the nudists were as bad as hippies for protests and sabotage. That a few might have gotten too high and wandered off course wasn't a difficult fabrication to sell.

Michael's aloofness grated on Becca, not that she would look his direction, except she was as aware of his presence as she had been last night when he had been lying with her. For whatever reason, she was painfully aware of his proximity to her since the night they'd met. Maybe it had something to do with him saving her life, some sense of obligation. She pushed off the suspicion that it had something to do with the whole servant and master thing Black had been talking about. The distance and complete lack of help he was giving her now clarified that it was a one-way appreciation. Whatever his mixed signals had been, this one was clear.

Part of her was glad she had not accurately predicted the timing of the raid in her vision. Singlehandedly she had recovered the stolen property and stopped the three shifters. It was a reasonably admirable feat, not that the arrogant son of a bitch would admit it, she harrumphed to herself bitterly.

Hopefully it would impress the admiral. He was really her ticket into the unit. Though whether she really wanted in with that crowd was in serious question.

After the wounded were loaded up and Becca was wiping her hands on the rag a medic had given her, she searched for her missing gun.

Danny regarded Michael with more than a hint of suspicion. "There's some paperwork I need to fill out. Why don't you go get your car and Becca can drive with us. It'll let us catch up."

Groaning, Becca considered running so she wouldn't have to spend another hour avoiding more specific questions from her partner while he filled out the lengthy paperwork she knew was necessary. And Danny's overt attempt at separating her from Michael proved he didn't trust him at all.

"You know we have to, Bec. You're a witness." Danny patted the fence and stepped away.

Michael reanimated, the suddenness of his voice making her jump. "Petty Officer Sauter and I will meet you at the office."

Trumped by rank, Danny couldn't disagree. "Fine." He eyed Michael with open distaste.

Danny's dislike for Michael was obvious and a surprise. Becca had never seen him react like that to anyone without being physically attacked first. She wondered if he came to that himself because of Michael's prickly exterior or if she was putting out a vibe he was picking up. Either way, she found it humorous and commented on it as her eyes picked out the solid shape of her Glock lying nearby. She grabbed it and they made their way briskly to the car.

Shrugging, he replied unconcerned, "Does it matter?"

Bristling, Becca broke into a jog. "It does to me. He's my partner and I trust his judgment. It's saved my skin more than once."

Michael let her pull ahead of him, letting her comment swirl around in his head. He hadn't thought about how dangerous her human job might be. He would like to know more about it *and* her partner.

A few humans were sensitive to his kind even if it was subconscious. They took an instant dislike to them whether they understood why or not. Danny might be an interesting complication.

What really bothered him was Danny's comment about Terry, and Becca's reaction. The comment had stopped her cold. She had been instantly upset at the mention of his name. Michael felt his rising jealousy picturing the arrogant human who had behaved so possessively toward the woman at the hospital. He had not treated her with respect but rather as something he owned. Snorting, Michael knew the human could not stop him if he wanted her. He stopped moving. Did he want her? Shaking it off as a lingering effect of having given her his blood and increasing his innate possessiveness. He kept it to a nearly human speed, in case anyone was watching, as he jogged to catch Becca already getting into the car.

She drove to the office, her assertion of power making Michael smile. He had to duck his head to hide it. Then his mood turned black upon arriving at the office. Becca parked, and he saw from the look on her face she had recognized the other car next to Danny's patrol car. Michael had smelled its owner through the open window.

Becca dragged her feet, a fact not lost on Michael. He stepped in front of her, entering the building first with Becca sluggishly drooping behind him.

Chapter 11

"Becca!" Terry breathed when he saw her. He had been anxiously pacing in the hall of the building outside the office door. From his rumpled hair Michael assumed he had jumped out of bed when Danny called him, something her partner had undoubtedly done as soon as he'd gotten back in the car. He obviously wasn't too worried about Becca if he could get a good night's rest.

Michael did not step aside when Terry moved toward her, however he did keep himself from lashing out and tearing his arms off when the human sidestepped him to wrap his arms around her. Michael twisted his neck to observe Becca's reaction. He worked to keep the satisfaction off of his face at what he saw there.

Dread. That was how Becca felt at seeing Terry again. She knew she owed him an explanation only she had hoped to let him down easily in the right time and place. The hospital hadn't been right and this didn't seem so either. Nor did she want Michael to see her failing in her relationship. He already believed her an inadequate addition to his unit. That was before tonight, she reminded herself. She would dare him to have done as well.

Terry was the only one who didn't sense Becca's lack of reciprocity. He loosed his arms only enough to lean back and capture her lips. Becca thought about not returning his kiss except she didn't want to hurt him more than she had to. Instead she broke it off quickly, turning her head to speak to Michael over Terry's shoulder.

"Could you go in and get started? I'll be right there." She saw his irritated expression at her dismissal. "I would like to speak to Terry privately, Sir."

His eyes narrowed at her formal address and he withheld comment. Michael opened the door and Becca swore she heard something crack when he grabbed the knob.

Terry went for her mouth again and this time she turned her head, giving him her cheek.

"Bec, where have you been? Who *is* that guy?" He stepped back, keeping hold of her hands as he examined her newly issued uniform, the jacket devoid of patches identifying her, her branch, rank or even country. "What are you some sort of black ops now?" His high-pitched laugh betrayed his nerves.

Becca wasn't sure how to answer and saw her hesitation register with Terry. His eyes widened. She let him think what he wanted. Wasn't it true? Hunting supernatural creatures was as off the grid as it got in her mind.

"Look Terry, I'm going to be gone for a while. I meant to call as soon as I was able but it's been a little…" What? What should she say about meeting a werewolf and two scary men, one of whom could heal in a day and move faster than a normal human? The idea of what he could be tickled on the edge of her consciousness only she didn't let it in. It was too weird for her yet. "Hectic."

He stared at her, hands tightening on her upper arms. "What do you mean *for a while*? Are they shipping you off somewhere?"

Her head started to tingle a warning, she broke her gaze from him to scan the office and saw nothing. There was no one there but Danny and Michael in the other room. "I really can't say where I'll be or how long I'll be with them." That was true. "I think it would be best for us to call things off for now." She dropped the bomb abruptly and held her breath.

"We should *what*?" His brows pinched together, his voice rising. "Wait, are you breaking up with me?" He pulled her forward and lifted her to her tiptoes.

Wiggling furtively in an attempt to hide her discomfort and reestablish her space, Becca nodded. "Yes, Terry. I think that's best. We don't know when we'll see each other again and it isn't fair for me to ask you to wait."

"Why don't we see how long this operation takes? We both know deployments and relocations are part of the job." Ever pragmatic, Terry was being difficult in her eyes.

She rolled a shoulder, trying to get an arm free from his tightening fingers but it was no good. He held her firm and her heart started to race as her adrenaline kicked in. The tingle in her head crossed over to a shooting pain, spots danced across his face. "Terry, let me go."

Eyes turning hard, Terry showed her a side she hadn't suspected was there. "No. Not until you tell me what this is really about. Is it someone else? Is it that guy in there?" He indicated the office with his head.

"What, Michael? No." She heard the hesitation, ever present when she lied, which is exactly why she tried not to. She was bad at it. Terry caught it, his fingers dug in and his jaw clenched.

"Stop it." She could feel the circulation in her arms being cut off and tried again to work loose. She didn't want to escalate things, although she was considering hitting him if he didn't back off. "Terry it isn't him, okay? It's me. I can't give you what you want. It was coming to this anyway, you had to know that." She was hoping to diffuse his emotions currently running too high for her safety yet was saying all the wrong things. Becca had been arresting people for too long not to see Terry getting desperate now. "Terry, don't to this. You don't want to go to jail over this." Becca softened her voice, trying another tact. "Let me go." Each word, layered with a double meaning, hit him like separate physical blows.

Unable to comprehend how she could leave him otherwise he lashed out, ridiculously grasping at justifications. "Did you sleep with him?"

Becca had no idea why she felt the need to tell him the truth. It came out before she thought through the repercussions. "It's not like that, we didn't have sex." Stomach twisting, sight narrowing and wincing with the pain in her head and arms, she wobbled on her toes. A blinking glance down showed his fingers were white with the pressure of his iron grip.

That was all the answer Terry needed. "You ungrateful bitch! No one else would have you before me. And this is what you do to thank me? I took pity on you." One hand let her go long enough to draw back and backhand her across the face.

The crack echoed in the hall and the door behind Terry shot open. The occupants spilled out, Michael in the lead. He grabbed Terry's arm still holding Becca and squeezed the wrist, instantly disabling the limb with a snap.

Freed from his grasp, Becca stumbled. Michael's face was dark, inhuman, and Becca saw a flash of long white teeth protruding from under his top lip as he spun Terry to face him. One blow sent him flying backward and his limp body slid along the floor stopping only when it ran up against the wall.

Danny dodged past Michael and caught Becca up in an embrace. "Bec, are you okay? What the hell was that about?" He shot a look at Terry, now lying motionless behind her in the hall.

Becca didn't trust her voice. To think she had been worried about hurting Terry's feelings. It had never crossed her mind he would lay a hand on her. Danny was rambling but her mind was on Michael.

He was a little confused on how to relate to women, but as a sailor he was honorable. She translated his actions to how he would command. He saw her at her worst before and as a result, didn't want her risking the lives of his unit. He had been angry, maybe rightfully so, about her sending him to the warehouse and handling the shifters alone. She'd give him that. But here he was, protecting her yet again as a human when she'd been unable to help herself. Personal feelings aside, she wanted to work for him. She felt that certainty settle around her shoulders, bringing with it a mantle of tranquility.

Danny was still going. "Never seen him hurt anyone before. I mean, yeah he's wound a little tight and maybe a little controlling but I've never seen him hit a woman before. I'm so sorry Bec, I didn't think he was that kind of guy." Danny was turning himself inside out. "I never would have put you two together if I knew he was like that."

Vision cleared, she looked at him and forced a smile, wincing when her cheek moved. It was going to have a hell of a bruise if she didn't get some ice on it soon. "It's okay, Danny. It isn't your fault, I know you wouldn't have encouraged him if you knew he was like that."

Becca's eyes wandered past Danny to Michael behind him, worrying about what she had seen when he had attacked Terry. Whatever he was, he had helped her and she had to do the same for him. It was part of being a team. You take the good with the bad, or the scary or whatever.

The storm on his face still raged and she saw him fighting to control it. His teeth were receding while his eyes remained darkest midnight. Instinctively she knew she had to get him out of there now. His control was tenuous at best. She pulled away and sidled around Danny.

"Danny, I think we should get out of here before Terry gets up. I'm going to fax you my statement, okay? Michael and I have to head back or we'll be in deep with the CO." She avoided mentioning Black's name.

Danny craned his neck to see Terry lying on the ground. "Is he going to be all right?" he asked Michael but when he tried to make eye contact, Becca stepped between them.

"Unfortunately," Michael growled out.

"We really need to go." Becca started forward and noticed Michael was not following. She turned back, saw him still eyeing Terry coldly and reached out to take his arm. "Come on, Michael. I don't want to piss off the CO, do you?"

Turning his furious eyes on her, Michael saw her balk at the monster she saw in him. Then, instead of shying away, she strengthened her grip on his forearm, frowned at him, and tugged. He wanted to kill the man who had put that mark upon her delicate flesh, but the feel of her hand on his body soothed him. He let her guide him out.

They moved quickly once they were out of the building. Michael intentionally held his speed even with hers down the steps to the passenger side of the vehicle and opened the door for her. Becca ducked into the car and watched his form blur as he disappeared from beside her to reappear a fraction of a second later at the door opposite hers.

Tires squealed and the vehicle's engine roared as it tried to keep up with the speed of Michael's demands. Sensing his rage drove him and fearing they would raise suspicion at the gate approaching it like they were a couple of drunk hotheads out for a beer run, Becca reached out. Her hand lay gently on top of his on the gearshift, "Please, Captain. Go slow until we're past the gate." He did as she asked without a word; the car's speed crept back down to within the normal range. Touching him made her pounding heart steady quickly. She tried to keep calm and make him so as well. It was taxing after the emotionally charged night they'd had.

After they cleared the main gate, Becca removed her hand from his and lay it in her lap. Michael darted his eyes sideways at her. He could see she was struggling to maintain her composure. She must be hurting from Terry's attacks, both physical and verbal. His hand twitched on the shifter. He wanted to reach out to her, to give her strength the way she had given his back with her touch, except he doubted he could have the same effect on her. Especially now that she had seen what he was. Why else would she be working so hard to get him away from all of the humans before he could harm anyone else? She was afraid of him and what he could do.

"What do you think is in the bag?" He gave her mind something else to focus on.

"Huh?" Her eyes were blank. "What bag?"

He pointed to the strap on her shoulder. "The bag the shifters were after. What do you suppose is inside?"

She blinked, the words gradually making sense to her. "I don't know. Do you think we can look?"

Michael nodded assent. "He didn't say we couldn't." He grinned, then quickly put his lips back over his teeth, not wanting to remind her.

Becca smiled faintly back at him, leaning forward to take the strap from her body and spin the small bag around. Unzipping it, she peered inside but couldn't see what it held. She flipped on the interior light and looked down again.

"What is it?" he asked, though her answer wasn't necessary. The smell was unique and unmistakable.

"It looks like shells." Her brow wrinkled. "Why would they go there specifically to steal ammunition? They could buy it anywhere."

"Because it isn't just ordinary ammunition," he informed her cryptically. "It's *our* ammunition."

"What do you mean 'ours'?" She turned to face him full on.

Michael did a double take. He felt the demon within him struggling to come back out as he watched the purple stain on her cheek growing darker. He was not the only monster among the humans. His fingers tightened on the wheel until it cracked.

"Our team requires a specific type of round for our missions. They are made by a particular laboratory and shipped here. We are the only individuals allowed access to them."

Becca stared at him, waiting for him to go on, to keep filling in blanks for her. He did.

"Supernatural creatures are not harmed by a normal round. Instead of standard rounds we use two different types. The one you carried tonight has only a trace amount of silver, which serves to incapacitate. The other is pure silver and delivers a lethal dose." He nodded down at her guns.

She turned off the overhead light and sat in the dark, mulling over what she was learning and piecing it together with what she was guessing. "How did you know I would have the right kind of bullets?"

"Black had the silver locked up when you arrived. He didn't want anything to happen if you had trouble adjusting to us."

"Would a regular bullet hurt you?"

"It would be painful but no, it wouldn't stop me."

They drove on in silence, the sun rising as they pulled in at the estate. Michael got out and flashed around to Becca's door, opening it for her again. She noticed he was not being careful to hide what he was from her any longer even if he hadn't told her in as many words. She continued to piece together what she had seen of him and her mind tried to push the word away as impossible. Impossible? How could she think that when she had met and accepted the existence of werewolves and shape shifters? Why could a vampire not be real?

The taste of the word in her mouth was not as repugnant as she would have anticipated. She had the same warm, giddy reaction each time he touched her. That night he had lain with her, she had had dreamed of Black hurting him again. She had called out for him, afraid to lose him. His actions tonight had reconfirmed for her that he would not hurt her. But did he still consider her a detriment to the team? He would protect her but she wasn't good enough to work with them. That thought ate at her.

Michael opened the door to the house where Ryan met them. His arm already out of his sling, he was looking perfectly healthy. And Gabrielle's mood had shifted to mild annoyance. An improvement.

"How's the other guy?" Ryan studied Becca's face.

Michael's voice was distinctly unhappy. "He'll live."

Gabrielle's brows rose. "Oh?"

Becca kept it short, knowing Gabrielle would probably find the whole thing funny. She wasn't in the mood to deal with her brand of nasty. "While we were on base we ran into some old friends."

Refraining from saying anything snide, Gabrielle cracked a hint of a smile and shot a stealthy look at Michael behind her.

Ryan was chuckling and rubbing his chin. "Well, will wonders never cease?"

Becca was fried. She pushed on past their inside jokes wanting only to get some ice and go to bed. "If no one needs me for anything else tonight, I'm turning in."

No one followed her to the kitchen. It took her only a minute to grab some ice and wrap it in a rag from the drawer. She snorted at the return trip. She'd had to dip into that drawer for first aid purposes twice now. This was going to be a challenging post.

And Becca didn't want to leave it. Strange and different as this was, it felt right. She was already beginning to feel at ease with the whole concept of policing this whole other world. "What does that say about me?" she mumbled with a roll of her eyes.

Chapter 12

Becca passed through the halls holding the cold bundle to her face, grateful it was numbing the throbbing ache in her cheekbone. The entry was empty when she came through again, which was mostly a good thing. Tromping up the long flight to her quarters, she felt the last of her energy draining out of her with each step. By the time she finally reached her door she was done in and barely got her shoes off before falling in to bed, fully clothed.

What seemed like only a few minutes later, Becca woke to someone knocking on her door. Rather than bounce out of bed, she shuffled to the door, feeling the wetness of her shirt and jacket where the melting ice had ended up as she slept. Tired fingers tenderly probed her face. The ice had helped with the swelling though the skin was still mildly tender. "I'm going to have to start keeping a cooler up here," she mumbled.

Michael stood at her door in clean fatigues. She smiled automatically, taking in the sight, wincing when her muscles tightened under her bruise.

A shadow crossed his otherwise cool face. "We're due for debriefing at thirteen hundred."

"What time is it now?" Becca hadn't checked the alarm clock on her bedside table when she got up.

"Twelve thirty."

"Okay, thank you."

He didn't respond, he only turned on his heel and began to walk away and Becca called out to him.

"Uh, Michael?"

He stopped and turned around.

"Thank you. For what you did. He took me by surprise, I didn't think he..." She saw him frown and wondered what she had said this time. Frustrated with herself and with him, she backed up and closed the door.

The door closed and Michael muttered in disbelief. She was making excuses for her abuser? How? He'd sensed her dislike for him. Humans confounded him.

Becca took a few minutes to clean up and put on clean clothes before reporting to the debriefing. At the rate she was running through them she was going to have to find the laundry room soon. The pair she had worn on her first mission were most likely ruined from the blood. She hoped that wouldn't be docked from her pay. She assumed she was being paid for this.

When she got downstairs she found she was the last one to arrive. Again. She would have to plan better to get there early. Admiral Black stood at the head of the table. Michael sat at the foot. Ryan and Gabrielle were understandably absent not having been a part of the mission. Michael turned his head at her approach. Becca felt her heart skip when she saw the sky blue eyes meet hers. She thought she knew the word that described what he was, and yet it did not strike fear into her heart. It became a word to describe him like any other, no more terrifying than tall or short, rich or poor.

"Rebecca, please be seated." Admiral Black began. He faced Michael. "Michael and I were discussing the fate of the shifters you apprehended. They are to be moved at nineteen hundred today to the facility in Boise."

"Boise, Sir?"

"As you can imagine, supernatural and preternatural creatures alike cannot be contained in a human prison. It would neither hold them nor would it be safe for the humans confined alongside them. We have several permanent facilities within the country and a number of temporary holding facilities throughout the world. These three have been stealing for some time from both military and civilian installments in the area, most recently focusing on our weapons. This particular theft would have been of great concern. I understand Michael explained to you why this would be the case?"

"Yes Sir." She kept it simple.

The admiral leveled his flat black gaze at her. She felt her insides crawl and struggled to keep her face straight. Black was the same type of creature as Michael, she knew that, only her reaction to him was very different. It was visceral. He was the nightmare that was the undead, the one she'd seen in horror movies and grown up fearing as the thing that would sneak up behind her on a dark street. Michael could be equally deadly, that she did not doubt. However, he was different than Black. There was good in him where there was none in the admiral. Her sight, she had grown used to the title, told her that and she trusted it.

"Rebecca, Michael told me of your performance. I am impressed." He nodded approvingly at her.

The aggravation at missing Michael's report was softened by the shock of it being a good one. She saw his eyes focus on her cheek and felt herself grow hot with shame at having her personal life so blatantly thrown in the faces of her new team and CO. Mercifully, he said nothing.

"You are a valuable asset to us, Rebecca. I would like you to join our team permanently. We will send for your things tomorrow." He reached down for the file sitting open in front of him, snapping it shut. He clearly did not expect any arguments.

The invitation was what she had been hoping for only now that it had been offered, she found herself questioning her place there. It wasn't enough for her to want to be with them, they had to want her too. Ryan seemed ambivalent about it, Gabrielle *couldn't* be happy with it although she hadn't said

111

anything. But Michael was their immediate commander. If he didn't want her, it wouldn't work.

Becca swallowed hard forcing herself to ask, "Sir, permission to speak freely."

Black looked up at her, cold face frozen in an unreadable mask, waiting. "Granted."

She kept her eyes aimed only at Black. "Sir, I wish to be a part of the team, however I must decline if my presence interferes with the cohesiveness of the unit."

"Do not worry that you are human." Black picked up the folder to leave. "We intend to give you more guns."

Becca persevered. "No, Sir. Captain Rossi expressed doubts about my performance. If he questions my suitability, then I cannot be under his command. Sir." She kept her eyes forward, struggling not to turn her head knowing Michael's eyes were on her.

One white eyebrow rose, his pale, thin lips twisted into a smirk. Looking past Becca at his captain, he waited.

She waited quietly as well. Taking the prolonged silence as her answer, Becca carefully placed her hands flat on the table, rising deliberately to her feet and took a breath, ready to tell the admiral of her wish to decline.

"I can find no fault with Petty Officer Sauter's performance in the field. Her skills would be a compliment to this team."

Michael's words were hollow not because of what he said, it was because of what he didn't. Becca heard his doubts ringing loud and clear in his hesitation.

"Thank you for your honesty, Captain." Turning first to the admiral and then Michael, who did not hide his surprise well, she saluted respectfully to them both. "I'll wait in my quarters to catch a ride with the next one going back to base, Sir."

A hushed pall dimmed the black room darker. Becca held herself to a businesslike stride, all the while wishing she could run from this place and the people in it. She wanted to be clear of all of them, two in particular. One purely out of fear, the other for so many more confusing reasons.

Once up the stairs and back on the main floor, Becca broke into a run and didn't stop until she reached her door. There, she promptly skidded to an abrupt halt. Gabrielle stood leaning, arms crossed against her doorframe.

"Gabrielle, don't start with me." She moved to open her door around her. "I'll be out of your hair soon enough, just let me get my things and you'll never have to see me again. Unless there's a troll hiding on the base or something, then I know who to call."

"Quitting so soon?" she taunted, not shifting out of the way. "I had you figured for more of a stayer. Guess I was wrong."

Becca sighed. "Look, if Captain Rossi can't trust me it puts everyone in danger. I'm not going to do that to you guys." She didn't say that it wouldn't surprise her if Gabrielle didn't trust her either. It was no longer an issue.

Gabrielle straightened. The effortless movement was less of a push off of the doorframe than a flowing upward. Becca felt horribly inept. Her hand reached behind herself and she pushed the door open. "Then by all means, let's get you packed."

Becca watched Gabrielle's hips sway into her room and felt an angry urge to put a boot right in the middle of them. Knowing that wouldn't end well for her, Becca walked to the dresser and removed the borrowed desert fatigues she had worn here from the hospital. Where she had met Michael.

The mere thought of him made her body react.

"Oh for fuck's sake, you *are* dumb." Gabrielle threw up her hands, rolling her eyes heavenward.

Becca turned to face her, her blank expression probably not helping the beautiful woman's assessment of her mental faculties.

"Every time you look at him, hell every time you hear his name, your pulse goes double time. Not to mention what else just warmed up. If that's why you're leaving, then that's just sad."

Becca learned a new mood of Gabrielle's. Judgmental. Her cheeks flamed. "It isn't like that. It comes down to who you can trust in a fight and if he can't trust my ability to keep any one of you safe, then I have no business being out there."

She snorted. "Of course you can't keep any of us safe. Not any more than we can keep you safe." When her voice dropped, softening, it caught Becca off guard. "In the end, no one can keep anyone else safe. And you being human complicates things, I won't lie about that."

Becca turned her back to her. It was easier to talk to Gabrielle indirectly. "So you see my point."

Gabrielle wasn't done. "Becca, the creatures we hunt are like us. They're stronger and faster than anything you've ever squared off against and most have had lifetimes to grow more skilled." She raised a finger at Becca's impending interjection. "But with you, we could see them coming. It could help us to fight them and keep everyone alive. Michael knows that. And like any good leader, he worries about his crew, *even* the humans. He doesn't want you getting into something you can't handle and getting any of us killed trying to protect you."

Speaking to Gabrielle in the mirror over the dresser was no longer enough. Becca turned to face the bed. "You aren't disproving any of my points about my inadequacy right now. You know that?"

A hint of a smile played at her features. "I am not here to be your friend, merely to point out that we could use someone like you. As far as danger goes, you could get shot on duty any night of the week. At least with us you would know you're saving lives, not just dragging drunks to the brig."

"Thank you for your sales pitch, Gabrielle," his unmistakably aggrieved voice called from the door.

Becca felt peace descend.

"I'll let myself out." Gabrielle sashayed calmly past.

Becca didn't turn around. "Captain Rossi." She moved closer to the bed to put space between them. Her things were by him in the dresser. Her arms folded across her chest.

"Why did you do that?" His voice was tight. "You asked a question and I answered honestly."

"I apologize, Michael." Becca kept her tone flat. She didn't know how to deal with him; her thoughts were all turned around again thanks to Gabrielle.

Black had told Michael to work things out with the human. He wanted her on the team and would not accept her leaving. Black had told him that, given the strength of her preternatural abilities, she would not be *allowed* to leave. The usual simple mind wipe was not an option. It wouldn't work on someone like her. She worked with them, or she would be eliminated.

"Do whatever you need to do to convince her." The admiral had noticed the way Becca looked to Michael for reassurance. "She has your blood in her and she is attracted to you, Michael. You can use both to your advantage. That doesn't pose a problem for you, does it?"

He couldn't think of her being killed, the blood exchange's power went both ways. And Michael was angry with himself

115

for not hiding his interest in Becca very well from the admiral. He would use it.

"Bastard knows everything," Michael had muttered to himself on his way up. Admiral Black's penchant for gathering intelligence gave him an advantage over his men and even many of those above him. Michael was fairly certain not a single world leader would challenge the admiral if push came to shove. He scared the hell out of all of them.

In truth, Michael *wanted* to convince her to stay. Gabrielle's remark about her being harmed in the line of duty even by chance weighed on his mind. At least if he was with her he could protect her. But the admiral suggesting he seduce her gave him pause. Playing upon his blood's hold on her rubbed him the wrong way. That he wanted her to want him without him using his nature's advantages surprised him. Then there was the fact that Black planned to use her to his own advantage in the same way he used the others on the team. That was different, *they* were different.

They had no real place in the world anymore. Human populations had grown and expanded exponentially through the ages leaving them few places to exist peacefully. For the most part, their kind was content to use humans for food and blend in. They didn't want the difficulty or responsibility their exposure would bring. Rossi and his team had found a way to serve their country, a desire that did not change with their natures, and to exist without persecution.

But for Becca it was different. She could hide her ability because she was otherwise human. Her ability was something that had not stopped her from living her life.

"What is it I can do for you, Michael?" Becca prompted him, her temper growing short.

"May I come in?" Standing there, her intoxicating smell filling his nostrils and the sound of her suddenly slowing pulse in his ears, Michael entertained the idea of carrying out the admiral's order. As a man who had kept to himself aside from the occasional physical necessity since before the war when things changed, Michael felt his need to protect her warring with his desire to possess her. If he had to, he would return her to her quarters and bind her to him there. He would not take her here, under Black's roof.

She turned and motioned him inside, carefully keeping her features hardened against him. She refused to let him know how much his insult earlier had hurt her or how his presence effected her.

"I'll take you home this evening." He stood just inside the door, eyes roving the sparse furnishings.

She let him see her dissatisfaction. "I'm ready now."

He traced his fingers over the dresser, barely affording her a glance. "I'll meet you out front after the sun sets." Michael's fingers continued to move in an unrecognizable pattern.

Becca shifted nervously from foot to foot. Unable to push him further without being outright rude, she could say nothing.

"I'll see you out there." He returned his hand to his pocket and walked out.

She watched his retreating back, not looking forward to leaving yet unable to think of staying.

Chapter 13

Neither one spoke the entire hour long drive back to base. The glow of the newly waning moon illuminated the desert landscape around them. It was the first cloudless sky in a week and Becca stared out, face resting in her hand on the window.

Michael approached the main gate, stopping to announce them to the guard on duty.

Ducking down, the Marine in the gatehouse raised an eyebrow though not the guard arm. "Petty Officer Sauter? I was told you were transferred." He frowned.

She leaned over to look past Michael at the familiar face working the gate. "Hey Gutierrez, no, it was a brief assignment. It's done now. I'm just heading back to my quarters." It hadn't crossed her mind that anyone other than her partner or CO would have noticed her absence. Or Terry. She let her thoughts graze past his place in her mind without stopping for unwanted introspection. She felt familiar tingling begin behind her eyes. The only reason the guard would have an idea she was posted off base was if something came from higher up, or if this was a repercussion from last night's events.

Lance Corporal Glen Gutierrez went inside and picked up the phone without raising the guard arm. Becca watched his mouth move and the tingling grew to stabbing inside her head. In a flash, Becca's vision skipped over the prelude of dancing spots and went completely white. She could see nothing. Then, a fast flash of Michael holding a gun in front of her, protecting her from an enemy just beyond her vision. Her decision was clear.

Becca rocked back, her head bouncing off the headrest. She felt her eyes rolling wildly in their sockets, searching for a glimmer of something while seeing nothing.

"Becca?" Michael's voice was anxious.

Blinking several times made no difference. "Something bad is going to happen," she whispered. "We have to go."

The engine revved and Gutierrez called out. "Sir. You have to wait Sir. I have my orders that Sauter is wanted for questioning in an ongoing investigation. She is not to leave, Sir."

Becca felt the car jolt backward, the tail end whipping around before the velocity of the vehicle's acceleration pushed her back into her seat. Becca stared around her, seeing only the vibrant white light the spots had merged to become. The engine drowned out all other sounds as they raced away.

"Becca, talk to me." He couldn't hide his concern. Becca could tell she had spooked him. "What did you see?"

It was hopeless to hide how terrified she was, she'd never lost her sight before. "Michael I can't see. My eyes, I can't see." How could she manage to help them when she was blinded by her visions? They were so much stronger now, her fears of bringing danger to Michael and his unit doubled.

A cool touch on her forearm and her vision was restored. Blinking, she stared down at the pale hand touching her, amazed and relieved that she could see it clearly.

"Is that a vampire thing?"

Michael didn't think he had heard the question correctly. "A what?" he choked out.

Her wide hazel eyes turned up to his face, studying him to find her own answer. "I couldn't see back there. My second sight, as you call it, literally blinded me and then, when you put your hand on me, it cleared it up. Is that something all vampires can do?"

"Not that I'm aware of. No." What she was telling him took him floored him. She knew he was a vampire and was not frightened nor did she cringe from his touch. By her own words it sounded like his touch actually helped her.

Her large eyes continued to examine him unflinching. Michael removed his hand from her arm.

Blinking, she moved her other hand to rub her arm where he had touched. The miles rolled past before Becca spoke again. "Do you think they've figured out who the shooter was?" She kept her eyes on the illuminated asphalt ahead. "A witness doesn't get stopped at the gate. He was calling the MPs on duty to come get me."

"Possible."

A phone appeared in his hand and Michael held it to his ear. "Admiral, we have an issue." He paused for Black's answer. "I believe they have some suspicions about last night's mission, Sir." He explained in short what had transpired and the admiral agreed with the assessment. Michael listened and hung up without another word.

She waited until she couldn't. "Well, what did he say?"

He shifted his hands on the wheel. "He said that is a non-issue if you come to work for us." Years of practice allowed him to keep the snarl from his voice. Admiral Black had gotten what he wanted. That he would no longer be required to sleep with Becca to bind her to them filled him with an unexpected rage. He wanted her more than he thought.

"He wasn't surprised, was he?" Some of her suspicions she'd had about the admiral's power were justified it seemed. "He did this on purpose to make me stay, didn't he?" Slowly she shook her head, "What wouldn't he do to get what he wanted?"

Nothing, he thought to himself. "I'm sorry Becca." He chanced a sideways look and was intrigued by what he saw. Outwardly she remained calm. Aside from a shake of her

120

head, he saw no evidence of upset whatsoever. "Does it bother you?" He wanted to know what she was thinking.

Becca was slow to answer. "Yes, it does bother me that he's so loose with my career and my reputation." She shrugged. "I'm sure he'll take care of things once he gets his way, even an admiral can't harbor a fugitive for long. Still, this'll get around and I'll have a mark against me whether it's written on my record or not."

Little did she know, Admiral Black operated so far off the grid he could do almost anything without penalty, even harbor a fugitive. Angry with the admiral for trapping her, he couldn't help the pleasure he felt at knowing she would be staying with him. Them, he corrected himself.

When they arrived back at the estate, Michael let her out of the vehicle before she could object. Knowing Becca was aware of what he was and was not afraid, he wanted to push her to see more of what it meant to be a vampire. Maybe if she knew all of it she would know enough to be frightened. If she was going to hunt them, she needed a healthy dose of fear.

She was not afraid when he came over the top of the car even quicker than before. She smiled at him. "How long have you been a vampire?"

Her unexpected boldness threw him off kilter. It had been decades since anyone had been truly unpredictable to him. Becca was proving both exciting and a challenge to him.

"Since the war." He glided effortlessly up the steps, holding himself to her speed out of respect.

"Which one?"

"The Second World War."

Her heart skipped once and settled quickly. "Can I ask how it happened?" Becca stopped with one hand on the door. She enjoyed hearing Michael's voice and, although furious with the admiral for his subversive tactics, she was getting the chance to work on the team like she'd wanted. She gave herself over to her new reality with surprising serenity. It was, after all, what she liked, orders to follow.

Michael stopped at the doors, letting one finger touch the iron handle. "I enlisted in March of '41; my family thought I was crazy. Most of the men enlisting were just boys. I was already twenty-six and had a college education. They wanted me to stay in the family business. The thought of working in our restaurant for the rest of my life was unfathomable." His eyes softened with mention of his family.

"A restaurant? What kind?"

He looked at her, mock disapproval in his eyes. "Rossi? Italian." He continued, face growing more serious and his voice dropped lower. "My mother had the sight, but not as strong as you. After I signed up, she told me I would die over there. Her prediction made me fearless; knowing I was going to die, I didn't have to worry about avoiding it. I moved up through the ranks, my superiors thinking I was brave when I was actually just resigned to the fact that I would not be coming home." His voice was distant, Michael's memories carrying him back to his final years as a human. "We were moving through Western Europe in 1944 after D-Day, trying to get to Poland where Hitler was accelerating his Final Solution. That's where the history books lose an important piece of the War. Hitler had an interest in the occult. That was relatively common knowledge. What's less well known is that he'd uncovered a long hidden truth. The monsters of legend were real." His eyes flicked up to Becca where he saw she didn't flinch at his mention of monsters.

"Hitler commenced a different kind of warfare. He tracked down a few vampires, all too willing to be unleashed upon the unwitting civilians. They were turned, and left hungry just before the advancing Allied troops. It was chaos. Those who didn't turn on each other fell upon the soldiers. Most were too wild to control themselves and destroyed the humans they attacked. However, on occasion, an established vampire would come out and capitalize on the frenzy. That was what happened with me." His hand went to his neck, subconsciously rubbing where he had been infected. "When I woke, the admiral's team was already in the village. They were eradicating all evidence of vampire activity. Nearly the entire village was wiped out. The few who had hidden had to have their memories erased."

"You can really do that?" Becca interrupted, her voice low to match his.

Her tone took his thoughts back to the pleasure Black's move had denied him this night. Giving his frustration no voice, he nodded at her question. Watching her features closely, he continued to wait for a sign of shock or displeasure from her at some point. She was an unusual human. Maybe it was the presence of her own ability that allowed her to accept the existence of monsters without fear.

"Wait, Admiral Black's team has been around for that long? How old is the admiral?"

He smiled tightly. "No one knows exactly how old the admiral is but he's led a number of teams in one form or another for the American government for as long as there has been an America."

"Why did they spare you?"

"The former team lead, Captain Torres, could smell that I'd been turned by an older vampire. It gave me a better chance at a successful outcome with proper guidance. Plus, I was young and hadn't been driven mad by my blood lust yet. He incapacitated me and sent me back to the base in Florida for training." He left out the details of his "accident," preferring not to share that part of himself with her. Being around a human again gave him reason to want to atone and finally move past the self-loathing that had ruled him since. Killing an innocent was never acceptable.

Becca didn't ask how one incapacitated a vampire nor what "training" meant. She wanted to know but held back, not wanting to ruin what felt like a truce between them. "Well, I'm glad he saved you." She ducked her head and reached for the handle on the front door.

He saw uncertainty in her, timidity in her demeanor for the first time. Humans are fragile, he reminded himself. Moving quickly, he opened the door before her and motioned her inside.

Smiling self-consciously, Becca thanked him and walked through. Together they went directly downstairs. The admiral was already at his place, Ryan and Gabrielle as well. They'd known he would have to bring her here upon their return.

"Welcome back, Rebecca." Black didn't gloat over his victory. He was matter of fact in his recognition of her return. He motioned for them to be seated.

Becca correctly assumed he didn't hear the word "no" often. Nodding coolly at him, she touched the file sitting at her place; the others' already lay open. She did the same, scanning the details, certain they could hear her body react to the gory pictures in front of her.

"There have been numerous reports of suspicious deaths in the Ukraine with the last two lunar cycles. We have reason to believe it is the work of one individual 'were,' however other secondary infections are a possibility." He glanced over at the two similarly natured individuals. "Now that the moon is waning, we are at full strength again. And Rebecca, this creature will not have the same amount of control as these two. It is younger, and it is wild. You will be carrying pure silver rounds this time. Do not be afraid to use them. Just be sure to aim carefully." Shutting his folder, tucking it under his arm, the admiral took a step back. "Wheels up in two hours."

After the admiral left, Ryan and Gabrielle stood. Gabrielle held out her hand to Becca.

"I see you've changed your mind." She smiled smugly.

There was no reason to tell her the real reason she had returned. "Yep. I decided this was a great opportunity for me." She took her hand, noting it was overly warm like Ryan's.

Ryan laughed. "Right. Everyone wants to hunt rogue monsters. It has great potential for advancement and is virtually risk free."

Becca blanched. She hadn't thought of it like that before. She trusted her sight, she only feared it might endanger them all should it prove incapacitating at the wrong time. Michael couldn't have a hand tied up touching her whenever it threatened. A quick flash of Michael's hand on her bare thigh gave her a start and her pulse jumped.

Becca's eyes followed Michael as he stood from the briefing table and went to the weapons room. The others left, Ryan mumbling about packing. She followed Michael.

Going out on another mission with him so soon, she was apprehensive. It was possible he maintained his reservations about her dependability.

"Michael, I wanted to reassure you that you can count on me in the field." She kept her doubts to herself.

He had laid out four black packs on the free-standing island in the center of the room and was busy loading them with weapons and incendiaries from the walls and drawers around them. Becca recognized most of the supplies but a few were new to her. One pack looked especially heavy with arms. She presumed that was hers.

"I know that."

She no longer heard doubt in his voice. Giving voice to her curiosity, she surprised herself by asking, "What changed?"

His hands stopped loading a grenade into her pack and, leaning on it, he looked up. "Before, I thought you had a choice as to whether or not you were going to be with us." He answered her honestly. "I have no misgivings about your abilities. I have valid concerns about your longevity as a human among us."

Becca told herself not to read too much into his fears for her safety. Gabrielle had hit the nail on the head earlier. He was considerate for the well-being of his team. It was one of the things that made for a good leader. It meant nothing more than that.

"Do you need any help?" she offered, eager to prove her usefulness.

Michael started to say no and stopped himself. He enjoyed having her to himself. "Sure. Come over here. I always pack the gear, but it is your responsibility to double check that I have everything since your life may depend on it."

She came around the table to stand next to him.

He pointed to a long cartridge about the size of a pencil and three times the thickness. "This is one of your most important tools." He pressed a button on the end and a six inch long, thin silver needle extended. "This is a pure silver stake. When silver enters our bloodstream, we die. That is the case with vampires, weres, faeries, elves; no supernatural creature is impervious to its effects."

She lifted her eyes to examine his. "You mean this is all it takes to kill any of you?"

His blue ones darkened. "It's not just you who needs to trust, Becca. We must trust you with our secrets as well. Humans knowing our weaknesses has not always ended well for us."

She reached out her hand, lightly touching his arm. The dark shift in the color of his eyes reminding her of that night when he had called to her for the admiral, a hint of that power danced through her veins. "I trust you with my safety. I hope you can feel the same for me."

Vampires are covetous and possessive creatures. Now that Michael had an object of desire and she stood within his reach, he virtually shook with the effort it took to keep his hands off of her. The place on his bare arm where she touched him warmed under her heated flesh. His fangs were not all that he felt stirring.

Becca felt the cool flesh, firm beneath her hand. His body was cool as if he had just stepped out of the ocean on a brisk day. It was not uncomfortable, only different. Her thumb stroked his flesh, feeling the smoothness of his skin combined with the texture of his dark hair. She hadn't imagined he would feel different from a human, but he did. Being very tactile, Becca rolled her thumb in a circle, pressing down. The pressure made no indent nor did it change color as it would on a human as the blood flow was interrupted.

Interest eradicated her timidity. "Where does the blood go? The blood you drink?"

Her wonderment was of constant fascination to Michael. He found it agreeable to discuss his differences with her, and it provided a distraction from the battle his mind waged with his nature. "It goes into my stomach and is processed much the same as a human body processes food. The constant supply of energy keeps the nerves in my body and synapses in my brain functional." His lungs filled with air, taking in the scent of her. Her body's natural musk flavoring the light clean scent of the soaps they all used gave her a unique smell he had committed to memory. He could track her if need be. It would be even easier if he covered her with his own scent. He was losing the battle.

"Oh." Sensing he was annoyed with her, Becca lifted her hand reluctantly from his arm. Her heart pounded in her ears despite his calming influence telling her it was racing from something other than nerves. Becca was embarrassed, knowing he could hear. She moved her hand to a clip. "Is this loaded with silver?"

Turning his head to see was unnecessary. The second she lifted the clip she stirred the smell of the silver within its steel shell. "Yes. Those are designed to explode on impact, releasing the silver into the bloodstream. The effects are irreversible."

The mortality of her fellow unit members struck her. These bullets made them just as easily killed as her. She pledged to herself to not only provide value to the team by way of her sight, but to protect them physically as well as she knew they would her. She would learn to overcome the blinding visions somehow.

Becca surveyed the pack's contents, pointing to a bullet-sized cylinder with a raised toggle in the center. "And that?"

"A vampire's version of a stun gun but it only works on newly turned vampires still paralyzed by the sun."

"It doesn't bother you, the sun?"

"Bother is a relative term. I feel it and it weakens me after prolonged exposure, but I've learned to function for short stints in it. Those newly turned can be temporarily halted by a sudden burst of ultraviolet light. This device has a ten foot radius, so is limited but useful."

"Are there larger versions then?"

Michael nodded, pointing to a small tangerine sized black object she had taken for a grenade. "This one has a fifty foot radius. Up close it's effective even on an older vampire due to its intensity."

"Are there any other weapons in there I need to know about?" She liked hearing him talk.

"No, the remaining weapons are standard issue." His fingers moved over the ballistic nylon of her pack.

"What are you thinking?" She pointed to his fingers when he looked at her questioningly. "You do that when something's bothering you." Becca was discomfited at her boldness. This unit wasn't formal but she was speaking to her superior as a peer. That couldn't be good. Fearing a reprisal, she held her breath.

"I am thinking you need to go pack some personal gear." His voice was gruff. Becca felt ashamed that she had obviously overstepped again.

"Yes, Sir." She turned to leave.

"Becca." His hand shot out to grab her arm, his fingers easily encompassing her bicep.

His hand accidentally pushed against the bruises Terry had made. She hid her reaction well, though not before Michael saw. He released her at once, jerking his hand back to his side. "I'm sorry. I only wanted to..." He stopped. Again he was at a loss when it came to her. It was hard for him to concentrate when his thoughts were with her and not where they should be.

Becca hurried to explain. "You didn't hurt me. I'm just a little sore." She saw his eyes go dark and misunderstood the source of his displeasure. "I apologize that you had to get involved in that. It won't happen again."

His jaw hardened and he felt his fangs grow, he'd been fighting himself for too long and his nature was turning the tide. "Do you always choose your mates so poorly?" he snapped.

"Mate?" She was incredulous. "Terry and I dated for a few months." His presumption that she had known Terry was a woman beater and stayed with him anyway was insulting. "He's a decent guy." She defended her choice, not the man.

"What I said really hurt him." She remembered the betrayal she'd seen just before his anger got the best of him.

Michael's Italian temper had gotten him into trouble as a human, yet it was nothing compared to his immortal sense of vengeance. "You're defending him after what he did? How could you lie in the same bed with a man and not know anything about him?"

Becca's hurt fueled her anger. "I'm not defending his actions, but I am asking you not to judge him, or me for that matter, by that one incident. What would you do if you'd just found out someone you loved did something she wouldn't do with *you* with someone she'd *just met*?" She spilled more than she had intended in her indignation. "How can I sleep next to someone who, love me or not, would freak out the second he found out I could see the future?" Becca's nerves were raw from the roller coaster that had been her last two days and she felt her eyes well up. "My career would be over and they'd probably lock me up like they did my Grandma."

Her honesty extinguished his heat immediately. "I spoke out of turn, I apologize."

She shook her head, swallowing and blinking back evidence of how much the admission had humiliated her. If it weren't for Black, Michael would probably have marched her directly back to her apartment at the base and washed his hands of her. "I have to go pack."

When she was gone, Michael traced a pattern in Becca's bag. He smiled to himself. She noticed his habit. It pleased him that she had been watching him. In his time worrying for her safety and future with their unit, it never crossed Michael's mind that she would have a better life with them than she had in her own world. She might have been safer amongst humans, but she was lonely. It made him wonder, was he any better than a human mate? Was he any more trustworthy? Every moment he was with her, the temptation grew.

Michael slammed his fist down on the table, cracking its surface. The need to have her was suffocating. His hard won control was slipping. Soon he would have no ability to stop himself from taking her, whether she was willing or not. Finishing the packs, he went to the kitchen to gorge himself on more blood. It was the only thing keeping her safe from him at all.

Chapter 14

Becca, unsure from where they were to depart, was in the entry nearly a half an hour early with her small pack containing two changes of clothes and her toiletries. She knew nothing of the duration of this mission or what type of quarters they would have. These would be bare bones necessities while letting her keep her appearance presentable should they be more urban than rural.

Ryan saw her and his generous lips curved. "You pack light. Gabrielle could take a few pointers from you."

The party in question answered his jab, rounding the corner from the kitchen hall. "You complain that I bring too much, but you would complain more if I let myself go."

He validated her statement with his blushing smile. Becca got a hint there was something else between the two she hadn't considered before. Were relationships okay between unit members?

Michael was the last to join them. He came from the other direction, easily carrying their four packs in his hands. He tossed first one, then another to the wolves before handing Becca's to her. At first she wanted to object to his deferential treatment, then the heft of the pack hit her. If he'd thrown it she would have gone down like a stone. Her respect for their strength grew.

She set it down and put her personal items in the small compartment below the section Michael had packed. The bag was not remotely close to full yet held an impressive arsenal within. Becca familiarized herself with the contents, counting the number of each item. Better to take the time now than be uncertain in the field. Ryan and Gabrielle did the same. Michael was not offended and stared off into the distance while he waited for them to finish.

The door opened and closed while she conducted her inventory and refilled her pack. Standing, she shouldered into it and tested its weight. It had to be close to fifty pounds, less than she'd carried in basic training.

Michael was standing at the door, waiting, when she looked up from her task.

"Where are the provisions?" She had noticed their absence in her inventory.

"We hunt," he said simply.

One human amidst three hunting creatures gave Becca pause. Ryan had been nothing other than personable until she had struck him. Would the same thing happen if they were under duress out on an assignment? Becca didn't want to think about either of the wolves sinking their teeth into her, or someone else for that matter.

Michael seemed to have better control over himself than Ryan. She hadn't seen him lose it even when angry, not the way she imagined he could what with the fangs. She wasn't afraid of him yet, as she'd seen with Terry, desperation could drive people to strange places.

Michael opened the door and waved her out. "When you're ready."

She brought her hands to the straps on her shoulders and shifted one more time before walking out. Michael followed, closing the door behind her.

***

The airfield was a short drive away on the estate grounds. The positioning of the house in relation to the drive and the hills behind them had kept it hidden from sight before. Granted, she hadn't exactly been looking for a runway or hangar. They reached the small airplane hangar on the plateau around the backside of the hill the house butted up to and removed their bags from the trunk. Gabrielle stepped into the plane first and took her seat.

"She's the pilot?" Becca asked Ryan.

"Don't look so surprised. She's one of the best." Unable to hide his pride, he practically beamed.

Definitely more than co-workers, she thought to herself. Becca watched Ryan lower himself into the middle aisle seat and hovered to see where Michael would sit on the small jet. There were four people, ten seats. Plenty of available seating but she didn't want to step on any toes by sitting in the wrong place. She'd done that on a jeep once and caused a rift between herself and an officer that had led to months of midnight patrols in a car with no heat.

"Please, take a seat," Michael spoke from close behind her.

She jumped, having been so lost in her own thoughts she hadn't heard his approach. Her heart fluttered at his nearness. It had nothing to do with her ability.

Experimentally, he laid his hand on her shoulder and heard the correlating change in her heart beat. She calmed on contact. Her eyes were soft when she looked at him, their faces inches apart. He saw flecks of gold in her irises he hadn't before. They glowed in the bright cabin lighting. Michael was captivated.

He stared at her, his recent revelations coming together in his head. Michael's reservations keeping him from giving in to his desire for her were crumbling around him. The only thing left was his fear that he might lose control and hurt her should his nature prove too strong once he let his passions loose. The memory of her calling his name in fear that night echoed through his head. Had it been her sight warning her?

"If the passengers can stop ogling each other and sit down, we can take off," Gabrielle's sardonic voice came through the overhead speakers.

Michael's eyes narrowed and he removed his hand from Becca who, reeling from the impact of her racing heart's sudden return, hurriedly found a window seat one row back from Ryan. Ryan snorted. She saw his eyes roll in profile. Michael sat in the row across from Becca, only the aisle and a seat between them. She shifted nervously, unable to settle her nerves, eyes continually roving to where he sat.

Ryan was his usual conversational self. Michael spoke only in limited doses, choosing to ride in front with Gabrielle after they stopped the first time to refuel in Philadelphia. Once he moved, she was able to relax only slightly. Mostly Becca dozed, waking once to her own mumblings. Ryan was the only one within earshot and she looked over at him, knowing whose name she had mentioned in her rather explicit vision. Feeling her eyes on him, he twisted in his seat.

The vision had been the one that had come to her repeatedly since meeting Michael, only this time it was much more than a few brief flashes.

Ryan smiled when she made eye contact with him. "Is it always like that? You talk like you're in a trance or something."

Becca felt her ears burning. "I'm usually asleep so I wouldn't know. It's been years since even my mom's been around to comment. She did bring me to a psychiatrist once for my 'sleep disorder'."

"People don't go to psychiatrists for sleep disorders."

She let her eyes drift to the window. "No. But sometimes there was screaming. It scared her."

Ryan waited for her to continue.

"When I was eight, I had a vision that my aunt killed herself. Mom said she couldn't wake me up for ten minutes, I screamed the whole time. Mom had me in the car before Dad could get home from his training junket. He always downplayed it as my imagination. I think he was scared of it. She told the doctor mental illness ran in the family." It had been a defining moment in Becca's life. Her rule became no slumber parties when she was a child or male overnight guests as an adult. She also made sure to go to sleep after her mother in an effort to hide the less noisy incidences. "When I saw my grandparents' car accident a few years later, I couldn't say anything." She rested her head against her seat.

He looked down. She could see him examining the backs of his hands through the gap in the seats. "That makes it easy then," he said quietly.

"How is that easy?" Becca asked, her voice too sharp.

Shrugging casually, he turned his head so she could see the side of his face. He let his teeth show, giving her a clear shot of his lengthened canines. "You couldn't go home if you wanted to." He waggled his eyebrows. "You know our secrets."

His statement rang true. Of course they wouldn't let her go back. If she gave away hints of their existence in front of the wrong person, they could be hurt. This was the only life for her now. Oddly, that concept released her instead of making her feel trapped. Her whole life Becca had hidden who she was. Now she didn't have to anymore. She felt light, unfettered.

She didn't let herself dwell for long on how that might bode for her love life. Becca knew where she wanted that to go but figured it was one-sided. She imagined that if she and Michael weren't even able to have a decent conversation without snapping at each other, a date would be impossible. Thus far, he tended to vacillate between friend and prick.

***

The flight was over eleven hours plus their two fuel stops in Philadelphia and Coleman airfield in Germany. It was a long time before they touched down in Odessa, her mind already on taking a shower to get the gross feeling of recycled air off of her.

They landed and taxied past several lingering snowbanks to a deserted hangar where a dark Mercedes was parked inside. While Ryan took their bags off the plane, Michael walked around the front of the car and pulled out a pile of clothing. He dug through and handed pieces out to each member of their party.

"Change fast, we'll head to the hotel for the night. We can break off for recon in town, see what we can decipher from mingling with the locals."

Becca took a long sleeved, short green dress with black leggings, holes randomly placed. It was a style she could wear with her combat boots. A chocolate wool coat lay beside it. She grabbed it and glanced around for a place to change. The hangar had no interior walls and her team members had split up to change already. Becca refused to ask for special treatment. She'd had to change publicly during basic a few times and told herself this time was no different.

That wasn't true. She kept feeling her eyes ranging over to where Michael had thrown down his pack a few yards away. She saw him strip down to his shorts and dog tags, light skin sliding easily over his well conditioned muscles. Her body responded and she saw him turn his head, catching her staring. Her heart galloped and her face burned as she stared down at her shaking hands, failing in their clumsy efforts to pull a few tools from her pack that could be hidden on her person. Gabrielle and Ryan changed and chatted on the other side of the car, politely pretending to be oblivious to Becca's discomfort.

Everyone dressed in their civvies, they packed up their clothing and each set their bag in the trunk. Michael took the wheel and Becca sat beside Gabrielle in the back. The beautiful blonde looked as fresh as when they started out; Becca envied her. She knew even in her change of clothes she looked like she had just rolled out of a sleeping bag.

The hotel was a brief drive from the airfield. Their files reported the bodies had been found at the edge of town. The thought was that their culprit would be a local resident or that someone there had at least seen something, either way it was the logical place for them to start. By posing as Russian tourists, they hoped to learn more.

Walking into the hotel, Michael switched easily to a Russian dialect and spoke in a barely audible tone to the others. Becca's language skills were limited to English and a smattering of Spanish, and therefore had to rely on visuals. Michael's hand dropped down to his side, fingers flexing at her. Taking the hint, she quickened to catch up, taking his hand in hers.

He muttered low in her ear, rubbing his nose on her neck and wrapping an arm around her waist. Temporarily, Becca forgot herself and melted into him; she could feel her nipples hardening with her arousal.

Michael whispered in her ear. "People are less suspicious of couples. We will pose as two couples visiting from Minsk."

They stepped to the front of the line ahead of Ryan and Gabrielle. Ryan, getting into his cover right away, started nibbling on Gabrielle's neck. She played her part superbly, tossing her head and giggling, sliding one foot up and down the back of her leg. Gabrielle was ravishing in her little black dress and fishnets, giving anyone looking something worth staring at.

Michael and the young man working at registration engaged in a pleasant and lengthy transaction ending in four keys being presented and Michael handing the man a credit card. The envious clerk could hardly keep his eyes from Gabrielle, still canoodling with Ryan, and seemingly lost in their amorous affections.

Becca caught the wink Ryan threw the clerk with a lascivious smile. The clerk flushed and concentrated on his computer, embarrassed at being caught lusting openly after a guest. Michael slid his arm around her waist again and led her to the elevators. Becca flushed at his familiar touch, only his unusual calming effect on her keeping her from hyperventilating. Her skin still tingled where his lips had touched the sensitive part of her neck.

The four of them had the elevator up to the twelfth floor to themselves. Once the doors closed Ryan and Gabrielle disengaged, as did Michael. Everyone was back to business. Michael switched to English and handed out the room keys. Becca's body ached at the loss of him.

"Ryan and Gab, you're in 1226, Becca and I will be across the hall in 1227. Gabrielle, bring the packs up the service entrance when it's clear. I've told the clerk the airline lost our bags when he asked about them. One look and anyone watching would know they're military." He told Becca while he checked his watch. "Feel free to order room service if you need it, they get started late around here. We meet back down in the lobby at twenty one hundred. We'll give them a chance to start drinking and feeling loose before we make our appearance in the club district."

Gabrielle glanced down at her wrist and one side of her mouth twitched. "That gives us three hours. What ever shall we do?"

Ryan laughed low beside her, snaking his arm around her waist and pulling her up tight against his body. Gabrielle's unexpected laugh lit up the enclosed space.

She caught Becca's reaction. "Don't look so shocked. You can do whatever *you* want now too. You're off the clock until twenty-one hundred, you heard the boss." She grinned openly at Becca's dumbfounded expression.

"Packs first, Gab," Michael said without taking his eyes from the doors.

The bell dinged at the top floor, the doors opened. Their rooms were nearly at the end of the long hallway. Becca hung back, choosing to stay out of everyone's sight. It was bad enough everyone present seemed to know of her schoolgirl crush. Now she was going to be acting the part of a girlfriend with him all night. She couldn't stop herself from picturing Michael nibbling on her neck, her tossing her head back like Gabrielle. Her physical response was immediate and she swore the men tipped their heads her direction, sensing it. Mortified, she cleared her head and pictured her drill sergeant from basic. He had not been a pretty man. She felt herself cooling at the thought.

Becca was no longer redlining when they reached their room. Gabrielle followed Ryan into theirs, winking at her over his shoulder. The lock on the door in front of Becca clicked as Michael slid the key card. He opened the door and Becca swallowed hard before walking inside.

Chapter 15

The room was predictably warm. Every hotel room was warm. She slid her coat off, hanging it over the back of the desk chair along the wall opposite the bed. Straight across from the door was a large wall of tall windows overlooking the city. The bright streetlights stared up from below. Becca stepped forward to move the drapes back to see the traffic and illuminated architecture, familiarizing herself with this foreign city and even more foreign operation. What would her father think of this if he knew, she wondered. If she could ever tell him she had gone beyond military police officer he might be proud of her.

His voice was barely above a whisper, in the stillness it made her jump. "Does it bother you, those two?"

She shook her head, keeping her eyes pointed at the windows even if she was no longer registering what she saw. "No. Like Gabrielle said, they're off the clock. There aren't any rules against it are there?"

"No. We're an isolated team. There isn't much opportunity to meet new people." The slap of their key cards hitting the desk behind her was followed by the sliding thud of the car key.

Becca didn't have anything to say to that. She considered going to the lobby bar and having a few drinks to pass the next few hours sanely. The thought of three hours in this small room with him sent a shiver up her spine.

"You're alone." His hoarse voice was close behind her.

She turned to face him, saw him standing leaning against the open door. "What do you mean?"

"You've had to hide for a long time, like us. Has there ever been anyone you could confide in?"

141

Ignoring the burn on her cheeks, Becca slowly shook her head. "Not until the other night when I told you and Admiral Black. I've told you more than I've ever told anyone."

He watched her curiously. "Does it bother you, sharing so much with us?"

Her brows knitted together. "I went through basic, which was hell because of the medications I took trying to block out the visions while I slept in the barracks. I have proved myself every day for the past three years with everyone but Danny calling me a cold bitch." She shuddered at the memory of her medication making her throw up on hikes and shake after a day of dry land training. Her instructors rode her incessantly, calling her a lost cause. "Then I met you, and the first thing you did was question whether or not I could do this job." She laughed harshly at herself. "And even with all of that, I'm more at home with all of you than I have been with anyone else, ever." Speaking so openly made her bold. "I've slept with you more than any boyfriend I've ever had," she snorted, "I even slept with Ryan. Poor guy got an earful on the ride over I'm sure."

"We all heard you." He watched her cheeks pink, the thought of her blood exciting him. Mention of their lying together brought his covetous nature roaring back. His muscles were rigid with the effort of holding his body in check.

She stopped short of asking how, making the connection that if they could hear her heart beating in the same room it shouldn't surprise her that they could hear a conversation a few seats away over the drone of the jet's engines.

Michael took a step toward her, his head cocked and frowning. "What did you see? When you called my name, what were you seeing?"

Giving him the more personal vision from the plane ride was too much. In its place she offered the flash she'd had at the office; it was the same as the one she'd had when she'd

142

laid with him. "You were protecting me from someone or something. I don't know, I couldn't see past you." Becca saw his eyes grow unnaturally dark and recognized the hunger she'd seen that night in the storeroom. Alone, seeing him in that state, she knew he would be receptive to her when he was like this. Not willing to lose the chance to be with him, she closed the space between them and reached out, pausing when she saw something close to alarm as he registered what she was doing.

"Becca, don't do this." His rough voice was strained.

She ignored what he said, taking her cues instead from what she saw in his eyes. They told her he wanted the same thing she did. Another step put her within inches of him and she looked up into his face, marveling at the lengthening of his fangs. He could hide most of them with his upper lip if he kept his mouth closed.

"I saw the way you looked at me when the admiral made you try to control me. It's the same way you're looking at me now." Her boldness made her dizzy, she could hardly believe what she was whispering.

He closed his eyes, his entire body taut. His teeth pierced his tight lower lip. Two tiny spots of blood bloomed on the pale skin. "You don't understand," he growled out. "I haven't made love to a human, not like this. I don't know if I can control myself with you."

"Who says you have to?" Becca rose on her tiptoes to touch her lips to his. She laid her hand on his arm, using him to settle her racing pulse.

He stood perfectly still. When their lips met, Michael's eyes popped open and he pulled his head back in surprise.

"I don't know what's going to happen either, but I can't deny this. Not anymore." She squeezed her hand where it rested on him. "It's like this is supposed to be." She hadn't consciously considered why he effected her the way he did, but as it came out she believed it.

Michael's eyes were open as he studied the face of the beautiful woman he wanted so desperately he ached. There were many things he saw in her eyes, none of which were fear or doubt. She wanted to be with him. Although she could not possibly understand what she asked of him, what she risked, he felt his hold over the animalistic monster inside him snap.

Becca watched his eyes turn completely black in the span of a second. His lip curled as he reached for her. He grabbed her so fast she gasped and, with a shocking violence, his mouth covered hers, stealing her breath with it. She felt his fangs prodding her lower lip as his tongue darted into her mouth.

He pressed himself hard against her, desire firing his brain as he tried to wrest control back from his nature and keep himself from consuming her physically as well as sexually. "Becca, I can't be with you." He breathed against her mouth. "I've lost control before."

Breathless, she stroked the back of his neck, wanting him more each second. "I trust you." She pulled back long enough to look in his eyes. "I've seen it and I feel it. You'll never hurt me."

Faced with her absolute blind trust he was lost. Nothing could stop him from taking her after her admission and Michael fought to ride the line, barely keeping himself from harming her while taking possession of her bodily. Grabbing her in an embrace tight enough it made her squeak, he loosened his hold only a fraction as he lifted her up to carry her to the bed. When the backs of her legs touched the mattress he stopped and slid his hands down to her hips. Wrapping his long fingers around her trim waist, he brought her up hard against his body and held her securely to him.

144

Becca's eager hands were running over his back and lower, rolling over his hips. There was only a moment's hesitation before her fingers slid into his waistband, clearing the way for the rest of her hands to trail down and grasp his cheeks. Pressing none too gently, she let her wants be known. Groaning, he threw back his head and Becca found the skin of his neck. She nibbled and nipped, turning his groan into a hungry growl.

Michael eased his hold on her and lowered her to the mattress, reluctantly taking her away from him for the seconds it took him to pull off his shirt and her dress. When he leaned over her eager body, his tongue flicked against her bare abdomen, making her suck in her breath in a gasp.

Chuckling, Michael reveled in the power he held over her body that had nothing to do with his blood being inside of her. Again he let his tongue taste her flesh, running it up the center of her body in a series of quick flicks until it reached her bra. A quick snap of his fingers and he tossed the material aside, his mouth eagerly taking its place on her breast. The other was treated to his thumb rolling over the nipple, teasing the sensitive nerve endings until they screamed in joyous protest.

Michael's other hand trailed down between them to loosen his pants when her eager hands proved too slow. Faster than Becca was capable he took over and whipped them off before he knelt down to do the same to the last of her undergarments.

Becca looked down her body to see Michael on his knees between her legs. Whimpering, she pulled at his arms to bring him back but he refused, smiling wickedly. She pulled again and he leaned forward, letting his tongue stroke lower. Becca's back arched and in moments she was flying.

Her body was not given a chance to recover because as soon as she'd had her release, she felt the length of him spreading out over her. His tongue ran up over her neck and he licked then sucked on her lower lip.

"Please Michael," she moaned. Becca didn't want these sensations to ever stop.

It didn't just yet. Catching the weight of his upper body on his arms, Michael used his hips to drag his shaft against her moist opening. Desperate to feel him inside her and give him his pleasure, Becca reached between them and grasped his erection. She smiled when he bit his lower lip, his eyes focusing on her and she saw his raw need. He lowered himself and she guided him slowly, inch by blissful inch.

As soon as he was inside her, Michael's nature screamed to be let out. His jaws ached with the desire to tear her tender flesh, his throat burned for her blood. Needing an outlet for his passions he drove himself into her hard and fast. Soon both of them were on the edge and he let her capture his face in her hands to bring his mouth to hers. Biting his lip, she pushed her tongue into his mouth and moaned his name, sending him over with her.

When at last they lay together, Becca pressing her overheated body against his cool one, he ran a hand through her sandy hair and rubbed it between his fingers. The other wrapped around her back.

Becca turned her face into his chest, kissing him. "We aren't going to be in trouble with the admiral, are we?" she joked. "I don't know the fraternization policy with a superior officer in the unit." She kissed him again, nipping him on the side of his neck.

Michael hesitated, hand stopping for a second before continuing to play with her hair. "I don't think Admiral Black should concern himself with what we do on our own time." He leaned his face down, kissing her head. Becca's breathing slowed, becoming more regular as she drifted off.

The silence around her was deafening. Becca couldn't see, the white light so bright it drowned out all but a number of grey shadows surrounding them. Michael stood, one arm holding her behind him, the other hand extended in front of him holding a gun. She said his name, not hearing her voice outside her head but knowing he could as his head tipped toward her. In that brief glance, she saw fear on his face and something else that frightened her more than whatever lay on the other side of the gun. She stepped around him, pushing his hands down, and walked straight toward the thing on the other side of the gun. Her mind screamed its objection.

Becca sat up in bed, damp with sweat, and heard the lock of the door click a split second before Michael was beside her, his arms wrapping around her. The peace she felt was an instant relief, the chill of his body a little slower to hit her.

Seconds later, a banging on the door interrupted them. Swearing, Michael jumped up, mumbled something at the door and was back. When her body lost its contact with his skin, the emotional memory of her vision came back and she felt the terror racing through her only to disappear again when he returned. His coming and going from her, trading horror for peace again made her feel sick, her body trembled.

"Becca," his face rested against hers, their cheeks touching, grounding her to the present. "Becca, what did you see? You called my name. Was it the same vision or something different?" Michael ran his hand down the side of her face, brushing her hair aside, not knowing what to do to help. He'd never been good with helplessness. "Are we in trouble here?" He pulled the blanket up around her damp, naked body.

She was shaking, her skin slick with sweat. Michael's hands helped to soothe her physically, though not entirely. Nothing he did could alleviate the true curse of Becca's sight; the memory of it. The awful, blow by blow detailed memory of it. Like so many other things she couldn't tell and had to live through over and again in her head before they came to pass, she would need to keep this vision to herself as well. Sharing the partial details with Michael would only distract him from their assignment here. Besides, what could she really tell him?

In her vision, the one that continued to plague her, she could neither hear nor see anything. The tiny snippet she'd been able to decipher, she had already given him. The baffling part she couldn't get over was why she went *toward* the threat, and what had she done to Michael? Her stomach twisted, Becca convulsively curled her legs to her chest trying to make it stop. She'd looked back as she walked away from him and it was the look on his face that hurt her. The look on his face was one of betrayal. She would betray Michael. Her captain, her team's anchor and now her lover. But for whom? Becca felt sick all over again.

Having gone the final step with Michael and crossed the line had unlocked the last half of her vision, finally letting her see what she couldn't before. The guilt tore at her as she locked the details away, determining to change her course. She would fight this one. Becca *would not* let this vision come to pass. It had never been something she was able to stop before. Details she could change, but the final outcome was always the same. This one was different. She understood what she had now with her sight. She'd been able to control the subject of the visions before, and she would succeed in altering the future this time. She had to.

Resolving herself to make this vision nothing more than a horrible nightmare, Becca pushed the image of Michael's stricken face from her mind and locked it away with the rest of it. Forcibly relaxing her muscles and bringing her breathing back under control, Becca came back to Michael with a weak smile.

"It's nothing new. It's the same one I told you about before. I didn't see what we were facing but you're holding it off, protecting me. The idea of you being hurt is a little scarier now, that's all." She tried a surer smile, throwing in a coy duck of the eyes to feign shyness. It was a relief to look away and not see the worry she'd caused and couldn't take away.

Michael softened toward her, relenting in his questioning. "Becca, you're not supposed to worry about me," he reassured her. "Remember, it's my job to worry about you."

His statement drove an icy blade through her ribs, straight into her confederate heart. "I know," she said quietly. "Who was at the door? I didn't mean to bring security down on us. I'm sorry. I hope we aren't in trouble with the hotel."

"It was Ryan. They heard you and thought there might be trouble."

Anxious her betrayal would harm them too if it came to pass, Becca cursed herself for being weak. Michael had been right in his initial assessment, she was going to be a problem for the unit. "Oh."

Steady blue eyes studied her, not entirely convinced she was okay. Michael kissed her softly on the forehead and rose from the bed. "We have to be downstairs in a half an hour. Do you need more time than that?"

She shook her head. He stepped away and she heard the door open and close. Becca sighed, hating herself and her cursed ability only Admiral Black seemed to value. Pushing herself up, she went straight into the shower.

Chapter 16

Michael made sure the door's lock clicked behind him before walking down the hall. His hand fished in his pocket to retrieve the phone he had hurriedly stuffed inside when he heard her screams.

Black answered right away. "What was that about?"

"She had it again. It's a vision for sure. She sees me standing in front of her with a gun but can't see the threat."

"That is not much to go on. Can she give you more? Do you have any idea the timeline or source of danger?"

"No, Sir. She can only tell me that she fears for my safety. There is no mention of the rest of the unit in the scenario." Michael knew as well as the admiral did, Becca was hiding something from them. Her concern for him was touching.

"Is there a reason she might feel some special concern for *your* welfare, Michael?" Black didn't hide his feelings well. Self-satisfaction practically dripped from the phone.

Michael wanted to go through the line and throttle his superior. Guilt compounded his need to respect Becca, yet the admiral had bound Michael to him long ago. Disobeying wasn't possible. He answered grudgingly, "Yes, Sir."

The low chuckle crackled in his ear. "Well done, Michael. I must confess, I had my doubts when she rejected my blood that we could bind her to us. Now she is mine through you. You have once again proven ingenious in your methods. Remind me to give you a raise."

He gagged on the words. "Thank you, Sir, but that won't be necessary." As much as he wanted to make Black eat his offer, to stop him from ever speaking Becca's name so disrespectfully, he knew he had no ability to do so.

Decades with Admiral Black had shown him to be resilient and impervious to all attempts at his destruction and also highly retaliatory. Everyone, human and non-human, who had ever crossed Black ended up destroyed, and not always physically. Michael had seen the admiral make a five star general who survived three years in a North Korean prison camp grovel and cry before his mind was warped, driving him to insanity.

Michael knew better than to try to fight his binding and rebel against Black. He was far more capable of protecting Becca if he lived. No one could completely protect her from the admiral and the fact that he'd tied her in with him in his eternal servitude grieved him. His only consolation was his buffering position between them. Hopefully it would be enough to keep the worst at bay.

"As I told you, we are still receiving intelligence but it sounds like this newest attack on the moon's zenith occurred not far from the Arcadia district. Are you familiar with it?"

"Mostly nightclubs, isn't it Sir? We were planning on starting there tonight."

"Good. The most recent attack was a female prostitute who worked several of the local clubs. Start at the Zirka."

"Yes, Sir." Michael waited for the admiral to hang up first.

That was four attacks in three days and the full moon had peaked the night before this most recent attack. Only a rogue or a newly changed "were" would be irresponsible enough to leave so many bodies in plain sight. Most of their kind hid what they were out of necessity. To cause so much damage and go after the bones like this one said that it was specifically a werewolf.

Secrecy was key to their continued survival. Most controlled themselves; werewolves feeding only on animals, vampires relying on blood banks or taking small amounts from people and wiping their memory. If you were supernatural and your activity caught the admiral's eye, you would meet Captain Rossi and his unit of soldiers. It was that simple. There were no trials and few options for punishment. If you committed a crime, you were brought to one of the containment facilities for questioning and evaluation. Those not considered a continued threat were released with a sudden death clause: one more slip would bring the executioner to your door. Murder or violence against humans carried an instant death sentence. This animal they sought had a certain fate.

Unpleasant call over, Michael returned to the end of the hall and heard the water still running in his room. Thoughts of Becca naked brought back the events of the past few hours. He had to force himself to ignore his urge to join her, instead knocking on the door across the hall.

Ryan answered within seconds. "Is everything okay?" His affection for Becca was clear in his concern. Ryan was relatively uncomplicated, truly a rarity for a supernatural being. By no means stupid, he was uninterested in politics or complicated double crosses. It was the reason Michael himself had recruited the wolf only a few years after he was changed. In the ten years since he had joined the team, he'd done the work of two and mellowed Gabrielle out as much as possible, which was a godsend.

She was Ryan's opposite. Her skill set was unparalleled and her mind for intrigue was unrivaled. She was also a huge pain in the ass to work with. Her background in Intelligence made her an invaluable asset although Michael could never tell if she was working her own agenda.

In addition to Ryan's charisma, he was also incredibly perceptive and a good judge of character. Not trusting himself to keep his doubts about Becca's forthrightness hidden, Michael only nodded in answer to his question. Ryan was dubious but quickly switched directions; he stuck his nose in the air, scenting.

"You dog!" He laughed. "You did it with a human? I'm surprised we didn't hear more screams." He frowned. "You didn't hurt her, did you?"

Gabrielle came up behind him, perfectly coiffed and ready to go. "That's because you were too distracted with your own sound effects, you silly pup." She never tired of pointing out their age difference. Gabrielle was nearly twenty years his senior and had been in the unit all of that.

Michael instinctively growled, protective of Becca and her honor. Ryan looked sheepish while Gabrielle remained petulant. She showed a little fang, establishing her own dominance. Their social hierarchy held more sway in the unit than did their ranks. The admiral had evened those out years ago.

Michael let some of his monster show as well, eyes black and hard. Gabrielle, a skilled politician, covered her teeth and twisted her full lips into a seductive smile. It had been such a rapid display, one might not have known if it had been imagined or real. She eyed him steadily and unblinking.

Ryan evaporated from the doorway, reappearing with their supplies. Michael took his and Becca's, double checking them both for content. Becca's was loaded differently than everyone else's. A mixup could be lethal when the time came.

"The admiral called. There's been another attack. It was two days ago." Filling them in on the details, Michael sent Ryan out on a stealth mission. "Meet us back here as soon as possible. Half an hour maybe. We'll meet in the lobby. Gabrielle, dress nice." They all knew it was better when Gabrielle worked alone on missions such as this one. Men were drawn to her like bees to honey. If Ryan were a jealous man there would be endless trouble. Michael could not think about the same lusting looks being poured on Becca. She was his now, his nature argued. He placated himself with the knowledge he would still be with her after this night. She was still his.

Finished with his instructions, Michael slid his card in his lock and flipped the deadbolt shut behind him. He sat on the bed trying not to think of his new lover in the other room and what he wanted to do with her in place of investigating werewolf attacks. Only for a brief moment did he consider sending the other two out alone before he recalled himself to his duty. And his allegiance to Black.

Becca heard the bathroom door open and close gently while under the water. Getting out, she saw he had put her personal bag of supplies on the counter. She smiled affectionately at his thoughtfulness, consequently taking extra care in her appearance. Her hair flowed free, a rarity for it. Long bangs swept to the side best accentuated her large eyes. Terry had told her it made her look older and she had latched on to that. She could have tried to fool herself into believing her extra care was purely for Michael's benefit when in truth, she was fearful of spending too much time alone around him. Her lying skills were severely lacking and she now blamed her curse for this newest vision. It was solely responsible for taking her one decent shot at happiness with him and potentially ruining it unless she could stop it.

They had been intimate less than three hours and she already had a secret to keep from him. She seriously considered the possibility that she had done something awful to someone in another life to deserve this kind of karma.

When her watch told her she was out of time, Becca heard Michael knock gently on the bathroom door. She stepped out and stared at him, feeling her heart flutter. He tipped his face down to brush her lips with his, black lashes resting on his pale cheeks. Her heart ached as he wrapped his arms around her, holding her securely against his body. It would be so easy to be unguarded around him, so unlike a human ignorant of things like second sight and prescient dreams. She sighed. Damn.

"Ready?" he asked, covering her small hand with his.

"Yes, Sir."

He shot her a look. "A little late to go back to that now."

Becca detected a hint of something strange in his voice. Maybe she wasn't the only one hiding something. "Yes, it is."

A brief dip into her pack provided a few more necessary additions to her wardrobe. Michael watched her slide the silver stake carefully into her sleeve, securing it with her watch. The small "stun gun" slid more interestingly into her bra. She caught him eyeing her, noticing his brief nod of approval at her choices. The dark glimmer in his eyes made her shiver in a good way.

***

They each ordered a drink in the hotel bar. Michael not touching his but Becca was making steady progress on her vodka tonic when Gabrielle showed up.

Curious, she pretended to watch the clientele in the lobby while surreptitiously studying Becca, who seemed rather pouty for just having had what had sounded like some very good sex with the vampire. That was a conquest she'd often wondered about, regretting briefly not having taken a more serious crack at him when she first joined the unit. That time was past for them but that didn't stop her from considering what it might have been like. She'd never been with a vampire. They were too cold for her taste. She preferred her men warm blooded.

Michael turned his eyes to Becca, unable to hide his consternation completely. Gabrielle's interest peaked. Their dynamic had shifted in an unexpected way. Something more than sex had changed between them. She ground her teeth. What she had heard in the hall after the human's vision had broken off everyone's activities didn't mesh with what she was seeing pass between them now. It wasn't just business for Michael like the admiral might want and that could spell trouble for everyone.

She was compelled to make sure it was not something that would affect the safety of the unit. Or Ryan. A personal dispute in Gabrielle's former unit in North Africa had led to the deaths of the entire unit apart from her. She would not stand by and let it happen again.

Michael's hand twitched toward her before he stilled it, returning it to rest on his leg. "When you're done, Becca."

Becca downed the last half of her drink, setting the glass back with a clunk and clink of ice and stood to go.

All three made their way to the nightclub district, Arcadia. Odessa was a smaller town and, unlike Moscow or Kiev, the prices for entertainment were relatively cheap. It made sense then that the clubs were well attended. Tonight was no exception.

Gabrielle entered Zirka first and took a position on the far side of the dance floor at a small round table, looking gorgeous and available. Michael held Becca securely on his arm and waited a few minutes to go in. They made their meandering way toward the back hall where it was quieter and they could overhear the chatter of those seeking quiet places. They posed as a couple deep in an intimate conversation, their bodies were glued together to make for a convincing show.

Becca's human hearing combined with a lack of language was useless in the loud nightclub. Fortunately, Michael and Gabrielle would be able to hear over the music. Becca imagined what it must sound like to their sensitive ears, all the pounding music, clattering dishes and so many conversations. She glanced up into Michael's face. His head was turned so that she saw his profile, perfectly relaxed and uninterested in their surroundings though she knew he strained to listen. Having no other function but to content herself with watching him and occasionally having him nuzzle her neck; running her hands across his back or chest for their cover allowed her endless opportunities to watch body language and wait for some hint of a vision. Even so, every touch of her fingers on his body, stroking him through his dark blue shirt and black pants kept their lovemaking fresh in her mind. With her mind and body in a constant state of arousal, it was a challenge to keep her thoughts on the mission. When he brought his head down to the curve of her neck, letting his teeth graze her sensitive flesh, Becca gasped and shuddered.

Minutes later, he disengaged himself from her. "There's nothing here. Let's go." He took her hand, leading her out.

Gabrielle joined them on the street. She took one look at Becca and frowned. "This isn't going to work."

"What?" Becca was instantly on the defensive looking down at her less glamorous outfit. The short dress and leggings combo accented her slender form without calling too much attention to her small chest and short legs. "I look fine."

Gabrielle was shaking her head. "That's not the problem. Five more minutes and you're going to be lifting your skirt. We all need to be ready if something happens, and you can't tell me you are, not like this. You're too distracted."

Shamefaced, Becca stared at the sidewalk. Gabrielle was right. Her body was ready for something but it wasn't soldiering. Her brain was having trouble functioning clearly as well. "What should I do?" Being the newest member, she deferred to their decisions.

Gabrielle hadn't said anything to Michael. She didn't need to. Frowning, he removed his hand from Becca's. "Go with Gab, you two together should be twice the draw. I'll play lone wolf. We can split up to cover more ground."

She knew he was making a tactical decision although it was hard not to feel rejected. Still, the less time she spent with Michael, the less likely he was to guess at her guilt inducing vision.

The second club, Stereo 23, was ice themed. Everything was white, the blue lighting casting everything in an arctic glow. Dance music was pumping when Becca walked in with Gabrielle, feeling the leering stares turn toward them.

Gabrielle curled her arm around Becca's, the extra heat of her skin a shock. "Back corner, to your left. Russian mafia," she whispered in Becca's ear, giving it a long pause for show. Becca jumped when the other woman nipped at her earlobe. At the very least, a group of businessmen straight ahead of them noticed and she saw Gabrielle's show produced the desired result. Plenty of attention was on them now.

Eyes searching nonchalantly as they passed over the crowded dance floor lit in flashes by strobing blue lights, Becca caught sight of the party Gabrielle had noticed at the "high roller table."

Three men in suits with twice as many attractive women in tight dresses and stiletto heels sat on the white couches; several bottles of vodka, champagne, and glasses littered the table. When Becca looked, she saw that the men had temporarily forgotten about their bevy of women and were blatantly staring at Gabrielle.

Gabrielle led. She steered them to a table not far from the mafia crowd. Having a beautiful woman as one's bar pal was both a blessing and a curse. All eyes were on them but service was impeccable. They ordered a local drink suggested by the leggy server dressed as an Eskimo in short white shorts, vinyl Go-Go boots, and a short fur trimmed parka. That was the last drink they ordered for themselves. The rest were brought in a steady stream until their small table held a ridiculous amount of alcohol no one in their right mind could consume.

"Wow, all that's missing is the paparazzi," Becca muttered to Gabrielle, thankful her partner's hearing kept her from having to shout.

The amber eyes trained on the drink her elegant fingers lazily traced, moved up to take in Becca's sardonic expression. She was listening carefully to the conversations around them. The women had kept their commentary between them down to a minimum to avoid missing anything.

Now she smiled at Becca. "These aren't all for me."

It was impossible not to roll her eyes at the idea that anyone might notice her in the wake of the blonde's superior appeal. "That's a nice gesture, really, but it's not necessary. I've never fooled myself about my appeal."

On cue, a short barrel chested man with an all too cliché gold chain and open shirt approached them, asking if Becca would dance. Gabrielle interpreted for her and, instead of honoring Becca's wish to decline, she motioned that she should go with him. The traitor's response to the daggers her fellow unit member pointed her direction was to wave cheerily.

The number was fast; her partner's skill was solid. Becca actually enjoyed having something to do other than watch Gabrielle listen to conversations spoken in a language she herself could not understand. This man was speaking a language Becca understood all too well. It was called drunken hookup and was internationally recognized by women everywhere. Her responses were polite but clear. She left him at the end of the track, staring at her retreating backside.

"Thanks a lot, you're a shit wingman," Becca snapped at Gabrielle when she got close enough. "I'm shocked that guy only had two hands, it felt like a lot more with all the grabbing he was doing."

She winked. "Admit it, you liked it. And there's nothing to feel guilty about, it's not like Michael isn't doing the same thing right now."

Actually, Becca hadn't thought about it as being unfaithful until the thought of Michael hitting on a woman, even for the good of the world, burned her. She caught Gabrielle eyeing her, gauging her reaction.

Chance cut Becca a break. The server chose that moment to bring another round. She sighed. Even sparsely drinking off of each one they were sent of the local favorite, which had more in common with gasoline than cocktail, Becca was starting to feel fuzzy from the influence. Gabrielle appeared unaffected.

"She says we're invited to join the gentlemen in the back corner," Gabrielle told Becca as the server walked away. Both ladies raised their glasses to the men in the corner. The man in the middle, the obvious leader, tipped his head at them.

Skillfully, Gabrielle shot them a disdainful look and flicked her fingers to the ladies already with them, her unwillingness to compete very clear. The leader said something to the man on his right who in turn stood, spoke something to the girls and doled out money. Alone now, the central man put his arms on the back of the couch on either side of him and smiled, patting suggestively in time with the music. He was clearly used to getting what he wanted.

Hazy or not, Becca recognized the tingling building behind her eyes and mentioned it to Gabrielle.

"Then we must be on the right track." Gabrielle nodded and began to saunter over anyway.

"Or this is just a really bad idea." She let Gabrielle lead the way.

In an abrupt self-motivating speech, Becca reminded herself she wanted to be part of the team and this was being part of it. She was in a unit that spent some time undercover collecting Intel; sometimes a little ass-grabbing would have to be tolerated.

Gabrielle extended a thank you and took the man's hand, lowering herself gracefully down on the butter-soft leather. Becca caught sight of their host's other hand disappearing under Gabrielle's rear just before it came to rest on the surprise. A quick glance showed the blond smiling flirtatiously at him, no indication she would have much preferred ripping his arm off. She was good.

The trio consisted of a central man, Mischa, the second was Alexi, and the third, Vlad. Mischa was tall, mildly portly, and sported a neatly trimmed beard, dark like his shoulder length wavy hair. He exuded an air of confidence as well as a dangerous edge to him, palpable even to a bystander. Everyone in the club gave this table a wide berth; no need for velvet ropes in this VIP section. Alexi was thinner built and taller. He had to be at least six three with a buzz cut and hard edge to his constantly moving blue eyes that screamed former Russian police or military. Vlad was harder to figure. His fairer hair and lighter complexion combined with a soft pair of caramel brown eyes to make him Becca's pick for least likely to kill them. It was hard for her to rely on her usually reliable sight due to the fact that it had been pinching her since they'd accepted the offer to sit with the three thugs. It made it very hard to single out which of the three, if any, was a safe bet.

Gabrielle was predictably snatched up by the leader while the second sat, legs crossed and eyes roving the crowd for danger. Becca assumed a seat on the edge of the couch next to Vlad.

Vlad said something to her and Becca shook her head. "I don't speak the language, sorry." She guessed that would be the end of that, shocked when she heard the same smooth voice speaking in a familiar pattern. Whipping her head back to him, she exclaimed, "What did you say?"

He smiled, his neat, even teeth too white to be Eastern European. "I asked you what was your name." His clipped English was very good and easy to understand even through his heavy accent.

"Rebecca." She held out her hand. "And yours is Vlad, right?"

Taking her hand, he held it lightly and squeezed. He did not let it go right away, letting his interest in her be known.

Extricating it gently and without offense took only a casual reach up to sweep her hair behind her ear. Vlad watched her, his eyes focused intently on her. She couldn't help but compare him to Michael and found the Russian lacking.

"Mischa likes your friend," Vlad offered, tipping his chin toward Gabrielle.

A quick glance and Becca saw that Mischa was already staking his claim. One hand around Gabrielle's back, the other on her knee, he leaned in close speaking in her ear. Her lips were curved in a smile, yet Becca saw the coldness in her eyes. Gabrielle was all business, and something told her if the mobster went too far he would be missing some fingers or more.

"Everyone likes my friend," she acknowledged.

He tipped his head. "How does an American come to Odessa with a Russian friend?"

"Cousin. She's from Minsk. I'm visiting and we heard Odessa would be fun for the weekend."

"Two beautiful women should not be alone in Odessa right now. It is not safe."

Dismissive of his compliment to her, Becca zeroed in on his words of caution. "How is it not safe? I heard it's one of the safest places in Russia."

Vlad's hand brushed across her knee as he leaned in, pretending to whisper in her ear. His alcohol-tainted breath rolled across her skin. Creeped out, she fought the claustrophobic feeling he gave her, wishing she could push him off and run. One of the team, she reminded herself.

"There is a devil in this town."

She felt her back stiffen and, seeing Gabrielle perk up, she leaned a little closer. "A devil?" Becca forced a laugh.

He needed no further prodding. Lips brushed her ear as he explained. "Yes, a devil has been killing people in town. This very night he has taken another soul."

"Has anyone ever seen it?" She sat back to pull away except Vlad took it as an invitation and eased closer, his hand slipping behind her neck.

"None that have lived. It comes in the night with the full moon, taking people one at a time and removing their souls. It tears them apart until nothing is left."

"That's just people talking. It's probably an animal or something." Becca leaned forward to capture her drink from the table where she had left it. "Back home they get hungry sometimes or sick and come into town looking for food."

That got Vlad's attention. He sat back, regarding her with a watchful eye. "Funny you would say an animal. It appeared much like an animal attack. Like something had torn the bodies limb from limb."

"You saw the bodies?" She took another sip of the kerosene. Its burn fought back the chill winding its way through her body at Vlad's story. Pins poked the backs of her eyes and she blinked at the sensation.

He bobbed his blonde head, smiling at what he thought was her winking. "Yes I did. My cousin is the chief of police."

Note to self, Becca thought. The local police had ties to the mob. "Is he close to catching it? Have they sent hunters out?"

The perfect teeth flashed again, a shadow darkened the soft eyes for a brief instant. "I told you, it is a devil. Men cannot catch a devil."

Gabrielle's hand touched Becca's arm. Twisting, she saw that Gabrielle had indeed been listening. "Tell your friend we must go. We're due at the hotel soon, Father will be calling to check on us."

"That is my cue, Vlad. It was a pleasure." Becca held out her hand, going on when Vlad looked ready to argue. "Her father is really protective and he refuses to call us anywhere but the hotel to be sure we're in for the night."

Vlad took her hand and rose with her, still holding it. "Let me escort you back then. A gentleman cannot let two beautiful ladies walk these dangerous streets at night. Not with a devil loose." He chuckled.

"That's very kind of you but I can assure you we are quite capable," Gabrielle said over her shoulder.

"Please, I insist." Vlad did not take his eyes from Becca's face.

Seeing the folly of arguing, Becca nodded a reluctant thank you. Vlad spoke something quickly to Mischa who laughed and waved, unconcerned. They had barely cleared the table when Alexi signaled to the party girls laughing at a nearby table to return. Mischa was going to resume his party exactly where it had left off.

Vlad led them to the coat check and, taking their claim tickets from them, handled the exchange. He slid Becca's coat on first and then helped Gabrielle before retrieving his own. Holding out both elbows, he stood between the women.

"Shall we?" His broad smile made Becca's head hurt. Her sight tingled somewhat less now that they were leaving the table though the pins had not gone away entirely. She had been right; those had been dangerous men.

Each woman took an arm and walked out into the chill of the night.

Chapter 17

The cold helped to sober Becca up, she tried to look around Vlad to see how Gabrielle was receiving his escort but could not get a clear view.

"Where are we going? What hotel?" Vlad inquired outside the front doors.

"The Mozart," Becca replied, wishing he would go somewhere else. Her tingling was coming and going like it was shorting out. It could have been the alcohol. She'd never used her ability while under the influence before.

"That is a good hotel," he approved jovially and then proceeded to hold up some self-absorbed banter about his schooling in London and his hope to someday move to New Jersey with an uncle operating a small family business out there.

Becca answered him absently, her head busily coming up with about one hundred different excuses as to why he could not come to her room at the hotel. The simplest was probably that she had her period, otherwise she was willing to claim venereal disease if necessary.

"Why are you going this way?" Gabrielle asked him. They had turned the wrong way at the end of the block.

"There is a better view of the lights at night this way." He did his best to plead with his eyes, adding a warm smile meant to reassure them. "It is the same distance, let us make it more pleasant."

Becca leaned forward, finally able to see Gabrielle. She wore a falsely pleasant expression and gave a small shrug to let her know she was okay with it. Becca's growing headache from the alcohol didn't leave a lot of room for her sight to help her out even if it did decide to cooperate. She found herself relying heavily on Gabrielle's werewolf senses, having pretty much ruined hers for the evening. A mistake she would take care not to make again.

They walked along the sidewalk. Becca was listening to the sounds of the street fade as they entered a quieter part of town, away from the busy clubs in the district. Her arm jerked as Vlad halted suddenly. Becca's headache exploded behind her eyes at the same time Gabrielle growled.

Something moved fast from around the building, the dark form charging from the darkness to halt, panting heavily a few feet in front of them. Becca's stomach twisted, not just from warning. She was afraid.

Vlad spoke loudly in Russian, his arms twisting to wrap around their backs, pushing them together in front of him. Gabrielle was allowing it or Vlad would have been dead by now.

"He's made some sort of deal with him. The human wants him to kill Mischa and Alexi, making him head of the local thugs," she translated for Becca, whispering rapidly in her ear. "He's planning it with his cousin he mentioned before, the chief."

That was all Gabrielle needed. Grinning wickedly, she pushed herself away from their captor, breaking his hold on Becca in the process. Becca threw herself to the side to give her partner room to maneuver. How their opponents would be divided didn't require any discussion.

With an angry roar and a shimmering of air around her like hot tar in the desert, Gabrielle's bones shifted and cracked as she transformed rapidly into a giant golden wolf. Her ears pinned back, she tossed her head, and howled.

Vlad shouted something. Becca got the gist of it; Vlad wasn't happy with Gabrielle's new body. He backed away, falling in his rush to escape. His eyes were wild as he gaped at the beasts and crab-walked backward, placing himself only

167

a few paces from Becca. She was fascinated, fixing her eyes on the forms circling each other in front of her.

The new wolf was dark grey and a full shoulder taller than Gabrielle. He growled back at her and began to circle. Her lips pulled back to expose teeth easily as large as Becca's fingers.

The male lunged for Gabrielle but what he had in bulk she made up for in agility, easily stepping aside and avoiding his rush. Once past, she reached out and bit his flank. It was a teasing move meant to incense. It worked. He roared in anger.

Becca watched them circle and lunge, snap and feign in a dance that was successful in producing blood on both sides. A hand she had stupidly forgotten about snapped onto her arm, knocking her roughly from her feet again and taking the skin from her knees in the process. In seconds she was back up, using his momentum to regain her feet. Metal clattered on the sidewalk as a weapon fell from her sleeve.

Vlad was cursing rapidly, spittle at the corners of his mouth, eyes wide in horror as he watched the wolves tear at each other. He thought Becca was Gabrielle's master, recovering himself enough to bark orders at her.

"Make her stop. You must make her stop or I will kill you," he commanded. His mouth was close enough to her face, spit landed on her cheek.

She tried to pull away from him, aiming a sidekick at his knee meant to disable. Inconveniently, her boot slid on a loose stone and her leg dropped and her booted foot connected with his lower leg instead. Vlad spat another curse at her and punched her in the face with his free hand.

The first impact split her lip, the second cut her cheek just freshly healed from Terry. Her eyes watered making it hard to see but she was trained for this and, having plenty of experience in the field, Becca fought back. Spinning her

168

body away, she broke his hold on her, grabbing his wrist and using his momentum from her pull to jerk him off balance. She wrenched his wrist straight and threw her weight into her elbow, striking him in the back of his. The resulting crack disabled the arm. He shrieked in pain and stumbled, breaking her hold.

He was in a panic and his adrenaline kept him functional. Vlad spun around, dropping and coming back up with a knife in his hand when he lunged for her again. Becca jumped back, very glad to be in her boots and not heels, her preference at the start of the night. She grabbed his arm when it came at her, swinging him around herself and squeezing his wrist in a death grip. Her hands were small and couldn't wrap around his thicker limb far enough to hit the pressure point that would have made him drop his weapon. Fearful that if she let go of him she might not see him through the tears somewhat blinding her, Becca held on for dear life, landing several kicks that resulted in pained cries. The knife caught her forearm once, then twice. She kept her hold.

She grappled with him, holding on to try to control him except she was overmatched, a fact that was steadily becoming apparent as they began to tire. Vlad's longer reach was getting the better of Becca as her speed flagged and she couldn't get out of the way as quickly.

Snarls and snaps were coming fast and furious beyond her but she couldn't afford a glimpse to see how Gabrielle was faring.

When he was raising his knife for a backhanded slice to her ribs, Vlad paused mid-attack and started backing away, knife held high. His skin paled in the face of something behind her. A blur of cinnamon sped past her and Becca heard Ryan's growl joining the fracas with the other furry fighters.

Cool hands touched her shoulders and Becca felt her head clear. He gave her a gentle squeeze and his hands were gone. The air moved beside her and Michael's back blocked her view of Vlad.

His voice was dark. Becca felt it pulling at her senses and knew he was using his influence on the human. Vlad responded calmly, entranced. It struck her that she hadn't succumbed to his influence yet he had definitely used them on her at least once. She wondered why that was for a fleeting moment before her attention was drawn back to the street in front of her.

There was a brief exchange and Becca heard a snap before she registered movement. Vlad's body collapsed to the ground, his head bent at an unnatural angle. Michael afforded the body no respect, turning away from it to focus on the battle still raging.

Becca turned just in time to see Gabrielle lunge low, skidding on her chest to bite down on one of the grey wolf's front limbs. He hopped back, dancing on three legs. The golden wolf rushed and the grey faltered. That was all she needed. One final lunge and she was on his throat. Ryan sat back, relegated to referee and leave Gabrielle to fight her own battle.

Becca moved to stand near Michael, his hand reached for hers and she clasped it gladly. Gabrielle and Ryan approached and sat on their haunches, Gabrielle panted heavily. She licked the blood from a wound deep within the fur on her chest while Ryan licked a wound on her shoulder. Becca had to fight not to be ill. Michael clutched her hand more firmly and she felt her head clear; she shot him a grateful half-smile.

He asserted himself as leader. "Ryan, Gab, take our coats and meet us back at the hotel. Ryan, your key is in the pocket." Michael slid his own key out of his long wool coat, re-depositing it in his pants pocket. They had planned for this, working through details a less practiced unit might miss.

He looked over at Becca busily shrugging out of her coat and noticed a slight tremor to her movements. She was shaken from what she had seen tonight though all in all she handled it and herself impressively. The marks on her face and forearms brought on his protective rage and he fought it back, not wanting to treat her as less than either of the other two. She would resent him for it. It was difficult when his nature was demanding he scoop her up and carry her back to their room where no one else could touch her.

The air shimmered. Becca averted her eyes and Ryan laughed. "Becca, you can look. I know you want to."

She wrapped her arms around herself, her club dress nowhere near warm enough for the chilly spring air.

"Leave her alone, Ryan," Gabrielle chastised him sharply. Her arm slid around Becca's back, radiating heat she couldn't help but press into.

When she glanced up, questioning, Gabrielle closed her eyes and gave a minute head shake. Obediently, Becca was silent. She felt the blonde's body shaking from her exertions or injuries or both but she could not see any sources of blood loss anymore.

"Ryan, you and I need to clean up here and go find the chief of police. Gabrielle, Becca, why don't you two head back to the hotel and we will be along shortly." Michael nodded at Gabrielle. "Are you okay to get back?"

She snorted in response.

Michael grinned. "Tough bitch."

Becca felt Michael release his grip and her giddy feeling slipped away to be replaced by uncertainty and guilt once again. She was glad to be going back with Gabrielle and not him. Gabrielle was less complicated.

As they walked away, Becca could hear the sound of a body being dragged along the pavement. She couldn't help but smile when she heard Ryan curse Michael for giving him the heavier of the bodies.

"You're naked, it's not like you're going to mess up your clothes. Why do you think I did mine clean? No blood," Michael teased.

Ryan continued to grumble. "I didn't do it, she did." Their voices faded.

They walked a full block before Gabrielle spoke in a low voice. "Are you going to tell me what's going on and why Black is so happy you two are sleeping together?"

"I don't know what you're talking about." She knew the woman heard her pulse jump.

"Please. I heard you." She let that sink in. "I've known Michael longer than you've been alive. You two slept together, that isn't the question. What I want to know is why the first thing he did afterward was call the admiral."

That brought Becca up short. "What?" Her worry that they would upset the admiral by being together was obviously unfounded, but happy? "Did he have to tell him what we did? Is it a," she hesitated, "requirement?"

"No Bec. After you started yelling, Ryan and I paid attention. You were in the shower and he snuck out to make the call. It sounded like he'd been on a call with Black when you started making noise and was calling him back." Gabrielle's amber eyes stared intently into hers. "I heard the admiral congratulate him for bedding you and then I saw you two in the lobby. You didn't look like a woman who's just been with a man she's been licking her chops over for days. I'm trying to figure out what's going on between you."

Becca felt ill. "I'm sure you heard it wrong."

Her forehead remained smooth and unburdened by doubt. "No, Ryan heard it too."

"I'm sure you two heard him talking about something else. You were listening through a door to a phone conversation.

You can't tell me you can hear *that* well." Becca tried to dismiss her suspicions as unfounded.

"We've gone to war on less reliable info. I'm sure of this."

Becca pulled ahead of Gabrielle. They were still about six blocks away and Becca jogged it. Gabrielle let her go.

The human hadn't known about Michael's admission; she was easy to read. That shock and hurt were genuine. But Becca had been upset in the hotel lobby about something else. Gabrielle was sure of it. What was *she* hiding? It wouldn't stay a secret for long. Gabrielle wouldn't let Ryan be killed like Luc in Algiers. Their unit was not going to be put in jeopardy because of some sick game being run by the admiral and his favorite captain.

Chapter 18

Becca got back to the hotel barely winded. By the time she reached the bar, she had recovered enough to order two vodkas and downed them in rapid succession. She gave the bartender her room to charge and ordered two more. He gave her a bag of ice for her face. Danger behind them, Becca didn't need her sight to work. As a matter of fact, she would like to have that short-circuited as well. And she was trying the only way she knew to do that.

Gabrielle pulled up a barstool wrapped in Becca's coat and nothing more. The bartender served her Cosmo and dallied, not even trying to hide the fact that he was trying to get a glimpse down her neckline. He was disappointed when she ignored him. Becca failed to acknowledge her arrival.

They were sitting silently beside each other at the bar when the other half of the team arrived. Ryan's hair was damp, his body cleaned of blood. He spoke first.

"I thought you were heading up. I saw you on my way through the lobby." Ryan's appearance in a man's dress coat and no pants was not being as well received as Gabrielle's. The bartender looked disgusted.

"Why don't you two head up?" Michael suggested, sidling up to lean on the bar next to Becca.

Gabrielle gave Michael a curious look as she whisked Ryan back to their room.

When they were alone Michael lowered his voice, giving his husky timbre more of a sexy growl than usual. "Was it that bad? This is pretty standard for our ops. Sometimes they're worse."

He was close enough to touch her. Becca didn't know if she wanted that or not and her lack of self-respect infuriated her. She shook her head angrily, downing the last half of her fourth shot. Her goal of being pass out drunk by the time he got there was successful, now she just had to keep her mouth shut until she could manage to pass out. Becca was hoping if she had enough alcohol in her system she could cancel out any sort of visions tonight. How she would handle things tomorrow was less clear.

Michael could see how inebriated she was even if he hadn't been able to smell it in her blood. She hadn't been squeamish at the scene, he'd seen her with that tall blonde. He'd heard her crack his elbow. It had been hard for him to hold himself back from snatching the guy off the street and tearing his head clean off when he'd seen him fighting with her. But she was trained and competent and just because she was his lover didn't mean he could treat her any differently than the others in action. It wouldn't be fair to her. Then again, Black would have his head if he let anything happen to her. Theirs would be a delicate dance.

Black. The unwelcome reminder of him and his involvement in their relationship dampened his budding happiness. Michael leaned in to keep his words between them and rested his hand low on her back.

Becca's reaction was instant. She jerked forward, away from his offending touch. She wouldn't give in to her body's desire for him, growing with his nearness. If he touched her, she might lose her resolve. Her head was going to win this one damn it.

"I heard *you* had another mission here tonight." Her words dripped venom.

His face fell and Becca felt her insides sink. Gabrielle had been right. Unable to be in the same room with him any more, she pushed her hands off the bar and slid off the stool, stumbling as her knees argued with her need for balance.

Michael's hand reached out to steady her but her glare stopped him. She hated the tremble in her voice when she spoke. "Don't touch me."

Storming out was not as effective as she might have hoped with her drunken stumbles. She went to the desk, got her own key from the clerk, who thankfully recognized her from earlier, and went to bed alone.

When she woke in the morning, Becca's head was pounding and her tongue was thick. Hesitating long enough to be sure she wouldn't fall or puke on herself, she stood up and went to the bathroom to shave her tongue and splash cool water on her face.

Her face wasn't as bad as she would have thought. The lip was swollen but nothing a little lipstick wouldn't help to hide if she had some and the cheek was dark pink and barely bigger than the other. It didn't really hurt unless she moved her face. The cuts on her forearms were superficial thanks to the thick coat. She gave them a quick washing just in case.

Becca was alone in the room. The only sign Michael had come in was another set of street clothes more appropriate for daytime than the dress from last night or her military garb. Tan trousers, green Henley and brown coat from the night before made up her wardrobe for departure. The bloodstains had been washed out of the coat sleeves. Changing took only a few minutes. Afterward, she checked with her stomach and they agreed that breakfast would not be a welcome addition.

In the lobby, coffee was available at the desk. She poured a cup and found a seat on a couch in an alcove mostly hidden from view by two large palm fronds. Anyone that needed her could smell her wherever she might be, so visibility was a non-issue.

Halfway through the cup she began to feel somewhat human and her head slowed its pounding. Gabrielle stepped into her little oasis, breaking her out of her pity party.

"Are you hiding?" Her teasing held no malice.

"No." Her voice was thick from disuse. "Not really."

Gabrielle sat down. "For what it's worth, I'm sorry." She managed contrition well enough.

Becca wasn't easily convinced of her sincerity. "Can I ask you something?"

"Sure."

"Why the sudden change? I mean, you hate me. What happened?" She watched Gabrielle for signs she was lying.

"It's true, I wasn't happy about the addition of a human. Especially a female." Her brows pinched for a tiny second and then were smooth. Breaking eye contact, she examined the palm frond draped beside her, rubbing its edge between two fingers. "I've seen you in action and I understand the need for you in our unit." Amber eyes burned intense when they returned to Becca, "Black has used any number of methods to keep us all here, but this one could blow up and hurt us all." The glow dimmed from her eyes and she raised a shoulder. "I thought if you knew it might save us all some heartache."

It didn't surprise her that Gabrielle's motives weren't guided by kindness. Her mention of Black's nefarious methods gave her cause to wonder what he'd done to the others to assure their allegiances. "Huh, um, thanks for the vote of confidence. I hope I help here. And, thanks. For the honesty. It's good to know someone's capable of it."

Gabrielle smiled sadly. "You're better off knowing. It'll save you some heartache in the long run."

Becca managed not to look completely crushed. "Well, you don't need to worry about us. It was a one time thing. You were right, I was just another assignment to him." She kept her back straight and her head up, but could do nothing about the sting she felt at letting herself be fooled. He had been so passionate. It was hard to think he'd been faking it. At least he'd been honest about one thing, Becca thought bitterly. He

177

had said he wouldn't let her go. She'd only misrepresented the why.

Done with the supportive sister business, Gabrielle clapped a strong, neatly manicured hand on Becca's small leg and smiled. "Come. It's time to move on." Rising, she held out a hand and, hesitating only for a second, Becca took it.

***

The four drove back to the hangar. Only Ryan was his usual happy go lucky self, undaunted by the dark moods surrounding him. The other three remained silent. Gabrielle flew them home, again making two fuel stops. Becca rode up front with her this time, leaving the men in the back. Becca appreciated Gabrielle's act of kindness but still imagined it was fueled by a hidden agenda. Either way she wanted a friend right now, false or no.

Once again on the ground, on home soil, Gabrielle taxied the jet into the hangar. Before they deplaned, Michael came to the front.

"We debrief with the admiral in one hour." He was curt and left immediately.

Becca grabbed her pack and trudged to her room feeling more tired than on her worst day in basic. She unpacked and heaped her laundry together in a pile. That would give her something to think about at least for a little while.

Heading next door to Ryan's room, Becca knocked. He whipped his door open and smiled at her. "Did you want something?" Dark eyebrows waggled playfully.

"Yes, as a matter of fact I do." She looked up through her long lashes at him, enjoying the much needed frivolity. "A washing machine."

Ryan had a great laugh, infectious. Becca found herself grinning. "Come on, I'm heading down too."

Becca put her clothes in her pillowcase to carry it down. The laundry facilities were just off the kitchen, before the storeroom behind a door she had thought was a large cabinet. The storeroom had its ghosts and she moved past it quickly trying to keep them at bay.

"It's an old house and sometimes you have to put things in strange places to make them work. This was where they found water pipes," he shrugged, "so this is where we wash."

The room was long and narrow, four sets of stackable frontloading washers and dryers were all that fit. A bottle of detergent sat on a small shelf protruding from the wall directly inside the door.

Laundry loaded with over a half an hour until debriefing, Becca accepted Ryan's offer of a snack. She hadn't eaten anything all day.

"Have a seat, let me cook for you," Ryan proclaimed grandly.

She did and watched him stuff his huge shoulders into the fridge and move about the kitchen with a grace that belied his hulking form. In moments, he produced two plates with cold meat sandwiches and carrot sticks.

"Ta da." He winked at her.

Laughing felt good, it let her forget. "You are a fine chef, Ryan."

Nodding very seriously, he replied, "You know that's what I'm doing if this whole soldiering thing doesn't pan out."

Although it wasn't high cuisine, Becca was hungry. She got up to pour them both waters and sat back down to sip hers and relax. It was difficult to keep her mind from the upcoming meeting when she would be at the table with Michael and the man who had orchestrated her seduction.

What Gabrielle had said about inspiring loyalty and the odd number of people sparked an interest.

"Hey Ryan, how long has the unit been three members?" She took a sip. "For working in pairs, wouldn't you typically want four? Like now?"

Rolling his eyes skyward in thought, he leaned back and crossed his thick arms. "I would say it's been just us three for the last six years, when Kenny left."

A carrot stick dangled in her fingers. "Was he killed?"

"No." He shook his head. "He was a younger vampire though. Couldn't handle all the humans around all the time when we were on operations. The admiral okay'd Michael to relieve him of duty." Ryan shrugged his shoulders and popped his last chunk of sandwich into his mouth. "This job ain't for everyone."

"How is Admiral Black to work for?" Now that she was in and had gained some traction with her fellow unit members, it was time to learn about their boss.

His expression was troubled for the first time. "He's tactically unparalleled. I think sometimes he has more people under his thumb than the President. But don't cross him. No one says 'no' to Black," Ryan warned her. "Not if you want to keep breathing."

Becca let that roll around in her head. It wasn't enough to make her forgive Michael his trespass, though it might possibly keep her from hating him. Maybe he hadn't meant to be cruel and had slept with her out of self-preservation. The conversation in the storeroom that night came back with new meaning. The admiral wanted her to feel some loyalty to the unit. Unable to bind her to himself, he had capitalized on her attraction to Michael. Her instinct told her she was right.

Becca was a big girl capable of understanding Michael's actions. That didn't mean she had to agree with them or like them but it helped temper the hurt she felt gnawing on her heart.

Chapter 19

The debriefing was awkward. The admiral watching her, his thin lips twisted in a smirk every time he glanced her way. She kept her face blank; not looking at Michael and not letting her outrage at the admiral show either.

Michael led, as would be expected, calling upon the others for their own accounts of their actions. Both Gabrielle and Michael were complimentary of Becca's information gathering in the club and her cool head in a fight. Despite her issues with the unit's leadership, she was proud.

"Well Rebecca, it sounds like you are a valuable asset even when you're not using your ability. I can only hope that your work with us brings you pleasure."

His blatant nudge burned, she felt her jaw clench. Nodding curtly she stared at the table. "Yes, Sir."

Michael spoke up. "I would like to make a request, Sir. The mission so soon after the lunar cycle has taken a toll. A few days leave for the team, Sir? We could use some time to heal."

Becca's eyes roved Gabrielle's flawless arms and face. She caught her curious stares.

"When we change back to our human forms, we heal. The more severe injuries take a little longer."

"What happens if you're hurt when you're in your human form?" Becca wanted to know more about her dual-natured comrades. She wished she had a touch of what they did, fingers absently touching her bruised face, different shades of purple and green on the one cheek complimenting the fat lip she sported. Oddly enough, they were healing faster than expected. Maybe it was contagious.

Ryan answered. "We do the whole thing backward." He flipped his hands. "Person to wolf."

"Forty-eight hours. I'm monitoring a situation in Canada," Admiral Black agreed, striding from the room. "Good work."

When it was the four of them, Ryan stretched his arms. "I think I'll sleep at least twenty of those."

Gabrielle crabbed, "What else is new?" She turned to Becca and asked her, with a raise of a single eyebrow.

Learning Gabrielle speak, Becca pursed her lips. "Well, I guess I should go get my things from my apartment since I'm moving."

"You're not to go near that base." Michael's response was harsh. "We've taken care of that already, your things will be here by end day tomorrow."

Becca bristled, spinning in her chair to gape at him. "So what do I tell my family? That I'm a criminal now? Where does my mother send my Christmas cards? How do I explain where I am?"

His eyes were cold and dark, belying his mild expression. Becca couldn't help but be wounded by his firm hand now that his mission was complete and he was back to being her superior officer.

"Your cover is that you're on a special security detail that travels frequently."

"Do you think they'll buy that?"

"Your father was Corps. He can read between the lines. Your brothers won't know enough to question it."

Her mouth fell open at his knowledge of her family. Becca felt twice violated. "You read my file?"

He nodded, glancing down at the table where his fingers traced. Catching himself, he stopped and lowered his hands to his lap. "We thoroughly vet all new recruits. You required a little extra due to the fact that you're human and have living relatives."

"Yeah, she did," Ryan guffawed.

"Hallbeck!" Michael barked angrily, cutting short any further comments.

The chair's wheels made a low rumble as Becca pushed it back to stand. "Permission to use a vehicle to go home, Sir. It's been a while since I've seen my family."

He felt his heart wrench at the shame and pain Becca was working so hard to hide. He saw her eyes shining brightly in the dim lights. Knowing that he was the cause grieved him immeasurably. "Granted," he said simply.

Without another word, Becca stalked straight-backed from the room.

Michael waited only until she had reached the top of the stairs before pushing back from the table. Standing in front of the remainder of his team, he considered what they had done together as comrades in arms and how closely knit they were. They'd all come from different branches of service, from different times and wars. Closer than a conventional family by far, united under a leader who was so singularly focused on his cause they could choose to share that purpose or die. That was why it infuriated him to think that one of them had betrayed him. One of them had taken his chance to have that with Becca, this human who had so swiftly wrapped herself around his heart, away from him. He had to know the source.

"Which one of you told her?" He leveled a no nonsense gaze upon them, not bothering to control the icy fury building in his rigid frame. His hands pressed into the tabletop, going white as he leaned into their space.

Ryan blanched, eyes wide. "What? Who told who what?"

Michael growled through clenched teeth. "Becca. Who told her?"

"I did, Michael," Gabrielle confessed, no hint of remorse on her face. "I heard you on the phone in the hallway. Black too."

Silently he cursed his stupidity. He hadn't wanted to go far after her scare and had been careless to remain outside their doors. "Why would you tell her that?" Her cold heart had no limits in his mind.

She studied his reactions closely. He was genuinely upset. Could he have *wanted* to sleep with the human? It was an angle she hadn't seriously considered. She had assumed his interest had been pure curiosity and Black's orders. To her knowledge he hadn't been with a human since being turned. That it could be more caught her off guard. "We were talking and it came up."

"Bullshit, Gab. You've been in intelligence and covert ops for too long for me to buy that 'it just came up' line." He felt his fangs growing as his nature fought to tear her perfect face to pieces. She'd heal but it would hurt like hell in the meantime. "No matter your personal feelings on the subject, you realize this might ruin her chances in the unit and if she can't cut it we can't turn her loose."

Gabrielle didn't flinch at his overreaction. "You can wipe her mind if it doesn't work. We do it all the time." She shrugged.

Michael's body quivered with his need for retribution. Her flippancy was pushing him to his tipping point. The table cracked under his palms. "Black wants her because of the strength of her ability. It's that strength that makes her immune to our influence. She can't be wiped like a typical human."

The ramifications were clear at once. This one knew too much to go back out among the humans. If she failed here, she would have to be killed. "I didn't realize." Her misstep bothered her more than she would like to admit, having another woman in the unit had been rather enjoyable. She couldn't meet his eyes.

"No, you didn't realize," he snapped back. Whether Becca forgave him or not was one thing but if it led to her destruction, he would make Gabrielle pay dearly. "Now both of you keep your damned mouths shut on the subject of Becca." He lowered his voice to a whisper. "Nothing is said to the admiral and nothing is said to her. Anything you want to talk to her about other than the weather goes through me. Do I make myself clear?"

"Yes, Sir," they answered in unison. Though in all fairness it didn't look like Ryan had any idea what he had just been accused of.

"Dismissed."

They rose and left without a sound.

After they were gone Michael slid down into his seat, the weight of his responsibility oppressive. He eyed the indents his palms had left in the surface of the table. From the moment Black had encountered her by chance, he had wanted Becca for his collection. Each member of the team had been handpicked by Black personally, each for the same reason. He saw things in them he could use. Most of them died in his service; it was a rarity for the admiral to let anyone go once he had his hooks into them.

Kenny, the last recruit to leave had been the first in over a century that Michael was aware of. The only reason the admiral allowed it was because he hoped that with age and maturity Kenny would be able to rejoin the team. He was one of the rare vampires who had had a gift in life, like Becca, and had kept it through the transition to undead. He had also had the sight but it had blinded him in his immaturity, showing him nothing except a bloodbath anywhere he would encounter humans. It had led to a few unfortunate incidents before the admiral turned him back out to pasture to mature for a few years. Once his blood craving was under control, the admiral might attempt to bring him back.

Now he had found a human with the sight. There was no way he was going to let Becca go. Michael worried Black would turn her before killing her in an effort to keep the gift alive, easily trading her out for Kenny if she suffered the same complication. But Michael remembered Kenny confiding the hellish turning for him. The heightened senses that came with being a vampire had made the sight more powerful. His visions had been maddening, the feelings he had on situations and people had been so strong they were paralyzing. Michael couldn't let Becca suffer that.

His need to protect her had only grown sharper after their lovemaking, his nature urged him to take her again and keep her close regardless of her feelings for him. Knowing Black's ways, he feared for himself too. Should the admiral push his agenda too far, Michael would be compelled to fight for Becca even knowing the penalty for his actions. He would sacrifice himself for her. It would be far more bearable than having to be the one to turn her. Surely that would be the case due to the Black's incompatibility with her or eliminate her altogether. The image of her tortured face, eyes wild with madness etched itself upon his mind. Would it be better to kill her than have her suffer that? He shoved the thought roughly aside.

Nervous energy made his synapses fire faster than even his blood-preserved body could handle. Electrified, he leapt to his feet and began to pace the room. He was marching back and forth, fixating on *his* Becca and the danger Gabrielle's little "slip" had put her in. Fury had his blood near the boiling point when he felt his phone vibrate in his pocket.

"Yes, Sir."

"Any ideas where our newest member is going on her leave, Michael?"

"She mentioned going home, Sir." Prescience was unnecessary to see where the admiral was heading and in Michael's state he grasped at it before it was even suggested. "Do you want me to go with her, Sir? Make sure she sells the cover?" Make sure she comes back, he thought to himself.

"That won't be a problem, will it Michael? I thought I sensed some friction at the debriefing. Things haven't soured so quickly I hope. We might have to be more drastic in our approach to secure her place with us."

Michael's chest tightened. Years of practice allowed him to keep his response calm. "No Sir, that won't be necessary. Her loyalty is guaranteed." He didn't add that the only thing that could get in the way now would be the very thing the admiral had hopes would cement the deal. Him.

"Good. Go with her just to be sure."

The line went dead.

Chapter 20

"Why?" Becca couldn't conceive enduring the drive up to Oceanside with him.

"The admiral wants to be sure we sell the cover. Convincing family can be difficult. We thought if you had something else to distract them they might limit their questions." He was dressed in civilian attire; tan trousers and light blue polo shirt. Daytime casual made him even more tempting, if that was possible.

It was hard to tell if Michael was as uncomfortable as she. Becca could feel her body trying to tell her he hadn't meant to hurt her and she hated herself, and her cursed sight, for it.

She saw that he wasn't going to give up, knew that once the admiral gives an order it was to be obeyed. "Fine. Do you have money I could borrow until mine arrives?"

His brows rose at the unexpected question. "What?"

Becca felt a small twinge of satisfaction having taken him by surprise. Not typically a borrower, she liked putting him on the spot. "My things aren't here and I can't go in looking like covert ops or like I'm fresh from the club so my current wardrobe is out. You said I need to sell this." She pulled her lips back in a large, fake smile. "I'll be downstairs in five minutes." Her smile remained plastered to her face while she shoved the door closed in his face.

***

Not surprisingly, Michael insisted upon driving. He punched her parents' address in to the GPS and promised to hit a mall on the way. They did exactly that and Becca stepped out, staring at Michael as she did so. Her chilly voice stayed his hand on his seat belt buckle.

"I will lie to my parents and be friendly with you for an entire day. However, unlike you, I can't fake my feelings

189

easily so if I could just put off having to do that a little while longer I would appreciate it. Let me do this by myself."

He removed his hand from the buckle and dug for his wallet, peeling out several one hundred dollar bills. She snatched them from him with another fake smile. Michael took his hands and placed them both palms down on the wheel, fingers extended. Becca wanted to scream, settling for slamming the door instead.

"Hurry back," he called out acerbically.

She didn't. Becca was a fast shopper, hating the experience usually. Her build had never been the one designers had in mind when they made their clothing. The trim waist was good, not so much the short stature. Short legs meant she could almost get by with no shoes when she bought jeans. The extra fabric typically encased the better half of her feet. Her tailor loved it. Just once Becca wished she could buy something other than shorts off the rack.

A new petite store advertised short length jeans in their front window. Becca went in and, shocked by the accuracy of their claim, ten minutes later walked out with three new pair of pants; two jeans, one pair of black trousers. Tops were easier. With a limited bust and small body she preferred the Juniors' department.

Becca combed the racks in the Juniors' section at JC Penney and found several long sleeved t-shirts. She figured if she couldn't *act* cheerful, at least she could dress it. Another detour provided her with some essentials for underneath her new clothes. Her black belt was fine as were her boots for civilian duty. When she checked out and hefted her bags, now clothed in her petite jeans and a spring green fitted tee, Becca detoured to grab a coffee. Finally, warm beverage in hand, she felt her heart sink.

She could put it off no longer. She had to go back and face him.

By the time she returned, Michael was ready to jump out of his skin. Not only was he unhappy about being left behind and not being at liberty to argue given his already raging guilt over her assumption that he was a pig who'd manipulated her feelings, he was also growing more uncomfortable by the second at the sun's growing intensity.

They had left the estate early in the afternoon and Michael had been in the San Diego sunshine for the better part of an hour. At least it wasn't full summer. He would've been unable to tolerate it more than twenty minutes. As it was, he was starting to get antsy. His body was demanding blood; moving the car into partial shade on the east side of the building offered limited relief.

Not that he hadn't planned for this. Knowing they would be the gone at least until nightfall, he'd packed a bag as well. He glanced behind his seat to confirm for the millionth time that the cooler was in there. And for the millionth time he told himself no. He didn't want to break into it yet. He would need to feed often if he was to be staying in her home with so many humans. He hadn't stopped to think about sleeping arrangements. A wave of regret mixed with sexual frustration broke over him at the thought.

His eyes locked in on her the second she exited the building. She held three bags and a coffee and added an extra hop to her step off the curb. She didn't know he was watching. He took the opportunity to observe her, the vampire liking what it saw.

She had taken her hair down the way he preferred it. It hung loose in light brown waves, brushing her shoulders as she moved. The sun illuminated the gold and red in her locks as she swung her head around, searching for signs of the car no longer where she had left it. Michael disliked the new sunglasses she wore, blocking his view of her eyes as they did. He did like the way the new shirt clung to her small breasts, revealing the soft curves she had willingly offered to him what seemed lifetimes ago.

Sighing in frustration, Michael pulled the car out and saw her face settle into her blank mask, hiding herself from him.

"Why did you move the car?" she asked benignly while loading her packages into the back through the seats.

"Shade."

She settled herself into her seat and buckled up. "I thought you were okay in the car, it blocks the light."

"It's Southern California, light's always a factor."

Becca twisted in her seat to face him. It didn't matter that she wore shades, he could tell she was appraising. "Is there anything you need?"

He imagined a hint of concern in her voice. "I have an emergency supply here in the car if things get too dire but I'm sure it won't come to that." Michael kept his voice unemotional.

She turned to face forward once again, walling herself off for the remainder of the drive.

Chapter 21

The Sauters lived in a small, post war bungalow, a style popular up and down the coast. The exterior was painted a sunny yellow with white shutters affixed to the stucco siding and a tan shingle roof.

"Does your mother garden?" Michael noticed the impeccably pruned rose bushes out front full of reds and pinks as well as a small, well-maintained yard. Shrubs and several flowerbeds dotted the cheerful space.

Becca remained seated. "No, that's Dad." There was a sense of something he couldn't pinpoint in her tone when she mentioned her father. Her file could only report the facts of who was inside, not what it was like in the trenches with the troops. Michael thought about his own family's complex dynamics.

They were a well-bred Italian family. Okay, half Italian. His mother, the source of his blue eyes, had been the daughter of an English diplomat stationed in Italy during the first Great War. She married his father against her parents' objections and immigrated to America, settling in New York during the Depression.

They found America no better off during the economic fallout. Gathering up the last of their reserves, they sent him off to college in hopes he would return and help expand their enterprises beyond just the one restaurant. A few years in business with his equally hotheaded father drove him to enlist despite his mother's tearful objections.

It was true she'd told him he wouldn't return; only she'd said it a little differently. She'd said that his soul wouldn't survive. Her prediction had haunted him after he'd been turned. As a human he assumed she meant he would die in the war. He'd had no idea what had happened was even feasible. Often he wished he could see her again but he couldn't face her after what he'd done. He had quenched his thirst on a number of civilians after his unit had been attacked and destroyed by younger vampires. Only he had reanimated, having been turned by an experienced vamp who had given him some amount of sanity over his thirst.

When the burning of the initial thirst was tamed, he had sought cover from the burning of the daytime sun so hot on his newly sensitive skin. The young girl, barely a woman, who had offered him her cellar to hide had been an innocent. Thinking of her bothered him. She had been able to hide from the horde of vampires created from the members of her town only to be killed by a soldier she had attempted to help. She'd only been stealing an innocent kiss from the handsome soldier and had gotten too close. He shut off that part of his mind, not needing any further distraction.

Breathing deeply in a practiced rhythm, Becca closed her eyes and took one last deep breath before exhaling powerfully and throwing open her door.

At the same time, a mature, well-maintained version of Becca with a short bob dyed to match her daughter stepped out from around the back of the house. Michael heard a gate latch. She wore denim shorts, a loose short-sleeved top and a wide-brimmed tan sun hat.

As soon as she saw Becca emerge from the car, a smile lit her face. There was only the briefest glimmer of worry in the lines on her face as she called out. "Bec! What a surprise." She held out her arms for her only daughter.

"Hey Mom." Becca let her mother fold her into her embrace.

Michael saw her shoulders relax, the tension flow out of her taking years off of her already youthful face. It was easy to picture her as a child, though never as carefree. He could remember little of his childhood, it had been so long ago, but seeing her in her mother's arms gave Michael a tiny nostalgic pang for his own mother's affection and warmth.

Her mother straightened, eyes rolling over Becca's face. "What happened to you?" She could see the faint traces of bruises fading rapidly from Becca's skin. She had no way of knowing, but Michael knew she owed her rapid healing to his blood she'd ingested a few days ago. The effects would fade over the next few weeks but, given her potential for danger with them, he was glad at the moment to have given her some extra protection.

Self-conscious, Becca touched her face. "It was just a training accident. No biggie."

Dubious, her mother's gaze moved to the driver's window. "Is there someone with you, honey?"

"Yes." Her response was crisp.

Michael took it as his cue and stepped out of the car.

"Mom, I'd like to introduce you to a friend of mine, Captain Michael Rossi."

Her mother studied him with pointed interest in her large hazel eyes. "Friend" was obviously a term she intended to define for herself. She politely held out a hand. "Hello Captain, I'm Melanie Sauter. Pleased to meet you." He saw where Becca got at least part of her spark.

"Please Mrs. Sauter, call me Michael." He smiled pleasantly at her and looked her directly in the eye, working to put her at ease with a small amount of influence which was inherent to his condition.

Her shoulders eased and he saw the small pinching between her brows smooth. "Only if you call me Mel."

As soon as they turned back to Becca, she took one look at her mother's face and Michael watched her eyes harden. To her credit, that was her only outward expression of anger. She flashed him a quick glare to show him she knew what he had done and didn't approve.

What she knew, he wasn't sure. He hadn't explained anything to her about his extra abilities and though pop culture had some of the details, they didn't have it down entirely. He would have to clarify some of that for her in her pending education on supernatural creatures. She'd already been learning a lot from pure observation but they would have to make sure to fill in the blanks so there could be no misunderstandings in the field.

He'd used his seduction on Becca, or attempted as it were. She had proven to be somewhat resistant to it. He had seen it make an impact that night in the storeroom. She had seen what he'd wanted her to, his desire and hunger for her, but yet she had not come to him. He could also erase a memory should he have the need and could affect people's moods, though all required direct eye contact making it an isolated sort of control mechanism meant mostly for prey. It had proven greatly effective in this type of work.

The three walked across the yard around a tall arborvitae toward the side gate from where Melanie had come to greet them.

"Your father's back here." She gave a short strained laugh. "You know him with his garden."

Michael picked up on the tension settling in both women's shoulders. He let himself drift back to observe. Becca set her jaw and stood ramrod straight, her mother shot several side glances at her daughter as they walked through the six foot tall cedar gate and into a veritable Garden of Eden, California-style.

Wisteria draped from beside the gate, lending instant shade for which Michael was unendingly grateful. An arbor to their left protruded from the house as an awning, boasting a canopy of pure ivy. More roses circled the sides of the porch and the smell of citrus assailed Michael's nostrils informing him the species of trees surrounding the yard. In the center was a small pool with attached hot tub typical of this area where intense heat drove people not to the crowded beaches but to their own backyards for relief.

A pair of skinny legs was visible sticking out of a pair of tan shorts below a lemon tree. One leg had a scar Michael couldn't see yet knew existed. A small basket below held clippings from the branches above. Several more were tossed in as the trio made their way under the canopy. The shade was a welcome relief.

"Ed, we have company," Melanie called out. "Becca's here and she brought a friend."

The legs didn't move.

She motioned for them to take a seat under the awning. "Michael, would you care for some iced tea?" The wrinkle had reappeared between her brows, her eyes lingering on the legs in the tree.

"That would be fine, Mel. Thank you," he answered politely, taking the seat she indicated.

"I'll be right back." Her light footsteps on the tile faded into the house.

Once her mother was out of earshot, Becca leaned forward in her chair, hissing at him. "Don't do that to her again."

"I thought it might help make things easier."

"Manipulating me is one thing, my family is another. Things are complicated here. You said you wanted to be here to make sure I don't give too much away, that's fine. But you don't get to mess with their heads. This is an admiral-free zone."

He was slow to answer. "Sometimes the admiral gives assignments I want."

"Yeah, I bet you do." She sat back, stewing.

"It wasn't like that." He kept his eyes focused on the pool's reflections dancing on the ivy above their heads. "What we did had nothing to do with him. He tried to take credit after the fact."

Becca stared at his profile. Not that his face would show if he was lying, he was well versed in deception. Age, nature, and time in this field combined to make him a master. She wanted to believe that what they had done, what she felt from him had been real. She couldn't, her doubts persisted. "Gabrielle heard you talking to Black in the hallway. You must have snuck out of bed to tell him you'd done it. The naïve human was under the sexy vampire's spell." She looked down at her hands embarrassed at having come so close to the source of her hurt.

He eagerly took the opportunity to explain himself. "Gabrielle heard me checking in, which I was duty bound to do before we went out that night. I can't lie to him, Becca. He asked if you and I had become intimate and I had to answer truthfully. He was pleased but that was the extent of his involvement."

Her eyes welled up, "She said you were offered a raise for what you did."

"Becca, please look at me," he pleaded softly.

She did. His eyes were soft and blue, no evidence of him trying to use any of his influences on her. "Black is a strong leader and an exceptional strategist, however, he is a sadistic bastard who's always trying to make sure he's got all the angles covered. I didn't make love to you because he asked me to. As a matter of fact, I thought about *not* doing it once he ordered it. I'd planned to tell him it was unnecessary. You had proven your loyalty during the mission." His eyes darkened, boring intensely into hers and he leaned forward, his hand reaching out to brush the back of hers sitting on the table.

She let him, her body thrilling at his touch regardless of her continuing reservations.

"But then you offered yourself to me and I couldn't hold back any longer. Things just happened from there." Michael's voice was rough with emotion.

"If he is so awful, why do you all stay with him?" Becca zeroed in on something less complicated. "Gabrielle said he does things to get you to stay with him."

His thumb traced the back of her hand, his eyes following its slow pattern. "He pulled us in however he could, that's true. Then, once we were in, we saw the good we did. We're doing work normal soldiers can't. We're keeping things at bay that have the potential for untold human destruction." Michael chose not to reveal the fact that he was *unable* to leave Admiral Black.

Her footsteps were intentionally louder on her return as Melanie carried a tray from the house.

Michael's hand removed itself from hers to rest in his lap.

"Please help yourselves. Becca, could you pour?" She smiled tightly. "I'll go get Ed. I'm sure he's just finishing up."

Becca felt her body tighten at the reminder her father was going to be joining them. Her hand trembled as she poured. He always did that to her. When she was in his presence, Becca was an awkward little girl again.

The familiar heavy march of her father's footsteps on the tile set Becca's teeth on edge. He sat down without a word.

"Hi Dad." She handed him a glass first.

He let her set it on the table, not bothering to reach for it. As usual, asserting his authority from the start. "Becca." Ed glanced over at Michael, brown eyes thoroughly assessing the newcomer. He said not a word about her bruises.

She let her glance slide over to Michael to see how he was taking it. He was completely nonplussed by Ed's examination.

Mel handled introductions. "Ed, this is Captain Michael Rossi. Michael, meet my husband Sergeant Ed Sauter, USMC, retired."

Only a man who lived and breathed military life would have his wife introduce him like that. Becca wished she wouldn't but it was too ingrained by now.

Her father misunderstood Becca's reticence to seek a commission. He couldn't understand that if she were an officer there would be no justifying the gut feelings she followed. She couldn't live with herself if she had to ignore her instinct to spare herself scrutiny and harmed someone as a result. No one she had ever known would understand that about her. No one until now; her eyes passed over to Michael again. He was smiling pleasantly enough at her father, unperturbed.

"It's an honor, sir." He extended his hand, rising to put himself within Ed's reach.

Ed did the same, curiously studying the young confident man with his daughter. He couldn't tell the details of their relationship exactly, though his daughter's affection for the man was clear. She might think she was hiding it but she couldn't keep her eyes off him.

The captain came off as confident, not arrogant. He had a firm grip and no aversion to looking a man in the eye. Ed liked that.

"Captain." He nodded, releasing the cool hand. They must have had the air conditioning on pretty high in the car for his skin to still be so chilly.

"Please, call me Michael." Glancing around him he complimented the man's obvious obsession from his seat. "You have a beautiful home, Sir." He nodded toward the backyard.

Ed grunted. "Had to find something to do with myself after I retired. We bought this place seven years ago, and it's been an ongoing project since." He surveyed the perfectly manicured yard. "It's coming along."

"So Becca, what brings you home?" Mel took a deliberate drink of her tea.

Becca ran her fingers up and down the sides of her glass making stripes in the condensation. "It's been a little hectic lately and I thought a visit might do me some good."

"Well this doesn't happen often. Your brother is actually in town for business and due any time." Mel beamed happily. "I actually thought you were him when I heard the car."

"Kyle's here?" She was visibly conflicted, shooting a nervous glance at her father.

Michael was curious at Becca's reaction. He knew Kyle was the oldest by three years and his career choice of software developer had proven highly successful in spite of his young years. But how that played within the family was a point of interest for him. Becca's reaction was telling. Her shoulders slumped, her fingers stilled in their nervous energy.

Chapter 22

Michael's ears picked up the car's engine before the family. When they did, Mel fluttered excitedly out the gate and Ed sat up, smoothing his shirt. Becca watched her father out of the corner of her eye.

Watching their dynamic change as each new piece was introduced was intriguing. It would be incredibly uncomfortable if Michael wasn't used to politics. Not so the case for him. He'd been there when presidents and dictators were brought down for their transgressions. Family politics were easy. If anything he focused on Becca, using the opportunity to learn more about the woman who fascinated him.

Moments later, a beaming Mel rounded the gate on the arm of a young man nearly Michael's apparent age and height with Ed's dark eyes and hair color. Unlike his father, the son had grown his hair out a few inches and worn in a contrived messy style held in place by significant quantities of gel.

Kyle must have left his suit coat in his car, his gray tie was loose and his shirtsleeves rolled up. Ed rose to shake his hand when he reached them and Melanie introduced him to Becca's "friend" Captain Rossi.

"Kyle." He nodded, liking Mel's emphasis on "friend". She had her suspicions, he gathered. Michael glanced around the table at her family. For a fleeting, excruciating moment, he missed his own blood kin.

Introduced to the interloper, Kyle rounded the table to his sister already getting to her feet. "Hey Bec."

"Hey Kyle." She smiled softly at him, her eyes untroubled as she let him scoop her up in a quick hug. The family's tension, it appeared, revolved around the father.

Kyle paused at Becca's cheek. Becca sighed. "Work," she said simply. Her brother said nothing. Michael didn't find it comforting that her family so readily accepted her arrival with signs of abuse as part of her job.

Mel had kept to her feet. "Ed, could you give me a hand in the kitchen please? We can let the kids talk while we get some munchies."

Ed joined her without a sound. He walked straight backed with a hint of the limp caused by shrapnel Michael knew he carried in his leg from what his family thought was a "training accident." Michael's clearance level gave him more insight into Ed Sauter than his family had. Like his daughter he had been Special Ops, his cover was an explosives expert responsible for training new troops in the field. It explained his frequent travel and occasional scrapes.

Michael hadn't been entirely truthful when he told Becca her father would be able to read between the lines when he assigned her cover story. It was a common cover in their line of work. As for the "why" he'd done it, he'd read that unbeknownst to his daughter, Ed had requested his daughter be put on the officer's track twice in the last eighteen months. Both times she had been declined. This was Michael's way of letting her father know she had advanced up the ranks. As far as Black was concerned, it was all part of removing the human's distractions allowing her to work that much harder at her post.

Kyle kept one arm around Becca protectively. Michael remained seated, allowing himself to be assessed again by the big brother.

Becca leaned against him comfortably. "What are you doing in San Diego, Kyle?"

Shrugging, he downplayed the reason for his visit. Curiously, Michael heard his pulse quicken at her question. "Just pitching some software locally. What about you? What brings you up here?" *And with this guy*? He left that part out but his attention was fixed on Michael. Instead of having it bother him, he was pleased to see Becca had another ally here.

"I hadn't been by in a while. Figured I'd check in." She smiled at him, playfully punching his side. "You should have called." Becca lowered her voice. "I'm on leave for a couple of days. We could have hung out."

Kyle shared a conspiratorial smile. "Want to blow after happy hour? We can meet up for dinner. I can move my flight to tomorrow morning and not tell Mom and Dad."

They grinned over their secret plan. "What about you, Captain?" Kyle raised his eyes. "Would it be safe to assume you will be joining us?"

"We were going to have dinner at a little place on the coast tonight. Do you like seafood?" He lied easily.

"Fish yes, nothing with a shell though." He grinned at his sister sharing some inside joke. "Doesn't end well."

Becca enjoyed seeing her brother. It was an unexpected treat to have him here even if she did have to endure her father's constant comparisons that left her wanting. Unfortunately, with him there she was more nervous about letting something slip. Her parents let a lot of things go. Kyle, on the other hand, always knew when she wasn't telling the truth and would push her until she broke. It was how he'd found her Halloween candy every year and eaten every last piece.

"Good to know."

Kyle took the seat next to Becca, placing her in between the most important men in her life. The thought unsettled her. Yes, Michael was important but his role was a little less clear, was he her boss or her lover?

"How are the girls?" Becca leaned back to regard her brother.

Predictably, his face lit up. "Des is great. She's back to working part time at the hospital. Sometimes she picks up an extra shift here or there when another nurse wants some time off. She likes the variety and she gets to spend tons of time with the girls." Kyle fished in his pocket for his wallet and proud dad pictures. Finding what he was looking for, he slid out a recent family photo with Kyle, Desiree, Maddie and Jessica. "Wow Kyle, they're getting so big."

Becca handed it to Michael, politely bringing him into the fold. "Des is his wife, Maddie is two and Jessica is just over a year."

"They're beautiful." A pale finger traced the youngest child's profile before handing it back.

Becca heard a wistfulness in his tone that caught her unawares. She hadn't stopped to think Michael might have wanted a family before he'd had the choice taken from him. It had come up during their night together when she'd told him she was on the pill. He'd promptly told her it didn't matter. Safe sex with a vampire apparently had nothing do to with birth control.

He handed the photo back to Kyle, turning his head a fraction toward the house. Becca knew her parents were coming and climbed back into her protective shell.

Kyle heard their footsteps and dishes clattering and took control of the conversation. "So Michael, how do you know my sister?"

She listened, as curious as her family what their story was.

He smiled pleasantly and rose to help Mel take the small plates she indicated he should hand out. Ed had a bucket with beers and ice to place in the center of the table. Mel set her tray down and laid out the chips, salsa, crackers and what smelled like olive tapenade around the table for sharing.

"I met Becca a while back when she was investigating a theft on the base. She gave me her card and I faked remembering something later so I had an excuse to see her again. We both had some time off and business up this way," he rolled a shoulder, "and thought we'd share the ride." His grin was disarming.

In one fail swoop, he had given them reason to be friends, insinuated his interest and left it innocent. She was glad he left her feelings out of it. It would have been incredibly uncomfortable to have him be the first man she introduced as her boyfriend to her parents. No one ever came home, not with Ed in the house. Michael was different on a lot of levels. Becca felt forgiveness pushing aside the hurt.

Kyle reached out and grabbed a bottle, twisting the cap off before handing it to Becca. She took a grateful gulp. He did the same for Michael next, who raised his bottle and took a small pull. Kyle placed two more in front of his parents.

"Captain, huh? You aren't Navy are you?" Ed kept his voice even, not blatantly giving a clue as to what Michael and Becca both knew was derision behind the question.

"No, I'm a Marine, sir." Just the slightest pause before the "sir" warning Ed he wouldn't be intimidated.

"When are you out?"

Michael's lips twitched at his private joke. "Never sir, I'm a lifer."

Becca watched the exchange, fascinated. She hadn't known Michael was a Marine.

Their conversation was relatively free-flowing after that. Her dad was on good behavior, she didn't know if her mom had asked for her sake or if he was being good for the officer she'd brought home. No one asked too many questions about Becca's new assignment. Her father gave her a strange look without comment when she announced it.

206

After two beers, Kyle stood and stretched. "Well, I have a plane to catch."

Everyone around the table followed his lead.

"Yeah, we'd better go too." Becca smoothed her jeans with her hands. "Michael has been kind enough to put up with my personal stuff, I figure he's earned himself the rest of the afternoon off." She glanced at him, winking. Between Kyle and Michael being there this had been one of the best visits with her family she'd had in years. The beers were helping to loosen up the last shreds of resentment in her. In the end did the "why" matter so much as the "what," she thought to herself.

Michael and she had sex. Black approved. Did it matter that Black wanted her to stay if she did too? She was looking at a long career with her unit, fighting over details that would probably become unimportant in time were pointless. Just like that, she felt light.

Her mom was disappointed to lose both kids again so soon. Ed stood to shake hands with the men, making very little noise. Mel came around to hug everyone, sticking her arms out again when she came to Michael.

Becca wasn't the only one surprised by the gesture. Michael was shocked, unable to hide his reaction entirely. Her mom wasn't normally a hugger except for those people closest to her. That she folded him in like he was family spoke to her acceptance of him. Becca saw his pleasure and wondered how long it had been since he'd had a friendly hug. He put his arms around her in return.

"Michael, you're welcome here any time." She kissed his cheek.

If he could have, Becca thought Michael would have been blushing. Lack of emotional obstacles, seeing him welcomed into her family, Becca had a picture of him putting his arms around her. She felt her heart starting to accelerate and saw him glance over. She smiled shyly at him.

Kyle shook Michael's hand, hugged the girls and waved his good-byes with Mel on his arm.

Ed sat back down, nodding briefly at Becca with a quick squeeze to her arm. He shook Michael's hand again, thinking it must still be cold from holding the beer. Not a big drinker or eater, that was good these days. It showed discipline.

Becca and Michael joined Mel in the drive to wave at Kyle's car as it accelerated down the street.

"Bye Mom." Becca reached for her again, giving one last hug. It was always harder to leave her mom knowing she would be lonely when it was just the two of them. She was used to it though. Melanie had been married to Ed for over thirty years, alone for many of those to raise the kids and run the house. With him outside all the time, she virtually lived alone now.

Melanie embarrassed her daughter, taking Michael's arm and looking him in the eye with a strength of purpose most people didn't expect by her mild exterior. "Becca's special. Be good to her."

"Mom." She felt her face burning.

"I will, ma'am." Michael answered her, serious at once. "I intend to spend a very long time showing her how special she really is."

His intensity took Mel aback. Her eyes sparkled and she hugged him again.

"Thank you."

Becca opened the car door, falling in to her seat. Her blood was rushing in her ears and she felt her body responding to his emotional declaration. It was the most romantic thing anyone had ever said about her.

Michael got in, put the car in reverse and waved once more back at Mel as did Becca. They were half way up the block when his hand found hers. Her heart calmed. Her body was another story.

The car eased out to the freeway and Becca's phone rang.

"Hey Kyle." She had nearly forgotten about their agreement to meet.

"Where and when were you thinking of dinner?"

Michael heard and suggested, "The Drunken Fish".

"Never heard of it but I'm in." Kyle had heard him.

"Do you have GPS?"

"Yep. What time did you want to meet?"

Becca studied the clock in the car. It was just after six.

Michael took over. "I have something I need to do first. Can we meet at eight thirty?"

He had heard again. "Yep. I'll get a hotel for the night and wash up first. See you two there."

Perplexed, Becca hung up and turned to Michael. "What do you need to do?" She hadn't remembered him mentioning any errands.

By way of answering, he pulled the car off the freeway at the next exit. Becca glanced over and knew right away where they were going. He followed a series of turns until he came to the entrance of the Hilton. Michael threw the car in park and looked over at her, the intensity in his gaze awakening physical parts of her that hadn't forgotten his kindness. She let go of his hand and stepped out of the car, her answer clear.

Becca was very careful not to touch him again, wanting to feel her pounding heart and twisting stomach. It had nothing to do with her sight. It was more base than that. She was a woman desiring a man. She wanted to experience all of the anticipation for what she knew was coming.

She stood beside him, not speaking while he announced them as Mr. and Mrs. Rossi. Her tentative smile was returned; his eyes were growing steadily darker. Becca saw him stare at the registration clerk and he blanched, questions stopped and he handed them their plastic keys.

"I'll take care of the rest, sir," he told Michael in an even voice.

"Thank you."

Becca followed him in the elevator. "That was the fastest I've ever checked in anywhere. What did you do?"

He turned the full weight of his gaze upon her and she couldn't swallow. "I don't want to wait."

The bell dinged and they stepped out on their floor. Michael unlocked the door and opened it for her. She stepped through and felt a dizzying sense of déjà vu.

"This is familiar." She spoke to him behind her without turning. Becca felt a temporary wave of uncertainty, wondering if this was just physical for him. Her heart told her it wasn't but she had a hard time letting go of the last of her fears about his motives.

His voice was unexpectedly in her ear. "But this time you know everything. No secrets."

"None?" She held her breath. They had time to discuss feelings and futures. All that mattered was now. Heat blossomed inside her and now was no longer soon enough.

"None." His hands touched her shoulders, his lips came down and the cool tongue tracing her neck from the top of her shirt to her jaw raised goosebumps in its wake.

Her body trembled for him. She leaned back and felt her heart steady while her desire raged. She moaned as her body caught fire.

He reached up under her arms to cup her breasts in his hands, pinching them roughly. Michael slid his hands firmly down her sides, sweeping over her stomach and stopping at the inside of her thighs, already slick with anticipation. Growling, he pulled her back into him. His equal desire was clear from the pressure against her back. Becca twisted in his arms, needing to wrap herself around him. She couldn't get close enough, his body pressed against hers made her desperate for him.

He picked her up and she coiled herself around him. Backing her up to the wall, Michael used it to keep her pressed tight to him. Freed, his hands ran down her body, taking the hem of her shirt and pulling it up over her head. Becca eagerly did the same. Their flesh touched, his cool skin burning into hers until she couldn't think clearly.

Hands and mouths explored until Becca wasn't the only one moaning. All at once, Michael stopped and pulled away, letting her slide down his body. Questioning, Becca blinked up at him, fearful she had done something wrong. That this wasn't going to happen. But before she could voice her questions he scooped her up and carried her to the bed. Changing gears and easing their pace to a torturous crawl, he kissed his way down her body, slowly working her jeans over her hips to slide them down her legs. The way he watched her eyes, gauging her reactions as he kissed her with little flicks of his tongue on his descent brought Becca nearly to the brink. She could feel the wetness between her legs and

211

rubbed her thighs together, needing him but too self-conscious to say. There was no need; he sensed her predicament. Standing up, he removed his pants and shorts with impressive speed. Becca watched his eyes flaring between dark blue and black. He was struggling to keep his fangs in, his other side hidden.

"It's okay," she said quietly. "Don't be ashamed of who you are with me."

Carefully he lowered himself to the bed, trapping her within his arms resting heavily on either side of her body, his dog tags lying cold on her chest. "I'm not ashamed, I'm afraid. I can barely control myself around you on a good day and the sun today made it worse."

She reached up to wrap her arms around his neck, pulling him close enough to kiss him, this time slower and with more behind it than just passion.

He pulled back, breaking her hold but letting her see how she effected him. Up close without hiding. The intimacy of the gesture more powerful than any words he could have uttered. "I'm not just worried that I'll hurt you," he confessed, "I don't want to drive you away."

"You won't." She put her arms around his neck again and he let her pull him down to her.

Reaching a hand down to where their bodies met he touched her, dipping a finger inside and pulling it out, circling while he used his thumb to rub her clit. Becca's mouth fell open and she gasped in rapturous agony as her body arched. With a whimper, Becca clutched his shoulders and spoke, "please." And with a growl, Michael removed his hand and drove himself inside her. At the change in sensation and the feeling of fullness Becca shouted. He kissed her as his steady strokes made her his, both of them knowing this time would be for good. She climaxed quickly and yet he continued. Pushing, licking and biting until her cries again reached a crescendo. The vampire clawed its way up, licking its lips as it began to ride them both.

Just as she reached orgasm again and felt Michael's body go rigid with his, she felt a sharp sting on her chest above her breast. Glimpsing down she saw two puncture marks, blood welling at the surface and Michael's look of absolute horror.

Staring at them, Michael apologized profusely. "I'm sorry Becca. I shouldn't have tried to be with you when I'm hungry. I never wanted to feed from you." He started to push away from her, ashamed of what he'd done.

But Becca didn't want him to leave her. She tightened her arms around him, keeping him on top of her.

"It's okay." Michael had always been in such complete control of himself, that she could drive him to lose control of himself flattered her. She'd never thought of herself as much of a lover, then again she hadn't been able to be truly intimate with any of her few partners. "I liked it."

He gaped, incredulous. "You like that I bit you?"

Becca smiled lazily, her body moved against his suggestively, not wanting to let him go. "Not especially. But I liked that you trusted me enough to let go. If that's all the worse you're going to do to me when you lose control, I can live with that. I told you before, I know you aren't going to hurt me."

His expression softened and Becca saw that he had been as lacking as she had in close relationships. He was a lost soul just like her.

They made love again, slower this time. When he lay down beside her, stroking her hair, Michael kissed her deeply. "Do you *need* to eat?"

A deep laugh bubbled up from Becca's chest. "Yes, and I want to see my brother. But we're coming back here afterward."

Michael grinned.

***

The Drunken Fish was a casual boutique restaurant on the water just up the coast. The lights were low, intimate. Also, Becca noticed, the tablecloths were assorted fabric remnants in nautical themes. Instead of being kitchy it catered to the illusion that the diners were on someone's porch ready to enjoy a fresh, home cooked meal.

"How does a vampire know about a seafood place?" Becca asked, nearly too low for her own ears. She had seen Michael's version of feeding in the car on the way over. It hadn't bothered her when she looked at it analytically. He was on a liquid diet, his food came in a bag.

He hadn't wanted to eat in front of her but after the display in the room, he could put it off no longer without risking a more serious incident. Michael ate quickly, drinking from a tube connected to a plastic bag not quite opaque enough to obscure the color for her tastes. He'd continued to shoot her guarded glances, expecting to see disgust. He never did.

His thumb rubbed the back of her hand entwined in his. "Because I have a wide and varied social circle."

She gave his fingers a gentle squeeze.

"I do. I meet with businessmen as well as people on both sides of the law. You should come along some time, it would give you an idea of how we function when we're not kicking asses." A shadow crossed his eyes. "And why we're a necessary part of this government, even if we are invisible."

"I know there are shady sorts. You aren't the only one who's seen things they didn't want to. My visions don't

214

usually involve birthday parties and pink ponies." Becca's expression was grim.

Michael leaned over and put his lips to her ear. "Now you're in a position to do something about it. You'll do great things with us, Becca." He kissed the top of her ear, curving his lips at the shiver he produced.

"You're awfully pleased with yourself, aren't you?" She was giving serious consideration to calling off dinner in favor of an evening in when he chuckled his reply.

"As a matter of fact I am." He indicated the tables in front of them with a jut of his chin. "Better behave, our date's here."

Michael straightened and Becca saw Kyle already seated toward the back of the restaurant with a table next to the floor to ceiling windows facing the ocean. The breeze coming off the water was chilly and the restaurant had closed the upper parts of the windows accordingly. As a result, most of the diners could only hear the roar of the surf distantly. Michael heard it perfectly.

He could also tell that Kyle's contrived outward pleasantness was contrived. The smile on his face was forced, presumably for the benefit of his sister. His jaw worked nervously, brow furrowed.

Becca saw enough evidence of her brother's upset even without hearing his conversation. A frown formed as she sat down in the chair Michael offered. Pushing it in, he took the one next to her.

He was careful not to touch her as he leaned over, half his ear on the phone call and the other for Becca. They were getting close enough for him to make out some of the conversation. "Vibes?"

She twisted to look him full in the face and whispered appalled, "About my brother?"

Michael was hearing enough to tell Becca she didn't know her brother as well as she thought she did, except he didn't want to be the one to burst her bubble. He shrugged and kept listening.

Kyle held out a finger to them, making an attempt at an apologetic eye-widening and stood, walking a few feet from the table. Their table was far enough from the other tables Kyle didn't have to go far to feel he had some privacy. That would have been true if it weren't for Michael's hearing.

Kyle's voice was low. He uttered a warning to the other end. "I told you I *will* sell the software. When I do, I'll have the money for you just be patient."

The voice on the other line was female and not human by the sound of her cadence. Vampires and humans had different speech patterns and not just the old vampires who had learned to speak in other times and countries. It was due to the different manner in which a reanimated body utilized itself. Their bodies were more efficient and could bypass other systems, which explained the strength, sight, all of it. Not a lot got in the way once a system was streamlined.

No pain receptors or fatigue meant they had more muscle endurance and power; less of the brain devoted to normal body functions meant more resources could be devoted to senses giving them hypersensitivity. Vampires' speech worked much the same way. Their vocal chords could vibrate much faster giving them a broader spectrum allowing them to speak lower and higher than most humans.

The phenomenon of rock stars captivating and seducing humans on a grand scale wasn't so mysterious if one understood what some really were. It also explained why so many switched partners often and "died" early. They had to move on before anyone paid too much attention to their "fast lifestyle" of no food or sleep, drugs and excessive alcohol use, their appetite for immediate physical gratification running unchecked.

The female vampire speaking to Kyle was old by her timbre, and very angry. "I won't tell you again Mr. Sauter, you sell that program to whom I say. No questions."

Kyle's eyes shifted to his party, both seeming to be enjoying the view. But Michael was completely focused upon the conversation between the mystery vampire and Kyle.

He turned his back to them and whispered hotly. "I told you, *he* found *me*. What does it matter if I hear him out? He's coming to my office tomorrow afternoon."

"It matters because you have a specific market and I do not want to see you selling to anyone else," she explained as if to a child. "Now do as you are told and you may have your life back."

The caller hung up and Kyle lowered the phone. He took several deep, steadying breaths before returning to the table. Becca's eyes held only concern for her brother as she studied him. He was pale and sweat beaded his forehead. Frenetic hands wiped across his head.

"Is everything okay, Kyle? Are the girls okay?"

His eyes went wide. "The girls? Yes, they're fine." He worked to calm his heart rate; Michael smelled the sweat continuing to run down his back and under his arms. "It was just work. We're on a pretty big project and there's a lot of pressure to wrap things up."

"Well I hope you can work it out, you don't look very good."

Kyle smiled tightly at her. "Thanks Bec." Abruptly, he changed the course of the conversation. "So Michael, this is your place. Tell us what's good." He picked up the menu the server had left for him.

Becca watched him cautiously before picking up hers up as well. She couldn't resist and her eyes sparkled with amusement at Michael. "Yes Michael, do tell me what is your favorite thing to eat here."

Michael neatly tucked his suspicions under his hat and twisted his lips at Becca before answering from memory. "The macadamia encrusted Mahi Mahi is probably the best item on the menu. I've also heard good things about the snapper in leek butter sauce. Kyle, I know you don't do shellfish but if you wanted good lobster or crab, Becca, this is the place."

The server arrived and Kyle indicated Michael should take the wine list. Amenably, he did and selected a Pinot Gris that would go with virtually any of the lighter fish selections he had recommended. Both Kyle and Becca confirmed they would choose one of his recommendations.

"If you two will excuse me." Michael stood, smiling at Becca. "I have a phone call to make and it would give you two some family time." He saw the uncertainty flicker in her eyes when he mentioned the phone call. He wished he could influence her to force her to believe him, sadly her immunity was making him have to do it the old fashioned way. He had to *earn* her trust. Smiling his reassurance, he squeezed her hand and saw her eyes relax at the corners. "It's just business."

Alone, Kyle was a little more himself and nodded at Becca. "So, something you want to tell me that you couldn't say in front of Mom and Dad?"

Michael had gone back to the entrance to the bathroom hallway and turned in time to watch her blush as he pulled out his phone to pretend to make his call. He adored her human side, finding it a perfect combination of pleasure and torment to watch her blood rise to the surface when she was embarrassed. He felt his fangs start to slide and carefully willed them back in.

When Becca didn't answer, Kyle pressed her. "Come on. I saw you two walking in. How long has *that* been going on?" His curious brown eyes flicked from her to Michael looking for his answer.

She darted a few furtive glances at Michael who pretended not to notice as he searched his contact list. She looked down at her hands, wondering if he could hear over the chatter and distance. "What? Michael and I work together."

Kyle snorted. "Do you make cow eyes at all of your coworkers? That's one way to make officer."

Becca's adrenaline surged as her anger flowed through her. "Kyle, that was a cheap shot and you know it."

Brother or no, Michael wanted to throttle the prick for insinuating his sister would sleep her way through the ranks.

Kyle's hand messed up his hair. "Bec, I'm sorry. I don't know why I said that. I'm an idiot and I'm freaking out about work." He smiled at her and Michael saw her frame loosen.

"I know you didn't mean it." She sighed, "Things just kind of happened, and with him being my superior officer it's not something I want Dad to know about. He wouldn't understand."

"I won't tell." Kyle meant it. His body exhibited no signs of deception. His gaze flicked over to where Michael stood, pretending to be absorbed in his call. "He seems like an alright guy. A little odd maybe, but okay. Do you like him?"

Michael's senses trained on her. He saw her glance up and held her eyes, sending her a smile.

With a visible effort, she pulled her eyes back to her brother and answered. "More than I've ever liked anyone. He gets me and he doesn't care about any of my hang-ups."

Kyle's mouth tightened at what he assumed was her mention of her sight. Michael had wondered how or if the family ever talked about that. It would appear it was only discussed in passing and it was definitely not considered a good thing.

"I don't want to say anything that might scare him, but I think I love him," she whispered, leaning in so he was the only one to hear her confession.

When she looked back up at Michael, he had to duck his head. He knew he couldn't hide his feelings. The woman he coveted, who had stirred so many long-dead emotions within him, loved him. He felt himself redeemed after an extraordinarily long period of self-doubt. He'd long believed himself unworthy of the blood he took to survive. Blood given by servicemen as mandatory monthly "donations." Theirs was a sacrifice given that he was sure they would abhor were they to find out the monsters it sustained.

Now to have this wonderful creature, this wonderful *human* creature, so good and caring validate him. Not the work he did, but him as an individual, it rendered him hers completely and totally. He knew that he loved her as well.

Watching his sister smiling at the captain, Kyle was happy for her. He also wondered, as he had earlier, if he could get a meeting somehow with the USMC through this Captain Rossi of hers. Kyle's call earlier rejuvenated the pressure on him to sell this software to the right buyer. He might have faster results if Michael was well connected and could get him through the proper channels to the right guys quickly.

His firm was well respected enough to get a meeting but it was a long, arduous process to get a government contract and Kyle needed this sale now before the biggest mistake of his life ruined his marriage.

He still couldn't understand how it had happened. Kyle was used to attractive women hitting on him. It came with the territory when a man was successful and young. His wife even insisted he was attractive. He never had trouble saying no yet when it had come to this one, he had not.

It had been the strangest thing. She seduced him at their New Year's Eve cocktail party when Des stayed home with the girls, too ill for a sitter.

Not only had Kyle been sick over the one nightstand, but then the woman had resurfaced last month demanding payment of a quarter of a million dollars or she would show his wife the pictures. Pictures! Kyle had freaked.

Her interest in his business had been genuine. She had asked numerous questions about his software programs and he had been foolish enough to tell her about his package designed to streamline companies' abilities to track purchases online. It was their biggest product thus far in its wide-ranging scope and data compiling capabilities. Their goal was to sell it to companies like Amazon or ebay to better follow up with additional sales that suited the buyer's tastes. He had also let her try it out while he went downstairs to the bar to retrieve the champagne room service could easily have brought up.

When their interlude had concluded, she'd informed him he *had* to sell it to the government. Frighteningly, he found she had some strange power over him. When he was with her he couldn't hear his own will. Then, as soon as he was away from her and he could think for himself again, he was mortified at what he agreed to do for her. Really though, even without her power over him he would do whatever it took to save his marriage and spare his children losing their father or worse. Kyle had no doubts about her willingness to harm his girls if it came to it.

Becca watched Michael's return to the table and straightened in her chair. She wondered if he could have heard what she said to Kyle. There was so much noise in here, she doubted it. Having actually said the words out loud that had been floating around her subconscious for days, no longer causing her pain at believing they'd been unjustified, she found it harder to hide her feelings for him. As he approached, she beamed at him.

"Did you two have a nice brother-sister chat?" Michael inquired with an innocent grin as he put his napkin in his lap. He leaned in and slid his lips along her cheek in a passing kiss as he took her hand under the table.

Becca gasped at the sensation. When he touched her, her senses were aflame. She didn't know if that was because of what he was or because of how she felt; only that it was mind-blowing. Since they had first made love she had been in tune with him, now after this last time she could almost sense him wherever he was.

"We did." Becca answered with a smile.

The server brought the wine. They ordered and were left to talk before their meal arrived.

Kyle took a gulp of his wine and casually inquired into Michael's military rank and chain of command.

"So you directly report to an admiral?" He was pretty sure that was unusual. "What did you say you did again?"

When Becca questioned his curiosity, worried he would get too close to the truth, Kyle laughed.

"What?" He put his hands out palms up, shrugging. "I'm just trying to find out more about my sister's new boyfriend."

Becca blushed; she hadn't put the term to Michael and somehow it seemed sophomoric to call it that.

"It's okay," Michael reassured her. "I've had people feel me out before, I think I can handle it."

He explained that he worked on a security detail, specifically in a special investigative unit, or SIU based at NAS Miramar with frequent trips to other military installments worldwide. He directly reported to an admiral who had the ear of Homeland Security and the NSA.

Kyle was duly impressed, making Becca proud. She enjoyed watching her brother chat up Michael while she sipped her wine.

Their meals arrived. They smelled and looked fantastic. Kyle and Becca both had chosen the Mahi Mahi, Michael the Snapper with a promise to let Becca try it.

While Kyle and Becca chewed their first bites, delicious by the looks of pleasure on both faces, Michael took a sip of wine. "I know Becca is too humble to tell you herself, so I wanted to let you know. She so impressed us when our professional paths crossed, that we began recruiting her at once for a place with our unit."

Becca stopped chewing. She was glad to have a mouthful of food as he went on. Kyle glanced back and forth between them.

Michael raised his glass. "I'm pleased to say it's official. She has agreed to join our unit and will be promoted to captain when her probation period ends in thirty days." Calmly he swallowed a mouthful from his glass.

"Captain?" Kyle repeated excitedly. "Bec, why didn't you tell Dad? He's gonna be pumped."

She stared at Michael, his calm demeanor helping her to ease the untruth through her lips. "I didn't want to say anything until it was official." It was easier than usual.

"Well, I'm happy for you, Becca. Things are going really well for you."

She couldn't agree more. They finished their meals and Kyle asked Michael if he could exchange numbers.

"In case I need to find you and you're traveling. It's always nice to have another point of contact," he assured Becca with a shrug when she gave him an odd look.

Kyle never saw the bill appear. Becca smiled at his confusion, knowing Michael had snatched it off the table before Kyle was aware it had arrived. Together they left the restaurant, stopping outside the front door.

"I'm proud of you, Bec." He hugged her and added in her ear, "He's a decent guy. You could do worse." And kissed her cheek, straightening up. "Give Dad a call about the promotion." Kyle smiled and slapped her arm. "Gloat a little, you've earned it."

Kyle stuck his hand out to Michael. "You're good people, Michael. Watch out for my little sister."

"Will do, Kyle."

***

"Captain?" Becca rolled her eyes when they were in the car. "That was a nice touch."

He turned the key and the engine roared to life. "About that." He stopped mid-motion as his hand rested on the gearshift. "That part's true. All of us are captains, it's the only way it works."

"What?" Disbelieving, Becca turned on him.

"Didn't I tell you that?"

She threw a half-hearted and easily deflected punch to his arm. "No, you did not. Besides, what does it mean if everyone is the same rank?"

He turned his face to her conveying his sincerity. "It means *everything* to be the same rank when you are all equally capable of destroying each other. The only reason I was voted lead is because no one else wanted to have to report to Admiral Black." He twitched his hand under hers to put the car in reverse. "And there's that whole full moon thing. *I* can be fully functional *all* month." Never mind he was the only one stuck with Black for all of eternity. Not that that was common knowledge. It could be dangerous in the wrong hands.

Vampire bonds had been used in the past to bring down powerful clans, which was why they were rare now. Most vampires were loners, preferring to take their chances moving around often and remaining under the radar from other supernatural creatures. With all of the old treaties and allegiances mostly defunct now after borders and lands had changed hands so often from human involvement it was, for all intents and purposes, a supernatural free for all. A number of them felt their lot would improve significantly if another group had its numbers reduced. All the more reason for the admiral's unit to exist so that none could grow too powerful and humans could not be alerted nor affected by their deadly power struggles.

The intricacies of this bigger picture were unknown to Becca. Thus far she only knew generalities. In time she too would learn all of the details encompassing this new service she had been pressed into. And Michael was sworn to protect her, as bound to her in heart as he was to Black in soul.

Becca couldn't believe what she was hearing. "So I'll be a captain even without going through OCS or getting a commission?"

He gave her a look. "Who do we answer to? Do you think the admiral cares what your file says? You will earn your title by merit instead of schooling; I hope that's acceptable to you." Michael put the car in drive.

"Yes. Yes it is." Becca sat back, letting her head take it all in.

Chapter 23

The prospect of forty-eight hours' leave spent in a room with a vampire who happened to be coming off of an even more severe sexual drought than her left Becca grinning from ear to ear with anticipation.

When they arrived back at their room, she had excused herself to the bathroom to freshen up when Michael's phone rang.

He stared at the caller ID, disappointed that he had known this was coming, before answering. "Yes, I can talk."

Becca knew from his tone it wasn't Black and paid little attention in her stroll through the suite. Pulling her other pair of jeans out of her shopping bag, she carried them and a change of clothes into the bathroom. In light of where they were, her only concern for his call was that it be brief. However, no sooner had she shut the door than her stomach twisted, her knees buckled, and sweat beaded her upper lip. She barely made it to the toilet before her dinner came back up.

When she emerged, Michael wore a troubled expression. He hid his eyes from her. "Are you all right?"

She stared at him, willing him to look at her. "You can't go." Her sight was in full upheaval. "Whoever that was, tell him no."

He muttered quietly, "I have to." He glanced up at her pale face. "I should get you back."

Becca wanted to scream. He was hiding something. Something with that phone call was very bad and he wasn't going to share it with her. Her entire purpose in this unit was to keep them from harm. What good was she if he didn't listen?

"If you go you're putting yourself in serious danger," Becca tried to reason with him.

She knew it without a doubt. Her sight was screaming at her that something horrible was happening and that it was warning her not for her safety, but for his. That call heralded great danger for *Michael* and he wasn't willing to take her warning. Whatever was happening, he was trying to keep it from her. However, he couldn't keep away the terrible sadness and dread she was feeling. Becca was not going to let him get himself killed. It was that simple.

He cautiously avoided her eyes, watching his hand as he tucked her hair behind her ear. "It was a contact of mine and he has some information for me. He can only meet today," Michael checked his watch, barely glancing at its face, "in an hour."

Becca's knees were trembling. Lightning was dancing behind her eyes, bright spots blasting holes in her vision. She sank down on the bed, momentarily weakened by the power of her sight. Using it seemed to be making it stronger. She had to push it away so that she could function. "Please, it isn't safe," she pleaded.

He offered her a sad smile. "I have to. Rain check on our evening?"

"Why don't we stop on the way back?" She felt her hopes momentarily lift. If she was with him for his meeting she could better isolate the source of the threat. "We're sharing a ride, remember?"

"You can take the car back. I'll go on foot."

She had no idea how far or fast Michael could make it on foot. Judging by how quickly she'd seen him move short distances, she assumed it was a lot. Without any helpful parameters, there was no way to accurately predict where his meeting might be or track him without his knowledge. Frustrated, she crossed her arms.

"Well, you'd better go then." Becca glanced up at him, catching a hint of something on his face before he hid it away again. Had it been regret? Did he *know* the danger he was putting himself in when he ignored her like this? He had sworn no more secrets and she believed him on a personal level. That left a gaping hole for *work* secrets.

"Right. I'll see you back at the estate." His hand was on the knob and he let himself out without another word.

Becca cleaned up her things, dropping her shopping bag three times and tearing it when it caught on the corner of the dresser she didn't see because of a blind spot. "Shit!" She felt frustrated tears prick her eyes. A glance in the bathroom for anything else and she threw the key cards on the bed behind her. Becca was at a dead run when she hit the front door.

Fine, she couldn't follow him. That didn't mean she had to let him go off alone when she knew something was going to happen. Becca was going to find him and she had an idea who to turn to for help. Herself. With a quick stop for weapons, of course.

Chapter 24

By some miracle, Becca didn't get stopped by the Highway Patrol on the way home. She had driven eighty and above the entire way back with the windows down and blinking profusely. If anyone had seen her they probably would have thought she was stoned off her ass.

"Where's the fire?" Ryan met her at the door. No spark in his eyes and his mouth was forced into a shadow of his playful smile. Ryan knew something and he wasn't offering it up.

There wasn't time for witty banter. "I have a headache, I'm going to lay down." Her feet carried her directly to her room where three brown boxes sat stacked against the far wall. Her few personal things had arrived.

It was nearly midnight; there was no need to darken the room. Becca flopped down on the bed, hands pressed palms down on her eyes to rush her visions toward her. When nothing came right away, she wanted to scream. Frustrated, she balled her hands into fists striking the bed beneath her.

"Well that's juvenile."

Becca hadn't heard the door open. "Remind me to fix the hinges so that thing squeaks." She sat up.

Gabrielle wore street clothes, fitted jeans that hugged her hips low and tight topped with a blue camisole barely brushing the tops of her jeans. She pushed off and approached; Becca held her breath in anticipation. Gabrielle stalked, her eyes focused on her prey. The animal waited close beneath the skin.

"What do you need, Gabrielle?" Becca's rising panic made her voice quake and she desperately wanted to get back to her vision quest. Gabrielle freaking her out wasn't going to help. "I'm kind of tired."

Undaunted by the less than warm reception, she sat beside Becca on the bed. Her amber eyes were hard and cold. "I was downstairs cleaning my equipment a little while ago when Black got a call from Michael. Can you tell me what business they might have that requires a meeting at two a.m.? Alone? I heard mention of your old stomping grounds." Her eyes narrowed. "Working a side deal already, are you?"

Becca felt the surging pain in her head and her spots doubled. Michael was bringing the admiral in? Nothing good could come of that. Whether the admiral was the source of the danger or the caller, Becca knew she had to help. She took a desperate chance, hoping she could trust Gabrielle.

"Michael is meeting with someone, he says an informant but it doesn't feel right. He got the call about an hour ago and left the hotel." She saw Gabrielle's brow rise at her mention of the accommodations and didn't have time to be embarrassed. "He's in trouble. I felt it the second he got the call."

Gabrielle studied her, blinked once and was on her feet before Becca saw her move. "Let's go. I'll drive."

Becca stood up, cursing her painfully human speed. "What about Ryan?"

Gabrielle hesitated for a fraction of a second. "We don't need him. We'll be back before we're missed." She winked mirthlessly. "Girls' night out."

Becca followed her departing figure, jogging to keep up. Instead of heading out the front door to the car she had left there with the keys in it, Gabrielle went down the hall to the kitchen where she made an abrupt left turn upon entering the storeroom. The memory of Michael hanging broken and bloodied sent an ominous chill up her spine.

There was a door Becca hadn't noticed when she'd been in there. It was no mystery considering what all she'd seen in there. Pushing everything else aside, Becca focused solely on making sure Michael was safe. Nothing else mattered.

The door flew open in front of her and Gabrielle disappeared into the darkness. Becca smelled gasoline and oil. "Are we in a garage?"

A light went on overhead and Gabrielle stood on the other side of the door, her hand lingering on the switch.

"You didn't think we had just the one car, did you?" Her affront was contrived. "Your lack of faith in our budget is disappointing."

Shrugging, Becca admitted, "I guess I hadn't really thought about it." Her eyes scanned the expansive space that appeared to have been carved out of the hill behind the estate. It would have to be at least a ten car garage. She could see several Chargers which blended in with the fleet vehicles used on the local bases, two SUV's, a jeep and some other smaller vehicles not clearly visible beyond the tall roof of the big Suburban in the back.

"Come on." Gabrielle had disappeared while Becca had been gawking. Her voice called from the far end of the space.

She followed the sound and found what the Suburban was hiding. Gabrielle straddled a motorcycle. She couldn't tell what kind, only that it looked unsteady and sure to kill the human.

Sitting astride the massive black death machine, zipping up a leather coat, Gabrielle was growing impatient. "Come on. Let's go."

"No way. I don't do bikes." She shook her head and took a step backward.

Unphased, Gabrielle tossed her the helmet resting on the gas tank and pulled her own off of her lap. "Don't be a baby.

We need to get there fast and this is our best bet." She let her eyes heat up, their intensity mesmerizing.

Michael's influence failed to work on her. Not so with the werewolves it seemed. Becca felt the pull. She wanted to be with her, even if it meant a fast, dangerous ride on something better referred to as a death trap.

"Bec, if you think something is going down with Michael and the admiral, and you have a bad feeling, then honestly we don't have a lot of time. The words "bad" and "Admiral Black" when put together usually means *very* bad. He *never* leaves here unless it's serious." With a blink she released Becca's will.

When Becca snatched the helmet from Gabrielle, she snapped, "Don't look so smug."

"Why not?" She brought the engine to life with a roar and pressed a button opening the door behind them. "I won."

Becca felt someone behind her and turned to cast a glance over her shoulder as they sped out the open door. Ryan stood, hand on the door with an uncharacteristically furious look on his face, the air shimmering around him.

Chapter 25

They made amazing time. Gabrielle had no regard for laws whatsoever and her sensitive reflexes allowed her to handle the bike in a way that would have made a stunt driver weep. They flew past mile markers and other cars so fast any details other than general glimpses of color were lost.

When they arrived at the south gate, Gabrielle showed her military ID to the guardsman who looked expectantly at Becca's helmet. She still had her shield down and he couldn't identify her. She recognized him.

She twisted her head to Gabrielle's other shoulder. "If he ID's me we're going to get hauled in for questioning. We don't have time and Black can't get us out if he's tied up." The knotting in her stomach and dancing vision flared in agreement. She had nearly lost her functional sight.

The engine roared and the guard reached out to miss the handlebars by a hair as Gabrielle shot the bike forward and around the guard arm. Becca was suddenly grateful for her push to take the highly maneuverable bike.

Their time was limited now that their presence was known. The base was huge; where the meeting was taking place was unknowable. Gabrielle slowed her speed and leaned the bike toward the airstrip and hangars.

It made sense. Most of military life after basic training took on a similar pattern to office life. The buildings closed in the evening and staff went home. The hangars would be no exception but they were far enough from the rest of the buildings that lights and activity could remain relatively undetected.

Becca was trying hard to stimulate a vision to no avail. Still she pushed. Her eyes were closed, her immediate surroundings had fallen away, no longer a concern. Then, as soon as Gabrielle committed to the path aimed at the hangar, Becca's body reacted violently.

Her vision went completely black and then came back, not a vision exactly. It felt different than they usually did, less ephemeral. It almost had a physical dimension to it, like she could turn the corner and come upon the scene. This vision was fully fleshed out in perfect detail, no white space or blurred edges. Fascinated, she watched in wonder.

She saw the interior of a familiar building. The safety lights were on as they always were, 24/7. The metal racking rose up on all sides, weapons of all types sat in crates awaiting deployment.

Her eyes were on Admiral Black's side as she walked next to him. Gasping in amazement, Becca realized what she was seeing. Through whose eyes she was watching the scene unfold. Had she tapped into something when she'd focused so hard on just him? It wasn't possible. A shadow moved in front of them and her breath caught in her chest. Her stomach lurched and she knew what had caused the violence of her reaction at the hotel.

"Kyle," she whispered in fear. Then, much louder, "Gab, the weapons supply. They're at the weapons supply." Panic clutched at her heart. "Hurry."

The motorcycle lurched beneath her as Gabrielle abruptly switched direction. They slowed to a near crawl, the engine quietly bringing them within a half a mile of the building's doors where Gabrielle hid it behind the dumpster outside.

Helmets off, Gabrielle motioned for Becca to take the lead.

"You're our best bet to find them."

Tightening her lips, Becca closed her eyes and breathed in and out. Her heart was hammering in her ears and her mind jumped frenetically from thought to thought. Aggravated, Becca gritted her teeth and pinched her eyes shut tight forcing her mind to focus on Michael. Solely on Michael.

As soon as she thought his name she felt a physical tug at her gut. Mind reeling from having to exist in two places, Becca took a deep breath, set her shoulders and let herself go.

The second she stopped trying to control her vision, Becca's head cleared and her feet carried her forward to where her instinct told her Michael was. Gabrielle followed close behind as she led the way through the maze of aisles and racks full of arms and munitions, across to the far end of the warehouse where the larger guns were stored.

Focused on Michael's scene, Becca forgot to look where she was going and tripped over a piece of a wooden crate. The combination of speed and obstacle sent her spinning to the concrete floor.

Picking herself up off the ground, she wiped her palms off on her jeans, leaving a small smear of blood behind. Without delay Becca began moving again, letting her feet carry her blindly forward through the tall doors standing open to the night. She would take the time later to figure out how to use both of her sets of "eyes." For now she was more concerned about saving the two men she loved from something horrible.

Gabrielle's hand reached out and grabbed her arm, stopping her at the edge of the tall steel shelving. Halted, Becca once again took control of her body and her eyes. It took a moment for her eyes to adjust. She saw nothing at first in the dim lighting and then Gabrielle's head was just beside hers, whispering "there, by the fifties," as she pointed to the fifty caliber guns waiting to be mounted on a mobile unit. They sat on the concrete floor where the racking ended and the warehouse floor was open for some of the larger weaponry.

Becca could easily pick out the tall, thin form she recognized as Admiral Black wearing his dress blues. On his other side, Michael was in his dress uniform as well. Black must have brought it for him, she thought in passing. She took a breath to steady herself, the abruptness of the change between sights had been physically unsettling and her stomach hadn't fully recovered from the messages her sight was sending.

When she exhaled strongly, she swore Michael's head twitched in her direction. His face remained impassive.

"Be still," Gabrielle warned in a whisper. The air moving past Becca's ear tickled.

The men stood maybe ten yards away, Becca strained to hear. A female voice spoke from the darkness, her silhouette partially hidden behind the guns.

"Admiral Black,"she drew his name out. "Thank you for agreeing to meet with me so quickly. As Captain Rossi might have explained, one of our employees stole the program and is trying to beat us to market. I am under some pressure from the other partners in the firm to sell our software package before that happens. That makes it a challenge to go through the usual channels."

"Why's she lying? Nobody stole anything."

Becca's impulsive remark drew a rough elbow from Gabrielle. "Control yourself, damn it," she hissed.

Her brother broke in from beside the shadow lady. "Captain Rossi has told me your department would be interested in the tracking portion of the software though we might need to tailor it to better suit your unique needs." Kyle was staring at Black, the whites of his eyes showing his nerves even in the low light.

"Introduce us to your partner." Black's voice was even.

Kyle stepped back, a tall figure suddenly stood beside him in the light. Her dark hair created a curtain hiding much of her face. All that was visible from where Becca and Gabrielle crouched was half of her bone white face standing shoulder to shoulder with her brother, easily making the woman six feet. Her appearance sent Becca's sight into overdrive. Her willowy figure was encased in black tights, heeled boots extending all the way to her knees and a fitted turtleneck sweater covered by a black pea coat.

Each minute, Becca's vision was becoming more obscured by the flashes threatening to completely obliterate her view. It was like trying to drive into a defensive line of oncoming traffic all flashing their brights.

A feminine voice, as ice cold as Black's, cut through the tense silence. "This is unexpected. Mr. Sauter, do you have any idea who you have brought me?" She stared at Admiral Black. "You have in fact found the most elusive man in the United States military. Most of them won't even admit they've heard his name, they think of him as a sort of boogey man." The side of her lips they could see curved up in a smirk.

Kyle's face swung from the woman with him to the men in front of him. "What do you mean? *Him*?" His surprise spoke of an underestimation of Admiral Black Becca wouldn't have thought possible considering her own visceral reaction to him.

The admiral spoke quietly, his voice carrying through the cavernous space. "Mr. Sauter, I believe it is time for you to go."

Chapter 26

Kyle was staring at the admiral. From the loaded silence, Becca knew the admiral was influencing him.

"I should go," Kyle agreed flatly.

Except when he started to walk away, the woman spoke sharply. "Stop."

He did.

"This one is mine. I prefer to keep him close."

Becca clapped her hand over her mouth to keep from being heard as she began to hyperventilate. Kyle belonged to her, what did she mean? And her interest in her unit leader had set Becca's teeth on edge. The ball in her stomach roiled.

"She's a vampire," she whispered.

"Duh," Gabrielle replied sarcastically. "Now shut up."

"But my brother." She couldn't tear her eyes away from Kyle, standing frozen and entranced in the space between the vampires. Becca prayed there wouldn't be any weapons fire, or a need for a snack.

"What do you want with him?" asked the admiral calmly. "You have made the connections you seek. The product is now in my hands."

The sexy vampire smiled. Becca felt the hair rise on the back of her neck. This was going to end badly. And now she had two dogs in the fight. Even the admiral had his value to her. "Better the devil you know," she thought darkly.

She answered coolly, "I find him useful and entertaining. Their kind is so concerned with unimportant minutiae. Sometimes I forget the guilt a transgression can induce. He has been easily directed with the mere threat of exposure to

238

his wife." Again she chuckled. "So petty, his concerns." Her head turned toward the darkness where Becca and Gabrielle crouched behind the container on the lowest rack.

Michael spoke sharply. "Why did you call this meeting? What is it you're after?"

Becca had pulled back to hide completely behind the container, fearing someone might have sensed her.

"It appears the human and I have a common goal. He needs to sell his software and I would like for you to buy it. I'm merely acting as a matchmaker."

"And your interest in this software is?" The admiral left Michael to handle most of the talking.

"That's not your concern. My request for you to purchase the software and load it on your system is a simple one. It is not too much to ask, is it?" The woman purred.

Michael's doubt was clear. "What do you stand to profit by this exchange?"

"The admiral here is going to pay me two hundred and fifty thousand dollars. My time is worth something after all."

"Why have you directed him to sell only to the military?"

Her hesitation was minute, and enough to announce her deceit. "It is a tracking program. I feel it would behoove us to track the humans who pose a threat to us rather than to waste such technology on the private sector." She spread her hands harmlessly. "I thought that would be right up your alley, Admiral."

"So you're giving us virtual radio collars for any human we deem suspicious?" Michael didn't sound convinced. "You'll excuse me for not being moved by your selflessness."

"Why should we not have an advantage? If it is available we should take it." A hint of emotion crept into her eerie voice. "If we could track those who move against us, we could better defend ourselves against attacks both from humans and creatures who wish to eradicate our numbers."

Becca risked poking her head out past the corner of the wooden container. No one was looking her direction any more. Her nerves were making her palms sweat and she wiped them on her jeans. Why would any of their number want to fight amongst themselves? Were they so similar to different human populations? There was so much she needed to learn. Becca sighed softly.

The female's head whipped toward her. "Is anyone else hungry?"

Everything changed in a heartbeat. The woman's fangs grew. She took a step and her motion blurred, but not before Becca realized she was coming right at her.

She stood, throwing herself backward only to smack into Gabrielle. A shimmer at her periphery told her she had seen the woman's intention and was taking her own defensive actions.

Within seconds, battle lines had been drawn. Becca stood with a wolf growling at her side, a very scary female vampire glaring at her just out of reach, and then there was Michael. He sidled in front of Becca, effectively blocking her with his body, while Gabrielle continued to snarl at the female.

During their standoff, Admiral Black strode calmly up to take a neutral stance between the two opposing forces.

The female hissed. Michael drew a gun. The spots stopped dancing and solidified. Becca's vision went white at the edges, leaving her a narrow field and she felt her stomach heave. She shook her head trying to clear her vision. Bile burned the back of her throat as she wrestled with her sight in a valiant effort to fight what she knew was coming.

"She is with *you*?" The surprise on her face would have been comical were it not for her long fangs and black eyes still staring unblinking at Becca.

"She is one of ours, yes," Michael growled back. "Put your hands in your pockets." He muttered over his shoulder.

Becca frowned down at her hands when she saw that what she had thought was sweat had in fact been blood from her scraped palms she had been mindlessly wiping on her pants. No wonder they had known she was there. She jammed her balled up fists into her pants pockets, cursing her stupidity.

The female scented the air. "You allow your staff to take a human courtesan?" Her question was aimed at Black. "Is that wise?"

Michael growled low in his chest, Becca could feel it through the few inches of air between them. She leaned into his back, meant to reassure him.

The female's lips parted, giving Becca a full view of those teeth. "There is no need to be defensive, I play with my food too, it's more fun that way." She was taunting Michael and enjoying his building rage.

Black spoke up. "Never mind the pursuits of my staff. Shall we finish our business here?"

Blinking, her eyes regained their color. From her nearness, Becca could see they were normally a bright jade green. When her fangs retracted, her beauty washed back over her. Porcelain skin set off by shining jet black hair and her vibrant eyes complimented her long, lean form. She gave a small incline of her head at the admiral.

Thin lips pursed. "Let's, I'm tired of dicking about." Seeming no longer concerned with them, she pulled a jewel case from her coat pocket and held it out. "You will load this software into your system or I will level this place and every

241

living thing within a two mile radius." All pretenses of friendliness dropped as she made her demand.

The admiral tipped his head, his curiously pale hand on his chin in thought. "I would assume you are going to tell me you have placed explosives of some sort in a central location?"

She nodded, producing a cell phone from her coat pocket. "How did you know? I had a family of shifters in my employ until recently. Before they were apprehended, they were able to liberate a number of valuable weapons for me." She smiled pleasantly. "I take it I have you to thank for the disappearance of my servants?"

"Now we know where the Semtex went," Michael grumbled.

The admiral returned her head bob. "As you can imagine, I cannot allow dangerous plastic explosives to just walk away without being curious. Certainly you can appreciate that."

"Indeed. And certainly *you* can appreciate the number of human lives I hold in my hands." She waved her cell phone in the air. "Your reputation is well known, Admiral Black and that gives me the advantage. Your primary objective is to protect human life, mine is to win. Your choice in this situation is clear."

Neither Black nor Michael responded. The admiral's countenance was grim and the female could see Michael's simmering anger.

She took that as acceptance. "Kyle, come here please," she called over her shoulder.

He shook himself, looking around as he came out of his trance and approached their tense configuration. His eyes searched their faces, attempting to figure out what had happened and how he'd clearly missed something. Kyle's eyes went wide when he looked into Michael's face.

Becca knew what he saw. She could picture Michael's black eyes and long white fangs and felt her heart grow sick. Kyle knew too much now. She feared for his safety. Michael had never told her specifically not to tell anyone, but given the extent they were willing to go to keep their operations secret, it went without saying that ordinary humans weren't to know about their existence. And now Kyle knew. She needed to get to her brother.

Becca started to move around Michael, wanting to explain to Kyle he didn't have to be afraid. They were different than the female. Was there a way to explain that these were "good" vampires? The mere concept of discussing good versus bad vampires was ridiculous.

Gabrielle grabbed Becca's shirt in her teeth to stop her.

"Gab, let me go."

That got Michael's attention and he wrapped an arm around his back to prevent her moving further. Though he held her gently, his muscles tightened to lock her against him. There would be no escaping his grasp. He pressed her tightly enough her breath was reduced to shallow gasps.

"Becca, what's going on?" Kyle had gone white. He stood beside the female, close enough to touch. "Vanessa, is everything okay? Do you have what you need? I want to go." The poor guy was clearly shaken. He had to be wondering how everyone had gone from a business deal to an armed standoff, with wildlife among other things.

Vanessa answered him in a purr. "Everything will be fine, Kyle. Why don't you give the admiral here your disk and he will take care of the money right away." Holding the case out to Kyle to make the actual hand off, she let her eyes drift to Michael, or rather, behind him. "Kyle could you tell me how you know the captain's woman?"

"She's my sister." Kyle's answer was distracted. His white-rimmed eyes were focused on the large wolf standing

243

beside Becca. The animal's head reached Becca's shoulder, her teeth still held the side of Becca's shirt. "Becca, are you okay?" he repeated. His face was nearly as white as the woman's next to him.

Vanessa watched Becca, patiently waiting for her to answer.

Becca swallowed. "Everything's going to be fine, Kyle. Just give Admiral Black the program and go home. We can handle this."

Watching her, clearly not convinced, Kyle decided she was the only one he could trust in this situation. He looked around before his eyes settled on the case Vanessa still held. Hesitating only for a moment, he reached across the distance between them and handed Black the disk. Vanessa maintained her safe distance from all except Kyle.

The admiral took it, tightening his lips in a flash of a smile before speaking. "Thank you, Mr. Sauter. Now, if you would please go we will handle this from here." His face went slack and Becca watched him project his influence on her unsuspecting brother.

With an earsplitting roar Vanessa reached out and grabbed Kyle's arm, pulling him into her so that his back was pressed to her front. "I told you this one was mine."

Where Kyle had been pale before, he now had taken on a decidedly green cast. If Becca didn't miss her guess, he was pretty close to puking. That was one thing she and her big brother had in common. Both had very easily stressed systems.

"You know I don't share well with others." She opened her mouth, putting her mouth to the base of his neck, and Becca watched in horror as the fangs penetrated her brother's flesh. His scream echoed through the warehouse.

The arm around her had prevented Becca from stepping away from Michael but as she discovered when her knees failed her, it didn't keep her from falling. When she collapsed, Michael moved to retrieve her and she scurried back, away from all of them.

Vanessa caught the movement and blessedly pulled her fangs from Kyle to watch Becca with a detached interest.

Becca picked herself up once she was out of reach and swung around her allies, inching closer to the enemy. A brief glance at Michael showed her vision coming to life. It hadn't been betrayal she'd seen on his face, it was the sickening realization that he couldn't protect her. One hand out, she continued closer to the woman and tried to bluff her brother free.

"You don't want to do that." She found her body's usual reactions to misdirection gone when her brother's life depended upon it. "Kyle told me about you. He has your picture from his phone downloaded to his computer at work. If you kill him they'll go through his things and they'll find it. They'll know it was you. They'll hunt you down."

The vampire's eyes faded back to green, her fangs retracting. "And do you think that makes any sort of difference to me? That a few humans will cause me any sort of inconvenience?"

Quelling the chill in the pit of her stomach, Becca stepped closer. Without a quiver in her voice she lied through her teeth. "No, but he knew you weren't going to let him off with a payout. He put you on that disk too and only he knows how to get you off of it."

Vanessa's eyes narrowed slightly, confirming Becca's assumption that the female didn't know the particulars of the program; the gears in her head working blindingly fast to sort the details.

"If they can flag you, Vanessa," she used the name for emphasis, "then they can freeze your bank accounts. It'll be hard to run if you have no money. Don't think we'd let this be handled by the local police either." Becca nodded toward the admiral. "We can have this handled by the United States military because it happened here. We can follow you anywhere."

Her eyes went black again and her voice quaked with fury.

"It seems you have me at a disadvantage," she spat. "Since I have no choice, I *will* let the boy go." Vanessa threw Kyle to the ground where he stared up at Becca, his eyes glazing in shock from the combination of blood loss and the fact that he was surrounded by nightmares.

While Becca watched her brother try to scoot nearer to Admiral Black she failed to notice Vanessa shift her direction. So concerned was she with her brother, she completely missed it when Vanessa streaked over to wrap her arms around Becca, the woman's incredibly strong arms pinned hers to her sides.

Taken off guard, Becca screamed. Her vision went white and she was blind. Her ears worked though. Michael roared, Gabrielle growled, and Black spoke.

"You cannot take my people." The menace in his otherwise calm tone was enough to make most people stop what they were doing and run in abject terror. Not so with Vanessa.

"Consider her my insurance that you will upload that to your server today, Admiral Black. When it is on and my name cleared, I will let your pet go."

She must have been running then because Becca felt her world shift and the cool desert air swept past her skin, hair blowing off her face. A sudden stomach dropping sensation explained how Vanessa had gotten over the fence. She had jumped it. Her awe of vampires grew. She hoped Michael was as fast as this one. If not, Becca didn't have much of a chance.

Chapter 27

Becca was gone. Michael was left holding a gun aimed at nothing. Gabrielle howled in frustration and a wounded human cowered at their feet. Only Admiral Black remained outwardly unaffected.

Michael started after them and Black halted him with a word.

"Stay."

The ties that assured Michael's loyalty as well as obedience tightened and Michael's feet lost their ability to move. In a rage, Michael shouted at the admiral, "God damn it, let me go!"

Admiral Black met Michael's furious glare with a glimmer of emotion that did not bode well for his second in command. "Michael, I have a vested interest in Rebecca as well. We will get her back."

Gabrielle spoke. She had changed back to her human form and stood naked by the admiral. They had both seen it numerous times before and were by now unmoved by the sight.

"Give me your phone. I'll call Ryan and have him bring some gear up from the storage unit by the front gate. He saw us go, he's probably almost here by now. We can track her before the trail gets cold."

"We have something we need to do before we can reclaim our witch," Black intervened, using an old term for Becca's kind.

Michael flinched at the word. That her sight made her not entirely human was something he had been waiting to tell her, waiting for her to be ready to accept it. It would be part of her education on the supernatural realm, her place in it. Now he only hoped he would have the chance to tell her anything again.

"We're really going to load this software of his? We don't know what it is but if that woman wants it, you know it isn't good," Gabrielle fumed, her hands on her hips.

Michael walked over to Kyle and knelt down where he lay, frozen on his side watching their exchange. By his glazed expression, Michael could tell he was quickly passing beyond their reach. He worked to maintain a calm exterior hoping he could draw the information he sought from the fragile mind. But as he got down to Kyle's level, the human cowered, closing his eyes.

He took a deep breath and fought back his nature, the one screeching inside him to shake the man. The vampire wanted to fly from here and chase down the one who had stolen his mate. Black's control over him helped for once. "Kyle, listen. We need your help. *Becca* needs your help."

Kyle opened his eyes at the mention of his sister.

Heartened, Michael continued. He used his name often to keep him engaged. "Kyle, I know you've seen some strange things here tonight but trust me, no one here is going to hurt you. Kyle, we need to find out what was on that disk before we load it. We want to get her back Kyle, but we can't do something that's going to hurt a lot of people. Even if it's for Becca." Michael told the vampire inside him to shut up, that they would do anything to find her.

Kyle was blinking at Michael, sitting up as if from a daydream. "Did she take Becca?" He was looking around.

"Yes Kyle. Vanessa has Becca. You have to tell us everything you know about that woman and what's on this software." He wanted to use his influence. If it wasn't for the damage it could do to his already fractured psyche, he would. The man needed time from the manipulation he'd already suffered. Becca would never forgive him for driving her brother insane.

"What *is* she?" He stared from face to face, taking a longer look at Gabrielle's naked body and flushing self-consciously. Eyes coming to rest on Michael, Kyle studied him evenly. "What are *you*?"

Michael knew he would be wiping Kyle's memory of this night so he gave him an honest explanation. Unlike his sister, Kyle was susceptible to their influences. Vanessa had proven that.

"We're vampires, Kyle." He pointed up at the admiral. "So is he. Gab's a werewolf." Michael pointed his chin at Gabrielle who raised her hand back.

Kyle stared at them all, his mouth forming a small "O". Michael worried he had been too straightforward in his explanation. If he'd had more time he might have taken the long way round. He didn't have that luxury. Amazingly, Kyle rallied. After a short pause, he gave a decided shake of his head and pushed himself to his feet. He wobbled and Michael started to catch him until he saw the way Kyle shirked from him. Kyle righted himself.

Her brother's fortitude lent her lover hope that they would be able to find a solution and get Becca back before any harm came to her. He bit back the anger, fighting back the creature inside him that pounded just below the surface demanding to be unleashed. It wouldn't help things with Kyle if he gave in to his monster, nor would Black allow that plan of attack. Black was the master Michael ultimately served.

Back on his feet, Kyle dusted off his pants and hands casting a sideways glance at Michael. "I knew there was something weird about you." He looked up at the admiral. "Where's the nearest computer? I think she's put something on it like a virus or a worm or something. It's the only thing I can think of to explain why she insisted on taking it and handling the sale." Kyle made eye contact with Michael, his gaze steady. "I might be able to separate it if I can see what we're dealing with."

The admiral answered. He had not moved. "There is a place here. Come." Turning on his heel, he led the way out without a backward glance.

The others followed to the car Admiral Black had parked at the back loading doors. Fortunately for Gabrielle, it was outfitted as were all of their cars, with a spare set of fatigues. These things happened often. As she dressed in the back, Kyle stared straight ahead, his self-control admirable. It had taken Michael a lot longer to get over the urge to look. Then again, he hadn't had a wife to be faithful to.

While the admiral drove them to the main office, the nearest building with a computer, Michael's thoughts turned inward. He needed to find Becca. He remembered their mission in Odessa. When he'd heard Gabrielle's howl he'd gone mad as he'd streaked through the streets. Then, when he and Ryan had arrived and found that piece of garbage had offered them up as meat to nothing more than an animal... It had felt good to snap the bastard's neck but not nearly as good as it would have felt to have the chance to take his time, ending him painfully. He'd stopped because he hadn't wanted Becca to see the monster in him. How he *could* be when he lost control.

Michael again had to push down the vengeful vampire struggling inside of him. Becca was a sailor, a soldier like him. She had proven capable of defending herself. If she was going to be a part of their unit, he would have to not only allow her to be in harms way but he would occasionally have to place her there. The knowledge ate at him yet he knew it was the only future they had together.

Michael could never leave the admiral and the admiral would never let Becca out of the unit alive. The only small comfort he found was that he could have her close enough to protect her from danger the majority of the time. It hadn't worked that well this time.

Now that she was gone, taken from him by a beast that had every intention of harming her, Michael was ready to kill. His nature struggled to be free, to run loose in the darkness as his kind had done for millennia and hunt Vanessa down. To tear her unholy body limb from limb, sink his fangs in to her tough, pale flesh to gratify his need for destruction. Michael shook with the desire to spill her blood. More importantly, he feared more than anything that he would be too late and would lose his Becca.

They pulled up to the building and, mercifully, the lights were out and the lot was empty of cars. All four spilled out with Black leading the way. Keys jingled in his hands and the door swung open. The others could see fine without illumination. Not Kyle, who struck his knee on the doorjamb and cursed. Gabrielle snorted and walked past him to turn on one row of lights. Kyle mumbled a thank you and followed her in, rubbing his injured knee.

Admiral Black strode down the hall, his shoes making barely a sound as he led the way to the back office on the left. He reached in, flicked on the light and waved Kyle to go ahead.

Nodding, Kyle scuttled past the team to go around the desk and seat himself at the computer sitting on top, a slide show of sunny beach scenes illuminating the monitor.

He held out his hand to the admiral, eyeing him expectantly. When Black did nothing, Kyle prompted him.

"The disk, please."

Black wrinkled his brow. "Can you look at its contents without uploading it to the system?" His concern for their lost member could not be cause for him to compromise the entire country's military, all of whose branches were linked through the same server.

"Yes, Sir. I have a back door built in that'll let me look at it before I launch anything."

Michael watched their exchange, frantically hoping Kyle would prove himself as resourceful as his sister. *She* could think on her feet *and* evolve her plan as the situation demanded it. He also hoped her brother was quick.

Hearing that Kyle had planned ahead to put in a back door was heartening. Maybe there was hope for the boy yet. Michael was gaining a whole new respect for humans. Or maybe, he thought of something he hadn't considered before, Kyle had some preternatural tendencies as well. It did usually run in families.

"Did you really input Vanessa into this software of yours? Do you know where she lives?" Black waited patiently for the human's search to bear fruit.

A wry smile crossed his features as he favored Black with a brief glance. "No, she made that one up. Pretty good, huh?" Then his expression darkened. "I don't know anything about her but her name. When she's gone, she's gone."

Shrieking inside his head temporarily distracted Michael's thoughts.

Kyle's "huh" interrupted his thoughts.

"What is 'huh'?" he asked.

Kyle was still staring at his screen. Black and Michael came around the desk to peer over his shoulder. "Huh." He leaned in to look more closely at the screen.

Standing behind him, Michael saw an ordinary list in a format similar to a phone book listing. Nothing special stood out.

Glancing quickly over at Admiral Black, Michael could tell the admiral expected him to take over. Taking a step back, Black lifted one brow at him and stared out the window at the deserted parking lot. He was listening and would miss nothing. They had learned that questioning humans always ended better with Michael conducting them. The admiral usually ended up scaring most people silly. Then again, Michael wasn't usually this close to losing it.

"Fill me in, Kyle. What am I not seeing here? All I see is a list."

Leaning in, still studying the screen, Kyle shook his head slowly from side to side. "That's the problem. I don't see anything new on it. This is *just* the software I created. The list pulls personal information from someone's credit card and catches similar entries to compile a list." He started keying different combinations. "Let me dig and see what I can turn up. There has to be something else here to make her want it on your server so badly. Is there anything she might be after specifically that you can think of?" Kyle looked expectantly over his shoulder.

Michael gave him a look. "This is the server for the United States Armed Forces. It's got troop locations, weapons, codes, anything you need is on there provided you know where to look. There's stuff on there *everyone* wants."

Seeing him obviously distracted, Michael was left again to his own devices. All of which led to one person and how he was going to get her back. Black faded into the background, disappearing somewhere in the building until he was needed.

Chapter 28

After a few minutes of running, loud crashing sounds blocked out everything else and the breeze no longer flowed over Becca's skin. The air around her grew cooler and she could smell the brine while the crashing sound became more concentrated. They were inside some sort of hard walled structure. She would guess a cave by the sea judging from the echoing sounds of the surf now coming from above as well as all sides. Hopefully the tide wouldn't come in while they were in here; unlike Vanessa, Becca needed to breathe.

Vanessa set Becca down on a rocky floor none too gently. Her legs, cramped and wobbly after being held over Vanessa's shoulder, let her fall gracelessly to her backside.

"Ow," Becca couldn't help herself from grunting.

Her inability to see remained a handicap. The blindness had retreated to tunnel vision and was a factor should Becca want to escape or defend herself from an attack. Both of which were definite possibilities in her near future.

Consequently, after scooting a safe distance away and putting her back against the wall of the cave, Becca began to slow down her breathing, hoping her nerves would follow suit. As she breathed, she busied herself with trying to take in her surroundings. From what she could see the cave was relatively shallow. It was maybe ten or fifteen feet deep, the ceiling closer to eight.

It was dark. The moon was waning and would have provided sufficient light were it not for the clouds. Spring in Southern California usually had a few weeks of rain and clouding, and damn if this wasn't one of those weeks. It would have been helpful to have the extra light. Fortunately, some amount of light reflected on the water's surface though not from celestial bodies. The lights along the edge where the street met the beach were evenly spaced and held an orange cast, illuminating a sign telling her which beach she had been brought to.

Calming herself down had opened her vision somewhat. Becca didn't trust it enough to try to handle an escape attempt from a vampire who could easily hear her, see her, and kill her before she got more than three feet. Any amount of hampered vision could cost her life.

Inspiration unveiled itself as she watched the lights dance on the waves crashing toward the shore not fifty yards from the mouth of the cave. Becca began to moan.

Vanessa spoke from the back of the cave. "Be quiet."

Becca moaned again, falling forward to her hands and knees.

"I told you to be quiet." Her voice was closer.

Committed to her plan, Becca crawled several steps toward the mouth of their shelter. "I'm going to be sick."

Feet appeared directly in front of her. "You are not going anywhere."

There was a permanence to Vanessa's words Becca found unsettling. Her stomach twisted in agreement. Vanessa was not going to let her leave here and she didn't just mean for right now.

Growing desperate, Becca put her hand up to her mouth, tipping her head down and away from Vanessa's sight line. As her face and fingers met, Becca promptly shoved her longest finger down her throat. Her body's response was immediate and forceful.

"Agh! Humans are disgusting." Vanessa jumped backward. "Get your stink out of here."

Becca felt a cool hand wrap itself around her arm, another vicelike claw took hold of her ankle and she was propelled outward. Vanessa didn't hold back for fear of harming her human captive. Becca hit the sand, hardened from the retreat of the waves. That was the answer to her question about the tide. She could hear the surf roaring very near by.

There was another sound. A soft padding that had once struck fear in Becca's heart. Now it lifted her spirits and helped her sight to clear. When she looked up to see the cinnamon fur approaching, she was confused. It wasn't the beach she saw in front of her, but the inside of the offices at Miramar.

She was looking at Ryan's approaching wolf form as he crept carefully from the shadows. Michael was speaking so quietly she could barely hear. She strained to hear over the crashing waves.

"Start at the weapons warehouse and follow from there. They haven't been gone long. Her trail should still be fresh. Black wants her alive for questioning."

Ryan's canine head nodded in understanding.

"Ryan," Michael's voice was strained. "If Vanessa has hurt her, bring her to me first. 'Alive' leaves a lot of room for interpretation."

With a short yip, Ryan spun and hurled himself off into the shadows, racing directly toward the interior of the base and heading straight for the warehouse.

Becca bobbled as she got to her feet, moving her head around to try to capture Vanessa in her narrow field of vision. With Ryan coming she had to keep Vanessa occupied. "What's so important about that software?"

She closed the distance, coming to a halt a few feet away. Vanessa's gloating smile revealed her perceived victory.

"There's nothing important about that stupid disk. It's what I've attached to it."

"What's that? Some sort of virus? Do you want to crash their server or something?" Becca's limited understanding of computers was a choice. She always let computer knowledge slide by without much consideration. If she needed help, she could always ask Kyle. That was his forte.

Vanessa laughed. "No, it's a 'tickler.' It catches very specific data." Her green eyes reflected brightly in the limited moonlight. "Have you ever considered how many of us there are? How we manage to hide among you?"

Becca's negative head shake didn't surprise Vanessa.

"There are a large number of us in the military. Think about it. With our special abilities, we are highly capable in Special Forces, Intelligence, even as an ordinary infantryman. Beings like you gravitate to service as well." She tipped her head and frowned condescendingly at Becca's shocked expression. "Why else would Black want a near-human? If you were only for sex and food they wouldn't have tried to protect you. Clearly you have preternatural gifts. If it weren't for his smell all over you I could tell what exactly you are." She frowned before continuing, pleased to have an audience for her brilliance. Obviously she wasn't intending to let Becca go by what she was giving away.

"It may not be common knowledge that there are beings like us in the service, but it is obvious once you know what to look for in their files. There is a small notation, a tag they call them now. It has been attached to each and every one of their files. My tickler can find them and make a list. Once that list gets turned over to the proper authorities, the hunt can begin."

Puzzled, Becca didn't understand what Vanessa hoped to gain by revealing those like her to the government. *She*, not the servicemen and women would be considered the problem. "They'll never believe they have vampires among them. You said it yourself. They're good at what they do. How do you plan on proving what they are?"

Not attempting to hide her annoyance at Becca's slow wit, Vanessa rolled her eyes and explained. "Don't be stupid. I have no intention of exposing us. There is no need. Kyle's little program is going to combine with my list and do everything for me." She grinned again, showing no sign of her fangs. "My device is going to find the tag and link a list of suspicious purchases to each of those files. The delivery address will lead the authorities to a number of warehouses full of enough weapons and bomb making supplies to blow up every state and federal building in the nation. I've been amassing the supplies for some time and your brother's software was exactly the delivery vehicle I was looking for. When I read about its upcoming release this summer, the idea came to me." She ran the toe of her boot through the sand. "Find a way to tie in to the program and let it do all the work." Smiling, Vanessa stomped the sand raised by her etchings.

Incensed both by her loyalty to her unit mates sure to be targeted and also her allegiance to her fellow soldiers, Becca forced a smile at Vanessa's obvious oversight. "You can report them but you know they can get out of any prison they put them in."

Vanessa's good humor was undaunted. "Right. They will put them in one of three prisons as a matter of fact. Only three in the country handle suspected terrorists. And I have arranged for each one to have a mysterious and unfortunate fire as soon as my kith and kin have arrived." Her eyes narrowed. "You know that fire is as effective as silver, right?"

Becca was sickened. "Why? What does it benefit you to have so many of your own kind destroyed? What could you possibly have against them?"

"You don't really know much about how our society works, do you?" She looked Becca up and down speculatively. "We are all predators. We are in constant competition and living undetected among you has only created more of a scarcity. Our need for blood cannot ever be totally sated or we call too much attention to ourselves. Instead, we must take small amounts, never quite enough to satisfy, only enough to keep us alive. We must steal and hide so we are not suspected by humans or our own, forced to live like scavengers. Some of us are tired of being hungry."

Vanessa's dark glare gave Becca an idea who she blamed for that one. The admiral's unit must be hated in some circles. Becca hadn't stopped to consider the politics before.

"Fewer predators means more prey for those who remain. And with more blood comes more power." She looked around, holding her arms out to encompass something beyond herself. "And in this world, what can we not have with power?"

The lunacy of Vanessa's plan was overshadowed by its ingeniousness. After years of public pressure to reveal a greater conspiracy from within, at least a few politicians would readily believe that the chaos on the home front was initiated by rogue members of their own military. If any number of higher up officials within the military, a fact Becca was sure would be realized, could be tied to the conspiracy a number of groups would eat it up. The political machine would speed their incarcerations and, as opposed to risking exposure, the accused would allow themselves to be taken. Of course they would figure to break out and disappear later. Except with Vanessa's plan there wouldn't be a later. They would all die, leaving her and other far more dangerous creatures to prowl among the human populace unchecked.

She prayed Ryan would get here soon so that she could warn him, there was too much at stake for them to load the program. Feeling the time sliding away from her, Becca grew anxious.

Vanessa mistook Becca's accelerating pulse. "Don't worry. You won't burn in prison. Your death will be more immediate." She smiled again, this time her fangs made indents in her lower lip. "And useful."

There was no mistaking her intent. Becca was going to be her first victim in this new world order Vanessa was creating.

Her visibility narrowed, her stomach rolled, Becca fell to her knees and angrily she shouted, "No!" at her body's attempts to cripple her. She could not lie there while her team unwittingly killed thousands of their own kind so that one greedy vampire didn't have to be hungry anymore.

"Don't worry, I will make it relatively painless." Vanessa smiled nastily. She assumed Becca was objecting to the idea of being eaten.

Becca thought about Michael, grasping at the new dimension of her sight she'd discovered earlier that evening. Having already been awakened, her vision readily extended itself to her lover. *As soon as she called it, his vision took over. It was faster this time, equally disorienting. Her immediate surroundings fell back and she stood tall behind her brother, watching him stare at the computer screen.*

"There's nothing bad about it but it's definitely there. I know I didn't put it there so that has to be what she wants in the system." Kyle was explaining. He'd found Vanessa's addition to his program.

"What does it do?" Michael's voice came from where she stood. "Why does she want it?"

The back of Kyle's head wagged back and forth. "I don't know. She's piggybacking it onto the program's compiling capabilities but what she's trying to grab is beyond me."

Black's chilling voice was low in the quiet space. "I know what she's after."

Becca's sight shifted and she saw Black entering the office. Black didn't speak, yet she felt something in her head at his approach. It was some oppressive force she couldn't put her finger on. Not quite a headache, it felt like a tight band was wrapped around his skull. Her vision blinked back to Kyle.

"It's a list of military personnel. Certain individuals have something marked in their files she would find interesting."

Kyle turned around and she saw the frustrated look on his face. "What is it? What would a vampire want with that?" The calm way he asked that question and said that word made Becca wonder if he had been influenced.

"I'm not sure what she would do with it just that we can't let her get it," Michael said quietly. "It wouldn't end well for anyone."

The admiral's murmured agreement sounded behind her. It made her head hurt again. Something the admiral was doing was having a physical effect on Michael. If she had any control over where he looked, she would have been staring at Black. Instead she had to remain an anonymous witness, seeing through his eyes by some bizarre shift in her ability.

He looked at his commanding officer and she felt the band tighten around the inside of her skull. A low growl escaped Michael's lips.

Black's eyes narrowed and his jaw tightened. "We can replace her ability, Michael. We have done it before."

"But not her." His voice was nearly impossible for her to hear. She was guessing they were speaking too low for Kyle to hear given his lack of reaction.

Without indication of sympathy, Black retorted, "She is mortal. Her death is inevitable. Ours is not," he inclined his head toward the monitor beyond her brother, "Theirs is not."

"She doesn't have to die." Michael's voice was tight with anger. "Not like this."

Black's face twitched, the only indication he was doing something and the pain in Michael's head doubled, burning its way through him. His hand shot out to catch his balance on the back of Kyle's chair. Something primal screamed behind her, terrified, she wished he would turn around.

"Hey, are you okay?" Kyle asked, no longer oblivious to the exchange.

Michael's gaze shifted to Kyle who was by now staring at them.

"What's going on? Are we going to call and tell her we're doing what she wants?" He sensed something was wrong. "Michael, you said we'd get Becca back."

"We can't, Kyle," Michael choked out, eyes locked on Kyle's. Becca saw her brother's despair.

He leapt out of his chair, face to face with Michael. "Yes we can. If you don't then I will."

Black spoke calmly from behind Michael. He watched Kyle turn to face Black, hatred in his eyes. "We have someone searching for her. Any further contact from us requires that we load this and we are unable to do that. Too many lives would be lost if that were to happen."

Kyle sucked in a breath to object, Black continued.

"You sister understood the risks involved when she joined us. You must understand them now and honor her sacrifice."

Black was right and Kyle knew it. Defeated and pale he sank down into his chair. Michael watched him eject the disk and move to shut down the computer.

"Uh oh."

"Kyle, what is 'uh oh'?" Michael asked quietly.

Kyle began typing frantically, the computer beeping at him with each keystroke. "I had no idea. I'm sorry."

Admiral Black hissed in his first real display of emotion. "What have you done?"

"It's the disk. I went in the back door and searched everything without initiating any sort of transfer but here it is. The disk uploaded itself." Kyle was hammering on the keyboard, not that it was helping. The computer was just beeping more.

Becca scanned the screen with Michael. It announced that indeed the new software had been loaded successfully. Black snarled in Michael's ear, Kyle was desperately trying to undo the data transfer and the computer objected with a constant stream of beeps.

"She's locked it off. I had no idea she could do this. This is really advanced stuff." Admiration crept into his frightened voice.

Black grabbed a hold of Kyle's collar jerking him backward and out of his chair. "Are you working with her?"

Turning to face Black, Michael's sight caught Black's eyes burning hot as he glared at Kyle.

Becca wanted to scream. Her brother was facing death over a mistake. It was an honest mistake. She knew it was. Kyle wouldn't knowingly work with this monster. He would for his family, her conscience whispered at her. His love for Des and the girls could have motivated him to do nearly anything.

Despite the crushing force from within his head Michael put a hand on Kyle's shoulder, staring at his superior. The admiral turned his fury on his second.

The hell his eyes promised was terrifying to Becca even across the distance that separated their physical bodies.

*Agonized, he challenged Black anyway. "Sir, you can hear it
as well as I. He didn't know." His voice was rough, tortured.
"Their family has to lose one already. Don't make it worse
out of anger."*

*Black stared at him for a long moment before finally
releasing Kyle with a cold command. "You wrote this. Undo
it."*

*Kyle started to argue that it wasn't possible and then
thought better of it. Straightening his shirt, he bobbed his
head. "Yes, Sir." He slid into his chair, the sounds of typing
and the computer rejecting his advances filled the office.*

He had said her family was going to lose one. Michael
knew she was going to die here. Did he have no faith in Ryan
or did he already know Vanessa had no intention of turning
her loose? His grief was palpable. Becca regretted that he
was going to have to live with the loss. She wouldn't.

She shook it off, pushing the vision out of her head. Becca
prayed for Ryan to come. He was her last hope and possibly
Kyle's as well. If he couldn't fix this, Black would not be
very forgiving.

As if summoned from her very thoughts Becca heard that
rhythmic sound again only with *her* ears. She willed her
psyche to return to her body, dizzy when it snapped back with
the recoil of a slap. Turning her head, she looked to see him
pounding his way up the sand at the water's edge, masking
his footfalls until he was within shouting distance.

Sadly, Becca hearing it meant that Vanessa had as well.
She too spun to face the fast approaching werewolf. "Go
home, dog," she snarled at Ryan.

So focused on Ryan was she, Vanessa didn't see Becca gain
her feet. She eyed her nervously as she began to back away,
keeping her departure aimed for the dunes on the beach
leading out of Vanessa's sight and up to the lights. And
people.

Becca sped up when she had escaped from Vanessa's immediate reach. Becca's flight carried her in a wide arc reaching above Ryan and he changed course when he caught sight of her. He was nearly to her when warning pains lanced through her head. Becca shifted her eyes to Vanessa in time to see her black eyes turn toward *her*, not the wolf. Furious, Vanessa bared her fangs.

At the increasing blur that was her visibility, Becca screamed and lashed out. In a knee jerk desperate measure, she once again stretched out and latched on to a more reliable, familiar psyche. When she blinked again she was galloping up the beach, pounding on four paws toward her blind body and Vanessa bearing down on it.

Becca, or rather her body, continued to move away. Orchestrating the movement when everything she saw was the mirror image had her certain she would feel the bony fingers clamping down on her any second. As luck would have it, her erratic darting gave the vampire pause and bought Becca the seconds it took to orient herself.

Her feet back under her, Becca angled up again, scanning the sand and the slopes of the dunes for a weapon to use against the creature. Up the sand hill a few more feet, the remnants of an old bonfire pit were visible, making ghastly shadows in the halo of the lamps above. Several pieces of driftwood had been left uncharred beside the fire pit.

The pile wasn't far but the question was whether or not she could make it before Vanessa got to her. She held no illusions about the vampire's speed. Michael had allowed her to see only a fraction of his and it was staggering.

Becca shook off her fear and turned to run the last few feet. Her shoes dug into the loose sand as she scrambled to get up the small hill. Using the impetus of her spin to add a burst of speed, Becca took a huge step and let her adrenaline drive her forward.

She had gone most of the short distance when the anticipated cold claw laid hold of her shoulder. Becca tried to shake it off to no avail. Ryan howled behind her, his eyes never leaving her or her would-be killer.

Vanessa was suddenly in front of Becca. Even her narrowed field of sight showed her fangs standing out bright white against her pale face.

She couldn't stop her eyes from trailing down to see some useful pieces in the pile of driftwood. Several pointed pieces of erosion fence lay in the pile, torn from their wire framework.

Vanessa smiled cruelly. "You lose." She reared back and sunk her fangs into Becca's neck.

In that jolting second, she was catapulted back into her singular person. Becca felt the searing tear of flesh as the points pierced her neck where it met her shoulder, the knee-weakening feel of tooth scraping bone. Giving blood was a painless process, having it pulled out forcibly and rapidly was unendingly painful. For the first time in her life, Becca considered death a relief.

Her hoarse cries were lost in the crashing waves. The fact that the tide was coming in struck her as ironic; she wouldn't die in that cave from water, it would be on the beach where she was perfectly dry. Eyes closing, Becca felt herself weakening and her legs felt heavy.

A heavy hit from the side broke Vanessa's hold, spinning her away to land in a heap in the soft sand. Grit filled her gasping mouth while her hair covered her eyes. Ryan's snarls filled her ears as he engaged Vanessa in a violent and bloody fight. Becca put a hand up to her injured neck and felt the blood while her fingers traced the punctures. The blood was already clotting, staunching the flow from the marks. The sudden panoramic view from her own perspective was almost too much.

Confused and weak but definitely alive, Becca reached down to take a section of the fence in both hands, untangling one thick piece of wood intending to use it as a spear. She had no idea if the legend of wooden stakes would help. It was worth trying. Using it to push herself up, she gained her feet to join the fight.

Turning around, Becca focused on the snarling, swirling mass of cinnamon fur and white flesh. Blood colored the wet shadows in the sand black beneath them, flashes of white showed streaks of red as their teeth found their marks.

Becca stepped closer, watching for an opening. Ryan whined as Vanessa's fangs dug deep in his throat. Becca raised her spear and thrust it into Vanessa's back, feeling the resistance her tough skin offered before it slid between the ribs where a human's heart would be. The smell of sulfur permeated the air.

Vanessa's body stiffened, arching backward as her fangs released the wolf. Her shrieks pierced the night air, rising above the pounding surf. Unable to move, Vanessa slid off of Ryan and fell to the sand with a solid thud.

Ryan was panting hard. Blood covered his fur at his neck and chest, numerous gashes showed on his front legs. He gave several choking coughs, rolling his tongue across the roof of his mouth in an attempt to get rid of sand or fur or both.

Becca stared at Vanessa's prone body. She lay on her side exactly as she had fallen, the spear protruding through her chest. Her fangs had retracted, her eyes returned to jade. To all appearances she was a normal human being who just happened to have a spear sticking out of her chest.

Overcoming her fear of the monster after she was paralyzed, Becca knelt down and picked through her coat pockets. Victorious, she raised her prize so that Ryan could see it.

The phone's face lit up the darkness around them. "I'll call Michael and get us out of here. Are you all right?" she asked, worry creasing her brow.

He nodded his furry head.

Becca moved to dial and laughed. "You know, I've never called him. I don't know his number." She dialed Kyle instead.

The phone rang three times before he picked up. Becca was starting to worry something had happened to him when she heard his monotone voice heavy with dread.

"Hello Vanessa."

"Kyle, it's me."

"Bec?" Kyle shouted just before she heard the phone being wrested from his hand amidst his pointless objections.

A new voice came on the line, equally anxious. "Becca? Are you okay? I thought…" Michael's voice brought back the vision she had seen through his eyes. He'd believed she was dead.

The memory joined with mental fatigue and Becca started to cry. "I'm fine. We're fine. Ryan's here."

"Where is she?"

"She's here too. I don't think she's dead but when I jammed a piece of wood in her back she froze." Becca still didn't quite understand but whatever had happened, it was good.

"You staked her?" Michael actually laughed, light with relief. "Who told you about that?"

Embarrassed, Becca had to admit she'd seen it in the movies and figured it was based on something. Everything else seemed to be.

Michael laughed again. Becca felt a few chuckles trickle out around her sniffles. Ryan grumbled and grabbed Vanessa's coat in his teeth, pulling her back toward the cover of the cave. Dawn was beginning to make its first hinting glimmers on the water heralding its impending arrival.

"Sorry, Ryan." She straightened up, her head spinning from her loss of blood. "Michael, could you come get us? Ryan's going to be naked if he changes and we have a paralyzed woman with a piece of wood sticking out of her. It's probably best if we don't try to walk or take the bus." Becca was feeling giddy with relief.

"Where are you?"

Glancing around them, Becca saw the sign under a light. Her vision was perfectly clear now that the danger had passed. "Half Moon Bay. We're down in a little cave on the water."

"I'll be right there. Get under cover and stay put."

The phone went dark and Becca pressed a button on her end.

"He's on his way, Ryan." Becca saw that he had dragged Vanessa nearly all the way to the cave and had left a visible trail in the sand.

She went up to the fire pit again and grabbed the section of fence. Carrying it down to where the scuffle had occurred, Becca dragged the fencing over the bloodied sand. Once the blood was turned under, she kicked it around to mess up the somewhat linear marks. Satisfied it looked like people had trampled the beach during their bonfire, she turned her attention to the thirty or so feet of trench Vanessa's small, oddly heavy rear end had made in the sand.

269

She had just finished up and was returning the section to the woodpile when she heard a car's engine racing up. Her heart skipped a beat fearing the beach patrol had come for an early morning tour. A hurried peek up at the lot above the rock line showed her it was the one person she wanted to see right now.

Dropping her fence section, Becca shamelessly ran toward him. He moved with the speed she had only seen in bursts and, in two breaths, he had her in his arms. She threw hers around him, her need to touch him nearly unbearable.

"Becca, you're alive." Michael kissed her forehead, her face and one hard press on the lips. With a sniff he pulled back abruptly.

"What? What is it?" Her arms pulled at him.

Michael let her draw him back until his face got near her neck. She heard him sniffing. Alarmed, she heard him growl as he pulled her shirt from her neck.

"She bit you?" Michael whispered hotly.

Discomfited at his scrutiny, Becca shrugged her shoulder up to hide the marks. "Yeah, it's okay though. Ryan got here in time."

His jaw clenched, fangs altering the line of his lips and his eyes went black as a growl rumbled deep in his chest.

Becca, although flattered by his protectiveness, saw the first rays of the sun breaking over the water and feared discovery. "Michael, we have to go. People are going to be up soon." She put her hands on his chest.

Face turning toward her, eyes still focused on the mouth of the cave just beyond her, Michael fought the urge to rush past her and tear Vanessa apart. Eventually, Becca saw him gain control of himself. His eyes didn't go completely back to normal, although she saw them beginning to fade as they fell upon her.

Relieved, Becca called out to Ryan over her shoulder.

"He's here, Ryan. Come on out."

Ryan limped into view. His muscles were already stiffening.

Michael reluctantly released her with a gravelly order to get in the car. She moved unsteadily on her feet, wading through the loose beach sand. Her legs were heavier than if she'd run five miles with full gear.

Hearing the pattern of the sand shifting behind her, Becca assumed Ryan was coming. His limping form came abreast of her, his front left leg dragging noisily in the sand. Something rushed past them and she saw the rear doors of the Suburban open, Michael paused long enough to thow Vanessa roughly inside.

Becca was struggling in the sand. She couldn't deny it. Her legs were dead and the loss of blood had made her dizzy. When she saw Michael slam the back doors of the truck closed, the relief she felt washed the effects of the adrenaline away and she collapsed to her knees.

Ryan stopped with her and nosed her arm.

She understood and laughed at herself. "Thanks Ryan. You're a life saver." Standing, Becca put an arm over his shoulder and leaned heavily on him as they made their way the last few yards to the rocks.

Ryan scrambled up, nails scratching on the rough surfaces and hit the top of the wall. Michael opened the door to the back row of seats and the wolf jumped in.

Becca's hands had just touched the bottom of the three-foot wall when Michael appeared beside her again.

"Let me help," he offered gently.

She was too tired to disagree or be proud. Instead she merely nodded, grateful when he swept her up against his body with one arm and jumped up the rocks with barely a grunt. He opened the door for her, watching her closely for signs of fainting as he lifted her into the tall truck.

Chapter 29

After one long look at Michael, the guards saw no need to get anyone else's identification. He influenced them to forget they saw any of them.

Admiral Black and Kyle were waiting in the office when they drove up. The admiral's stern face told him everything he needed to know about their efforts to find a way to disable the tickler pulling together all of their information hidden so carefully since the inception of computers.

Michael cursed the machines silently. He lacked the common affinity for the benefits of information at one's fingertips. Yes, it made for fast research but it also made hiding their identities incredibly complicated. Every decade or so they had to take established soldiers, fake their deaths and reintroduce them in another role far away. Usually they ended up in covert ops to reduce their chances of running into familiar faces. Fingerprints had to be faked, blood types, back stories; it was highly complex and involved the assistance of several generals with the highest of clearance from a number of countries in a weird sort of witness protection.

With their prowess they were well suited to covert ops where they became ghosts, allowing them to live somewhat productive lives with more freedom of movement to hunt as their occasional wet work allowed. That was where their old teammate Kenny had ended up, a better fit for the time being.

"Bec!" Kyle met her inside the doors. He hugged her before he took a long look at her. "What's wrong?" He looked up at Michael, questioning. "What happened to her? Why is she so pale?" Kyle's eyes slid down her neck, resting on the punctures at the edge of her shirt. Eyes and mouth opened in shock. "She's not a..." He couldn't finish, his hand sliding absently to his own punctures. He didn't exactly flinch although he gave a wide berth to the large wolf trotting unevenly behind them and padded down the hall into an office.

Michael shook his head, putting a supportive arm around her shoulders. "No. Vanessa's goal was consumption, not conversion." He kept his outward appearances calm, his voice quavered only slightly with the beast inside him wanting desperately to break something.

Becca let him steer her to a long bench lining the hall. Her legs gave out just as she reached the seat and Kyle helped her to lift them as Michael lowered her head to lie down.

"Kyle, we have a timeline. Homeland Security is going to start hitting these alleged terrorists soon and while I can de-emphasize unusual behavior on an individual basis, a group this large is going to draw the kind of attention I am going to have to have a very difficult time explaining away." Admiral Black stepped out of the office. "We need you in *here* getting rid of this thing *now*."

Giving his sister's leg a final pat, he returned to the office and his work.

Black remained in the hall after Kyle left them. Michael felt his eyes those eyes boring into him as he continued to crouch, stroking her hair back from the marks already nearly healed. He couldn't deny the draw her blood held for him. The one time he had tasted it it had been intoxicating.

"She is important to you." He wasn't asking.

Michael's head fell forward. He hadn't wanted to give Black any further hold over either of them. "Yes, Sir." He stood, back still to the admiral. He was listening to Becca's faint heartbeat. She had lost a lot of blood and the strain of the night's adventures had taken their toll on her human body.

The admiral's next words took Michael by surprise and he turned to face him. "She needs strength, Michael. Give her your blood." At his captain's bewildered reaction to his suggestion, Black shrugged. "I am many things Michael, practical being one of them. We need her."

He was torn. Michael knew Becca needed blood. He also knew it was a dangerous thing to give a human vampire blood too often. It could lead to madness or addiction. The temporary effects of enhanced senses, strength, and rapid healing all had the potential to be addictive, much like a street drug that made one feel invincible.

Black saw his apprehension and made the decision for him. "I would give her mine if I didn't think it would kill her. We have proven her chemistry is incompatible. She has value to all of us. You must put your personal feelings aside for now, Michael. I am not asking you to change her, merely to get her well fast. We might need her if her brother is unable to reverse the program."

"What about her brother, Sir?" Michael had been thinking about Kyle's computer savvy. He was willing to wager his knack for computers was more than mere skill. There had been no outward indication of this tickler Vanessa had attached yet he had found it within the first few minutes of his search. Michael was no expert yet he doubted the average software developer would be so quick even if it *was* his program. Kyle would figure this out too. The only question being whether he would get to it before anyone was the wiser. Kyle was not the only computer genius in this world. A number of them worked for Homeland Security monitoring their systems for glitches and new patterns that might indicate a hack or cyber attack. So many were coming from Asia of late, they were watching closely.

"He'll be handled when he has righted his wrong." He nodded at Becca's pale body. "Take care of it, Michael. I would prefer you take point with our helper in there. You know I have limited patience for how slow they are."

"Yes Sir," Michael replied stiffly. The admiral made no bones about his distaste for the mundane. Daily drama failed to hold his interest. Black limited himself to the bigger picture sorts of intrigue: political positioning, power struggles between nations, and strategy were the areas where he excelled and utilized his exceptional skills. Captain Rossi handled the daily tasks and smaller minutiae involved in running their unit. That was Michael's strength. More than just the tasks, Michael could inspire the loyalty of his men to get them to work for him in situations where other leaders would face mutiny.

"Have you heard anything from Gabrielle, Sir?" He changed the subject. "Has she been able to find anything on Vanessa?" They'd sent Gabrielle out searching for her base of operations as soon as they had left the warehouse. He had yet to hear from her.

Black shook his head. "Vanessa was able to confuse her tracks. I am afraid we are facing a dead end. Ask her when she wakes, she might know something." Pointing at Becca to remind him his task, he turned on his heel to return to monitoring Kyle's progress.

Michael knew his patience was finite and he was working with a limited amount of time. Gazing down at her again, Michael focused on the faint rising and falling of her chest wishing they had more time to let her recover naturally. From a mobility and function standpoint he was right, of course. They needed her healthy. If something happened and they lost one of their number or if they lost *her* because he didn't do this, he wouldn't be able to forgive himself. "Yes, Sir," he called quietly to the admiral's back.

Kneeling down beside her, Michael drew his fangs. It was as easy as breathing for him at his age. The pain was minimal when he pierced the flesh of his wrist. His other hand slid under her head, bringing it up to meet his wound as the blood began to leak out.

After the first few swallows Becca's eyes fluttered open and Michael watched her absorb what was happening. Her hazel eyes grew enormous when the taste of the blood registered. She turned her head away and closed her lips, rejecting any more of it.

Michael retracted his fangs, removing his arm and licking his wrist to seal his wounds. He sat very still, waiting for her to react.

Becca came back to her senses from being mostly passed out for all intents and purposes to taste blood in her mouth and see Michael hovering over her in the dimly lit hallway. Pale green paint on the walls lent his pale skin an eerie cast in a trick of the light.

Her first instinct had been to spit when she tasted blood. Then as she came fully awake and saw Michael staring at her, vulnerable, she held back. In those seconds, she felt a surge of her pulse and heard her heart hammering in her ears. The faint smell of ammonia filled the air, a fluorescent bulb hummed down the hall. Becca squinted against the glare of the lights shining too bright in her eyes.

Fearing she was beginning to have a vision, she tried to distract herself. She focused on him and felt the newly familiar shifting of her perception as her ability recalled him and attempted to jump again. Carefully she reined it in, she had neither the need nor the strength for that at present.

When she woke with Michael's blood in her mouth, senses sharper, she understood the connection between his blood in her and the quick healing, increased strength in the Odessa street fight with Vlad, and even possibly the boost to her ability.

"Why are you feeding me blood?" she inquired. She was sure to keep the accusation from her voice, telling him nothing more than mere curiosity fueled her question.

Michael continued to watch her nervously for signs of disgust or fear. "Black. He wants you strong fast. A taste of our blood will do that and we've already seen what his does to you. That leaves me."

Becca frowned at him.

"That night at the estate, when I gave you medicine." He so clearly didn't want to tell her. She felt him struggling to honor his promise to keep no secrets from her. "The admiral had given you a serum concocted from his blood in an effort to heal you faster." He pointed to the injection site on her arm. "That was what burned."

There was no need to remind her of that. Becca had felt that burning through the haze of exhaustion and sickness and still it burned like nothing had before in her life. The relief when Michael had sucked the poison out had been cool water in a parched desert. He had saved her then too.

"That was his blood? How did you know yours wouldn't have done the same thing?" She studied his expression, pairing it up with the sensations she was feeling from him; on some level she didn't fully comprehend.

Michael hid his expression, studying the floor. "With age, we don't need as much blood to survive. The older vampires have highly concentrated blood and it can get pretty dicey when a human ingests it. I'm younger, my blood less potent, and you've tasted it before and lived. Do you remember what happened after the injection that burned?"

The memory of that night came back again. The burning, the blissful cool as the poison left her system and then some sort of medicine being fed to her through mostly sleeping lips before she fell asleep.

"You gave me your blood?" Again questioning, fascinated.

Michael watched her, waiting for her to panic or scream at him, waiting for the bubble to burst when she realized the monster he was, and the liberties he had taken with her body without her knowledge or permission.

Instead, Becca shook her head slowly in disbelief. "You've saved my life twice."

He was trying so hard to keep his mask in place, to hide his worry and doubt, and she saw through it. She sensed his self-loathing for what it was.

Becca sat up and leaned forward. Michael kept his hands clenched at his sides, still kneeling by the bench. To his amazement, she scooted forward to the edge of the bench and put her hands on his knees.

"Michael, I get why you did it. It's weird but hey, I have this whole sight thing and I work with vampires and werewolves now. It's *all* weird." She gave a short laugh before her brow pinched and she put her hands on the sides of his face. "Thank you for doing what you needed to do to save my life."

He was staring at her in utter disbelief. "It doesn't make you sick? You aren't upset?"

She shook her head. "No. I told you I knew you wouldn't hurt me and I meant it. I trust you." Leaning forward, she pressed her lips lightly against his. "I love you, Michael."

At their touch, Becca appreciated the enhanced senses. The sensitivity of her lips as they met his cool, firm set was twofold at least. Where her hands touched his face, Becca reveled in the feel of the unusual firmness of his skin under her fingertips. Getting lost in the intensity of the sensations, both how he felt and how it was making her feel, she ran her fingers down his jaw, swirling around his ears before sliding down the sides of his neck.

As her fingers met the top of his collar, Michael gave a small grumble of pleasure in his throat. Smiling at the victory, Becca brought her hands up to grab the back of his hair and curl her fingers into it, pushing him into her while holding him captive.

Her reaction released the pacing beast inside Michael. Her return had placated its need for violence. It continued to demand satisfaction. Forgetting everything else, he pulled her off her seat and onto his lap straddling him. Michael's hands slid up her arms, cupping the sides of her face tenderly while he kissed her.

"I love you too, Becca," Michael responded between his physical devotions. Even though he'd heard her say it at the restaurant, Michael couldn't believe his ears. She was declaring her love for him and, as much as he feared she would live to regret it, he let himself live in that one fantastic moment. Michael let himself believe that she truly did love him despite being a horrible monster.

The heady scent of her mixed with his blood on her lips and acted as an aphrodisiac. His arms tightened around her, Becca's breasts crushed against his chest. Michael slid his hand down her back, his tongue moved to find the marks on her neck and tenderly he sealed them, leaving no residual marks while extracting another eager utterance from her.

A car door slammed, Michael's ears perked up but he did not stop his lovemaking. His teeth grazed her chin. The sound of approaching footsteps on the steps outside made Michael reluctantly loosen his hold on Becca. She'd heard the same thing and was in the process of sliding off his lap back onto the bench when in walked her former partner, alone.

Becca darted a sideways glance. "You have got to be kidding," she muttered, breathing hard.

Danny took one look at them and his shoulders drooped. "A vampire, Bec? Really? Do you *want* to die?"

Chapter 30

"What did you say?" Becca felt her jaw go slack.

Unguarded loathing in his eyes, Danny came to a halt beside Becca and looked down at Michael who stared back unblinking.

Michael, however, did not seem surprised. "You know what I am. I thought so."

Danny gave him half a nod. "Yep, I've seen auras since I was a kid. Mom always told me that was how I could tell what everyone was up to." For a moment the amiable Danny broke through then was gone again. "I was a great tattletale. Made me good at my job, figuring who was up to something."

Becca was staring at him. Her whole world continued to tip on its end. The strange thing about this whole thing was, the two people in her life she had felt the most at ease with were both things that shouldn't be. *She* shouldn't *be* according to how she'd been raised. This sort of stuff just wasn't real.

Becca didn't remember much about her Gran, a very limited access topic in their home. And before she could ask any advice from her, she'd been gone. She did remember her saying something that made no sense at the time. Becca had been eleven. It had been one of their semi-annual trips to the institution. "You'll find what's right for you," she'd told her. She must have known something.

"You can see auras?" she asked him.

He nodded again, pointing at her. "Yours is funny. It fluxes from a nice happy gold to super dark when you have one of those weird little daydreams you have."

Becca stared, astounded at the accuracy of Danny's observations "I have visions about what's gonna happen."

Becca was astonished to discover she wasn't ashamed of admitting the truth she'd hidden her entire life.

Michael moved his body closer to Becca protectively.

"Relax," Danny shook his head, laughing harshly. "I'm the last person that would hurt, Bec." He frowned, suddenly serious. "That's why I hope you can believe there was *no* warning with Terry. I swear. I've known him forever and had no idea he would lay a hand on you."

His effusive concern on the subject made Becca self-conscious. "Danny, it's okay. I forgive you. Everyone gets one bad decision and now you've used yours." She aimed for levity. This was all too intense. "So, don't make another." She gave him a look, hoping he'd caught her warning.

He flipped a hint of a grin at her, still a little of her friend in there. "So you're one of us, huh, Bec?" Danny reached out, pausing only a second to make eye contact with Michael. They had a small but obvious battle of the wills before he asserted himself and leaned over to touch her arm. "No wonder I liked you."

Becca was fascinated to have someone to talk to about being different. "Does your family know? Are they cool with it?"

"Both of my parents are and a ton of people on Dad's side." He rolled his eyes. "Isn't yours?" Danny's open, honest face brought her guard back up.

"No."

"Just, no?"

Feeling awkward, Becca attempted to shut down the family exploration. "It isn't something we talk about."

He looked shocked. "Never? Really? How did you explain all of the kooky stuff growing up? Didn't you have questions when you first started to see things? My cousin has the sight and when it came on he thought he was hallucinating. He accused his brother of putting acid in his Coke."

She shrugged, watching her knees wiggle. "It didn't come up."

Regarding Danny coldly, Michael intervened. Seeing her growing discomfort, he rested a soothing hand on her leg. "What are you doing here, Danny?"

The quick flash of annoyance that crossed Danny's face wasn't hard to miss. She didn't know if it was because Michael was a vampire or there was some more normal reason, like his possessiveness. It didn't bother her, she'd had a hell of a night and a little comfort was more than welcome.

"I'm done with my shift. I always come back here to write up my reports at the end of my shift." He inclined his head toward his old partner. "Bec knows that."

Kyle chose that moment to stick his head out the partially closed door. "Bec, Michael, everything okay out here? Admiral wants you in here, like now." His dark eyes were bloodshot, bags developing rapidly from lack of sleep and the strain of staring at the computer.

He glanced around the door at Danny. Poor Kyle was already on edge and the extra stress of the admiral watching over his shoulder wasn't helping his nerves. His hair stood out in new and comical ways. Combined with the greenish cast of the walls and fluorescents Kyle looked a little like a ghoul.

Becca kicked herself for having forgotten about him while she made out in the hall like a hormonal teenager. Michael had that effect on her, when he touched her she forgot about everything else. Now that she was feeling stronger from the blood and they weren't licking each other, she refocused.

"Danny, meet my brother Kyle. Kyle, this is my old partner Danny. Kyle is helping out with a computer problem."

Kyle gave him a nod. "Are you here to help too?"

Danny shook his head. "No, but I can. What are you working on?" He was openly staring at Kyle

Kyle, for his part, was growing increasingly uncomfortable at his absence from his station, glancing over his shoulder waiting for the reminder he knew was coming.

"We'll be right in, Kyle." She felt her face flush. "I'm sorry." She turned to her former partner and sent him off with genuine remorse. "Really Danny, we're working on something that you probably shouldn't be involved in." Her brother was already in too deep, there was no reason for Danny to get sucked in as well. The less involvement Danny had, the better. She intended to get Kyle free of here as soon as possible. Becca was counting on Michael to help her convince Black to let him go when this was over. The idea of having his memory erased worried her. Hopefully there weren't any side effects, like him forgetting who he was or something.

Danny's eyes narrowed and he glared at Michael. "Bec, can I speak to you for a minute? Alone?"

She spared a glance at Michael and saw that he was focused entirely on Danny. His blank expression, she was learning, spelled trouble. Squeezing his arm, she called his attention to her. "Michael, give me a minute?"

He turned his head toward her, blinking once before nodding. "We have work to do." He stood waiting, motionless in the hall.

She smiled tightly at him, feeling torn between duty and loyalty. Could this night get more complicated? "I'll be quick." There was no way to satisfy all of the demands on her.

They walked to the far end of the hall. Far enough a human would believe his conversation safe from curious ears. It didn't bother her that Michael could still hear them. She only worried for Danny's safety if Black overheard something. He was the *real* danger here. Where was he?

Danny reached the far wall and stopped immediately, getting right to the point. Turning to face her, his eyes burned with a fiery intensity. "Is this your new assignment? Are you *working* with that thing? I had a feeling when I saw him the first time. Then, with what happened with Terry, I didn't get a chance to talk to you." He shook his head, clearly distressed. "I don't know what they've told you but vamps are no good. They may convince you they're okay with their mind games," he aimed a particularly hateful glance at Michael, "but in the end they're nothing but killers, Bec. Cold blooded killers. You've got to get out of this now, before you get hurt." His brow furrowed. Raising a hand, he cupped her chin and twisted her face in the light. "Unless it's already too late." Danny released her as if she burned him and took a step back from her. "You sure don't look like a girl who's been smacked around."

Becca blinked at him, not sure what to say. The blunt way he pushed her away needled her. How could she tell him what had happened and make him understand that she hadn't been at some sort of gothic sex party sucking on a vampire for fun, it had been a necessity. And she was hopelessly in love with that necessity.

"Michael won't hurt me."

Danny was sure of his position and tried to lay it out for her. "Who is he anyway? He comes out of nowhere, scoops you up and takes you out of the hospital before you're ready. And now he's with you whenever I see you, like you can't be left alone or you'll go AWOL on him. Can't you see what he's doing? Is *this* what you want to do with yourself, let him have you until he's taken what he wants and you're a shell or worse?"

Her hackles were coming up fast, frustrated that after a year and a half of trusting each other, Danny now questioned her ability to judge for herself. For the moment she left out the whole "in love" bit. "Captain Rossi is my new unit commander. And yes, it's what I want to be doing. I can't tell you any more than that."

His eyebrow rose. "Gone to the dark side, huh?"

She couldn't tell if he meant her inference that she'd gone into a covert division or if he was referring to the company she was keeping.

"My mother has a gift like mine," he began more gently. "She taught me about auras and how each living being has one, they're all just a little bit different." His dark eyes broke off from hers to study the floor.

"We were at the beach when I was a kid. We saw a swimmer disappear under the waves. I was closer and swam out to help. I didn't want to leave him out there so I kept diving, looking. He didn't come back up and Mom started yelling for me to come back. I was thinking he was drowning, I didn't think about sharks or anything until Mom yelled. Then I got scared and swam hard back to the shallows. About an hour later the Coast Guard pulled the body out, minus the head. I heard 'em say it'd been chewed off. We all assumed a shark. There didn't seem to be any other logical explanation.

The crowd was busy gawking at the headless corpse and Mom grabbed my hand, hard." He winced at the memory. "When I looked at her, she was staring down the beach. Out came this guy. I didn't get it. I mean no one had been in the water since the victim went under and this guy just comes walking out, down the beach about a hundred feet away. No one paid any attention, even I didn't see the big deal until it clicked what had Mom so upset. This guy had no aura. I mean nothing at all. Some people who are pretty dull have a faint one, but they have one. This guy was cold.

286

I asked my mom why and she didn't say a word. She just grabbed me and pulled me up the beach. It wasn't until we were in the car with the radio going that she told me why he didn't have an aura. He was a vampire. Only the dead and undead don't have one." Danny pointed at Michael. "That guy does *not* have one."

His story disturbed her, true. The concept that they hunted was just that to her. A concept. She hadn't seen them attack and kill in their "vampire form" so to speak. Michael had even killed the Russian using very human means. And when he'd bitten her in the throes of passion it still hadn't been violent. Maybe that was why she found it relatively easy to live among them without running away screaming. She preferred to believe it was because other than their quirks of genetics they were good people.

"That was one guy. They're like us, there are some bad ones and there are some good ones too. We're all interested in the same thing Danny. We all signed on for the same reason, to protect our country from the bad guys."

He continued as if she hadn't spoken, "Mom told me about the guy that worked with her and her gift. See, she was an orphan. When she hit puberty and her gift came on, she ran away from her foster family. She was ashamed of it. Thought something was wrong with her."

That was something Becca could understand.

"Well, she found this guy. Kind of a good samaritan who used to talk to the runaways on the streets. He was sensitive too and knew Mom had the sight. He taught her how to use it and became a mentor to her. Sometimes she would go with him at night when he walked the streets looking for lost kids. One night they saw a couple behind a dumpster in an alley. She said he tried to break it up because it looked wrong. He told Mom to hide since sometimes people don't appreciate the interference, you know? He got close, tried to break it up and Mom said the lady dropped the guy when her friend got close. He was dead. She had blood on her face and grabbed her friend. He was a big guy. Mom said he was like 6'2" and maybe two fifty. She picked him like he was nothing and threw him into the building next to her. He didn't get up. Mom didn't move, she was terrified, which is probably what saved her life. That and the fact that some other people happened to walk by. Mom followed them until she got to a coffee shop and she stayed there all night. She said that was her first vampire and she's steered clear of anything missing an aura since. They'll kill you just as soon as look at you."

He shot a look over at Michael. Becca followed his glance. Michael was standing where they'd left him, appearing to be waiting patiently. She knew he was hearing every word. Danny might know how to identify them but he hadn't a clue about all of what they could do or he wouldn't be speaking so loosely.

Becca answered him softly. "I can't leave, I want to be with them. I hope you can understand. They're good people."

He groaned. "They aren't people. Haven't you heard me? They're animals. Horrible, murdering animals."

Just at that moment, the front doors opened and in walked a large honey-colored wolf. Becca smiled and raised a hand in greeting.

Danny's eyes widened in fear, he grabbed Becca's arm got right in her face and whispered hotly. "Are you stupid? How many of these devils do you surround yourself with? I'm taking you out of here. If you can't think clearly enough to save yourself, then I will." He started to walk, dragging her behind him.

Becca planted her feet and twisted her body, breaking free. He grabbed at her and she sent a warning shot into his ribs.

The quickness of her movement caught him unawares. Collapsing at his waist, Danny gasped for breath. His eyes told her she'd proven him right, she was one of them now.

Ryan's head popped out of a janitor's closet a few doors down. He was human again and wore black fatigues somebody must have brought or he found. Gabrielle stayed down at the far end and Michael was in the middle, watching them closely, his face deadly calm.

Becca feared for Danny's life. "Danny," she spoke urgently. "You have to get out of here. I don't expect you to understand it, but they aren't going to hurt *me*." She looked from one end of the hall to the other, not liking what she was seeing on their faces. "I can't say the same for you. You have to go."

Still trying to catch his breath, Danny held his hand to his side and looked up at her before turning his head to survey the threats on either side of him. "You think they'll let me walk out?"

Her stomach twisted, Becca felt her heart pick up its pace. She couldn't let Danny get hurt because of her. "Michael, please," Becca called out low. She wasn't sure what she was calling for, only that she needed him. Maybe he could reason with the team, back them down.

A small breeze and he stood beside her. "No one will harm him if he goes now." Michael touched her hand.

The instant their skin touched, Becca felt her heart slow down and her mind clear. She flicked her eyes up and saw that he was watching Danny. The indeterminate set of his jaw puzzled her. Focusing intently on him, she found herself slipping and jumped.

His field of vision was filled with Danny. Becca watched him regaining his breath, his chest rising and falling a hair too quickly, his heart beat too fast. From months of working as his partner she could almost hear him thinking. Running through his options. As much as Danny believed he wasn't walking out of here, he hadn't given up.

"Bec, what the hell!" Danny grabbed her shoulders. He stared at her, dismay and revulsion equally represented in his expression.

Danny's touch shocked her out of her connection and she was cast back into herself. Switching perspective so fast brought with it a healthy dose of vertigo.

"What?" She threw her hands out to steady herself.

Danny raised his finger to point at her, unable to hide the tremor. "Your aura just disappeared." His eyes roved sideways to take in Michael's tall, still form. "You were like him."

Found out, Becca found herself unable to make eye contact with either one. She knew at some point she was going to have to discuss her new capability with Michael or even Black. They would want to know and it would be a tactical advantage on missions. She'd wanted to find out more about it first, like if there were limits or if she could jump into anyone. So far she'd only gone into people she knew, she'd touched. Knowing she'd tasted vampire blood, blood that made her stronger brought with it new understanding. On the verge of an "aha," she didn't answer Danny's accusation.

While Becca reeled she heard the sound of a door opening down the hall accompanied by the sudden silence that followed and she felt her heart sink. Only Black could hush a room like that.

Chapter 31

After what felt like the longest moment of her life, Becca finally heard that cold voice creep down her spine. The hairs on the back of her neck rose and her vision began to dance. As much as she didn't want to do it again, Becca didn't want to be blind should there be a battle for Danny's life.

As soon as she jumped, Becca heard Danny's gasp. She blinked to acclimate herself to the change in perspective.

"What are you doing?" Danny panted. "That isn't possible."

She saw movement on both ends of the hall out of her periphery. Gabrielle was still in her wolf form and approaching slowly. Ryan's human bulk came from the other side, equally intimidating.

"Rebecca, I am pleased to see you well enough to function. Might I point out, however, our computer whiz is attempting to secure the safety of our entire society and you are distracting him. Do I need to handle this situation myself?"

"No!" Becca nearly shouted and finally forced herself to face not Danny, but Michael.

The look on his face combined with the mix of feelings she sensed from him served as a bitch slap of guilt. He could feel something happening, though she didn't think he understood what exactly she was doing. "No, Sir. My old partner was on duty tonight and we were talking. He was just leaving."

"I don't think things are so simple. It sounds to me like he has some information about you that interests me." The obsidian eyes regarded Danny flatly as he loomed tall and green in the lighting. The bulb over he and Michael hummed and flickered, the only sound breaking the silence of the suddenly crowded corridor.

Becca stared at Black for a long moment, trying to figure out a way to explain her jump without making it seem like she was a psychic spy in Michael's head. She squared her shoulders, facing him straight on. "Since Michael has," she paused flustered to say it out loud, "helped me heal," Danny gave a choking cough, "I've been able to kind of 'jump' into you and use your eyes." Unsure why she felt the need, Becca kept the jump to Ryan quiet. Black might not like to think she could get into anyone's head. Michael gave her blood, they'd had sex, who knew the whys of it all, but that was the one she'd admit to.

She lifted her face to put her narrow field of vision on him and watched his blue eyes flickering back and forth from light to dark blue before settling at midnight. Becca clung to the fact that they were not yet black. Good. He wasn't completely furious though she could sense a pretty strong vibe of anger with maybe a hint of fear. His tone was becoming more difficult to read as he flattened out his voice, hiding himself away. In order to better predict her partner's safety, Becca maintained her connection to her lover, feeling all the while she was intruding upon his privacy when he surely wanted it.

Black chuckled, distracting her from Michael's tumultuous reaction. Michael followed the sound and Becca could see his thin colorless lips pulled tight into a smile. But instead of looking at her, he was scrutinizing Danny.

The first time Danny saw Black, his face went ashen. It didn't take preternatural abilities to see how the admiral could scare someone absolutely witless.

Michael took control of the situation. "Sir, this is Petty Officer Second Class Danny Yamamoto. He served as Becca's partner for the last year and a half. He has preternatural abilities as well. Danny can read auras."

The admiral's flat black gaze bored into Danny. "It seems we have an unforeseen complication." He spoke to the others without removing his focus from their trio. "Ryan, please look in on Kyle. See that he does not need anything. Gabrielle, go get changed please. I will make certain there are no further distractions out here."

The wolves, one actually still a wolf, followed their orders. Black stepped closer to the remaining three.

Michael watched the admiral approach, his mind spinning. Becca could be in his head. What did that mean exactly? Could she use more than his eyes? Could she hear his thoughts? Was that why his head buzzed sometimes? Was it her? He wished they could discuss this in private. He didn't want Black knowing any of this. What if it meant she could connect with Black through his bond with Michael? There was no telling how Black would take that. He could see it as fortuitous or he could see it as dangerous. If that were the case, the outlook for Becca's future was grim.

"Sir, if I may," Michael began. He fully intended to spin this new element of their dynamic to the positive both for Becca's safety, and also Danny's. He could see what her friend meant to her. "Becca and Danny both have impeccable service records." He ignored the curious look Danny gave him; Becca didn't appear surprised to hear he'd researched her partner. "And Becca has already proven to be of great value to our unit. I would imagine Danny's unique talent would give us the advantage of seeing living from undead from a greater distance. His ability used in conjunction with Becca's would significantly enhance our capabilities in the field." He forgot to pretend to breathe.

Admiral Black pondered his suggestion, remaining as still as death and focusing straight ahead. Michael, for all his concerns that Black would see their personal relationship deepening, couldn't prevent his hand from seeking Becca's. Her small, warm fingers slid between his readily.

Smelling her fear, though not as well as Danny's, Michael forced his feelings down and hushed the vampire inside of him. It wouldn't help to escalate anyone's emotions right

293

now. Black needed to see their ability to remain calm in the face of danger.

He couldn't profess an undying love or loyalty to the commander. His was deeper than that, a blood bond that could be broken only by the death of one of the two. That being said, he did know him probably better than anyone living or undead. He was the humans' best bet for survival.

This new turn of Becca's had Michael shaken. He hadn't anticipated such a thing. What was it and what could she sense through it? The pluses and minuses were numerous and he wasn't entirely sure which side was greater. The thought that she might discover how tightly he was bound to the admiral frankly scared him. She wouldn't use it against him, he knew that. However, it might cause her to question his motivations with her. Michael would have to find out how extensive her access might be and soon.

Black spoke again, interrupting his thoughts. He felt Becca start and stroked the back of her hand with his thumb, feeling her relax. Danny was practically vibrating next to him but there was nothing he could do there. Influencing a preternatural was always a fifty-fifty shot assuming, if by some off chance, he had an opportunity to do so without being caught by Black. To take the liberty of influencing the man in front of the admiral would be the equivalent of giving an order in front of an outranking officer. His most recent punishment was still fresh in his memory. Instead, Michael could only hope the man would be smart. There hadn't been much precedence of that.

"I like your line of thinking, Michael. However, we do not have the same option for promising Petty Officer Yamamoto's loyalty."

Inwardly, Michael cringed though he kept his face smooth. He heard Becca catch her breath. The fact that the statement continued to affect her bothered him more than he let on. Honesty was something he hadn't practiced for a long time and he was surprised by how important it was that she believed him that he hadn't slept with her at Black's urging.

Becca interceded, pleading for Danny. "Admiral, *I* will guarantee Danny's loyalty if you'll spare him." Her desperation was clear in her voice.

Danny finally spoke up for himself. "What if *I* don't want to work with *you*? I don't want any part of this business." His disgust was biting.

Michael's touch having cleared her own sight, Becca was back in her own head. Jumping so much was nauseating. She'd have to wear some sort of Dramamine patch if this was going to be a thing. "Danny," Becca began, as she renewed her grip on Michael's hand, seeking his calming influence. "I think you should hear me out. If you knew what we do, I think you would actually *want* to work with us." She willed him to listen.

Glancing only sparingly at Admiral Black who had stopped a few feet from him, Danny looked back at Becca and gave a decidedly hesitant nod.

"This group *is* made up of special individuals," she was careful not to call them people, "but they're the good guys. We *catch* the bad ones."

A quick glance at Black tempered Danny's open sarcasm. "And what, send them to the brig? They'd break out as soon as you lock them in. Not exactly a big threat there."

She shook her head. "No, there are places, strong enough to hold anything. And if they're *really* bad guys, they don't make it that far." Her voice wavered on the last part, her discomfort clear.

"No vampire is going to take down his own for the sake of a human."

Becca caught sight of a black-clad Gabrielle emerging from the janitor's closet. She held up a finger for her to wait. She had an idea, even if the thought of torturing someone ate at her. It could guarantee Danny walking out of here. "Why don't you wait and see for yourself? Sir," she faced Black, "I wonder if we could bring Vanessa in here?"

Willing to give her run, Black's lips spread in a thin smile before he gave the one word command. "Gabrielle."

Michael nodded his agreement. "We need to question her anyway. Soon if Kyle doesn't crack the program."

Gabrielle accepted the command, her face fixed in its usual sour grimace. While she was gone they heard a whoop from the office where Kyle was still hard at work.

Black disappeared back into the office before Becca saw him move. Michael and Becca exchanged glances and hurriedly followed him inside. She heard footsteps following close behind them.

The small office was crowded with so many bodies. Danny was the last one in and preferred to stand with his back pressed tightly to the door. There was only room for Black and Ryan behind Kyle at the computer.

"Well?" Becca asked her brother expectantly.

Positively beaming, Kyle was pointing at the screen as if they all could understand what they were seeing. It was just a bunch of screens with names, rank, addresses; it could be a mailing list for all Becca understood. "I found it. Whoever she used is pretty good." His voice faded, they all knew that person was long gone. Vanessa wouldn't have left a witness alive. Subdued, he started again. "The tickler was so simple I missed it at first. It just grabbed every file with a tag on it and built a list. It hid itself in the email piece of the program."

"Can you remove it?" Black wanted to know.

Kyle nodded absentmindedly, his eyes glued to the monitor. He'd never stopped typing and clicking around.

Michael didn't miss the hesitation in his pace, the tensing of the shoulders.

Nor did Becca. "What's wrong, Kyle? Can't you take it off?"

"It isn't that. The program was set to send once it had compiled all the data and, if I'm not mistaken, it sent." His dismay was palpable as well as genuine. He wasn't helping solely because of Black. His dedication and now his disappointment gave Michael an idea for when this was over. If they weren't too busy running from the government they were sworn to protect, that is.

"An email?" Admiral Black's chilling question caused everyone in the room to stiffen. "To whom?"

"Um, I'm trying to figure that out." Kyle's brow wrinkled as his fingers flew over the keyboard doing who knew what.

A knock reverberated on the door and Danny jumped forward, bumping into Michael. The human recoiled immediately.

Gabrielle stuck her head in. "I have the prisoner, Sir. Should I put her next door?"

"Yes, I'll be right in," Black told her. He spent only another few seconds watching the screen jump as Kyle flipped between who knew how many programs. Finally, he moved in front of the door. Michael slid out of the way and Danny stepped aside to allow him passage.

Danny followed the stream of observers who followed Black, curiously extending his neck to scope for this mystery prisoner.

Vanessa was being dragged to her destination. Gabrielle held her wrists in her hands and hauled her unceremoniously through the neighboring office's door. Black was on Vanessa's heels, Michael and the humans followed close behind.

When they were inside, the incapacitated body propped in a chair, the admiral gave a quick nod at Gabrielle and her hand flashed down, twisting and removing the fence post Becca had stuck there. As soon as it was removed, Vanessa's eyes blinked and her hands flew to the hole already starting to close.

Danny made strange noises. Michael chose to ignore him. His attention was focused on Vanessa. No longer paralyzed, hungry from her wound, she was a threat to the humans and if the glare she was aiming at Becca standing beside him was any sort of indicator, she wouldn't hesitate to attack.

Admiral Black got her attention. "Welcome back, Vanessa." The small smile he gave was more a show of fang than pleasantry. Black clearly saw the threat she posed, he was giving her the full force of his monstrous nature. Michael had yet to see it fail.

It didn't now. She shrank from Black's show of power, remaining silent as she let Admiral Black lead the conversation.

"This program of yours is a threat to our kind as well as the other non-humans who have found safe haven among our ranks. The penalty for your treachery is death. It is your choice now whether it is lingering or brief." He paused to let his words sink in. "Who else is working with you?"

Astonishingly, Vanessa pushed back. "You assume I will give up the identity of my employer?" Shaking her head, Vanessa flashed a seductive smile at Admiral Black. "Even your fearsome reputation can not convince me to give him up, Admiral."

The admiral held out his hands, bowing sardonically. "I appreciate the compliment to my skills." His face hardened. "Give him to me. I will make your end quick."

Michael watched the shudder run through her as she refused. "Nothing you could do to me would be as great as his punishment." For a moment he considered whether Vanessa could be blood tied to her employer, as he was the admiral. Were that the case there was nothing they could do to get her to speak. He kept himself from touching Becca, thinking their touch would let her see into his mind.

Black moved fast. His hand lashed out, long white fingers tightened in a fist as they struck her shoulder with an audible crack. The bones shattered and her arm drooped, useless.

The female didn't make a noise. The humans whitened.

"All you must give me is his name. In death you have nothing to fear." He let his long, thin fangs extend halfway to his chin. "Even *we* can only die twice."

"He can follow you down to the very depths of Hell. Death is no safe refuge from him."

Again Black's fist flew, over and again. Each connection brought forth the sound of breaking bones, the last a wet smack of tearing flesh. With it came the strong scent of sulfur. It burned Michael's eyes and nose. He snorted. Nothing would make her speak again. Defeated, Admiral Black held out his hand and Gabrielle placed the stake on his palm. Spinning it deftly to bring the pointed end forward, he slid it into her body through the same opening left in her clothing by its previous residence.

When she went still, Black leaned in and whispered in her ear so that the humans couldn't hear. Michael did.

"I know *what* you are working for, I smell him in your blood. When I find him, I will tell him you betrayed him. Wait for him in Hell, Vanessa." He straightened, glanced up

299

at Gabrielle and ordered, "Take her out to the desert and leave her to the sun. In her state a few hours will be sufficient." He looked out the window, seeing the sun's rays becoming more pronounced as full dawn approached. "Be sure no one sees. We already have our fill of humans as it is."

Giving a quick nod, Gabrielle picked up the limp vampire and dragged her by the arm, making a point of touching her as little as possible. Vanessa made not a sound as she was carried unceremoniously to face her end.

Black straightened his jacket and turned to face him. "Ryan, take the humans back to the estate. Michael and I have some tracking to do."

His decision to bring them to the estate either spoke to the admiral's acceptance of them or meant he didn't intend for them to live beyond his uses. Becca felt her vision trying to flare. Michael stood perfectly still at her side, carefully avoiding her touch.

"What's going on? What estate? I'm not going anywhere but home." Danny frantically scanned the faces around him. He landed on Becca.

She saw the break looming in his eyes as they grew wild. Guilt lent her the bravery to gulp down her own fears and speak up. "Why do we have to go back to the estate? I thought you brought me in to help." Ignoring the warning look in Ryan's eyes she stared at the admiral's chest, fighting the tangible compulsion to close her mouth and obey.

Admiral Black waited what seemed an eternity, the whole of which Becca imagined one of those bony white fists the size of both of hers together smashing in to her like he had done to Vanessa. Stoically she waited, not letting him see her cringing inside. All of her faith was behind the clear vision with which she continued to stare at the rows of color on navy covering his chest.

The officer's jacket in front of her turned sideways and left the office. Only the banging of the door in its frame could be heard at his departure.

A pale hand reached out to touch the side of her face and stopped, falling back to his side. Becca forced herself to meet his eyes and wrapped her arms around herself at the sight of his cold exterior.

"Becca." Michael's words were hushed, wanting to keep his warning private. Other than Ryan, it was. "Please trust me, what we are after is something far too dangerous for you to hunt." He kept his eyes above her head, hiding from her.

"No Michael, I can't just wait while you guys hunt down whatever evil thing is responsible for all of this." Her sigh was ragged. He was right; she wasn't ready. Odessa had been luck and Vanessa had proven that wasn't always enough. Before she went back in the field after one of them Becca need more specialized training. There was no way she was admitting that to him.

Keeping his chin up, eyes straight at the wall he answered. "No." He didn't raise his voice while his stern tone left no room for argument. "And stay out of my head," he added brusquely.

She bristled at his abruptness, bowing to his seniority. Again she wished she could have explained what she'd done in private where she would have had a chance to tell him she used the jump to keep herself clear, not to spy. She wouldn't use it to keep tabs on him or find out anything that wasn't related to someone's safety. She prayed she would have an opportunity to explain herself.

"Ryan," he called out a little louder. Stepping back and spinning on his heel, Michael treaded lightly out. The door banged shut again.

Left alone with the humans, Ryan barked out authoritatively, "Humans, front and center."

Taken aback by his volume, Becca was staring at him when she heard Kyle come out of the office. Danny and she stood shoulder to shoulder at attention in front of Ryan. Kyle rambled up beside her.

Ryan surveyed his mortal unit and broke into a grin. "Come on humans, let's get you out of here for safe keeping."

"But I'm getting close on tracing the server," Kyle objected.

Rolling his eyes, Ryan chuckled. "Wait til you see the computer you'll be working on. It makes this thing look like an Etch a Sketch."

The smile on Kyle's face was positively glowing. He practically vibrated with anticipation, the gravity of his task forgotten in his excitement for new technology.

Shooting a sideways glance at Danny, Becca noted the tight lines of his face and his pallor with a twinge. She couldn't help feeling responsible for his being there. She should have remembered their habit of coming back and filling out reports at the end of their shift. Routines of her life from less than a week ago were fading fast in the face of her new life.

Chapter 32

They parked at the front steps of the large house. Ryan stepped out, waiting at the base of the stone steps while the others emerged from the car. Becca paid close attention to the reactions of her brother and partner.

Kyle was visibly holding himself back, his eagerness to get inside and see this computer Ryan promised outweighed any hesitation he had about entering a house at Admiral Black's direction. As was to be expected, Danny had locked himself down, refusing to make eye contact with her.

Becca was losing her battle with the crushing fear that she had lost Michael. His curt treatment of her could be explained away, something he would get over as he adjusted to the idea. But nothing except blatant distrust would cause him to tell her to "stay out" of his head. The rejection tore its way through her, leaving holes all through her insides worse than any her vision left in her sight. It took all she had to keep her outward appearance calm and cool for her brother and Danny, like Michael. The searing pain in her heart surged back.

Barely containing himself, Kyle held himself to a walk with his fingers already keying the air in anticipation. Danny took a quick step to stay ahead of her leaving Becca to bring up the rear and wallow. Becca held her back straight, her head high.

The great wooden doors swung open under Ryan's hand and in they walked.

"Wow, this place is great," Kyle murmured, his head swiveling to take it all in.

Danny's spine was ramrod straight, what she saw of his jaw had her waiting to hear his teeth crack.

Together they made their way straight for the bank of advanced technology in the basement. Descending the spiral stairs single file, Kyle was the first to see the room open up before him and gasped in pleasure.

"Oh whoa. This is amazing."

Ryan brightened, delighted to be showing off their toys. Holding out his hands to the walls, he continued, "That's right, we have it all. You'll be working on that station over there." He pointed to the console in the center of the room.

Kyle twisted his head, gaping wide-eyed at his sister. "You've been holding back, Bec. This is almost as good as we have back at the lab." His dark eyes twinkled in the dim light.

"How can you see anything down here?" Danny mumbled sullenly.

Blinking, Becca realized with a shock the room was no longer dim to her. Not nearly as much so as that first night. Consuming Michael's blood had enhanced her senses significantly. She turned slowly in an arc, studying the room now so much more visible to her human eyes. Becca wondered if this was how Michael saw and heard all the time or if his senses were even stronger. The concept of having drunk blood only gave her a moment's pause before she whisked past it in her mind as just another thing she'd done, like going through training.

"Your eyes adjust."

Ryan eyed her strangely, saying nothing. He must have understood what drinking blood did for a human's senses.

"May I?" Kyle's fingers trailed the console's outer edge.

"By all means." With a few keystrokes to disable the password protection, Ryan stepped out of the way to allow Kyle access.

Eagerly he rolled the streamlined black chair up to the computer and his fingers began to fly. Ryan watched over his shoulder, a curious look on his face. Danny looked huffy. The instinctive way Kyle maneuvered his way through the foreign defense software was uncanny. Within less than a minute, he was where he needed to be, trying to find the path of the message that was sent out by his hijacked software.

"You've got it too," Ryan said clearly over Kyle's shoulder.

The typing faltered only for a heartbeat then recovered quickly. "I don't know what you're talking about. Quit distracting me."

"Seriously, this is your thing. Like, *really* your thing. It took me weeks to get used to this system and what's it been for you, like thirty-five seconds?"

"Kyle? Are you *different*? *Like me*? Have you been like this the *whole* time?" She was incredulous. All those years of her family pretending they didn't hear her at night, the exchanges over her head when she accidentally let something slip. And he had stood idly by leaving her all alone when he was the same. She had always considered him her protector, her buffer from her parents. He'd done the same for their little brother. "Is Jared?"

Her brother spun his chair around, painfully slow. His shoulders slumped with a weight he'd carried for a lifetime. "Yeah, sort of. But mine's different. It's more of a sense. It's not like I have dreams or anything. I just get this sense when I get around any piece of tech. I've never had it happen with anything else. And besides, what could I have done to make them treat *you* any different? You had your thing, Jared was a total flake and high half the time; I had to be the normal one." He shook his head. "I honestly don't know if Jared has it or not. He dealt with it in his own way. By not dealing with it."

Their kid brother Jared's recreational drug use was a constant concern to all of them. He graduated high school, only just barely sliding through the system; a fact Becca credited more to a few teachers' fudging than her brother's efforts. As soon as he was done, he was gone. Fast food in Aspen while he played as a mountain bum, busboy in Taos when he tried painting, currently construction in Arizona where he did who knew what. Becca lost track. Jared was the lost one.

"I suppose they needed that," She conceded. Three out of three nutty kids would probably have driven her mother over the edge.

"If you two could be done with the family reunion, we need him to use his mojo to track this routing so we can stop this list getting out. It's kind of important." Ryan crossed his arms.

Tight lipped, Kyle spun back around and got to work. With the more powerful system used in conjunction with the unknown boost of his ability, Kyle worked for only a few minutes before exclaiming excitedly. "Got it!"

They all gathered, even Danny.

"They bounced it across three different continents but I followed the IP address and it's right here in California. If I use the satellite link on this system I can give you an exact address." Lifting an eyebrow, he asked permission of the keeper of the computer.

Ryan harrumphed. "Did you figure out the satellites with that gift of yours?"

Kyle colored and nodded.

Ryan harrumphed again.

He kept working. Ryan turned to Becca.

"Talents like these aren't that common anymore and you've naturally surrounded yourself with nothing but preternaturals." He put an arm around her. "That makes a weird sort of sense. I'm glad I didn't eat you." He snapped his teeth playfully.

She caught Danny staring open mouthed at her. "It's okay. It was the full moon, that's all."

Her tidbit didn't appear to comfort her partner.

"Don't worry, I wouldn't bite her now unless she wanted me to." Ryan grinned wolfishly.

That did it for Danny. "What's wrong with you? Cavorting with monsters like it's a joke. It isn't funny. You're going to get killed. It's only a matter of time. Think of the risks they take on missions, risks they can survive but you can't." Pointing accusatorily at Ryan his voice rose. "You heard him, he almost did it already. What if he can't stop himself next time? There's a full moon *every* month, Bec."

"You have no clue about these guys. Your hatred is based on a story and one kill. What if the guy you saw get killed was a bad guy and the one you saw was a good guy, huh?" Becca's back was up. This jaded side of her usually congenial partner was an unflattering aspect of his personality. She couldn't stand seeing him like this. They *were* more dangerous and *did* have the capacity to kill if they chose to but how many *humans* were like that? She tried to explain. "They're just like us. Some of them are good, some bad. Some kill for fun and some try to keep things safe for mortals like us." She motioned to Ryan. "That's what these guys do. They go all over the world stopping bad guys. Like I told you before, they're the *good guys*. I've done more good in the short time with them than I've done in the last three years. How about you Danny? Do you think you've changed the world arresting weekend drunks and trespassers?"

He watched her nostrils flaring, hazel eyes narrowed in anger and Danny hated to admit it but he knew she had a point. He'd wanted to do something more with his ability but

307

he'd been urged to hide it. "Normal people don't understand," his mother had told him. "Find something you can do with it but nothing obvious," his father had urged.

Using it was one thing. Working side by side with these guys was a whole different deal. His mother had never steered him wrong and she was sure of their evil natures. Yet Becca's certainty was causing him to waver. Ryan didn't seem that bad, the woman was bitchy, and that admiral was freaky scary. Michael, the one Becca seemed to have taken up with, bothered him the most. It was like Becca was blind to him. He was trying to control her and now she was using her ability to get in his head? If he didn't get her out he was never going to get her clear of them. He would have to bide his time. Even then, he hoped with time he could convince her to go.

"Our patrols may not be earth shattering but it's an honest living. One I can go home at the end of the night and tell Michelle about without lying. My family is proud of what I do." He stared evenly at Becca. "How about you? Would your father be proud to know you work with monsters?" That you're fucking the undead, he left out.

Her answer surprised her. "I know that more than anything my dad believes in protecting our country and working here with these guys is doing more to protect our way of life than patrolling the base on any given Friday night." Crossing her arms, she finished determinedly.

Unable to argue against that, Danny let it die. Pissed, he growled at no one in particular, "Are we supposed to stay down here forever? I've been working all night and I want to get some sleep."

"Sure, we've got space for you," Ryan replied unperturbed. Happily leading the way, he marched past and waved for him to follow. Danny tagged along grumpily.

The day's toll had been exhausting and Becca felt it catching up to her. She collapsed into a chair at the console beside Kyle.

Sitting there alone with her brother, Becca was able to relax and close her eyes. She felt the stress starting to ebb into the background. She faded into a dead sleep for a few minutes.

"Bec."

She tried ignoring the sound of her brother's voice.

"Bec." Kyle's hand touched her arm, the physical reminder of her body ripping her from her peaceful state.

"You'd better have something freakin' amazing." Her eyes opened reluctantly.

"Huh." Unphased, he used his eyes to point at the screen. "Well, maybe this will help wake you up. I have an address for you." He pointed.

Her frustration was forgotten. "Really?"

"Yep. It's up in the Chocolate Mountains not far from the eastern edge of the Salton Sea. Looks like it's in the middle of BFE. Nothing's out that way." He pointed at the screen, using a nail tip to tap it. "But this says it's right. They have internet way out there. You have to love the advances of modern technology."

"Show me the aerial." Becca rolled her chair closer.

They were studying the area, looking for signs of civilization with little success when Ryan's voice boomed behind them.

"What do you two have your little heads together for over there? Planning a global takeover or next Fourth of July's perfect family picnic spot?"

"No, just trying to figure out the best way to grab our bad guy," Becca shot back without turning.

Ryan's tone switched to excited. "Really? You found him?" He came up behind them, leaning in to see.

Kyle's finger showed him the specific area where they were looking.

"Boy, there's nothing around there, just that one little cabin. Looks like a ranger outpost or something."

"That's what I'm thinking." Becca was pleased to have been thinking along the same lines.

Pounding his big hand on Kyle's lean shoulder, Ryan chuckled. "You two are handy for humans. I wouldn't mind keeping *you* around too."

Kyle cocked his head in thought. "Well, I would love the chance to play with this system but family duty calls." He turned his head to speak over his shoulder. "I *would* consider consulting here and there."

Ryan guffawed. For all her talk, Becca didn't like the idea of her brother being in Black's sights. She listened to the quiet of the room for a tic before slapping a hand down on the table.

"We know where Vanessa was sending the list and here we sit." She pushed herself up out of the chair. "I for one vote we have something to show the admiral when they get back."

"What are we going to show the admiral?" Gabrielle's voice purred from the stairs.

All heads turned toward the newcomer striding toward them. She closed the distance gracefully; Kyle was trying so hard not to stare but Becca couldn't blame him for watching the way she moved. Hell, she couldn't deny it was a little bit of a turn on to see her strut.

"How was the desert?" Ryan teased.

Amber eyes rolled. "I had to poke a few extra holes to speed things along." The discomfort of Becca and Kyle amused her. "The older they are, the longer they take to cook even in the California sunshine. Get them weak enough and it's like a microwave versus a slow cooker."

Gulping, Becca changed the subject. "Kyle found where Vanessa was sending the list. We were thinking of checking it out."

"I like it." Gabrielle shrugged without any hesitation. "No point sitting around."

"Are you sure the admiral would approve?" Ryan wasn't so sure. "He's tracking it already."

Becca thought she saw Ryan and Gabrielle exchange a look. Gabrielle's eyes narrowed and Becca felt her willingness fading.

"Look, we don't know how Black and Michael are doing. We've got the Intel, we should move on it. What if they can't get there and this guy starts making calls, handing out names and arrest warrants? I think we go and check it out. If it looks like it's too much to handle, we turn back and wait for the others. If nothing else, we call it recon and send Black and Michael in better prepared."

Ryan shrugged. "I'm game."

Gabrielle and Ryan disappeared into the weapons room to pack bags when Becca felt her heart sink. Danny. She had forgotten about him completely. How would he react? Part of her thought this might be the best way to show him the benefit of their unit. They were going out, working together to rid the world of another bad guy. Maybe, though with their firepower she couldn't imagine anything being too much for them that might force them back empty-handed.

Reaching the top of the stairs, Becca went to the door of the room Ryan said he had put Danny in. She knocked gently on the ancient wood.

The bed creaked, footsteps sounded on the hard floor. Danny's voice was at the door when he spoke. "What."

Great, he was still pissed.

"Hey Danny. Can I come in?" She made her voice gentle.

The door opened. He didn't step aside, sticking his head out instead. Danny raised his eyebrows expectantly at her.

Not a warm fuzzy exactly.

"We've found the physical location where the message was sent. We're going to check it out."

He kept staring at her.

The tension she was carrying, worrying for him, fearing she'd driven her love away, concerns her brother was Black's new computer expert, it all exploded on Danny. "Quit being such a twat and man up. Like it or not, this is your mission today. Deal. Ryan's getting a pack for you. Be at the front doors in an hour." Wheeling on her heel, Becca stalked to her room and slammed the door.

Chapter 33

Ryan threw the bags into the back of the black Suburban, all of the passengers piled in and he took the driver's seat. Kyle hopped into the front passenger seat before anyone else could lay claim. Becca and Gabrielle took the middle and Danny sat in the back alone.

Kyle and Ryan chattered happily, Kyle working the stereo until finally settling on a classic rock station. The desert sky around them was the brightest of blues; Becca thought of Michael's eyes when he was happy. Her heart stuttered.

"Try not to think about it," Gabrielle murmured to her.

"Try not to think about what?"

"Him."

"I wasn't."

She made a noise that sounded like "bullshit."

Becca stared pointedly out the window.

"You're a traitor to your kind," Danny snarled. "We're traitors for being here with them. If we injure a single human for them I hope you can live with that."

Gabrielle spun to face him, her beautiful face altered as her canines showed under her tight lips. "You are woefully misinformed about who the real monsters are here, Danny." She spat his name. "Humankind is as capable of atrocities as ours. You've had some great examples of humanity over the last century alone. All humans." Amber eyes narrowed, Gabrielle appeared to be growing inside the vehicle, the air around her beginning to shimmer. "And those are just the men who acted against humans. What about those who have campaigned against *our* kind for millennia?" She pictured Luc's face, destroyed by bombs. Bombs made of silver by

313

human hands. "Where's *our* justice? When do we avenge *our* fallen?"

Ryan glanced up in the rearview mirror. "Gab, keep it together back there," he warned her evenly.

Throwing herself back into her seat, she respected the rules. Black wouldn't abide killing an innocent, even if he was a whiny pussy. Gabrielle steadily regained control of herself, her features settling back into their beautiful human facade. She was quiet the remainder of the ride.

The hot desert landscape rolled by. The reddish hues of the clay mixed with the tans of the sand in a multilayered palette dotted with the browns and greens of the sparse scrub, the only plant life able to survive in this harsh place where desert meets mountains.

What kind of person would want to live out here, Becca pondered quietly. Vampires couldn't take much heat or direct sun so it couldn't be one of them. Maybe a shifter or a were was a better guess. Or a human. Her stomach tightened. That made the most sense. Who would have better cause to hate these creatures than a human? Becca, in her infinite social naiveté, believed it could only be someone who, like Danny, didn't know them like she did. Or maybe, like his mother, they saw something that turned them against the entire race.

Race. The word struck her when it ran through her conscious mind. That was indeed how she thought of them all. They all retained some of their humanity; they just also had a dose of something else, something inhuman in their makeup from an accident of sorts. They were still partially human like her. If she had abilities that were different than other "normal" humans, then she was not much different from them.

The vehicle came to a stop at an overlook point around the backside of the hill they wanted and everyone piled out.

They met at the back doors to grab their packs, even Danny. He looked surprised when Ryan handed him his.

"You need something to defend yourself against whatever this is, human or non." Ryan started digging out a few items to show Danny and Kyle how they were used. "Remember, there are more of us than you. We're not going to have any friendly fire incidents here, right? Any problems we have can be handled when we get home, alright?"

Becca asked, "Do you have any idea who or what would really want this list? It'll tear the country apart. It'll destroy what trust we have left. Who would want that? What good would it do?" Vanessa's monologue about power echoed in her mind. No one had power in that kind of anarchy. Only destruction could come of it and her logic saw no advantage there. Michael's warning that it was incredibly dangerous came back. Something like that might benefit from chaos.

Ryan put his hand on Becca's shoulder as he walked past. "Sometimes we tangle with crazy. We've seen some pretty messed up stuff."

Gabrielle finished checking her pack, answering more pragmatically. "It would be worth a lot of money if it were sold on the open market. Any number of agencies, governmental and private could use it to blackmail each other or sift through the files to create their own private armies. What rebel or terrorist with money and a hard on for power couldn't use some super soldiers?"

Becca blinked and wagged her head. "What about the fallout for the one who sells it? I mean, at some point doesn't he worry someone is going to find him and destroy him?" Kill didn't seem the appropriate word for such a beast.

Gabrielle and Ryan exchanged a look before she answered. "As far as worrying about himself, I would just say money buys safety in most parts of the world."

She remembered how strong Vanessa was and she'd been terrified of whatever commanded her. "Aren't you worried this thing could be too strong for us?"

Gabrielle shrugged into her pack and smiled bitterly. "We've been fighting enemies and friends alike since the beginning. Eventually, we all run into something stronger."

Chapter 34

They hiked up the side of the mountain, the sand and clay baked hard enough to walk easily. The sun was low on the horizon, just beginning its evening light show no more brilliant anywhere in the world than right here in the desert; the pinks and golden yellows visually stunning as they fell over the bleak landscape, shadows giving depth and character to the otherwise stark terrain.

It was a long haul. They had chosen to hike up the far side of the hill in order to stay out of any sightlines. The cabin they sought was on the other side, a short drop down from the peak. Their march was mostly in silence, a necessary safety precaution given the excellent hearing of the supernatural being that could be waiting on the other side.

When they did crest the peak, Becca stopped, crouching with the others to take in the view. It was amazing. She could see the dark waters of the Salton Sea, the edge of the sand dunes, a few clusters of civilization that must have been Brawley and Indio. Their lights were just coming on for the night giving an eerie glow to the dark masses of homes all shoved together, huddling for safety against the heat and solitude that personified the desert just outside their artificially green lawns.

Gabrielle touched her arm, motioning her to follow. Becca fell in behind her. Kyle and Danny were next with Ryan bringing up the rear. He was most likely to keep Danny in line. He hadn't said much thus far since Gabrielle snapped at him in the truck. Not that Becca much cared at this point. His brooding was getting old.

Partner or no, Becca had no patience for a bigot. His espousing hatred for the men and woman who had accepted her, defended her and fought with her because they were different was unacceptable.

Before she could get too worked up over him Becca had to pay more attention to her feet. Going up had been relatively easy but on this side, the lee side of the mountain, the winds and small amount of rainfall had fluffed the sand into unpredictable mounds on top of the clay. The loose piles slid under their feet, making for a treacherous downhill descent. They slipped and slid several times as they made their way down.

The group of five stopped at an outcropping. By Ryan's figuring they were to wait until full dark to continue to the cabin. It was a long, painful wait. Her watch said it was five. This time of year full sunset wouldn't be until after seven. The unstructured downtime was horrid and to compound matters, they were to keep their noise to a minimum.

She'd been leaning against her pack, comparing finger lengths and seeing how many stars she could block when her vision began to play with her. Sitting up in a rush, Becca assessed their camp. Nothing was amiss, no one doing anything eventful. Eyes and ears, even her nose strained for a hint of some other danger. Nothing.

The answer came to her and as quickly as it came, she knew it was right. The danger wasn't hers, it was Michael's, and judging from the mildness of the warning it wasn't urgent. Not yet. How had her ability tied in with Michael as a warning system? Did that happen when she jumped into someone? Maybe some residual connection remained or it was tied to the blood she'd taken from him. Whatever had given her the insight didn't matter. Becoming familiar with the process, Becca closed her eyes and jumped.

At first she thought it hadn't worked when nothing but views of the desert at dusk appeared in her head. The scene was like a dozen she'd seen all day. Becca was ready to give up when she noticed the perspective was wrong. She was looking up the hill, not down and the figure to her side wasn't any member of her party. It was the tall pale figure that always made her vision dance and her stomach turn. It was the admiral.

She had done it! Becca had made the link again and with it she felt the familiar surge of lightening in her head and twisting of her stomach. Being in Michael was much more powerful than Ryan. This time, instead of trying to overcome it, she welcomed it. Absently, her hand rubbed itself over her middle, caressing the roiling mess it had suddenly become.

A hand laid itself on her arm and Becca started. She caught herself before she lost the connection. Carefully, using his eyes to be sure nothing dire was happening just at that second, she withdrew. She was hesitant to leave him and found it comforting to know she could be on the lookout for him even at a distance.

When she opened her eyes, she saw the entire party was watching her. Even Danny had dropped the attitude in his curiosity. Gabrielle was glaring at Kyle. She seemed to know what Becca was doing and what Kyle had done by interrupting. That was interesting.

"What are you doing?" he whispered. Concern was etched plainly on his face. "You looked totally freaked out."

"Did you see them?" Gabrielle asked, barely making a sound.

Becca nodded. "They're here. On the mountain, downhill."

Confusion creased Kyle's brow. He hadn't been there when they'd been discussing the whole "jumping" thing and she didn't know how much he would understand. Now wasn't the time to explain.

Ryan scooted over to crouch between Gabrielle and Becca. "Where?"

She shook her head in frustration. "Don't know. I didn't get a chance to see. They weren't in trouble, just waiting it looked like. Like us."

319

They nodded, both frowning in thought.

"Can you tell him we're here?" Ryan asked.

"It doesn't work like that." Becca sighed. "I'm there but all I can do is see." She didn't add that with him she could sense something else. Why tell them when she didn't know exactly what it was she was feeling?

"Damn," Ryan growled. "We'll have to suck it up and call." He fished his phone out of his pocket. He held it up, cursing. "What good is all this stuff if we can't get it to work."

"We'll have to keep our eyes on them then to make sure we don't accidentally blow somebody up." Gabrielle gave Becca a meaningful look.

"Before we go after this thing," Becca's eyes held hers, "Michael said it was dangerous, more than usual. Is there anything you think we need to know before we go any further?"

Gabrielle and Ryan were so tense the air around them shimmered in the fading light. Both refused to answer.

"What are we up against?" Swallowing her frustration, she kept her voice even. There was no point getting into a fight amongst themselves.

"A demon," Ryan answered just as plainly.

Becca was glad she was sitting down. At once, heeding Gabrielle's assignment as "eyes," she jumped without hesitation.

"They've moved east. They'll attack from that direction." She felt somehow that was right. "Should we join up with them or stay on the other side should they need support?"

She heard them discussing strategy, Danny even taking part. Kyle remained quiet, his tactical experience the most limited of the bunch. For her part, she watched Michael and Black's movements through Michael's eyes.

Black moved first, Michael went where he was told. There was a small washout and Black wanted to go around while Michael pointed out it would save time. He argued that it was worth the brief time they would lose sight of the area they were focusing on. Michael attempted to take a step, Black said one word and just like that she felt the tension in his head and the physical pain at resisting Black's command.

It was both fascinating and disturbing. A faint whispering in her mind told her what it was and she saw everything slide into place as she let it unfold in her head. His loyalty to Black. Black's willingness to give control and trust to one over all the rest. Michael was being held hostage somehow, tied to Admiral Black by some unseen tether. He had no choice but to follow orders, disloyalty wasn't an option.

Admiral Black was a cruel bastard. The only vindication Becca saw in Black was his willingness to do whatever it took to protect their country and those willing to live by its laws. At the same time she assumed his patriotism wasn't merely an act of selflessness. No one willing to do what he'd done to Michael could possibly be so altruistic.

By allying himself with the U.S. government Black gave himself unlimited resources and guaranteed his own safety. He alone could say that. No other of his race could because he was the global authority in supernatural and preternatural affairs. They were all at his mercy. In a way, Black was the leader of the entire non-human population worldwide. The ramifications were staggering.

Becca kept her revelation to herself. She wasn't sure if the wolves knew of the bond between master and servant and she could see how it could be used to manipulate Michael if the wrong people found out. She wouldn't be responsible for giving anyone else power over him if she could help it.

"Bec," Kyle stage whispered. He was careful not to touch her this time, she noted.

Looking up and blinking, Becca saw that full darkness was finally upon them. Standing as a group and pulling the straps of their packs over their shoulders, the five were ready to head down.

Gabrielle led again, half jogging over the slippery sand. Becca noticed if they kept to the faster speed, and let the counterweight of their packs pull them back on their heels it was actually relatively easy to move along. Her dual vision took some getting used to but the nice thing about having to concentrate was that it kept her mind too busy to worry about the fact that they were running toward a demon.

They agreed that if they could signal their comrades without risking either position they would, otherwise they would have to operate independently. The burden of monitoring both positions was theirs. Becca constantly kept checking the visuals of each set of eyes against each other; if anyone took any damage because of an oversight it would be her fault.

Roughly a half-mile from the little cabin located up the hill from them in a diagonal trajectory, Ryan and Gabrielle took up their positions. Becca couldn't see it with her human eyes, but the set that could make it out clearly was just as close.

"How can you tell where it is?" Danny asked her, dubious but less confrontational. Time or exhaustion was taking some of his steam away.

"Can't you smell the sulfur?" Gabrielle asked.

Becca shook her head.

"It was how Black knew her master. When she was staked we smelled it. She was bound to it."

"When someone is bound is it forever? Can it be broken?"

322

Gabrielle kept her binoculars trained on the cabin. "Only death can break a bond between servant and master."

With that to chew on, Becca went back into his head.

Chapter 35

Michael and the admiral had taken only enough time to change into the fatigues they kept in the trunk of the car before beginning their hunt. It hadn't been hard to know where to go.

Unlike Gabrielle's attempt to track Vanessa's scent before, her sulfuric scent had given them direction. That and the admiral's close proximity that had told him where she'd been spending her time.

Her scent was nearly drowning in creosote, a bush common to southern California and he had smelled something else. While he had been working on her, he took a piece of her clothing where he had smelled something he didn't recognize. It was organic matter, that he knew. The what was less defined.

While the others drove back to the estate, Black and Michael made their way over to the storage facility on the far edge of the base. It was a nondescript building most people believed housed excess paper goods. No one was ever seen going in or out carrying anything more than a briefcase. What they didn't know was that the lower level, one not marked on the elevator, led to a laboratory accessible only with the highest of clearances.

Black swiped his card in the elevator and down they went. When the doors opened to release them into the white and silver expanse of sterility, Michael saw a handful of white lab coats milling around their stations. Some were at microscopes, others tinkering on metal tables. A supervisor approached.

The nametag on the white coat said Harris. His glasses were rimless, leaving an unobstructed view of his dark eyes. Dark hair, closely shorn, stood up a fraction higher on the top than the sides. The muscles under the white shirt, tie, and lab coat marked him as a strong man. As he drew closer to Black, his confident exterior began to crumble.

Nervously, Harris cleared his throat. "Sir. May I help you, Sir?" He paused before each "Sir" and his tongue flicked across his lips. A tic maybe.

The admiral handed the strip of Vanessa's black turtleneck to Michael. He knew his place. Obediently, he took point.

"Harris, we need this fabric run. The admiral needs an analysis on organic matter. Specifically to pinpoint location if that is possible."

The lab technician held out his clipboard, Michael placed the fabric on it. The tongue flicked over his lips again. Definitely a tic. "Your timeline, Sir?"

"Yesterday."

If Harris considered that a challenge he showed no sign. He gave a brief nod. "Sirs," he said then retreated, briskly making his way to his station equipped with a microscope, centrifuge and several other items he hoped would give them their answer quickly.

Black's phone appeared in his hand. "I trust you can handle things from here, Michael."

"Yes, Sir."

He watched the admiral dial and glide in his creepy manner off into a quiet corner. Michael wished he could wipe the smug grin from those thin pale lips. It would have been a great pleasure to smash his fist into that grim white face.

Ever since the admiral brought him into the fold after the War, Michael had been forced to serve under him. He hadn't known what he was doing when he'd agreed to serve under Black. Michael had assumed he meant in the same unit and thought the blood exchange was a vampire version of enlistment. Kind of gross, but what wasn't once he had to survive on blood? If he had known what allowing that bite would do to the rest of his eternity he never would have agreed. That blood exchange had firmly and finally bound him to the admiral for the remainder of time.

Michael settled himself to wait. Being a vampire brought with it certain special abilities. People usually fantasized about the strength, hypersensitivity, of course the near indestructibility; few people realized the advantage of the patience an endless life afforded. He stood with his hands clasped behind his back and every so often remembered to breathe in case anyone happened to be watching.

In a holding pattern, he turned his thoughts inward to the things foremost in his mind. His unit. And Becca. He thought about units past. How many had they had lost over the nearly sixty years he had been in, commanding for most of those? This batch was a good mix.

Ryan was strong both mentally and physically. And despite his joviality, he wasn't a fool. Gabrielle more than balanced out his optimism with her astounding cynicism. She saw scandal and deceit around every corner, whether it was political or personal. He knew she watched the admiral and him closer than was necessary. It had even crossed his mind more than once she was informing on their doings to someone higher up in the chain of command.

And now they had Becca. Adding a human, preternatural or not had been a bad idea. He'd told Black as much years before when they'd tried it the last time. Michael's responsibility was to his unit, he wanted to keep them alive and a human was a liability, he'd said. Becca was different. From that first night when she'd challenged Black for him, taking the risk for *him*, he had felt his long dormant heart stir. After their test run when she'd taken out the three shifters, she'd proven she was worthy of a shot. The entirety of the unit had slowly been changing their minds about her, not the least surprising of which was Gabrielle.

The fact that the ice queen was being social and even concerned for a human was beyond his understanding. Even if he didn't understand her motives, the outcome was groundbreaking. Becca was accepted by the unit, protected by the unit, and helpful to the unit. Those details were not lost on the admiral.

Initially Michael wanted to keep her with him to best protect her humanly frail body. Quickly it had become for more personal reasons. He could no longer argue that he wasn't in love with her. Yet he couldn't believe he had confessed himself to her. And now Admiral Black knew. Hell, he'd seen it all over Michael's face when she'd been taken. There was no way of keeping him from using the knowledge to control her too. Sometimes, even when Black knew something, he made Michael tell him if for no other reason than to drive home the point, "I own you."

The continued unraveling of her capabilities was going to be a huge area of interest to Black as well as a sticking point for Michael. She was getting stronger every day in her ability. Michael had to wonder if it was the blood he'd given her; he'd never given his blood to a human before her. How it effected one like her was beyond him and he definitely wouldn't want to ask Black about it. Concern for what Black might use it for overshadowed his personal reservations about her dual residence in his head. Until he understood it better, it was safer for them both if Black didn't use him as the middleman to manipulate her. "Stay out" as he'd told her, was the safest play for everyone. Michael wasn't sure he could live with himself if Black used him to bring her to harm.

"Sir." Harris' voice broke into his internal meditation and Michael realized he hadn't been breathing. Within a blink, Michael reanimated. Unnerved, Harris clicked his pen and tapped it on his clipboard.

Michael's countenance, darkly reflecting his thoughts, brightened to avoid frightening the man. "What did you find Harris?"

Harris flicked his tongue over his lips again before indicating with a head gesture that Michael should follow.

Michael didn't have to speak or gesture to Black, once Michael started moving, the admiral started moving. In an instant he stood beside Michael and proceeded to follow Harris to his station.

Harris was visibly excited. "This sample had some unique plant matter in it from an especially rare plant, the Chocolate Lily." He pointed at the microscope on the table and Michael leaned in to examine the slide.

On it he saw some darker bits of powder that must have been pollen by the smell. It wasn't entirely sweet. Like most flowers, it held a hint of musk as well. He let the thought swirl in his head and watched the admiral react. It was the smell that had caught his attention during his interrogation. Michael felt the impulse from Black and followed it.

"How rare is this flower? Where can it be found?" he asked, knowing that was exactly what the admiral wanted him to ask. They'd done this so many times by now it was automatic.

"It's extremely rare except for a place not far from here. Are you familiar with the Chocolate Mountains?" he asked, continuing when neither of the men answered his question. "Well," he waved his pen, "it's from the mountains."

Michael hid his disappointment well. "Can you isolate it any more than 'in the Chocolate Mountains'?" The name called to mind a children's board game.

Tongue flick. "Yes Sir, I can." Harris pulled out a lower drawer on his table, popping it up to waist level. On it was a laptop. Long fingers typed incredibly fast, navigating through the internet search to stop at an aerial photo.

Further study revealed it to be the Chocolate Mountains and surrounding area.

One long finger pointed to the right side of the monitor. "Do you see here where the mountains begin and the Salton

Sea area is here?" He pointed to the western edge of the mountains.

"Yes."

"That is where the soil changes. The soil content on the plateau where the inland sea lies is high in salt, but here, where it begins to move up into the mountains, there's a drastic reduction in content." He saw Michael beginning to interrupt and held up his finger. "The soil on the fabric you brought in has a mixture that tells me it spent some time right in here. I would say there's about a two mile radius where it could have picked up that particular mixture."

Michael glanced back at Admiral Black. He gave one brief nod. They were done.

"Thank you, Harris." Michael slid the fabric sample from the table and put it in his pocket before the technician saw his hand move.

Outside the building, they made their way to the vehicle Admiral Black had been driving, a black Mercedes. There was no point in him trying to blend in with a fleet vehicle and he liked his comfort. The trunk contained all of the firepower they would need to stop a creature like themselves. A demon was something else entirely. Michael had only heard stories about them. He'd never actually met one much less tried to fight one.

"Sir, have you ever dealt with demons before?" he asked once they were inside the vehicle and safe from uninitiated ears.

Black drove fast, speeding through the gears; he drove stick as he wanted to control every detail of the vehicle. Not surprising given his penchant for controlling everything else within his reach.

"I have. They are not an easy opponent, nor are all of them alike. We cannot know what we will be faced with when we find it," Black spoke to the windshield.

"What type did you encounter, Sir."

"Water demons. They were more common in Andalucia before the war with France. There were fountains in every town and many of those were used as hiding places for demons.

We were a relatively new arm of the military, what with the country being fresh from its own revolution, but the team was a good one. They tried several different methods but found the most effective to be pouring lamp oil into the fountains and setting them on fire. The fire purified the water and burned the demons as they tried to escape. But I cannot imagine we could destroy a fire demon in the same manner, we will need to do the opposite and extinguish his fire. Let us hope it isn't that one, though the sulfur has me concerned." The pale-haired head tipped to point forward. "As does the lack of water out here."

Michael watched the scenery whip past at over one hundred miles per hour. They were leaving the well-irrigated paradise that was San Diego and entering the desert that rode beside it. The sun would have been debilitating were it not for the special tinting the admiral had installed in his windows. As it was, they were comfortable.

"Will she hold it against you when you have to kill her brother?"

"Sir?" Michael had been expecting this.

"He is preternatural, we both sensed it. I would assume we cannot completely erase his mind, though he is more easily manipulated than his sister. He knows not only of our kind but also more about our operations than I care to consider." His tone was airy, absentmindedly running through a "have-to" list.

"Sir, I've given this considerable thought and I believe Kyle would be a useful resource for us."

Black twisted his neck to stare unblinking black orbs at him.

"At present we have no reliable technologically savvy assets who can compare to him. You saw how he operated in there. His knowledge is unparalleled. I would guarantee his ability encompasses more than just computers."

"And how can you guarantee his loyalty?" The taunt in his voice confirmed for Michael that Black already knew where he was going and he was going to make him say it. Control freak.

To let the words implying he would be responsible for harm to Becca come out of his mouth nearly caused Michael physical pain and to utter them would save her brother. "Because Sir, if he were to betray us we have his sister."

Black smiled. Michael hated his smile.

"Then that only leaves us with her partner. Unfortunate that one had to come at such an inopportune time."

He couldn't save them both. Michael only had so much pull with the admiral and at present he had exhausted that. He would try to help Danny later. Maybe he would be able to earn some leeway by proving himself useful. If Danny would cooperate, he thought grimly. "Yes Sir."

They arrived at the base of the mountain, stopping the car at an overlook at the edge of the Salton Sea. There were no other cars in sight. The admiral handed Michael a pair of binoculars from his center console.

It was no use arguing. Michael opened the door and stepped out into the baking heat. As much as he tried to prepare himself, it was never enough. The heat of the direct sun was excruciating. In minutes he felt his body beginning to fade. It would decompose with too much heat. There was only so far one could push a corpse, animated or not. With not much time to mess around, Michael moved quickly.

He was using the researcher's search radius to define his parameters. Another sniff of the piece of cloth gave him more specific criteria upon which to base his search. At his fourth vantage point, partway up the side of the hill, he spied a small cabin. It was barely visible so well did the faded wood blend with the reddish brown sand around it. Once he saw it, he couldn't lose sight of it. There was no movement or signs of life from within. Creosote and the strange musky sweet smell of chocolate lilies wafted in the late afternoon breeze. Without a doubt he knew this was what they were looking for.

Using his full speed, Michael made it back to the Mercedes and blissful shade. The admiral had a thermos ready for him. They always traveled well stocked in this part of the country. There was no telling when one might get caught in the heat and need something. After he drank his fill of nourishment, something strange niggled at Michael's awareness. He shrugged it off and reported his findings.

"I've found a cabin on the hillside. It appears to be abandoned."

Black smiled again. "I believe we have found our demon."

Chapter 36

Becca was getting tired of waiting. She crouched in the darkness, staring up at the stars. Out this far from the bigger cities the skies were huge. Millions of stars were visible in the dark night and with a waning moon and cloudless sky it was easy to feel overwhelmed.

And she did. She had been keeping her connection to Michael in order to keep track of their movements yet thus far they had made none. Her previous jumps had been brief, lasting only minutes. Tonight she had been holding her focus for over an hour and counting. It was taxing.

Becca could see that Michael was maintaining a position a healthy distance downhill from the cabin. Black was beside him. Neither spoke, Michael stared at the building, only occasionally averting his eyes up to the dazzling sky or down to catch the activity of a scorpion just waking or lizard seeking warm shelter for the night.

In their camp, the wolves stood vigil, binoculars in hand awaiting something either from the cabin or Becca. Danny and Kyle were sitting on rocks and flicking the random night creatures away with sticks. The moon provided some light, though it was reduced by the presence of the outcropping casting its long shadow over them all.

Looking for a change of scenery, she rose and approached Danny and Kyle. Danny grunted and got up, walking a few paces away to crouch again.

"What the hell, Danny. We were partners over a year and you're going to be like this now?" she whispered hotly at him.

The whites of his eyes flashed in the light as he rolled them at her. "You're not you when you do that." He waved a hand at her. "When you do your mind meld thing with him, you're just like him in my eyes."

That he meant that hurt her more than she cared to admit. "I'm still me," she pouted stubbornly.

"Not to me you're not." Danny poked intently at something in the sand with his stick, his side of their argument over.

She growled, kicking the sand in frustration. She'd forgotten about her brother and her kick landed a dusting directly in his eyes.

Kyle stumbled backward, clawing at his eyes in surprise. Spitting the grains from his mouth, he coughed and choked. "Agh!" he shouted before he could stop himself.

Becca recognized her mistake as soon as her foot flew and she raised her eyes to see the trajectory but there was nothing she could change once the spray was airborne.

When Ryan and Gabrielle spun around to see the source of the commotion, they refrained from cursing, barely. Ryan was on Kyle after his first sound, clamping a hand down hard on his mouth. Gabrielle zeroed in on the cabin and Becca heard her utter an oath.

Just before her concentration was broken and Becca was pulled from Michael again, she saw his sight change. A lack of soft grasses and leafy trees offered poor sound absorption and the sound travelled far. He had heard them from all the way over there. That meant more than likely so had the demon. That was when she lost him.

Gabrielle's mouth began to move in a constant stream of what Becca learned when a few she recognized flew past, were oaths in languages she'd never even heard of before, as well as some more popular favorites. Swearing herself proud, Gabrielle launched herself and took Becca to the ground.

Once Becca was down, Danny dropped under his own power. With a glare that could have dropped an ox, Gabrielle left Becca lying in the rapidly cooling desert sand to look again upon their target.

Becca watched the binoculars shifting more frantically in the blonde's hands between dancing white lights and she felt her stomach drop, knowing what that meant before Gabrielle announced it.

"They've moved in but it's ready. The door's open now but I didn't see it come out. I lost it."

More than what she was saying, it was the inflection in Gabrielle's voice that made Becca's blood chill in her veins. The unflappable soldier was scared. Becca felt her own racing pulse pounding in her ears and part of her longed for Michael's touch to calm her body's reactions. She was on her own on this one.

Kyle was busily apologizing, muffled beneath Ryan's hand still slapped over his mouth.

"What do we do now?" Danny stood, brushing sand off of his pants.

Ryan asked the same thing Becca was thinking. "We're a 'we' now?"

"Well, I would assume a demon is worse than a vampire, right?" was all he said with a shrug.

"We move in a scatter formation. Put in your earpieces, we stay in constant contact." Gabrielle took control with no argument. "Anyone sees Black or Michael, alert the others. We stay in contact so no one gets hurt."

"What about the demon? What if we see the demon?" he wanted to know.

"Humans," she said through tight lips, "need to go in with an incendiary. Only one type of demon cannot be destroyed by fire that I know of and that is a fire demon." She cut a sharp look at Becca. "Be damn careful with those incendiaries. You can kill any of us with one misaimed device."

Becca watched her eyes dart toward Danny before she could stop herself. It was a rational fear Becca didn't know the answer to and she knew him better than anyone there. Would Danny use this chance to kill one of theirs?

Swallowing, Becca tossed off her pack to dig inside for an orb about the size of her fist. The grenade was filled with napalm and would stick to and burn anything within a ten foot radius. She held it out for Kyle and Danny to see. "Dig in your packs, you're looking for one of these."

Kyle took a matching device from his pack before returning it to his shoulders. Danny didn't have to look. He knew these types of weapons well enough to pick it out by feel; they'd worked with them in training.

For her part, Becca couldn't help but see the dummy they had incinerated with one of these grenades. The sticky fluid inside had splashed up upon hitting the ground, spattering the dummy and instantly igniting. Flames quickly engulfed the plastic man on contact. She could see Michael's face on the burning figure and shook her head violently to clear the image.

Chapter 37

They spread out to form an arc, communication devices in their ears and weapons ready. Ryan and Gabrielle carried high-powered rifles loaded with silver shot. The grenades were better for those without the night vision who might be using the scattergun approach.

Ryan was to her left, Danny to her right, with Kyle and Gabrielle after that. They thought it best for the two strongest to remain at the outer edges, which also kept them the safest from any misdirected flames.

Moving steadily forward as a cohesive unit, they closed the distance from a half mile to a quarter mile without incident.

"Anyone seeing anything? We're awfully quiet out there," Gabrielle spoke suddenly, causing Becca to startle.

"Nothing here," Kyle whispered tightly.

Danny reported the same, as did Ryan.

Becca was just about to give her identical comment when something caught the light in front of her. Quickly, she dropped into a crouch to hide, though behind what, she didn't know. There was nothing around save sand and some minor scrub.

Again the thing flashed but it was not heading for her, it was heading to her right. Straight for Danny!

"Danny," she called in her "com" device. "Danny, I saw something coming for you. Heads up."

Before she could say another word she heard his anguished cry in her ear and saw a flash of fire not far away.

"Danny!" Becca screamed, taking off at a dead run over the questionable terrain. She stumbled and slid in her haste, falling twice over loose rocks. The sharp stones cutting into the palms of her hands barely registered in her haste to get to her partner.

The grenade had worked. It had burned a ring of shrubbery, the edges of which still glowed in flames. Inside the ring was a black mark where a form had absorbed the impact and the flaming liquid. Sagebrush stood untouched in two places in the center roughly in the shape of feet. To the side of the ring was a singed trail that swung past it and ended nearby next to another pile of ashes.

Gabrielle and Ryan were there, having approached with more caution, Kyle was last. When they all stood at the burning spot, Ryan cursed.

"Fire demon." Gabrielle pointed at the ash pile outside the charred ring.

"Damn. Don't know how we kill a fire demon." Ryan was frustrated, staring at the uncharred footprints with his hands on his hips.

"Water," Kyle replied simply, as if it was obvious.

Becca hunched over the remains of her friend, reduced to ashes. Her fingers touched him as he was carried away by a breeze. Sickened, Becca shoved his dog tags into her pocket and stood.

"Where do you propose we get enough water around here to douse a fire demon?" Ryan asked Kyle sarcastically.

Kyle snapped his lips shut.

Becca barely heard their frustrated exchange. She was staring at the ground, unable to tear her eyes away from Danny until he was gone. The wind had picked up, gusting just enough to play with Danny's ashes, casting them about between their dejected party. Her fingers stroked his dog tags, clicking them together in her pocket.

Danny may have been adverse to her present company but he had been a friend to her when no one else was willing. What has passed between them that night was forgiven with his death. Vengeance wasn't something she usually took much stock in but in this case, in this meaningless death, she wanted it for him and for his family.

Straightening her shoulders, Becca steeled herself and shifted her pack. Hands unencumbered by a weapon other than the grenade, she could move quickly. Reaching behind herself, she tucked the grenade loosely in her pack and aimed herself directly at the cabin.

Without a word she took a step. The soft scuffing sound of feet following her told her of her unit's solidarity. They had the same purpose, different motivations. Hers was purely selfish and for that she felt no guilt. There was no room under her grief and fury.

"Bec," Kyle called out to her quietly, jogging to catch up. "Bec why are you going this way?"

His question stopped her. Hesitating, Becca realized she hadn't thought about what direction she was going. Why *would* she go to the building where they knew the demon had just come from in order to attack one of theirs? She had no clue why or how she knew but with absolute certainty she knew it had returned.

"It's there," was all she said and marched on.

The party followed, trusting in her sight. Senses left hypersensitive by two infusions of vampire's blood inside a week guided her. Her feet found a more secure path with barely a conscious effort. In her head she thanked Michael for sharing.

At thought of Michael she felt a twinge and took it for a warning to focus in on him. Spots started dancing and anger, hot and fresh, rushed up as she thought "not him." Emotions made seemingly more powerful by loss and heightened awareness filled her until she felt as though her chest would burst and her nose began to bleed. Debilitating physical symptoms that rendered her helpless were not going to cost her another loved one. No one else was going to die, she raged at the wretched, worthless, goddamned spots!

Michael was in trouble, she'd sensed it and checked in with what he was seeing. She felt the warnings strongly when she thought about him. Her body warned her again and with a swift, decisive mental side block she sent the unwanted blindness down to cower far from her consciousness. Her liberation was cathartic. Mastery of her ability was hers! In place of screaming pain and holes in her sight, a polite twinge was her ability's way of alerting her to impending trouble. It was Michael. The demon was with him. She didn't have the luxury of time to plan on the safest line, instead picking up her pace to find the fastest one.

When she was a stone's throw from the door, Becca paused. The others caught her.

"What do you think?" Gabrielle deferred to her ability in this blind situation. That was why they had her after all.

If she hadn't been so worried that she had impulsively led them into horrible danger, she would have been flattered. They trusted her to get them the best possible outcome. She took a moment to gather her thoughts and feel out the interior.

That turned out to be unnecessary. Just then the darkened windows flared with sudden light. Flames plumed then went out.

Ryan cursed. "Kyle's right. Let's throw some water at this thing."

"How are you going to get it here?" Kyle queried curiously, unaffected by Ryan's revisiting his very idea. The same one Ryan had so unceremoniously shot down ten minutes ago.

Ryan was fumbling in his pocket for a phone. "We're in California right? Land of wildfires?" Fingers flew across his keypad and he put the phone to his ear. "Yes, Captain Ryan Hallbeck for Admiral Black." He barely had to pause before they were asking for his codes and what he needed.

The part on the other end of the line must have been familiar with the admiral's rank and power.

Ryan gave an order for a water dump on their location. Hanging up, he smiled grimly. "They'll get some water on us as soon as they can."

Becca wasn't the only one hoping that wouldn't be too late.

The flames flared again.

"Come on Bec, what are we looking at in there?" Gabrielle purred reassuringly. She was trying to relax her.

Her power over her ability was still settling in while Becca tried to make sense of what she was seeing inside. The layout of the house mapped itself in her head as he scanned the interior for escape routes.

"They're right inside the back door, the demon is fending them off with fire. It knows they won't come through it." She described what she was seeing. "The hallway of the cabin where the demon is holed up is off of the main living area behind this door. It pinches down and turns right to get to the back door. That's where Black and Michael are pinned down. Now that they're inside they can't go back or they'll be exposed. It looks like it can throw the flame a good distance." Her eyes widened seeing a volley of fire coming at her face, it was no less disconcerting to know that it was not actually her flesh that was at risk.

Ryan was on the move. He ran in a crouch to the side of the front door. Becca watched with her physical eyes as the demon heard the door handle click. Ryan ducked inside before she could shout a warning.

She turned to Gabrielle. "It heard him. It's moving away from the other two to check him out."

Any question of how Gabrielle felt about Ryan was eliminated as Becca watched her panicked eyes flash to the door. Without pause, she rushed inside to help.

"Damn," Becca cursed. That left her and Kyle outside with her entire unit inside. And as much training and experience as she'd had in her short career she couldn't hold a candle to the experience those four had.

"What do we do Bec?" Kyle sidled up to her, equally at a loss.

His faith in his little sister was flattering even if, she feared, ill placed. Scanning the structure she was grateful for her enhanced vision. She missed it on the first pass. On the way back, Becca saw it. All of the scrub around the perimeter of the cabin was burned to blackened dirt and smudges of soot. The demon's food source.

Pointing, she showed Kyle. "Does your super secret ability extend to generators?"

His eyes were worried. "I don't know. It's gas powered. I've never tried anything that wasn't electric."

"Well, this makes electricity so try now. We need a huge power surge. Enough to blow up the generator." She explained, "Fire needs fuel to survive. If you burn everything around it, it will die.

"I'll try." Kyle deferred to her again. "What about the others? They won't survive a fire will they?"

"I know. Just start working on it and give me two minutes. If I'm not out by then, blow it anyway." Ignoring the alarm in his wide brown eyes, Becca made for the cabin.

The demon was aware of threats from both doors. He would be too distracted to fight both competently. Becca went to the side window and looked around for something to break it. Seeing nothing, she took off her pack and wound it up over her shoulder, swinging it hard at the glass. The sound of the shatter was lost as another surge of fire shot toward the front hall.

Becca climbed up and into the room, landing behind an overstuffed recliner. It was the kind her father loved and her mother hated but at the moment, Becca had to agree with her dad on its usefulness. Peeking out around the sides, she guessed she was in the cabin's office.

The front entrance led straight into a hall. The cabin was essentially a shotgun house with several doors off the sides for bedrooms and offices. It was perfect for a standoff such as this, giving the defender full advantage.

Looking left, she saw the front entrance. The wood paneling had flames licking up the sides, melting the finish to give off nauseating fumes. With her head sticking out in the hall, Becca signaled to the Ryan and Gabrielle. She waved them back, pantomiming an explosion. Ryan nodded, tugging at Gabrielle's arm as he army crawled backward.

After they'd gone she had second thoughts about her idea. There would be no way to hide *and* warn the others. She glanced at her watch. Less than a minute to go.

She racked her brain for ideas. Something she could use to hold off the demon for a precious few seconds. That was all she would need to get its attention and allow Michael and Black to back out of the cabin. Thinking beyond that was more than she could handle so she didn't.

Becca had a plan. Digging in her pack, she came out with hands filled with grenades. Just like Danny, she would threaten it. That should get it to follow her long enough to get them out.

Grenades in hand, Becca stood up and stepped out into the hall. Other than the haze of smoke and flames illuminating various pieces of the walls, it was empty. She hadn't expected that. Temporarily thrown for a loop, she lowered her grenades and stepped forward. A few feet past the doorway of the room where she'd been hiding, Becca saw the demon as it turned the corner, coming from the back hall where it was holding off the others.

Clearly it hadn't expected her to be there either. For a few seconds they both stared at each other. It wasn't what she'd expected.

She didn't know what she thought a fire demon would look like. Maybe some sort of dancing flame or matchstick, something with horns maybe, she hadn't really thought about it. Instead, the demon was human looking, and male. Very male. It, he, was garbed only in the burnt remnants of trousers. He was built like an underwear model with a face to match. Too delicately boned to be handsome, Becca stared at its beauty.

She hesitated in her strike. She couldn't set fire to a human. Even if he wasn't really, he would burn like one and that would be the image she would see in her nightmares.

He didn't have the same objections. His arm came up, warning Becca just before he threw his flames. She jogged back, hand along the wall, searching for the open doorway through the smoke. She found it just as she watched him throw a ball of flame growing from his palm.

A quick check and she confirmed Michael and the admiral hadn't come closer, they remained out of the line of fire.

Shaking fingers pulled the pin from her grenade and she closed her eyes, throwing it down the hall before yelling. "Michael, get out of here. The whole place is gonna blow."

She couldn't hear if there was an answer because the grenade detonated, flames engulfed that end of the hall and the fire roared. Taking a breath and forcing herself to move, Becca stepped out again to face the demon.

Nausea and fear that had nothing to do with any sort of prescience mixed and bile rose up the back of her throat. Smoked stung her eyes, her lungs itched with the heavy air. She began to cough and gag. The demon's human body was burning. Instead of having the good sense to fall down, it was advancing. As the flesh and hair burned away, it left a blackened exterior flashing red where it moved. It was a walking lava flow, its furthest extremities cooling to sleek black moving rock. The wooden flooring smoldered with each step.

It's hand came forward again. Becca backed away instinctively, taking her further down the hall. The grenade was in her hand. She kept her eyes on the demon as her hands moved together, intent upon pulling the pin from it.

Then the thing spoke. A deep voice scratched out rasping sounds as it moved its black lips. Its dark tongue flashed, showing liquid hot magma behind it.

Becca was transfixed. She forgot to cough.

"You oppose me? A weak human, burned away as easily as my host and you attack me? You are as foolish as the others," it cackled, confident enough to toy with her.

Biting back the acidic taste in her mouth, Becca told herself it would have burned away its human host as soon as it was done with it anyway. It didn't help. She had incinerated another human just like this thing had done to Danny.

A flicker of rage blossomed in her breast as she thought about the humans this thing had destroyed. She reminded herself why they were here. This thing had enslaved a vampire who had used her brother to gain information that would expose her friends.

The flicker grew to a bonfire. Becca cultivated it, letting her mind run rampant with images of Danny's charred remains blowing away in the wind and Michael's face melting away as the host's had.

Enraged, Becca felt her fear sliding away. She pulled the pin and threw one grenade, then another at the walls on either side of the creature.

It realized what she was doing and roared as the cabin burned around it. It couldn't move when the wood beneath its feet was charred. It required a constant source of fuel. The fire grew behind and on all sides of it. Both of them were trapped in a small section of the hall with no doors and no windows to escape.

A flash of movement on the other side of the wall of flames behind her caught her eye. Two tall dark forms, one with a bone white face joined the other three and Becca smiled. She had done it. Her unit and her brother were safe. It hadn't been her intent to sacrifice herself but it was worth it if it saved those she loved and those they served alongside in one form or another.

The fumes from the melting paneling on both sides of her were making her dizzy. Becca watched the demon roaring furiously as he shrank steadily into a hard black rock that barely came to her knees. She had her arm up, trying to get clean air through her shirtsleeve. It didn't work; it was too thick. While her eyes studied the dying demon, her knees buckled bringing her eye level with it. The surface was cool and glassy like obsidian stone.

Becca's consciousness was fading. She leaned forward on the cool surface of the black stone. The flames roared around her and she felt her skin prickling in the heat, her lungs burned and grew exhausted with the effort of moving the thick air. She dry heaved from the noxious fumes.

Becca said a quiet prayer, unable to hear her own hoarse voice over the fire before she closed her eyes.

Chapter 38

Becca was floating. She heard distant sounds of voices and feet shuffling quietly. Once in a while she caught the sound of crinkling plastic.

She wasn't dead. Instead of being elated, she was frightened. Becca had seen bad burns before. If the person lived it was an incredibly painful process of skin grafting and debriding of dying flesh, all in vain if secondary infection set in. Terrified of what she would find if she opened them, Becca kept her eyes closed.

The monitor attached to her beeped erratically as her pulse raced. She couldn't feel the flesh of her arm where something put pressure on bandages and she heard the beeping echo the slowing of her heart.

She swallowed. Michael had survived. With the crisis behind them she felt her tightly controlled emotions unraveling. A tear leaked out from under her lids, burning as the salt ran across the scalded flesh of her face.

Michael's voice was rough and close when he spoke. "Becca, open your eyes."

Becca held her breath, not wanting him to see how close she was to imploding. If it weren't for his hand steadying her, she would completely lose it.

"Honey, please. Open your eyes."

The desire to look upon his face won out over her fear of seeing herself. Becca cracked her eyes, the corners burned as the seared flesh stuck to itself.

Michael's dark blue eyes were less than a foot from hers, filling her entire field of vision. He failed to hide his concern from her.

"The helicopter got there just in time with the water bucket. Black and Ryan wouldn't let me go in after you." His eyes went black for a flash, he blinked and the returned to blue when he opened them. "I thought I lost you."

Becca wanted to tell him it was okay. She could feel the damage in her throat and she didn't want to lie. He still might lose her if the burns were as bad on the rest of her body. The fact that she wasn't intubated told her the medical staff most likely agreed and were letting her say her good byes.

"The doctors have you pretty doped up on morphine for the pain. Can you feel it?" His eyes searched hers.

Not wanting him to suffer more than he already was, she closed her eyes and moved her head only the tiniest of increments to either side.

Relief never touched his features.

She wanted to know and she didn't. But Becca wasn't really one to shy from reality for long. Finding the well-worn path in her mind, she jumped. *And saw her face. It was impossible to hide her reaction.*

Most of her hair had burned away. The red, shiny flesh of her face was waxy and tight. Michael must have anticipated that she'd do that because he kept his eyes on her face, not giving her access to the rest of herself.

Ignoring the pain in her throat, Becca tried to talk. "Look at me."

Michael might not be able to cry, that didn't mean he didn't want to. To grieve for her, to have that release that tears offered and the cruel fates reserved only for those among the living. These were the last words he would hear from her before they intubated. It had been a fight to get in here to even have these few moments. He'd been around enough doctors to know why they'd allowed it. He was being given his last good byes.

Obediently, giving her need to know priority over his need to protect her from the pain of the truth, Michael took a step back. He moved away as far as his arm would allow without taking his hand from her arm. He would keep her as calm as he could. It was the least he could do.

Michael let his eyes move from her face down her body nearly entirely wrapped loosely in gauze. Enough red, damaged flesh showed to tell her what she needed to know.

He couldn't bring himself to give her another look and closed his eyes while he brought them back to hers, only opening them again when they were safely back at her eyes. Pain faded in the face of the fear she had of her own death. Michael wished he could kiss her but her lips were so burned the skin could easily tear away with contact.

She mumbled something so faintly even he had to lean in to hear.

"What, honey?"

"Is there anything they can do?"

"No, the doctors are doing everything they can." *He* could do several things and he had been wrestling with the vampire's selfish desires all night. If she wanted him to alter her in any way, he would. And he would wait for her to ask. He would never bring any part of his curse upon her unwillingly.

Another set of tears leaked out from under her lids and he watched her flinch, imagining how the salt burned.

"Is there anything *you* can do?"

There it was. The question he had hoped for and dreaded.

Placing his lips close enough to keep their conversation private without touching what was left of her ears, Michael told her all that he knew.

"I can turn you and you'll have to die but you will become like me." He hoped she didn't want that. "Or I can give you some of my blood and you will heal. It will still be painful but depending how much I give you, your recovery will be fast and you might not even have much scarring."

Michael remained at her side, watching the monitors while she decided.

The doctor parted the plastic tent around her bed.

"I'm sorry sir, it's time. We need to intubate her now before the burns in her trachea make it impossible."

Michael looked into Becca's eyes for a sign of what her answer would be. True to form, she lifted her chin and croaked.

The doctor stared at her, shocked.

"I want to go home."

Shaking his head, the doctor was emphatic. "Rebecca, you can't leave the hospital. You have severe burns on over sixty percent of your body. Without proper medical care you'll die."

She didn't flinch. "I'm dying *now*." Her eyes met Michael's and he saw her decision. She trusted him to save her.

"Give her enough morphine for me to get her out of here," he commanded.

The doctor started to argue until he made eye contact with Michael, then his eyes glazed over and he nodded dumbly.

A drawer in the white cabinet by the bed opened and the doctor fished out a syringe and bottle. He filled it, shot her full of the painkiller, and within a minute, Becca's eyes closed again.

Without delay Michael pulled her IV and monitors off. Scooping her up in her blankets as carefully as possible, he stepped out of the plastic sheeting. Going down the hall would draw too much attention.

It wasn't quite three in the morning and there was very little traffic around the hospital. Michael looked out the second floor window and made his decision. He only had to shift her slightly to open it and step out. He landed softly, absorbing all of the impact in his legs to avoid shifting his precious bundle and ran.

He never broke stride until he reached the estate. Even with his speed and stamina, he was taxed with his efforts by the time he crested the stone steps.

When he entered, Ryan met him at the doors.

"How is…," his voice trailed off as he saw and smelled what Michael held so tenderly in his arms. "Oh my God."

The surety of her fate he saw in Ryan's eyes infuriated him. Michael streaked past him shouting over his shoulder, "Bring me blood. A lot." And he brought her to his room.

It was at the end of the hall and larger than the others. Ryan had joked that was the least they could give him for having to be the go-to for the admiral. Gently he laid her down on the bed, taking a moment to listen to her thready heartbeat. Raising his wrist to his mouth, he flashed his fangs and tore his wrist wide open for a rapid blood flow.

Michael fought the urge to pull his arm away when she moaned painfully at the pressure on her melted lips. At first, he watched the blood leaking out the sides of her mouth, so effectively had the morphine dulled her reactions. Softly he stroked her throat to force her to swallow.

After a few swallows, there was a knock at the door. Michael didn't answer right away and heard it open behind him.

"Here." Ryan held out a donor bag of blood. In his other hand were three more.

"Thanks." Michael barely looked away from Becca.

"Are you turning her?"

He stared at her. The look in her eyes had been fearful but sure. She wanted to live. He was certain she wouldn't be angry if he turned her, however, he had interpreted it to mean that she wanted him to help her survive. If he was wrong, so be it. She would be alive enough to fight with him and if she was determined to be a vampire like him, he would turn her then. Not until she actually uttered those words.

"No."

"Good. I like her human." He turned to walk out and called over his shoulder. "She smells better than you."

Michael grunted at him. Vampires did have a hint of a musty odor but it was easily masked with cologne and daily washing. Only a supernatural creature would be able to smell the faint lingering odor of death under that.

The door closed and Michael was left with Becca.

He drank all four pints. Becca had to have consumed at least two from him before he finally pulled away.

Even his immortal patience was taxed as he waited for Becca to awake. The morphine steadily wore off. He smelled it leaving her system and the smell of charred flesh began to give way to hints of her sweet smell he loved. By increments the old gave way to the newly repaired.

It was a full three days before she roused. When she did, he watched her carefully for signs of pain or discomfort. He'd had Ryan bring him a syringe of morphine some time during the day. He'd lost track of the hours.

Her eyes fluttered and slowly opened. Seeing him, she smiled without wincing.

He felt his hope surge as she turned her head toward him with only a small twinge of pain.

"This isn't my room."

"It's my room."

Her eyes roved as far as her limited mobility allowed. "I've never been in your room before."

He tried to smile at her. "What a man has to do to get a woman to his room these days." He watched her reaction, listened for wheezing hinting at lung damage.

"You did it."

Automatically he knew she was referring to the fact her heart was still beating. "I assumed this was what you wanted. You didn't want to be like me."

Closing her eyes, she nodded. "That doesn't offend you?"

"No. I'm glad."

She opened her eyes. "Are you sure?"

Nodding back, he found it easy to grin. There was strength under her hoarse speech. "Ryan says you smell better than us."

Becca chuckled weakly. Her brow furrowed. "How is Kyle?"

Michael thought of the conversation he'd had with Admiral Black after they had med evac'd Becca. He'd secured a place for Kyle although not without cost. If ever there was a question of loyalty it was Michael's duty to guarantee it with threat of bodily harm to Becca. That meant he would be the one to make good on it as well. He hoped his gamble was right and that Kyle wouldn't betray his sister. Besides, the kid in the candy store attitude when they turned him loose on their systems downstairs would at least buy them time before that became an issue.

"He's going to be consulting for us. He's actually waiting downstairs for word on you. He won't go home until he can see you with his own eyes."

"I'd like to see him too. He needs to get home to his family."

"What about you? Do you want to go home for a little while," he asked, hesitant. "A few days off to be with family would be understandable considering all you've been through."

"I'm staying right here. You're my family now. All of you." She averted her eyes shyly, flashing a glance up at him.

"Yes we are." Michael's teeth flashed in a wide smile, he made no effort to curb his relief.

Becca smiled again and tentatively raised a hand covered in the same healing silver and purple marks that covered the better part of her body. Cautious not to stretch the new skin, she set it lightly behind his neck. Michael leaned in, wanting nothing more than to touch her lips, soft once again, hoping this would be one of many more to come.

End

The Admiral's Elite
book 2,
Into the Light

Summer 2013

About the Author

HK Savage fills her days with stories. When she isn't reading, she's writing. On the off chance she isn't doing either, she's riding her horse, practicing in martial arts, or taking a breather with her family.
On occasion she can be found at an odd writers' conference or teaching a workshop to up and coming authors.

Follow HK Savage on Facebook to keep up on all of her titles and signings.